# THE VALLEY OF UNKNOWING

Philip Sington was born in Cambridge. His father was an industrial chemist and his mother an officer in British Intelligence. After studying History at Trinity College, Cambridge he worked as a business journalist and magazine editor for nine years. He co-authored six novels under the pseudonym Patrick Lynch, selling well over a million copies worldwide. His solo novels include *Zoia's Gold* and *The Einstein Girl*. To date his work has been translated into twenty-one foreign languages. He lives in London with his family.

www.philipsington.com

PHILIP SINGTON

# The Valley of Unknowing

VINTAGE BOOKS
London

Published by Vintage 2013

2 4 6 8 10 9 7 5 3 1

First published in Great Britain in 2012 by
Harvill Secker

Vintage
Random House, 20 Vauxhall Bridge Road,
London SW1V 2SA

www.vintage-books.co.uk

Addresses for companies within The Random House Group Limited
can be found at: www.randomhouse.co.uk/offices.htm

The Random House Group Limited Reg. No. 954009

A CIP catalogue record for this book
is available from the British Library

ISBN 9780099535829

The Random House Group Limited supports the Forest Stewardship Council®
(FSC®), the leading international forest-certification organisation.
Our books carrying the FSC label are printed on FSC®-certified paper.
FSC is the only forest-certification scheme supported by the leading
environmental organisations, including Greenpeace.
Our paper procurement policy can be found at:
www.randomhouse.co.uk/environment

Text designed by Joyce Yee and Grant Carruthers

Printed in Great Britain by Clays Ltd, St Ives plc

For my father, Peter, in memory

# FOREWORD

*The following pages represent the last completed work of Bruno Krug, the celebrated (and reviled) East German novelist, who spent the final ten years of his life in Ireland, and who died in a still unexplained tragedy twelve months ago. It is also his only work in English. I interviewed Herr Krug a few weeks before his death, the last journalist ever to do so and one of the last people to see him alive. It was on account of our meeting that his manuscript came into my possession.*

*My involvement began a little over twelve months ago, when I was contacted by Mareike Becker, a college friend from Munich. Now working on a local Bavarian newspaper, she told me of some extraordinary revelations that had just surfaced from the files of the East German secret police (popularly known as the Stasi). In the dying days of the communist regime, many of these secret records – fifty million pages in all – were torn up, shredded or burned by Stasi officers. Their main aim was to protect the identities of key informers in the general population, of which there were in all some 180,000. After reunification in 1990, a Federal commission was given the job of preserving the Stasi files, and reassembling the mutilated documents. Mareike had a contact inside the commission, which is based in the small town of Zirndorf, and was able to send me copies of eleven reconstructed pages, all recovered from Stasi Regional Headquarters in Saxony.*

*These pages came from a series of reports by an unidentified informer whose code name was 'Nachtigall' (Nightingale). It was clear that 'Nachtigall' enjoyed a position at the heart of the East German cultural establishment. In briefings with his or her handler, 'Nachtigall' made allegations that could easily have resulted in the harassment, trial or imprisonment of the individuals named. This was not the only point of interest. From the same source came a startling suggestion of literary theft. According to 'Nachtigall', a well-known international best-seller, originally published to acclaim in West Germany (and subsequently adapted for the screen in America), was not the work of the supposed author, but of an East German citizen who – for reasons that will become clear – was in no position to assert his rights.*

*A common thread running through all these reports was the name of Bruno Krug.*

I did not know until Mareike contacted me that Krug was living not in Germany, but a few hundred kilometres away in County Cork – reportedly as a recluse. For me, as for many students of post-war European literature, Krug's masterpiece The Orphans of Neustadt (Die Waisenkinder von Neustadt) was not only a set text, but a favourite one. The juxtaposition of harsh and gritty realism, drawn from the author's own boyhood experiences, with the youthful passion of its young protagonists, made this love story irresistible. The critic George Steiner described the work as 'a flowering of hope amidst a wasteland of brutality, deprivation and fear'.

Krug's life story was as intriguing as his fiction. Losing both parents in the war, he was rescued from the streets and given shelter by a great-uncle who taught modern languages in the city of Halle, famous as the birthplace of Handel. When his great-uncle died, Krug completed his childhood at a state orphanage, before training as a plumber, a trade he continued to practise on a freelance basis for many years.

For all his talent, Krug was a controversial figure in the West. Unlike many artists, he remained in East Germany until its demise and was handed a plethora of awards by the state. With access to foreign currency, he enjoyed a standard of living normally available only to senior functionaries in the ruling Socialist Unity Party. In the early 1980s he was repeatedly attacked as a propagandist for the regime. One American columnist famously described him as 'a Potemkin village in prose'. In response, left-leaning commentators defended him as a man of principle who had chosen not to abandon his ideals for the sake of a Western lifestyle. Krug's later works, collectively known as the Factory Gate Fables, enjoyed little success outside the Soviet bloc, but supporters continued to praise them as examples of literature aimed not at academic or critical elites, but at ordinary working people.

After extensive enquiries, I learned that Krug had taken up teaching at an adult education college in Bantry. The staff were anxious to shield their local celebrity from unwanted attention, but in the end I succeeded in contacting him. I explained in general terms what had prompted my enquiry. The writer came over as wary, but agreed to meet me. Afraid he might change his mind, I drove down from Dublin the very next day.

I recognised Krug at once. The squarish face, the full head of grey hair, the dark eyebrows, the pupils like black glass, the suggestion of self-parody (or was it mischief?) in his smile and his gaze – those same features that had appealed to me as a teenager – they were *unmistakable. His struck me as a quiet but forceful presence, his dry good humour interrupted by moments of reflection and sadness, which he did not explain and struggled to conceal. I was reminded of what the actress Martina Hagen, with whom Krug had a brief affair in the 1970s, wrote in her autobiography: that Krug 'was at heart a romantic, but in a time and place where romantic ideals were very hard to sustain. I sensed that behind his encroaching cynicism lay disappointment, and I worried where it would lead him.'*

*To begin with I focused my questions on issues relating to the writer's life and work. Krug mentioned that he was writing something about his last years in East Germany, but the book was apparently incomplete, and he declined to say more about it. Finally, I felt able to put before him the documents Mareike Becker had sent me, and to raise the issue of the Stasi informer known as 'Nachtigall'.*

*I had the strong sense that something in the information from Zirndorf came as a shock to him. He stared at the papers for a long time, saying nothing, seemingly oblivious to my presence. My questions from that point were greeted with polite reticence.*

*I returned to Dublin without the breakthrough I had hoped for, and shortly afterwards left for a lengthy assignment in London. When I got back two weeks later, I found Krug's manuscript waiting for me. Its appearance came as a complete surprise. Its contents surprised me even more.*

*Long before I had finished reading, I picked up the phone and called the author's number. I tried again the next morning. On both occasions, for reasons which are now well known, there was no answer.*

Olivia Connelly, journalist
Dublin, Republic of Ireland

# PART ONE

## 1

One November morning, while the schoolchildren outside were going through their gas mask drill, the telephone rang. It was my editor, Michael Schilling. I knew something was wrong right away.

'Are you coming in?' he said, referring to his dingy offices on the southern edge of the Altstadt.

There were certain times in the publishing cycle when coming in was something I did often. The trip from my decayed but roomy apartment in Blasewitz took no more than twenty minutes, and in summer especially I would combine it with a trip to the Hygiene Museum or a picnic in the Volkspark, with its ornamental lakes and decorous imperial woods. But this was not one of those times, because my last book had been three years ago and my next was intractably stalled. Something had happened, but Schilling wasn't going to tell me about it over the phone.

'I thought we could have a coffee somewhere,' he said. 'There's this new place off Wilsdrufferstrasse.'

The opening of a new café was, in the Workers' and Peasants' State, still something of an event.

'All right. When?'

'How about . . . *now*? If you're not doing anything.'

I had promised to make a remedial visit to Frau Helwig, an old spinster who lived across the road. She had what she quaintly referred to as a 'weeping toilet', which I took to be a routine ballcock problem, but I had not specified the hour when I would call.

I arranged to meet Schilling at eleven. Frau Helwig's plumbing would have to wait until the afternoon. From the sound of it, Schilling thought he was in some kind of trouble – or I was, or we both were. Fleetingly I pictured intimations of official displeasure, perhaps some ideological shift in the wind. Schilling tended to worry about things like that. He was the worrying sort. Still, as I hurried down the road and squeezed myself aboard a tram, I found my stomach squirming in anticipation of bad news.

The publishing company operated from the fourth floor of a concrete office block overlooking Ferdinandsplatz, a windswept semicircle of asphalt and puddles bounded to the east by tramlines. The area, like many in the city, was one of perpetual reconstruction. Every second lot was piled high with earth, mixers and diggers and generators standing idly about, like children's toys in a sandpit. Occasionally a gang of workers carrying shovels and pickaxes would jump down from the back of a lorry and march off to one site or another – only to disappear again for weeks or months, leaving behind no discernible evidence of their stay. Meanwhile the pale yellow trams, dirty and sparking, moaned back and forth, adding to the air a smell of burning and a din of grinding steel.

I arrived fifteen minutes early, pressed the buzzer and began the slow climb towards the office (the lift hadn't worked in years). I was less than halfway up when I saw Michael Schilling peering down at me from the floor above.

'Stay where you are. I'm coming down.'

I watched him descend: a tall, bony man with a high forehead and grey hair that flowed over the back of his collar like a superannuated rock star, a look that complemented his long-standing attachment to an old MZ motorbike. The symmetry of Schilling's face made him almost handsome, but his teeth were crooked and years of squinting at typescript had obliged him to hide his blue eyes – his most striking asset – behind a pair of thick lenses. He had already put on his raincoat and was clutching beneath his arm a document wallet made of brown imitation leather.

Schilling and I enjoyed a relationship that is rare in capitalist countries between writers and editors. There the relationship's very existence depends upon cash flow, specifically the writer's ability to generate it, and may therefore be undone at any time by the unpredictable gyrations of market forces. Whereas under Actually Existing Socialism, where security of employment was an inalienable right, the cultural worker needed only to fulfil his cultural quota to be confident of maintaining both livelihood and status. True, there was still a readership to think about, one capable of dangerous reactions and perverse dislikes, but on the whole I found it more predictable than its Western counterpart and easier to please. I could even name a good many of the men and women who made up its number; for they worked for the Ministry of Culture and the *Büro für Urheberrechte*, and their names often appeared on the licences that granted permission for publication. Schilling had been my editor ever since I submitted *The Orphans of Neustadt* for publication more than twenty years earlier. We had risen together, we had faltered together, and now (though this we had yet to acknowledge openly) we were drifting together, living neither in anticipation of the future, nor in fear of it. In short, we were not just business partners. We were friends.

We left the building. Since my last visit a large hoarding had been erected outside, bearing a slogan in red capitals:

## TO CYCLE EACH DAY
## IS THE SOCIALIST WAY!

Ignoring this inspirational statement, we crossed the square on foot and continued to Wilsdrufferstrasse, a bland, well-swept avenue of sandy-hued apartment blocks and a sprinkling of shops. Schilling led me into a pedestrian alley where the wares of various retail outlets – reconditioned watches, alarm clocks, lace, tableware – were on display in free-standing glass cabinets. By now I was expecting a quiet tête-à-tête in a shadowy drinking hole, but the establishment Schilling was anxious to show me turned out to be a glass-fronted *Eiscafé* that went by the name of Tutti Frutti. Inside, melting under bright lights, were three varieties of ice cream. Behind the counter sat an impressive-looking coffee machine, but there was no coffee to go with it; so Schilling and I each bought a cone and perched on a pair of stools, catching glances from the children and bleach-blonde matrons who made up the rest of the clientele.

Schilling started in with a series of routine questions concerning my health (tolerable), my work (officially ongoing, actually dormant), my social life (satisfactory, if repetitive), responding to my answers with earnest nods of the head, slow licks of his ice cream and frequent glances out of the window. All the while, the document wallet sat tightly wedged between his thighs, like a bomb that needed pressure to keep from going off.

Eventually silence fell.

'Michael, what's the matter? You're acting strangely. It's making my stomach hurt.'

Schilling blushed. 'I'm sorry. Paul's coming down this weekend. At least he said he was. You know how he . . .'

Yes, I did know. Paul was Schilling's son, now twenty-two, the sole issue from a brief and disastrous marriage to the lovely Magdalena Bonner – her post-nuptial loveliness proving skin deep, as I'd suspected it would. Schilling loved his son, but the best I could manage was to pity him, stuck as he was with a selfish, materialistic mother and an absent father. Paul brought to Schilling little these days but grief. After his military service, which he had been lucky to complete without a court martial, he had abandoned the maternal flat in central Berlin and taken up with a pack of dropouts in Pankow.

I would have taken less interest in the whole sorry business had I not felt in some degree responsible. The truth is that Magdalena Bonner would never have taken the slightest interest in a bookish myopic like Michael had it not been for his connection to *The Orphans of Neustadt*. For a good few years the success of that book lent us both an aura of glamour and distinction; qualities that more than made up for any deficiency in looks. I'd had just enough experience with women to be on my guard against mercenary love, but poor Schilling who, as far as I could tell, had never had a proper girlfriend (and only a limited number of sexual encounters, mostly of the fumbling, outdoor variety) was easy prey.

'Does Paul have a job yet?' I asked.

'Oh, yes. Caretaker, at some sort of gun club.'

'A gun club? Is that wise?'

'Don't joke. I just hope he sticks with it. You know, until something . . .'

Until something better comes along was the unarticulated sentiment; one we both knew was best left uncritiqued.

On the other side of the street a man in a grey anorak was taking a long time lighting a cigarette. Schilling watched him intently, his tongue frozen on the rim of his ice cream.

'Someone you know?' I asked. (Such instances of paranoia always irritated me.)

My question went unanswered. The stranger discarded his match and walked away. Schilling's tongue returned to duty. 'By the way, Bruno. There's something I'd like your opinion on.'

I pointed at the bulky wallet between his thighs. 'That?'

Schilling pushed it further under the table. 'Yes. It's a novel. It's . . . well, I don't want to influence you. It's important you have an open mind.'

A novel. So that was it: nothing threatening or sinister – boring most likely, but no worse than that.

'What's it about?'

'The future. At least, it's set in the future. *A* future. The whole thing has a mythic quality.'

The last mythic novel I had tackled had been written by the leading literary *grande dame* of our little republic: an ancient Greek legend revisited from a Marxist-feminist perspective. I hoped it wasn't one of *those*.

'You think I'll like it?'

'I won't predict your reaction, although . . .' Schilling checked himself. 'Let's just say, you're uniquely qualified to appraise it. I mean that literally. I'm very anxious to know what you think.'

I wasn't a critic, at least not the kind whose name appears in newspapers and literary journals. My views on contemporary literature were given sparingly and always off the record. But it was hard not to be touched by Schilling's faith. He had never given up the hope that I would one day write something as heartfelt and successful as *The Orphans of Neustadt*; that the old creative force still dwelt within me, waiting only for the appropriate socio-intellectual conditions to burst forth.

'So who's it by, then?'

Schilling looked cagey.

'Wait a minute.' An idea had occurred to me, one which, for some reason, I found comic. 'It's you, isn't it? This is *your* book.'

'What's so funny about that?'

I must have laughed, which was not polite.

'Nothing,' I said. 'I'm surprised, that's all. You never said anything about . . .'

Schilling leaned closer. 'It's not my book, all right? I haven't written a book. For God's sake, what would *I* write about? What do *I* know?'

Melted ice cream was running over his knuckles. He cursed, switching the cone from one hand to the other.

'I didn't mean . . .'

'It doesn't matter. Look, if you're too busy . . .'

But I wasn't too busy. I hadn't been too busy in years. We both knew that very well.

I was still feeling guilty about my hurtful outburst when we left Tutti Frutti and hurried back towards Ferdinandsplatz. By this time it was raining in earnest and soon Schilling was sneezing. His raincoat was old and leaked at the seams. After use it left him looking as though he suffered from a terrible sweating problem, with wet patches under his arms and down his back.

'I meant to tell you,' I said, as we ducked into a doorway. 'I bought this new raincoat at the Intershop. A good one, English. Then I got it home and found it didn't fit. Would you believe it? Too narrow at the shoulders. You can have it, if you like. It'd fit you much better than me.'

If Schilling wasn't convinced by my story, it wasn't for lack of effort on my part. After I had extemporised upon the difficulties involved in obtaining a refund he said, 'I could certainly do with a new one. How much would you . . . ?'

'Don't be silly,' I said. 'I'll be glad to give it a good home.'

It was time to go. I held out my hand for the manuscript. Schilling began extracting it from the document wallet, then changed his mind and gave me the whole thing.

A tram pulled up at a nearby stop, passengers spewing out as if under pressure. I shook my friend's hand and jumped aboard.

'Bruno!' he called after me. 'Be careful with that, will you? It's the only copy.'

I made a big show of tucking the novel under my jacket and gave Schilling a wave through the closing doors. It didn't strike me as odd that the manuscript had not been copied, the right to textual reproduction being restricted in the Workers' and Peasants' State to the organs of government, the church and public libraries. If Schilling had not made a copy, I assumed this was due to the technical and bureaucratic difficulties involved. That he might be anxious to protect the author (and himself) from some unspecified threat occurred to me hardly at all.

# 2

'Have you ever considered a sequel, Herr Krug? If it's not an impertinent question. I'm sure you must get asked it all the time. But is there *any* chance?'

I was lying on my back in Frau Helwig's lavatory, attempting to fit a new spud washer to the back of the toilet bowl. The apartment was cold and my fingers painfully stiff. Frau Helwig herself, seventy-four and silver-haired, dressed in sheepskin slippers and a floral-print smock, stood at a respectful distance, a copy of *The Orphans of Neustadt* sandwiched between her palms like a book of prayer.

'I've thought about it,' I said, which had been my standard answer for the best part of twenty years. 'I'm still thinking. Nothing's been decided.'

'Oh, I *am* glad,' Frau Helwig said. 'I feel – I've always felt – that, yes, it does end. It ends beautifully. But there's so much one doesn't *know*. What happens to Sonja? And to Thomas? Will they be happy in the end? One is so desperate to find out.'

At that point I grimaced, not at the simplicity of her literary criticism, but because the old spud washer, being made of an inferior grade of rubber, had glued itself to the ceramic and could only be removed with a tug. In the past, when I plumbed professionally and wrote on the side (instead of the other way round), my work had been channelled into the heroic projects of mass reconstruction: the apartment blocks, schools and factories of the new society. Where sanitary ware was concerned, installation and modernisation were the order of the day. Now, twenty-five years later, it was all patch and mend, effluential disaster threatening on every side. I had never been more in demand.

'Forgive me, Herr Krug,' Frau Helwig said. 'Such trivial considerations. What must you think of me? *The Orphans* is so much more than a story. It says so much about the human spirit, about history. And here am I demanding you tell us what happened next. Like some silly romance.'

I wiped the purée of rotten rubber and limescale from my hands. 'What would you like to happen, Frau Helwig? What do you think *did* happen to Sonja and Thomas?'

There was a long silence. I looked up, craning my neck round the outside rim of the bowl. Frau Helwig was still there, but her reverential bearing was now supplemented by a beatific smile, her shoulders hunched and her eyes cast upwards, seemingly towards some divine entity that dwelt behind the mouldy plaster of her ceiling.

I should explain, for those unfamiliar with *The Orphans of Neustadt*, that the ending is an open one, at least by the standards of popular literature. Thomas Schwitzer, the teenage black marketeer, who has survived and prospered in the bombed-out ruins of the city through a combination of guile and petty thuggery, finally abandons his criminal gang for Sonja Bruyn, a young communist organiser who is devoted to the cause of rebuilding a new society. The ending is ambiguous in several ways, at least according to the various introductions and commentaries that have appeared in Western editions. Firstly, we do not know if the bright future the young people envisage will prove attainable, or if disillusionment will set in. Secondly, we do not know whether Thomas's decision to abandon his predatory way of life is motivated by idealism or by his desire for Sonja. There is optimism and belief, but the survival of their love is ultimately as uncertain as the future of their world.

Open endings appeal to certain kinds of novelist, myself being one. They are more true to life. Human experience rarely conforms to the demands of narrative structure. It is messier, less focused. There is little that begins or ends cleanly, inviting the credits to roll (besides death). Justice is elusive. And the redemptive arc, the path to self-discovery so beloved of Anglo-Saxon films and Anglo-Saxon books, is stubbornly absent from real lives, no matter how bravely lived. But an open ending is destroyed by a sequel. The ambiguities are cleared up, the possibilities reduced to one. To every question there is now an answer, definitive and inescapable.

Frau Helwig's speculative reverie continued for a few moments longer. Having Thomas's and Sonja's future in her hands was an opportunity not to be squandered. 'They run away together,' she said at last. 'Far away, to an island, where all the houses are white. Brilliant white in the sun. With blue roofs.'

'Greece?'

Frau Helwig looked at me, sprawled out on the linoleum, and her smile vanished. 'But of course that's ridiculous. And foolish. Sonja would never be so irresponsible.'

I shrugged, although, given my orientation, the gesture was probably futile. 'People can change. Maybe Sonja changes.'

'Not Sonja,' Frau Helwig said. She sounded panic-stricken. 'Sonja is a good person, a wise person. Sonja would never run away. Sonja is a socialist.'

I propped myself up on my elbows, partly so as to communicate more effectively, partly to relieve the cramps in my stomach, but Frau Helwig had already gone. She reappeared a few moments later bearing a large jar of pickled artichokes, delicacies she cultivated with great care on her small allotment half a mile away.

'Now, I've some gherkins for you too,' she said. 'My nephew grew them. They're sweet as a nut.'

I always refused such payment-in-kind from widows and the elderly, as I'm sure Frau Helwig was aware, but it seemed she was anxious to move on from the Sonja and Thomas discussion as quickly as possible.

I went back to work. Frau Helwig had nothing to fear from me. I was not about to repeat her musings, indiscreet or otherwise. But then, the old lady couldn't be sure of that and any attempt to reassure her would only have made her more uneasy still.

'My nephew's a great admirer of yours too,' she added, still audibly jumpy. 'And his son Heiko absolutely loves the *Factory Gate Fables*. They're his favourites.'

'Really?' I said. 'And how old is Heiko?'

Frau Helwig thought for a moment. 'Nine next birthday,' she said.

# 3

That evening I sat down in my favourite armchair – an ancient leather affair, alternately scuffed and shiny, positioned in front of the main window with its view across the rooftops – and took out Schilling's manuscript. At first glance, it looked like any other: three hundred and fifty pages, held together with a rubber band, typed, double-spaced, with amendments and corrections made by hand in blue ink; here and there a sentence struck out with black felt pen. But something was missing. There was no title, no authorial name, not even a date; just a blank page. Then the story began: *They kept always to the edge of the road . . .*

I turned the manuscript over. It ended in the same way, with a blank page. I checked the document wallet carefully, but there was nothing else inside.

I turned back to the beginning, curious to see how the first sentence ended: *They kept always to the edge of the road, where their shuffling, silent progress was hidden among the shadows of the trees.*

As opening sentences went, it wasn't bad; the use of two adjectives was extravagant, but the alliteration was quite effective.

Schilling hadn't wanted to influence me, he'd said. It was important I had an open mind. Was it in that spirit that I had been deliberately deprived of the title page? Or had it simply been mislaid? On reflection, some kind of accident seemed most likely. All books have titles and all novels have authors, even if those authors don't always choose to be honest about their identity.

Page 1: seven people on a road, walking. A child holding his mother's hand; the others in single file. It is dusk, the sky overhead ash-coloured, the sun a red smear across the eastern horizon. Most of the group wear backpacks. The mother carries a suitcase. They are bedraggled, weary but alert. They hug the side of the road, which is bordered by a slope of brambles and dark trees. As the road bends, one of them, a youth called Alex, goes ahead while the others hang back. The mother holds her son close. No one speaks. They listen. The trees creak in the wind like old timbers. There is no birdsong. The birds are all long gone . . .

Why *was* there no title page? The question would not go away. It was annoying to be kept in the dark, deliberately or not. I told myself it didn't matter. A title was just a title. A name was just a name. Read on.

Page 2: Alex is alone now. The others are out of sight. But the bend has become a corner and still he doesn't know what lies round it. He feels in his pocket for the greasy black revolver. Should he go back for the others or scout a little further? They have only the one gun between them. Old Tilmann has a hatchet, which he hides up the sleeve of his big overcoat, but what good will that be if they're caught by surprise? Alex is hungry. They're all hungry, but what they need most – what they need *first* – is more guns.

Maybe Schilling removed the title page for a different reason, it occurred to me: because his name was on it. Maybe it really was his book after all. I couldn't go on without knowing.

It was eight o'clock. Schilling's apartment in Südvorstadt enjoyed the dubious privilege of a party line (telephonic, not ideological), but there was a chance I could still catch him at the office. I picked up the receiver and dialled the number. It was Schilling who answered.

Anxious not to repeat my earlier mistake, I started with the question of the title.

'It doesn't really have one yet,' Schilling said.

'What do you mean, doesn't *really*? Either it does, or it doesn't, Michael.'

Schilling sniffed. 'It doesn't.'

I was not convinced. Would any writer who had laboured to produce a full-length novel really leave it untitled? Symphonies might have numbers, but novels, paintings and children have names. Without a name a book is incomplete and unrecognised. It has no place in the world.

'Why not?' I persisted. 'Why isn't there a title?'

'It's undecided.'

'Then who's it by? Or are you going to tell me that isn't decided either?'

There was a pause on the line. I heard a voice in the background, someone saying goodnight. A door closed.

'No one you know,' Schilling said. 'Does it really matter?'

'I imagine it matters to him,' I said. 'Or to her. What is it, a state secret?'

'Of course not. It's just . . . Well, never mind. He's a screenwriter, a local boy. I don't suppose you've ever seen *Two on a Bicycle*?'

'I don't think so.'

'Well, he wrote it. Wolfgang Richter's the name. He just moved back here from Berlin.'

'I can't say I've ever heard of him,' I said, which was not true.

In fact, I remembered Wolfgang Richter only too well. During the previous decade he had turned up regularly at public meetings organised by the Writers' Union to discuss and critique my work. He would sit at the side, making pointed or ironic remarks that made everybody laugh. It seemed he was not a fan of the *Factory Gate Fables*, which, at the age of eighteen, he clearly considered too unsophisticated for his literary palate. I was sure he only turned up because my meetings always had a larger contingent of young women in the audience than most of their kind. More than once, thanks to him, the generally indulgent mood of the crowd turned quite hostile. I was never accused of abandoning the socialist viewpoint, but my work was called patronising, simplistic, unconstructive. It was unpleasant for me and embarrassing for the organisers. It also made the social dimension of the occasion much more awkward. To put it another way, Richter might have left with girl in tow, but his presence invariably ensured that I did not.

As for *Two on a Bicycle,* a mildly satirical farce set on a collective farm, I had seen it, although it was not until the credits appeared that I noticed Richter's name. I was dragged to see it by one of his youthful conquests (as it turned out), a girl called Anna, whom he had brazenly picked up at one of my public meetings. Though it was years since Richter had moved to Berlin to take up a job with the Gruppe Babelsberg film company, it was clear that she still harboured feelings for him: she left the cinema with tears in her eyes ('cigarette smoke,' she claimed) and became too depressed to sleep with me. Nor was this the worst of it. In *Two on a Bicycle,* one of the characters – a gap-toothed peasant possessed of an earthy wisdom one is supposed to admire – is seen reading the second of the *Factory Gate Fables*. Later in the film there is a close-up of the selfsame volume dangling upside down from a metal hook. The camera zooms out to reveal that the book is now in the gap-toothed peasant's lavatory, its pages intended not for pre-evacuatory reading, but for post-evacuatory use. It was a throwaway moment, a sly joke most audiences wouldn't notice. But *I* noticed it.

I said goodnight to Schilling and closed the blinds. Richter's manuscript lay where I had left it, on the seat of my favourite armchair. It looked quite at home, nestled between the cushions, protected by the white cover sheets that I had lovingly shielded from the rain. And it came to me that it was not just a book in embryo, but an egg – a cuckoo's egg slyly planted in my writer's nest. I was supposed to nurture it, to bless it with my good opinion and my good name, to treat it as one of my own – without stopping to ask from whose rear end it had dropped.

Was this Schilling's plan? Was this why I had been kept in the dark: so that I would read Richter's novel without prejudice? But if Schilling knew I would be prejudiced, why send me the book in the first place?

I stared at the manuscript and the answer came to me: it was Richter's idea. He had wanted me to see his work. He wanted me to give my assessment, to put it on the record where it could not be retracted. I was still the author of *The Orphans of Neustadt*. I could still be useful. But I had to be useful unwittingly.

I swallowed two shots of plum brandy and carried on reading. My hands trembled as I turned the pages. Many novels started with a strong opening scene, I told myself. Such visions were often the inspiration for writing a book in the first place. But then came the hard part. Focus and momentum had to be maintained even as the canvas widened, through the passages of explanation and explication, through each new introduction of character and circumstance. And then came the yawning chasm of The Middle, that graveyard of the inexperienced and the underprepared, where developments had to seem natural – even, in retrospect, inevitable – and at the same time unexpected. People like Richter, who wrote films, might encounter these problems, but only in miniature. Their middles were one hour long; fifty or sixty pages. A novelist's was two or three hundred. And the novelist had no music, no lighting, no hushed movie theatre in which to work his magic. The best he could hope for was a comfortable chair and silence. Richter was a novice. The odds were stacked against him.

The story leapfrogged forward effortlessly, taking in years, decades. A new world was being made and Alex was in the vanguard of those who were making it. He grows older, more powerful, more ruthless. He falls in love with a girl called Tania, but will love be his undoing or his redemption?

I read on, page after page. Every run-of-the-mill sentence, every glimpse of awkwardness brought new hope that his novel would fail, that I would not be finally and decisively eclipsed, as Richter surely intended. But these promises of mediocrity were never fulfilled. Reading late into the night, I found humanity, truthfully and tenderly drawn. I found passion and anger and hope against all odds, such as I hadn't felt in years. I had no way of knowing how anyone else would react, but for me the experience was strangely moving – the way a rediscovered memory can be moving, when it shows us in sudden, vivid colours how we used to be.

And then, about halfway through, it dawned on me why this book, of all books, gave rise to such nostalgic feelings. Alex, the protagonist, was none other than Thomas Schwitzer, *my* protagonist, grown older, if no wiser. His was the same mixture of grit, resourcefulness and naivety, the same moral emptiness. His beloved Tania was none other than my Sonja Bruyn. She was no longer a true believer. Her hopes for a better world had turned to dust. Her dreams were now only of escape. But still I knew her. I knew her gestures, her voice, her heart. It was not an imaginary future world she and Thomas inhabited; it was Neustadt, *my* Neustadt, its uncertain destiny now realised in full.

I couldn't read any more. I got up from my chair, letting the pages fall to the floor. Whether Schilling knew it or not – but of course he knew it! – what Wolfgang Richter had written, what he had presumed to write, was nothing less than a coded sequel to my most famous work. What had become of Thomas and Sonja? It seemed Wolfgang Richter had taken it upon himself finally to answer that question.

# 4

If I could illustrate this story with two photographs, they would both
be of women, the first being of my mother. Unfortunately I have no
picture of her, nor of the other woman either, for different but related
reasons. It is the lot of those who flee to leave such inessentials behind.
The main requirement of the refugee is to travel light.

The day after I read Richter's manuscript was my mother's
birthday. It was an occasion I always marked with a visit to the
Neumarkt, at the heart of the city. Since Eva Krug had no grave
and no resting place that I knew of, I went to where I had last seen
her, namely by the ruins of the Frauenkirche. These lay still in a
scorched heap where they had fallen forty years before, the main
addition besides an unkempt hedge being a smudge of weeds, which
topped the mounds of shattered masonry like an ill-fitting hairpiece.
Once at the spot, I did what I had always done, which was to walk
round the ruins, first one way, then the other, just as I had done on
the morning my mother disappeared.

My memories are sketchy, but they offer a better account of the
event than has often appeared in prefaces and introductions to *The
Orphans of Neustadt*. I was eight years old. It was February or March
in the last year of the war. My mother and I were fleeing westwards
from a part of Germany that was soon to be a part of Poland. By the
time we reached the city there were half a dozen of us, the others
being neighbours and an old woman called Dora whom we had met
on the road. We had only been there a day, and had gone into the
centre because we'd heard they were handing out supplies. It was
windy, and I remember how the dust and ash from the bombed-out
buildings would blow up in great clouds, stinging my eyes. I had
expected the Neumarkt to be bustling – like a market, in fact – but
I was disappointed to find it almost deserted, except for boy soldiers
in baggy fatigues and a few old men with shovels. Most of the debris
from the bombing had been gathered into heaps, heaps far taller than
I was, leaving cobbled pathways from one side of the square to the
other. We were close to the ruins of the Frauenkirche, distinguishable
by the two surviving fragments of wall, which jutted, black and jagged,
fifty feet into the air. My mother must have seen something, or someone,
up ahead. She told me to stay where I was and wait for her. She would
be back in a little while. Then she walked away, still carrying her
suitcase. The last image I have is of her stepping over a beam of

19

charred wood that lay across her path. I think she glanced back over her shoulder, to make sure I was still there. Then another cloud of dust enveloped us and she was gone.

After a while two of the others in our party went looking for her. 'Don't worry,' Dora said. 'She'll come back for you.'

I ran round and round the ruins, anxious to search as far and wide as possible, but afraid to stray too far, in case my mother returned and found me gone. Eventually we were all moved on by some men in uniform. We spent several nights in a warehouse near the railway station (since demolished), but I kept running back to the Neumarkt, because I felt sure that whatever had happened to my mother, she would reappear sooner or later, or at least send word. This went on for a week or two – how well I got to know those ruins, the landscape of debris; charred timbers, broken columns, the fragments of carved stone – until one day I woke up in the back of a moving truck without any idea how I got there.

I was taken to a field hospital and treated for chronic dehydration, pneumonia, a urinary tract infection and head lice. I stayed there for almost a month until my great-uncle Kristof came from Halle to collect me. Somehow Dora had managed to get word to him. How much my great-uncle knew about my mother's (to me, utterly inexplicable) disappearance I cannot say. I expect he had suspicions. But they were not suspicions he shared with me.

'All we can do is wait,' he would tell me. 'Everything will become clear in time.'

Uncle Kristof, as I called him, had been a schoolteacher. In decades past he had taught English and French in the local high school. He lived alone on the northern side of the city, with a view of an old half-beamed water tower that, in the best neo-Gothic tradition, resembled the turret of an enchanted castle. His apartment was full of books – beautiful books, many illustrated, the plates lying veiled behind sheets of translucent paper. In other circumstances I might have been happy there, but I knew my duty lay somewhere else. I had to get back to where my mother was waiting. I had to get back to the ruins of the Frauenkirche, a hundred miles away.

After my third attempt at escape – I was twice apprehended at the train station and once while hitchhiking on the road – Uncle Kristof decided it was time I faced facts.

'Your mother is not coming back,' he said. 'I'm sorry, but that's the way it is.' I remember how he put his hand on my cheek, by way of consolation. It felt cold and callous. 'You must think of your mother as a casualty of war. One among millions.'

He was right. Mine was a common fate. We were a nation of orphans, the nature of whose orphaning was frequently obscure and rarely, if ever, investigated. But I could not think of my mother in statistical terms. I demanded to know if she was dead and, if so, who had killed her. Perhaps surprised at my vehemence, my great-uncle admitted that he did not know for certain if she was dead or not. He knew only that she had disappeared.

'It's possible that she just couldn't cope, Bruno,' he said.

If this was supposed to make me feel happier about never seeing my mother again, it did not have the desired effect. It simply added another horrifying possibility to those that already haunted me: that I had been taken to the Neumarkt for the express purpose of being abandoned.

Either way, my great-uncle was adamant that I should put the whole episode behind me. 'A lot of people disappear,' he said. 'They vanish off the face of the earth. It's no good asking who's to blame, over and over. It won't bring them back.'

There were tears in his eyes as he said this, but even these were not enough to convince me that what he said was true. It was many years before I could accept that my mother was really gone; and many more years after that before I was prepared to give up all hope of learning her fate. Even then, on my regular returns to the Neumarkt, I often caught sight of her – or rather of women who fleetingly, magically, resembled her. I would always take off after them. In those brief moments of pursuit my elation, my conviction, obliterated all reason and all doubt. I can't say that I ever really gave up hope. Hardly a day went by when I didn't picture the moment when I would turn a corner and find her standing before me, for real.

On this occasion, perhaps because of the mist and the rain, I saw no ghosts, no women with suitcases vanishing into the mist. What I saw mostly were lines of parked buses, that and young people in bulky jackets, smoking cigarettes and talking at the tops of their voices. Bratwurst was being sold from a trailer, filling the square with a smell of cabbage and boiled meat. Synthesised pop music, blaring from a loudspeaker, obscured the hammering of the generator. I took my usual bouquet of dried flowers from inside my coat and, when I felt sure no one was looking, threw it high up on to the tallest heap of debris – high enough, I hoped, to be invisible to passers-by. This was necessary because the authorities did not encourage unofficial acts of remembrance where wars of fascist aggression were concerned and any flowers placed at or near the ruins of the Frauenkirche were always quickly removed.

# 5

Who is the other woman whose photograph I do not have? If my mother was the first in my life, she was the last: my lover and my downfall, my hope and my despair. Her photographs I burned in an ashtray, one at a time – some might say to be rid of the evidence. Her name was Theresa Aden: Theresa like the saint; Aden like Eden, complete with snake.

I first laid eyes on her a few days after reading Richter's novel. It happened at a cultural event organised by the regional committee of the Cultural Association, at which I was to be awarded the title 'People's Champion of Art and Culture'. Originally, according to the notification I had received that summer, the title was to have been People's *Hero* of Art and Culture (my italics). Although 'champion', to my mind, carried pugilistic and mercenary connotations, the change didn't bother me. I assumed the reason for it was arbitrary and trivial, even if it was not simply a bureaucratic error. It never occurred to me that it might be a harbinger of disaster.

The venue was a large civic building, which had been burned to the ground in 1945 and recently rebuilt. The outside, colonnaded, monumental and sooty, looked much as it must have done before the war. But the interior was devoid of classical splendour. The walls were blank, the light fittings modern; where once there was marble, now there was flecked linoleum. Even the door handles, L-shaped in galvanised steel, would not have looked out of place in a prefabricated office. I arrived with ten minutes to spare, was briefly greeted by the secretary of the Cultural Association and took my seat in the front row. Behind me sat row upon row of prominent citizens: men sweating in their bulky suits, women shiny beneath voluminous perms. Finally the house lights went down and the stage lights went up. It was then that I saw her.

At first, all I could make out was the top of her head. She was playing the violin in an orchestral ensemble situated below the stage and partially hidden behind a curtain. I saw blonde hair, parted down the centre and tied behind. As she swayed gently back and forth, the tip of her bow dipping in and out of sight, I glimpsed large brown eyes, wide with concentration, and high cheekbones, slightly flushed. I straightened up to get a better view. Even with her chin clamped to her instrument, I could appreciate her slender, graceful neck. (Would it, I wondered, carry the violinist's signature pressure bruise, so like a love bite?) She was dressed in black, her arms pale, the neckline just stiff enough and low enough to hint at the swell of her breasts. But it was not until the piece was finished and she put down her violin that I got a clear view of her face.

In the preceding minutes my imagination had completed the picture, one in which she appeared as a beauty of neoclassical perfection. In profile she was divine. Face on, she turned out to be human: her jaw strong, almost masculine; a dimple in her chin; even a faint, but discernible depression on one side of her temple. In short, she was not classically beautiful, merely pretty (that complex, double-edged adjective, so close to *petty*, and which, when the English first coined it, meant *deceitful*). Still, she had those eyes: clear, brown, blameless eyes that narrowed when she laughed, hinting for an instant at the exotic, the erotic and the forbidden.

The event got under way, starting with a showcase of Saxon cultural talent. There was music, dance (ballet and folk), gymnastics and a reading of awful poetry. I watched the violinist through it all, becoming aware only as I mounted the rostrum, the applause ringing in my ears, that she had not been playing a violin at all, but a viola. I was surprised. The viola is the Cinderella of the string section, the butt of cruel jokes. It is always in a supporting role, never centre stage, being blessed with neither repertoire nor romantic connotations. But she had chosen it. She had chosen the shadows over the limelight, the toil over the triumph. It was, I thought, a very good sign.

She looked up as I passed, noticing me for the first time. The next few seconds, when I felt her gaze follow me across the platform, the sweet, intoxicating weightlessness, are all I remember of the ceremony: the speech given by comrade President Pischner, the handshakes, the solemn presentation of the medal, which was hung round my neck, these things I cannot even picture. My mind was elsewhere.

What I remember next was standing with a glass of sparkling wine in my hand, talking to Frau Jaeger, whose husband was something in the Ministry of Trade. Drinks were being served to performers and guests, the company forming a crush below the stage. The orchestral ensemble, now in plain view, was playing in the background – or at least they had been. For when I looked round I saw that they had stopped. Several seats were empty. The viola player had gone.

I wanted to go in search of her at once, but Frau Jaeger, whose name was Barbara, was someone I preferred to keep on side. Her husband was widely believed to be a member of the HVA, the elite foreign espionage department of the Ministry of State Security. Certainly he went away a great deal, leaving Barbara, a languorous redhead with a taste for entertaining, to her own devices. I was invited regularly to soirées at their spacious apartment in Loschwitz, where foreign alcohol, olives and superior charcuterie were usually on offer. The guest list consisted of university professors, musicians and artists (what Barbara called her 'cultural circle'), mixed with a sprinkling of Party people. To oblige Barbara, I would wear my velvet jacket and a black roll-neck sweater, in an attempt to look writerly. But the occasions were always marred by her incorrigible flirting, which grew more and more audacious as the evening wore drunkenly on. I had the impression her husband didn't care what she got up to. I expect he had a mistress in Berlin or Moscow or Beirut. But without written permission, duly notarised by the appropriate ministerial officials, I was not about to lay a finger on her.

'I'm a little disappointed, you know, Bruno,' she said, as I stood scanning the hall. 'I was looking forward to calling you *My Hero.*' Barbara took hold of the medal that was still hanging round my neck. '*Champion* makes you sound like a boxer.'

'I feel the same way,' I said. 'But it would be churlish to complain.'

'And pointless. Heroes are off the menu, indefinitely.'

I refocused on Barbara's wintry grey eyes. 'What do you mean?'

'Haven't you heard? But I keep forgetting, you're a *writer.*'

I had no idea what she meant by that.

'Heard what?'

Barbara lowered her voice. 'About Manfred Dressler.'

'The sculptor?'

'The *last* People's Hero of Art and Culture. They let him have an exhibition in Yugoslavia.' Barbara let go of my medal. It clinked cheaply against the button on my jacket. 'Big mistake.'

Manfred Dressler worked in bronze. He was the man behind many of our most politically inspirational – not to say heroic – public monuments. An exciting new talent, it seemed he had run away to the non-socialist abroad, as it was officially known. I hadn't heard about it, but then again, it wasn't the kind of news they carried on the front page of *Neues Deutschland*. The story might have been broadcast on Western television – Dressler was famous enough for that – but the city where I lived was out of reach of their transmitters, lying as it did deep in the valley of the Elbe.

Barbara drained her glass and waved it in front of me. 'Drink up,' she said. 'We're supposed to be celebrating.'

I elbowed my way towards the makeshift bar, once more searching the room for the pretty musician. But there was no sign of her. Earlier that evening I had contemplated various ways of approaching her. I had even considered the desperate ploy of spilling a drink over her, as a way of starting the conversation. Even so, when someone else's beverage splattered over my shoes, wetting my socks and several inches of trouser leg, it never occurred to me that it might be a ploy.

'I'm *so* sorry,' said a female voice.

It was the musician herself. She was on her way back from the bar, carrying two full glasses in each hand. For a moment I was speechless. I had been looking in the wrong place, yet here she was. I had been searching for an entrée, and here was an entrée served up for me. Perhaps the ease with which one step followed the other, without any effort on my part, planted in my mind the seeds of entitlement.

'*So* clumsy of me. What must you think?' The musician bit her lip, her cheeks flushing.

'I think you're carrying too many glasses. Let me help.'

I stole a tray from the bar and together we loaded it down with glasses of sparkling wine. Then, with a smile on my face, I carried it shoulder high to where the other musicians were packing up. People in the crowd laughed amiably as I went by. The People's Champion was not too grand for proletarian toil, even on the night when he was honoured – that, at least, was the inference with which I veiled my less public-spirited intention.

'I'm Bruno, by the way,' I said, as I handed out the drinks, which the other musicians accepted gratefully. They were mostly young, student age, with unruly hair and skinny frames.

'I know,' the girl said, still blushing. 'Bruno Krug. I got your book from the library. I'm in the middle right now.'

My book. As if there had only ever been one.

'The middle is always the hardest part. Keep going.'

'Oh, but I'm loving it. I read it before I fall asleep.'

'I'm afraid that happens a lot.'

'I mean, I read it *in bed*.'

With the mention of bed, her cheeks burned even brighter.

'Novels go to bed with whoever pays for them,' I said, quoting myself. 'They're the prostitutes of the art world.'

The girl laughed nervously; then, after a moment's hesitation, held out her hand. It felt cool, in contrast to the mood, which was warming nicely. 'Theresa Aden.' She spoke softly, her head slightly downturned. 'I'm studying here.'

She was not a native of Saxony. I couldn't place her looping, sing-song accent, but it made me think of meadows and cattle. There were other clues besides: hints of perfume more refined than I was used to, hair with a deeper sheen, teeth that were whiter and straighter than any in the room. And she was tall, broad-shouldered, straight-backed – like some of our famous lady athletes, but without the Adam's apples and the lusty baritone voices.

I wanted to ask where she was from, but the other musicians, grateful for their refreshments, gathered round, eager to join in the conversation. It turned out they were all students from the Carl Maria von Weber College of Music, which used to be the Royal Conservatory before Saxon royalty was collectively vacuumed by the wind of revolutionary consciousness into the dust bag of history. I felt obliged to act the avuncular pedagogue, and the best I could manage by way of private conversation was to touch Theresa on the shoulder and ask her to wait for me, before an impatient stare from Barbara Jaeger sent me scuttling away across the room. Theresa smiled again and pointed reassuringly at the floor where she was standing, as if to say: *I'll be right here.* I knew then, for the first time, that everything was going to work out just fine.

The sensation of triumph, breathless and uplifting, did not last. Barbara was soon up to her old tricks, introducing me to a succession of supposedly well-connected people. I don't know who was supposed to be more impressed, they or I. In any case I remember nothing about them. I was anxious to pick up where I had left off with Theresa Aden and barely managed a minimum of conversation.

Barbara must have noticed what was going on, because as soon as we were alone again she put a hand on my arm and squeezed. 'I'd forget about her, Bruno.' She followed my gaze in the direction of Theresa. 'If I were you.'

'You think she's too young for me, I suppose.'

'Not necessarily. Although, now you mention it, she is a little wet behind the ears.'

I shrugged and turned my back on the girl, though it took an effort of will. 'Then what's the problem?'

'The problem is: she's a Westerner. An Austrian.' Barbara laughed. 'Honestly, Bruno, where do you think she got that accent?'

'So that's an Austrian accent? Well, so what? You think she's a *spy?*'

Barbara regarded me coolly. 'You don't know what she is, Bruno.'

'Even if she is a spy, what's she going to learn from me? The secrets of punctuation?'

I turned round again, but instead of Theresa I saw Michael Schilling shouldering his way towards me, an ingratiating grin on his face. And there just behind him, evidently *with* him, was none other than his new discovery, Wolfgang Richter. He had put on a little weight since our last encounter (most of it muscle), his ugly shaving rash had cleared up and his brown hair was longer; but it was unmistakably him, dressed now in a black roll-neck sweater and a dark grey corduroy jacket. I took care not to catch his eye.

'Hello, Bruno,' Schilling said. 'Congratulations.'

We shook hands in a curious puppet show of formality, which was certainly not for my benefit.

'Frau Jaeger, a pleasure to see you again.'

'Likewise,' Barbara said. It was obvious to me that she had entirely forgotten who Schilling was, in spite of having met him on at least two previous occasions. 'Who's your young friend?'

We all turned, but Richter had been waylaid by some old acquaintances, and was being slapped on the back and handed drinks from several directions at once. It seemed *Two on a Bicycle* had been a bigger hit than I'd thought.

'Wolfgang Richter,' Schilling said. 'He's a writer.'

'Another writer?' Barbara said with pointed enthusiasm. 'How interesting. What's he written?'

'Screenplays mostly. Although I *believe* he's also working on a novel.' Schilling gave me a knowing look, which I ignored. 'I don't suppose you caught *Two on a Bicycle?*'

'Oh, yes, of course. Very droll. Have you seen it, Bruno?'

'No.'

'You know, I thought it was a bit like your *Factory Gate Fables*; only funnier.'

It was then that Richter saw me. He looked me up and down, friends either side of him still intent on their conversation, took in the medal, and laughed – not a loud laugh, not a laugh that anyone but me would even notice, but a small, involuntary laugh, just big enough to wound.

Then another of Barbara's cultural circle appeared. I saw my chance to escape. But no sooner had I turned away than I found Michael Schilling tugging at my elbow. 'So? What did you think?'

'About what?' I said, though I knew.

'The manuscript.'

'To be honest, I haven't finished it. I'm reserving judgement.'

Schilling frowned. 'I'm not looking to quote you.' He parked himself square in front of me, looking me straight in the eye. 'Seriously, Bruno, it's good, isn't it?'

'That depends on your definition of good. An age-old philosophical question, of course, and a difficult one in the cultural sphere.'

With his index finger Schilling pushed his huge glasses up the bridge of his nose. 'You know, I thought . . .' He shook his head. 'I thought you of all people . . .'

'I told you, Michael: I haven't finished it yet. I'm only halfway through. Besides, I thought you didn't want to influence me.'

'No, no, I don't.' Schilling sighed, his deflation obvious and almost touching. 'Take your time.'

'I tell you what,' I said, with a great show of generosity. 'I'll press on with it tomorrow. That's a promise.'

After so many glasses of wine I needed to empty my bladder, an exercise that involved traipsing up to the second floor, because the men's lavatories in the basement were closed for maintenance. I had plenty of time to reflect on my reticence regarding Richter's novel. It had never been my intention to disappoint Michael Schilling. I fully intended to rhapsodise about the book at the appropriate time and place. But then and there, on that night (*my* night), in that company, it was verging on the insensitive to expect an ovation. The sneaky business with the title and the identity of the author, the fact that I had not been trusted with either – these things still rankled. And then there was the whole business of the content, its debt to *The Orphans of Neustadt*. Schilling seemed to assume that I would be perfectly happy about it, about being, in effect, supplanted, my story colonised and taken over – as if the only thing that could possibly matter was the quality of the resulting work; as if fiction had a life of its own.

I returned to the party, determined to let nothing keep me any longer from Theresa. I wasn't put off by what Barbara had said. Barbara liked to be the centre of attention and was instantly jealous of any woman who threatened that position, no matter how innocently. Besides, I wasn't thinking about some conjoined future with the student musician, or about where a relationship might lead. My thoughts were not of romance. Theresa was a beautiful object I wanted to possess for a while and then let go of, the experience leaving me with a comfortable glow of affirmation and achievement. She was, I had no great trouble acknowledging, too young for me in any case.

I felt sure she would still be waiting for me, just where I had left her. But in spite of her promise (it had seemed like a promise) she was not there. In fact, she was not anywhere in the room, which was beginning to empty. I went out into the lobby, then out on to the front steps. I looked up and down the street. I waited, as discreetly as possible, outside the ladies' lavatory, hoping she would eventually emerge, having perhaps applied a new coat of lipstick. But several minutes went by and all I got for my pains were dubious looks from the women going in and out.

There was no sign of Theresa anywhere. She had left. And so too, I soon noticed, had Wolfgang Richter.

# 6

The following morning, a Saturday, I was woken by the telephone at a quarter to eight.

'I'm ringing to remind you about the pool committee,' a voice said.

It was Frau Wiegmann, a vigorous and efficient female who worked at the local high school, teaching mathematics and dialectical materialism.

I had slept very badly, partly on account of too much alcohol, partly on account of Wolfgang Richter and his novel, mostly on account of Theresa Aden, whose picture I couldn't keep out of my mind.

'I thought the meeting was this afternoon,' I protested.

'It is. But last time you were late. You said you had written down the wrong time. So I thought this time I'd make *certain* you have it down correctly.'

'Very kind of you, I'm sure.' My head was in a bad state. Standing up was making it worse. 'What time is the meeting, then?'

Frau Wiegmann sounded shocked. 'You mean you haven't written it down this time *at all*?'

I knew I had, but at that precise moment I could not recall exactly where.

'Two o'clock?' I ventured.

'*One* o'clock, Herr Krug, *one* o'clock! At two o'clock we have to make way for the chess club.'

Even Champions of Art and Culture, I should explain, had occasional uses in those days. One such was to sit on committees, like Frau Wiegmann's, adding celebrity ballast to petitions and appeals to the authorities: for an improved supply of bathtubs or batteries, for better toilet facilities at a factory or a school, for fairer holiday allocations, housing, pensions, for cleaner air or fresher eggs or coffee that was made predominantly of coffee beans. In the Workers' and Peasants' State the appearance of a Champion's name on such *Eingaben*, so it was believed, lent them intellectual weight – even a degree of political and cultural relevance – making them harder to ignore.

Frau Wiegmann's committee had been going for three and a half years. Its aim, a noble one in my opinion, was to bring about the restoration and reconstruction of an old indoor swimming pool that lay fenced off and derelict a few blocks from where I lived. Although in past eras Blasewitz had been an affluent neighbourhood, its outdoor leisure facilities were meagre, obliging the local children to travel long distances for exercise and recreation – much further than those who dwelt in the new housing developments to the south and west, with their abundant playgrounds, gymnasia and sports halls. I would see them often, traipsing on and off the trams at unsociable hours of the day and night, looking sleep deprived and weary in their grubby sports clothes, their latch keys hanging round their necks. Such supervised activities were important in the Workers' and Peasants' State, not just for fitness reasons, but because the right and duty of women to hold down full-time employment left the family home empty not only at midday, but usually well into the evening. My upstairs neighbour, Frau Liebegott, made rice pudding every morning for her children's lunch and placed it in their beds to keep it warm.

The old swimming pool itself had taken a direct hit during the firebombing of 1945. Like many such sites, I had never seen it other than in ruins, but at one of our first meetings Frau Wiegmann had produced some old photographs, taken before the war. They showed lines of grinning children queuing outside a squat brick building with a vaulted roof of wrought iron and glass. The pool had remained open until the invasion of Russia, when the oil for heating could no longer be spared. But the water had not been drained, which was fortunate because when an incendiary crashed through the roof, exploding on contact, most of the phosphorus landed in the deep end. The remainder started a fire that brought down one wall and half the roof, but the rest of the structure had remained sound. All that was needed to restore it were voluntary labour, materials and official permission.

'One o'clock,' I repeated. 'I have it down now. Thank you, Frau Wiegmann.'

'Really, Herr Krug, I do think you should write these things down *immediately*.'

'Oh, I will, I will, rest assured.'

But as I hung up, I knew that Frau Wiegmann would not rest assured and that from now on she would call me first thing in the morning every time a meeting was scheduled, until either the pool committee achieved its objective, or one of us died.

*

It is often said in the West that the central planning system under Actually Existing Socialism deprived the population of any need for initiative. With education, employment, housing, health care and pensions all parcelled out by the state, and with almost all forms of commerce monopolised by state enterprises, what room was left for personal goals? How was the citizen supposed to strive, assuming he or she was of a striving disposition? What was there to strive *for*?

It is true that when it came to the basics, a sense of entitlement was deeply inculcated, which in turn led to a good deal of moaning, especially when expectations were not met. Official encouragement of *Eingaben* – which the Party saw as an important channel of communication between the people and the planners – formalised and normalised the moaning phenomenon. Moaning became not only socially acceptable in the Workers' and Peasants' State, but practically desirable. Skill in moaning – moaning creatively, with the optimal blend of political, social and personal ingredients – was highly prized, because it could occasionally get things done. If the *Eingaben* had been a recognised literary form, like the epistolary novel, the haiku or the Rustavelian quatrain, our little republic would have led the world.

And this is not where the initiative ran out. There is very little initiative involved in going to a shop that has everything you want – a bathtub, a boiler, a battery – and buying it. When the shops have *nothing* you want and you do not have the spare cash to pay for it anyway, *that* is when initiative is required. That is where improvisation, barter and adaptability become essential. The West may have had the better of us when it came to supply-side initiative, as an economist might put it, but in demand-side initiative we were in a league of our own.

I permit myself this politico-economic digression only so that you may appreciate the difficulties Frau Wiegmann's committee had faced, and the initiative required to overcome them. It was not merely a question of raising money, though money was needed; nor of obtaining the necessary permissions, difficult as that was. Every brick, every roof tile, every bag of cement and tin of paint had to be procured through the exploitation of contacts. Likewise every shovel, spade, skip, cement mixer and paintbrush, and the labour – skilled and unskilled – to use them. So long was the list of requirements that the committee was forced continually to recruit new members. Frau Wiegmann had begun with just seven. My addition (the original crew had turned up on my doorstep en masse, each

armed with a lovingly dog-eared copy of *The Orphans of Neustadt*)
made nine. Since then nine further members had been enlisted,
although the total stood at only sixteen, Herr Baumgartel having
died from a myocardial infarction and Frau Springer having
succumbed to dementia. The loss of these two stalwarts had set the
project back months. Herr Baumgartel had spent his working life
in the construction business and enjoyed excellent contacts in scaffolding; while Frau Springer's brother had access to large amounts
of electrical wiring.

In spite of many such setbacks, Frau Wiegmann battled on like
a true socialist heroine: exhorting her followers with visions of the
promised land, banishing despair and crushing dissent with her
indefatigable energy, enormous bosom and complete absence of self-
doubt. In this she had always reminded me of Sonja, the young
communist organiser in *The Orphans of Neustadt* – not in the enormous bosom perhaps (although I had always pictured Sonja as
physically voluptuous), but in the way she saw every setback and
every challenge as an opportunity to make things better.

I was on my way to the committee meeting, my thoughts of Theresa
shrunk to a dull ache of regret, when the first winter snows began
to fall – lazy, feathery snowflakes that tickled as they brushed against
the skin, promising all the childish pleasures of the season ahead:
sledging, snowball fights, Christmas. All the other members of the
committee seemed affected by it. The greetings at the door were
heartier than usual, accompanied by much theatrical shivering and
stamping of feet. This meteorological bonhomie added to a general
sense of anticipation. The rubble had already been cleared from the
swimming pool site and in less than a week's time reconstruction
was due to begin. Everything, so we thought, was ready at last.
Nobody noticed, until we had all sat down on canvas chairs in the
brightly lit gymnasium, that several of our number were missing.

Frau Wiegmann wasted no time in giving us the bad news. Herr
Begler, the construction site foreman who had been drafted in two
years earlier to replace Herr Baumgartel, had been officially repri-
manded for drunkenness following an accident at work. Consequently
he was no longer in a position to procure either the cement or the
cement mixer he had promised us. Without cement, we could not
repair the pool. We could not even begin to repair the pool.

We had suffered many such reverses in the past, but for the first
time I thought I detected a trace of hopelessness in Frau Wiegmann's
demeanour.

'And that isn't all, I'm afraid,' she said, over the muffled sighs and groans. 'As you know, the council granted us leave to develop this site nearly two years ago. They have just informed me that if the swimming pool is not near to completion within four months, they will find another use for the land.' Her voice became softer. 'And we will have to give up on our plans.'

Nobody spoke. Frau Wiegmann, I couldn't help but notice, was looking at me.

'We'll find another Begler,' I said finally. 'Or we'll find another source of cement. Look outside. The city's full of the stuff.'

Frau Wiegmann smiled and nodded. I saw now why she had been so anxious that I should attend the meeting that day. She had been counting on me to take up the banner, to help carry the torch in this hour of need. And I would too. It was either that or my battle-weary Sonja, who had already lost so much, would lose her faith as well, the one thing she had left. I felt a joyous compulsion to rush to her aid, to be the champion – in fact, the hero – of that dark hour.

'What do you propose, Herr Krug?' she asked. 'Is there someone you could talk to?'

Everyone in the room was looking at me, the People's Champion. I couldn't disappoint them. 'There's always someone. Someone who knows someone.' My face was burning. 'We must press on as planned. The cement will come!'

'Well, that *is* encouraging,' Frau Wiegmann said, addressing us all. 'I knew we could count on Herr Krug in a crisis. I would like to propose a vote of thanks.'

And, in spite of my protests, a vote was taken and passed, after which there was a wholly unexpected round of applause. Then discussions moved on to the subject of electricity.

I said nothing else for the rest of the meeting and left as quickly as possible. By that time my sudden flush of ardour had all but disappeared, to be replaced by a weight of obligation. But as I trudged home across the soft, new-fallen snow, I felt increasingly confident that the cement could be procured somehow. It was simply a question of petitioning the right people and doing something for them in return.

# 7

The next Monday morning I had business in the city centre and stopped off at the publishers on the way. It was an opportunity to give Michael Schilling the promised raincoat, and to find out more about Richter and his book. Why didn't I drop off the manuscript at the same time? Firstly because I wanted to reread it. Secondly – and perhaps this was less than magnanimous – because I didn't want to admit that I *had* finished it, not in a matter of two days. That would have meant that I had liked it – loved it, in fact – and I was not sure I did love it. It is very hard to love something that unsettles you, even if the unsettling (like the loving) stems from its manifest power.

I was surprised to find Schilling's son Paul slouched in the corner of the office, smoking a cigarette and reading a magazine. His father explained that he had taken the day off from his job at the gun club and would be catching a train back to Berlin that afternoon. From the shifty look on the boy's face, I felt sure this was a lie. Most likely he had simply done a bunk.

'We're going to have lunch together first,' Michael said, smiling down at his progeny, his hands braced awkwardly against his hips. 'I want to try and fatten him up a little, as my mother would say. Put a good meal inside him.'

I laughed supportively at this display of familial normality, but it seemed to me Paul Schilling was in need of more than a couple of bratwurst and a dollop of potato salad. The fact was he looked awful. He wasn't only thin (arguably a family trait); he was very pale, his skin waxy and pimply, and beneath his eyes were dark pouches that looked like the aftermath of a fight. As a boy, even as an adolescent, he had promised to be much more handsome than his father, having inherited most of his looks from his mother, the dark and lovely Magdalena. But none of that counted now. What remained of his youth was clearly being eaten away at a terrible rate. It was no wonder his mother had been worried.

I attempted some light conversation with the boy, enquiring after his mother and his putative new job, but my efforts only seemed to make him uncomfortable and in no time he shuffled off, muttering something about buying cigarettes.

'He should give that up,' his father said, watching him go. 'Filthy habit.'

I nodded, not wanting to suggest that an overfondness for nicotine might not be the sum total of the problem, and reached for the raincoat.

'Not quite the thing for midwinter,' I said, holding it open, 'but it'll keep you dry come the spring.'

The fit, to my surprise, was good. Schilling ran his hands over the cloth and the heavy silk lining. 'It's a beauty. You must let me . . .'

'Absolutely not,' I said. 'I can't have an editor with pneumonia. I'd be sure to catch it, for one thing. Apparently microbes can live on a sheet of paper for anything up to a month.'

I sat down and watched as Schilling paraded up and down, trying to catch his reflection in the cloudy windows. The mood was already more relaxed. The gift was a success and, for the first time in days, Schilling wasn't thinking about his son.

'So, I've been reading that manuscript,' I said casually, though just the mention of it produced a prickly heat across my entire body. 'Enjoying it, actually. It's very well done.'

Beyond the glass, the towering phallus of the *Rathaus* loomed blackly out of the mist.

'I wanted you to be the first to see it,' Schilling said, 'for obvious reasons.' Literature, a new raincoat: I could almost see the clouds lifting. 'I hope you feel flattered.'

I shrugged, ignoring the extraordinary presumption behind this remark. There was a fine line between *hommage* and misappropriation, one to which Schilling seemed quite insensible. On the other hand, was it reasonable to object to Richter's theme and argument when I myself had left them unresolved for twenty years?

'I haven't finished it yet,' I said. 'Let's not praise the day before nightfall.'

'I don't mean to rush you,' Schilling said. 'But I do want to discuss the issues when you're ready.'

'Issues? Like the title?'

'Yes, that too. And whether we can really call this novel science fiction.'

Schilling had stopped pacing and was now looking straight at me. I had been so preoccupied with my own reaction to Richter's book that I had hardly stopped to consider anyone else's. Now, all at once, it was clear to me what was on my friend's mind.

'Michael, it's not science fiction. It's not set in the future, not really.'

Schilling bit his lip. 'No.'

'What *is* the title?'

Schilling pulled up a chair beside me and sat down, still wearing the raincoat. 'Originally? *The Valley of Unknowing.*'

He looked sheepish, as well he might. The Valley of Unknowing was not, as you might think, a fictional, mythical or poetic name. As far as we were concerned, it referred specifically (often sneeringly) to the place we inhabited, a place where, for topographical reasons, it was impossible to receive Western television transmissions. Why did that matter? Because it made the whole book metaphorical, contemporary, *relevant*. It might appear to be about an imaginary time and place, but it was really about the here and now, about our society, our system, our state. The non-political setting concealed a deeply political intention and the title gave that intention away. Richter's story was not a vision of a war-torn future; it was a vision of the war-torn past and of the present – a present in which peace and order were maintained only by violence and the threat of violence.

'The story has so much momentum,' Schilling said. 'You feel instinctively that you're looking forward. And everything is so focused on the individuals, it comes over as a study of human psychology, of character. Nothing political at all. It's not until you stop to think about it . . .'

'Which most people won't,' I said, 'you hope.'

'Well, that's the question. The question I have for you, Bruno: do you think the ministry *will* stop to think about it? In your experience, do you think they *will* see . . .' – he fingered the lapels of his new raincoat – 'if they're not told?'

I shifted in my chair. This was a difficult question. I had seen the connection to *Orphans* almost at once, but then I was bound to. The functionaries at the Ministry of Culture might not see it at all. Outside, in the main office, I could hear Schilling's colleagues talking quietly, a steady tap-tap-tap from an electric typewriter. Now I understood why Schilling had been so furtive about handing over the manuscript. He was the only person in the company who knew of its existence; and that was how he wanted to keep it, at least for the time being. Reading the novel must have been almost as painful for him as it had been for me, albeit it for very different reasons. Richter's book was trouble, but it was also a discovery, a rarity, a gem. Schilling must have wanted to embrace it and run from it, to celebrate and bury it, all at the same time. *The Valley of Unknowing,* I now realised, had been pulling him apart.

'I need to finish it,' I said. 'You can't talk about a book until you've finished it.'

Again, Schilling looked disappointed. Perhaps he sensed that I was playing for time. I was only too happy when the door opened and his son shambled back into the room with a pack of cigarettes in his hand, forestalling any further discussion.

# 8

The last meeting of the pool committee had not been a complete loss. On the way out I had noticed a hand-decorated poster advertising a Christmas concert by a school orchestra and it had given me an idea. If an ordinary high school was putting on a musical event, surely a college of music would do the same.

It turned out that giving concerts and recitals was a central plank of the curriculum at the Carl Maria von Weber, the aim being to train public performers rather than recording artists. Unfortunately there was no way of discovering which, if any, of these events would involve Theresa Aden. So for the next week or so I turned up almost every night at one draughty venue or another, full of expectation (much like the parents, friends and teachers who made up most of the audience), only to be disappointed. There were, I discovered, quite a number of viola players among the alumnae of the college. Every quartet, quintet and sextet had its own. I heard a lot of Beethoven, Mendelssohn and Brahms – passionate, romantic, melancholy music that deepened and gave noble lustre to my otherwise commonplace frustration, so that by the end of each performance my failure to locate Theresa had all the tragic profundity of Isolde's tryst with Tristan or Romeo's with Juliet. And when at last I caught sight of her, instrument in hand, taking her place in a full-sized orchestra for a concert at the Kulturpalast, I felt as if Fate itself had finally stepped in to help me.

By this time my mental image of Theresa was all but worn out. All I remembered was the excitement I'd felt when we met, an excitement I wanted to feel again. Seeing her now, features reanimated and refreshed, gave me a physical rush. It was halfway through the first movement (of what I can't recall) before my heart rate and breathing were slow enough for me actually to hear the music over the blood thrashing in my ears.

This reaction, I knew, was ridiculous for a man my age. Passions are like loud clothes: only the young can wear them and get away with it. I can't explain why I allowed myself such romantic licence at this particular time. Perhaps it had something to do with Richter's book, the way it seemed to connect me with my past. Perhaps I had already sensed something about Theresa that I would later see more clearly: a reticence and modesty born of incompleteness, of a deep, unspoken need. In any event, I did not resist my feelings – though I did my best to camouflage them, you can be sure – because I did not expect them to last. I expected youthful passion, like youth itself, to prove ephemeral, likewise Theresa Aden's power to disappoint me.

Even from a distance she looked more alluring than before. The imperfections I had detected were no longer imperfections: the defiant jaw, the dimpled chin, these were now part of her, which made them indispensable. Proudly I watched her tuning up. Impatiently I watched her play. Jealously I watched her between playing, when she would whisper remarks to the violinist next to her: sly, musical jokes that I couldn't share. Sometimes she would glance up at the audience, scanning the rows of faces, causing my heart to leap into my mouth. Once, when she was looking squarely in my direction (what could she see beyond the glare of the lights?) she smiled, which was unfortunate, though it thrilled me at the time. For I passed the rest of the concert waiting and longing for her to do it again, which she never did.

As soon as the final encore was finished, I went in search of the dressing rooms. The Kulturpalast was a modernist building of lofty, derivative design, but the backstage area could only be reached from the audience side of the building via a bewildering series of corridors and tunnels. By the time I found it, the last of the orchestra had left the stage, creating a euphoric crush of players and instruments: a double bass being carried shoulder high, a clarinettist playing a jazz version of 'Silent Night', a pair of trombones interrupting with ironic cartoon asides. To make matters worse, several of the string players recognised me from their earlier chamber concerts and took this opportunity to introduce themselves. Unintentionally I had acquired a reputation as a music lover and my opinion was eagerly sought.

I moved away as quickly as I could, but there was no sign of Theresa in the crowd. I was checking the last dressing room when a stout girl with short dark hair came up to me. 'Looking for someone?' she asked, a hostile edge to her voice.

I may have blushed. 'Theresa Aden. She plays the viola.'

'Yes, I know what she plays. You're too late. She's gone.'

'Already? Are you sure?'

'Gone home to pack. She's leaving tomorrow for the holidays. I can take a message if you want.'

I hurried back into the corridor. None of the other players were in a hurry to leave. Someone had cracked open a bottle of vodka and was passing it round. Distinctly unmusical singing came from several of the other dressing rooms. I headed for the stage door, stepping over instruments and cases, unable to believe that my chance had really gone, that Fate could be that much of a tease.

Then I was outside. Snow was falling, the drifting flakes caught in the cone of a solitary street light. This was the back of the building, a small yard in which a van and three cars stood parked, their windscreens and windows frosted up. A single pair of footprints – too small for a man's – led across the yard and turned right along the pavement in the direction of the river. My overcoat still over my arm, I set off after them, my feet slipping and sliding.

Theresa was standing in the darkness a few yards further down the street, silhouetted against the dim façade of the building opposite, her viola case in her hand. I was about to call out to her when she turned and walked back a few paces the way she had come. There, under the street light, a man had appeared, a man I recognised with a heavy, sickening feeling as Wolfgang Richter. She had been waiting for him.

I was sure neither of them had seen me. I stepped carefully into the shadows beside the van. They exchanged a few words; I couldn't make them out. Then Richter reached into his coat for what looked like a book and handed it over. Theresa looked at it for a moment, then slid it into the pocket of her coat. They said a few more words and, for a moment, I thought they were going to say goodbye. But then Richter threw his arms round her and buried his face in her neck.

I would have stayed to see what happened next, but I was afraid the loving couple would turn back towards the concert hall and discover me hiding in the shadows. I didn't want to imagine Richter's triumph at that moment, or my own humiliation. So, shoulders hunched, head bowed, I left, my heart as cold and heavy as a fist of stone.

# 9

In my regular circle of acquaintance there were only two people who expressed unqualified admiration for the *Factory Gate Fables*, and who counted them among their favourite books. Herr Andrich and Herr Zoch described themselves as employees of the city council. Their precise function was never clear to me, but every time we met, which was roughly five times a year, my less-well-known titles would come up in conversation. Herr Zoch, in particular, was always anxious to know how the latest novel in the series was coming along, what new characters would be in it, and upon whom these characters were based. He even took notes. My inspiration and research methods were a subject of constant fascination for him; so much so that, in any other circumstances, one would have thought he harboured literary ambitions himself.

I should explain that the *Factory Gate Fables* – a series of interconnected novellas, in which certain characters, like actors in a theatrical company, pop up again and again, sometimes in minor roles, sometimes in major ones – drew its inspiration from the lives of people I knew. At least, that was the widely held belief. My characters were not created to suit the story. Instead I created stories with the aim of portraying real individuals as fully as possible; their dreams, foibles, struggles and triumphs.

Like many widely held beliefs, this one was nonsense. My characters were fabrications. So was everything else in the *Factory Gate Fables*. I had not, in reality, been anywhere near a factory gate, let alone a factory, for many years. My starting point, it is true, was very often people I encountered in daily life. I drew on their mannerisms, habits and appearance (and not infrequently their smell); but as far as their inner selves were concerned, I relied entirely on my powers of invention. I had no way of portraying their inner lives and no desire to do so. In the East, this lack of factuality, this reliance on pure imagination, was a small but guilty secret. But then, I was only dimly aware of the ready excuses available to authors in the West, where individual self-expression is all that counts, no matter how disconnected from reality. A writer's words might not be literally true, the argument goes, but they describe a greater truth, an artistic truth that soars above the contradictions and inconsistencies of real life. In this sense Western fictions are like news bulletins used to be in the Workers' and Peasants' State: they might not be literally true, but they propagate a useful message, which is to steer its audience in the right moral, philosophical or ideological direction.

Herr Zoch often asked why I did not include more artists and writers in my books, since that was the world I knew best. My response was to say that writers were too few in number to be socially significant. This answer did not stop him raising the subject every time we met. The one time he didn't ask was two days after the Kulturpalast concert, when he and Herr Andrich turned up at my apartment unannounced. On that occasion he and his companion had more pressing matters on their minds.

'I expect you've heard about Dressler,' Herr Andrich said.

He was, I think, the more senior of my two handlers: a fat, middle-aged man with a bald head, pouchy bloodhound eyes and a permanent odour of stale cigarillos. He had probably been bullied at school – but not by the likes of Herr Zoch, who was half his size, bespectacled and slight, and who sat, when he was not taking notes, with his hands cupped over his kneecaps, as if the latter had been secured by cheap adhesive and were in danger of popping off.

'Manfred Dressler?' I said, feigning ignorance. 'The sculptor? He hasn't died?'

'It would be better if he had.'

'He's fled,' Herr Zoch said. 'From Yugoslavia. Using a false passport.'

There followed a few moments of head shaking, mine actual, the others' implicit.

'A People's Hero of Art and Culture,' Herr Andrich said, looking quite hurt.

'A hero,' Herr Zoch repeated. 'Like you.'

I briefly considered correcting Herr Zoch on that point, but decided against it.

'Unbelievable,' I said. 'And he showed such promise.'

Herr Anders nodded. '*Such* promise. Still, I always say it's the promising ones you have to keep an eye on. More subject to temptation. Didn't you know him?'

I explained that I had met the sculptor on a couple of occasions, but that we were certainly not friends.

'A pity,' Herr Andrich said.

'A *great* pity,' Herr Zoch said. 'We might have seen it coming, if you'd kept your ears open.'

I hurried away to the kitchen to fetch the coffee and the *Lebkuchen*. Usually my discussions with the agents of the state security apparatus were of a general nature. I was encouraged to set out my views on the direction of cultural activity in our country and to offer earthy critical appraisal of literary works. I had never been asked to draw out people's secrets or to note down gossip. It was not, I thought, part of our understanding. I supposed the Dressler affair had been embarrassing, a failure by whichever department was responsible for cultural affairs. And perhaps there had been other failures like it that I knew nothing about. In any case, I sensed that Herr Andrich and Herr Zoch were under pressure to up their game. My attempts to steer the conversation in a less concrete direction were unsuccessful.

'You really should put yourself about more,' Herr Andrich said. 'Among the artistic community. A writer can't live like a hermit. A hermit serves no useful purpose at all.'

I agreed that hermits were not socially useful, but protested that I was more at home with ordinary working people. I reminded him that I had grown up in an orphanage and trained as a hydrodynamic technician long before it ever occurred to me to write a book.

'The truth is, I've never felt very comfortable among the intelligentsia,' I said. 'So often they strike me as . . . They have a way of being . . .'

'What?' Herr Zoch asked, taking out his notebook and ballpoint pen.

'Well . . . arrogant, I suppose. A cut above. Didn't Lenin say . . . ?'

'Like who, for example?' Herr Zoch readied the ballpoint with a flip of his thumb. 'Give us a name.'

It was snowing outside: big, fluffy flakes like the aftermath of a celestial pillow fight. I pictured myself outside, walking arm in arm with Theresa Aden, the chill of the air a delicious contrast to the inner glow of companionship and love. But Theresa was lost to me now. Wolfgang Richter had got to her first. He had snatched her away while I sat around listening to chamber music and admiring his literature. All I was left with was the cold and a feeling of emptiness deeper than I was used to.

'I'm not talking about anyone in particular,' I said. 'I'm just not one of them, that's all, the intelligentsia. I never have been.'

Herr Andrich sighed and reached into his coat pocket for a pack of cigarillos. He smoked only Sprachlos, the local brand, a name which in English means 'speechless' (branding was not an advanced science in the Workers' and Peasants' Republic).

'This is very disappointing,' he said. 'Your observations on the artistic scene are *so* highly valued. Your opinion is trusted, more than you know. Yet you prefer to keep your head buried in the sand.'

To avoid further awkwardness, I thought it best to hold out some hope of change. 'I talked to Frau Jaeger the other day. She'll be having another one of her soirées soon. There'll be plenty of intellectuals there.'

'We're not interested in Barbara Jaeger,' Herr Andrich said. 'Her husband's . . .'

Herr Zoch coughed. The sentence remained incomplete. Herr Andrich frowned and stared at the end of his cigarillo, as if having doubts about the wisdom of lighting it. For a few moments nobody spoke. Then Herr Zoch said, 'Tell us about the swimming pool project. How's that coming along?'

I was happy to change the subject. 'Quite well,' I said. 'We're due to start work on the site very soon. Although we have had a bit of a setback.'

'Yes, we heard about Rudi Begler. Drunk on the job, wasn't he? Great shame. Still, someone could have been killed.'

'So they say.'

'Where are you going to get your cement from now? And the mixer? You can't make cement without a mixer.'

'I'm not sure,' I said. 'We were counting on Begler. He was our lynchpin.'

I shook my head, remembering now my rash promise to Frau Wiegmann and the rest of the committee. Soon she would be calling me – or, worse still, calling *round* – wanting to know how I was getting on with my string pulling. I had made a number of calls; so far all without results.

'Such a worthwhile project,' Herr Andrich observed. 'A swimming pool. It'd make all the difference to the children around here, poor little devils.'

He sniffed his cigarillo and looked at Herr Zoch. Herr Zoch looked back. Both men sucked their greying incisors.

'I suppose *we* could ask around,' Herr Andrich said. 'See what we could come up with. How about that?'

'Yes, how about that?' said Herr Zoch.

I had to acknowledge that this would be a great help. When it came to pulling strings, Champions of Art and Culture had nothing over employees of the state security apparatus. Theirs was a very network of string, one that reached into every corner of life, like cobwebs in a neglected attic.

'We'll see what we can do,' said Herr Andrich indulgently, finally mustering the courage to light up.

'So.' Herr Zoch looked at his notes. 'You were saying: arrogant, a cut above. Examples?'

'All I meant to say was . . .'

'You really *must* give us an example. If only for the sake of clarity.'

'For the sake of clarity,' Herr Zoch repeated, as if there were some danger I hadn't heard the first time.

'It goes without saying that anyone talented and clever is going to have a high opinion of themselves,' I said. 'It's only natural.'

'And who in your circle of acquaintance would fit that bill?' Herr Andrich looked at me with his pouchy eyes, his chin dropping on to his chest. 'Or are you simply making all this up for our entertainment?'

That was when I mentioned Wolfgang Richter. Put on the spot, I couldn't think of anyone else. 'He's young, of course,' I added. 'The young are often . . .' But what were they? Threatening? Usurping? Physically superior? 'He'll learn anyway.'

'Is that Richter with an "i"?'

Neither Herr Zoch nor his colleague had ever heard of Wolfgang Richter. I had no choice but to fill them in on his curriculum vitae.

'I liked *Two on a Bicycle*,' Herr Andrich said. 'Very amusing film. Not unlike your *Factory Gate Fables*.'

'Only funnier,' added Herr Zoch.

'Yes, that scene when the chickens get on the roof . . .'

Both men laughed heartily. I found myself thinking of Theresa Aden, she and Richter embracing in the snow.

'He's writing a novel too,' I pointed out, instinctively hedging by way of the present tense.

'A novel?' Herr Zoch made another note in his notebook. 'Have you read it?'

'I was asked to look over a few pages.'

'What's it called?'

'The title hasn't been decided on.'

'What's it about?'

'It's set in some unspecified place in the future.'

'So science fiction, then?'

'Of a kind.' I wondered if I would ever actually see Theresa again and, if not, how long it would take me to forget her. 'The whole thing has a mythic quality.'

Herr Zoch sniffed and made another note. He seemed to have run out of questions.

Herr Andrich watched me, eyes narrowing as he exhaled a pungent plume of smoke. 'How would you *describe* this unfinished book in a word?'

I considered my answer, my stomach gurgling all the while. 'I thought it was very . . .'

'Original?'

'Not exactly. The word I'd choose would be . . .'

'Would be?'

'Promising.'

Herr Zoch looked at Herr Andrich. Herr Andrich looked at Herr Zoch.

'Promising? You're quite *sure* that's the word?' Herr Andrich asked.

Everyone was a fan of Wolfgang Richter, it seemed, even the employees of the state security apparatus; and all thanks to one comic film.

'Yes, promising,' I repeated, sticking to my guns.

# 10

Autumn had finally given way to winter by this time, but when I look back at the Workers' and Peasants' State autumn is all I see. This was especially true of those later years, when our anti-fascist liberators cut their annual shipment of Caucasian oil by two million tonnes, obliging us to burn brown coal instead – coal that we gouged and scraped with terrible haste from the green hills of southern Saxony. To autumnal mists we added gritty miasmas, the one indistinguishable from the other, except for the carboniferous taste. The sky above – yellow, russet, dusty pink, depending on the time of day – had a persistent autumnal tinge, its colours mixed by the same celestial hand on the same celestial palette.

Aesthetic shocks, it could be said, were eschewed generally in the Workers' and Peasants' State, at least where the colour scheme was concerned. Contrast was contained, partly by accident (if soot can be called accidental), partly by design. Colours stood in fraternal relation one to the others, none enjoying more than its fair share of attention. I have only to close my eyes and there they are, the distinctive hues of Actually Existing Socialism: grey, brown, grey-brown, caramel brown, rust brown, brown ochre, burnt sienna, coffee, beige. These were the colours of the apartment blocks and factories, offices and shops, of construction and decay and all points in between; of stucco and brick, roof tile and render, nylon, polyester, acetate and rayon, wallpaper, linoleum and squeaky velveteen.

And then there was red. Red, the exception to the fraternal rule, denoting as it does fraternity itself. Red to be used sparingly: on flags, emblems, May Day carnations and the scarves of the Thälmann Pioneers. Never on party dresses, socks or hats. And certainly not on underwear. There are no red knicker days in the socialist republic. The workers' flag is deepest red (it shrouded oft our martyred dead), but the workers' pants are greyest grey. Red hogged the limelight on all occasions, big and small, fluttering from flagpoles and balconies, stamped on to posters and Party exhortations. Pure red, arterial red. Politically, as visually, it triumphed in our urban spaces through sheer absence of competition, an unflinching reminder that we are all one flesh and blood, all brothers and sisters; and that, from the highest to the lowest, we all bleed the same way, chromatically speaking, when we are shot.

The interview with Herr Andrich and Herr Zoch did not play unduly on my mind that Christmas. If there had been any clear thought behind my mentioning Wolfgang Richter's name, it was only that publication of his book might be delayed, pending revisions. As an act of vengeance this would have been thoroughly petty had I not also believed that to produce a less politically charged version was in his best interests and, more importantly, Michael Schilling's. Once a book is published it cannot be *un*published. Schilling might have succeeded in slipping the novel past unsophisticated officials at the Ministry of Culture, but what if the subversive nature of the work had been revealed subsequently? He would still have shared the blame. And the greater the success of the book, the greater that blame would have been. If the authorities paid Richter more attention than they might otherwise have done, what would that cost him? If he had nothing to hide, he had nothing to fear.

On the other hand. I had gone behind Schilling's back. He had given me the manuscript in confidence (although those words were never used) seeking my opinion as to whether the book's political character would be noticed. I had rendered the question academic, because it was certainly going to be noticed now. *The Valley of Unknowing* would need more than a new title. Its connections to the history of our republic would have to be rendered invisible, its relevance excised. There could be no agenda, no message, subliminal or otherwise. In its new incarnation, the novel would be a fantasy, an entertainment, nothing more – or rather, nothing *else*. For who in this modern world really cares for the message anyway? The notion is quaint. Who buys a novel to be lectured?

Schilling had to be told, but the difficulty was how to go about it. My occasional meetings with Andrich and Zoch, harmless as they might be, were supposed to be secret. I could have asked my old friend to share that secret, but it came to me on one of several solitary walks that complete honesty served no useful purpose. It only exposed me to risk. Besides, how could I ask Michael to share my secret when I had just failed to keep his?

I decided a fiction was called for (fictions were my business, after all): I would say I had heard something. Better still, I had *over*heard something – at one of Barbara Jaeger's soirées. One Party man to another: something about Wolfgang Richter, something about a novel. Enough to know that the authorities were aware of it and that they were on the lookout. The who and the how were not important. The important thing was that Schilling watched his step, avoided sticking his neck out, took evasive action – the result being that he and Richter would stay out of trouble, not just this year and next year, but indefinitely. In the end, what mattered more than that? Certainly not, I decided, the integrity of a sequel, even one so brilliant I wished I had written it myself.

I did a lot of walking during those weeks. The stomach pains that now regularly plagued me were alleviated, I found, by exercise and fresh air. I walked several times all the way to Schilling's office, but was finally told that he had taken a spell of leave in Berlin and would not return until January. I left messages, asking him to call me back. Finally, one evening, he did.

'Happy New Year,' I said. 'How are things in Berlin? How's . . . ?'

'I've got news,' he said.

'About Paul?' I felt sure if it was bad news it would be bad news about that. The sudden dash to Berlin, just the state of the boy. It was good news that would have been surprising. 'What's happened?'

'It's not about Paul. It's about Wolfgang Richter.'

'I've finished his book,' I said. 'But I really think we have to . . .'

'I just got a call from his father.' Schilling drew a long, unsteady breath. 'Wolfgang Richter is dead.'

# PART TWO

## 11

The facts were these: upon his return to the valley, the young screen-writer had reportedly contracted a rare and deadly disease. It had incubated in his blood or his lymph for a week or so, then struck at the lining of his brain. According to his father, he had collapsed on a quiet street in the district of Loschwitz, on his way back from a party. He had been taken unconscious to a small hospital nearby and placed in intensive care. Treatment with antibiotics proved ineffective. He never regained consciousness and was dead within twenty-four hours. The microbe responsible was reportedly a meningococcal bacterium, one the authorities feared might be highly contagious. That was one reason his father had telephoned Michael Schilling: to warn him.

'And now you're warning me,' I said.

By this time I was in my chair, staring out at the steely blue dusk. Fingers of sleet were running down the window, gathering soot as they went.

'Yes,' said Schilling.

'We didn't meet. I never spoke to Richter. I didn't even shake his hand.'

'Maybe you wouldn't have to. Maybe this bug spreads through the air. We were all in the same room with him when you got your award.'

'So we were.'

'Although what we're supposed to do about it, I don't know. Get a blood test, I suppose.'

'Right. We should definitely do that.'

I put a hand to my forehead. It felt distinctly clammy. And there was an unfamiliar tension in my shoulders and my neck.

'There's something else,' Schilling said. 'The funeral. Wolfgang's father asked if you were going to be there.'

'He did? Why?'

'He was a great admirer of yours. *The Orphans of Neustadt* was one of his favourite books.'

'The father or the son?'

'The son. It was the reason he took up writing. Apparently he was always talking about you.'

How little fathers knew about their sons, I thought. How little they understood. If Wolfgang Richter had talked about me at all, it would have been the way Lenin used to talk about the Tsar, with a view to his overthrowing him, and the sooner the better.

'But I didn't *know* him,' I said. 'We were virtually strangers.'

'Herr Richter just asked. Still, I got the impression it would mean a lot to him, and his wife. Maybe it would be a kind of validation for them.'

'What are you talking about?'

'Their son was an artist. They want to think he'll be remembered.'

For *Two on a Bicycle*? It didn't seem all that likely. As artistic legacies went, it was decidedly slim; another tragic case of promise unfulfilled. Except, of course, there was his unpublished novel . . .

'I still don't understand how my name came up,' I said.

'They knew where you're published. I expect Wolfgang told them. Look, it doesn't matter. I just thought if you didn't have anything better to do. It's this Wednesday at the Tolkewitz Crematorium. Two o'clock.'

'The day after tomorrow? That's a little quick, isn't it?'

'The authorities at the hospital arranged it,' Schilling said. 'Apparently they don't want to take any chances with this bug.'

It was a cold, grey afternoon. I took a tram to the Johannis Cemetery, then walked up the long avenue towards the crematorium, the east wind cutting through my frayed old suit, so that my bones soon felt as cold and numb as those of the permanent residents. Monumental in soot-streaked granite, the Tolkewitz Crematorium was one of the few buildings in the city that the Royal Air Force could have firebombed into oblivion with my blessing. Of late imperial design, it hovered in its likeness between a massive pressure cooker and the entrance to a Wagnerian Valhalla. This was to be Wolfgang Richter's final destination, as if, with his last breath, the part-creator of *Two on a Bicycle* had become a devotee of tragic opera and wished to be borne away like a dying hero in the arms of a Valkyrie.

The Richter party – I counted twelve of them – stood at the bottom of the steps, waiting for their turn to go in. Either side of the avenue mourners from earlier funerals wandered about, singly and in pairs, among the trees and the graves. Some placed flowers, some held quiet conversations with the headstones, some even took photographs. One of them, to my surprise, pointed his lens at me – an opportunistic fan, I told myself. The presence of these strangers was unwelcome to me, though I was little better than a stranger myself. It made the occasion too public and too routine – one more funeral in an endless succession of funerals. Like the architecture, it prohibited intimacy.

Schilling was already there, dressed in his new raincoat, which, new or otherwise, wasn't warm enough for the prevailing conditions. He came over at once, shook my hand and led me towards a late-middle-aged couple standing arm-in-arm on the bottom step.

I had expected Richter's parents to be elegant, even in their grief. I imagined urbanity and sophistication, or at least a touch of the bohemian. Nothing of the kind was in evidence. Frau Richter was a fat woman with a disastrous home perm that reminded me of a wet poodle. She was dressed in a pale blue trouser suit, over which she wore a black anorak. Herr Richter, older by some years, gave off an air of awkwardness and timidity, accentuated by a double-breasted jacket that was too small for him. Short and bald, with red, elfin ears, he was afflicted with a stammer, which he had learned to control with telltale breaks in his speech – breaks that I at first took to be the effect of trauma. Had Wolfgang really sprung from the union of these two people? Or was he a graft, an orphan, adopted in childhood the way my great-uncle had adopted me – the main difference being that my great-uncle had only lasted a few years before dying of a brain tumour?

I briefly surveyed the rest of the company, searching for the cultured and stylish mourners who I had imagined would be there: the Berlin literati, the film-makers from the Babelsberg studio, the host of beautiful women (now all in black, veiled) that Wolfgang Richter always seemed to have at his command. But I saw only old people and pimply youths in sports clothes. It was possible that the Berlin crowd hadn't yet learned of the tragedy, I reminded myself. It wasn't necessarily the case that they thought it was too far to come.

It had crossed my mind, I must admit, that Theresa Aden might be among the legions of beautiful women in attendance. But that was not my reason for being there. At the universities, the new term had not yet begun. I thought she would still be at home in Austria, oblivious to what had happened. Besides, if we were ever to renew our acquaintance, I wanted it to be as far away from Wolfgang Richter as possible. I had no wish to be connected with Richter in her eyes. It was bad enough that Richter was connected to her in mine.

But then I saw her. She was walking up the path towards us, her hands in the pockets of her overcoat. I hadn't recognised her at first; her blonde hair was shorter and mostly hidden beneath a black beret. She looked pale, her eyes puffy. She came and stood at the edge of the crowd, but no one came forward to greet her. I had never expected to see her look so vulnerable and alone.

'Frau Richter, Herr Richter,' Schilling was saying, 'allow me to introduce Bruno Krug.'

Herr Richter grasped my hand with both of his. 'So good of you to . . . come, Herr Krug. So good of you to m-make the journey.'

Ten minutes on the tram; that was the journey (and ten minutes back). But then the poor man wasn't to know that. Nor would it have been kind, in the circumstances, to enlighten him.

'Wolfgang would have been so proud,' Frau Krug said and, without warning, she hugged me, her teary face brushing against my cheek, her hand flapping against the back of my neck like a freshly landed fish.

I had prepared my condolences in advance. The potential for saying the wrong thing is never greater than when dealing with the recently bereaved. But faced with the reality of grief, my carefully balanced words deserted me.

'He . . . he was a . . . a great talent,' I stammered. 'He showed such . . . such extraordinary . . .'

'Promise?' Schilling suggested.

A troublesome picture leapt into my mind: Herr Zoch, perched on the edge of my sofa, his notebook and ballpoint at the ready. *It's the promising ones you have to keep an eye on.*

'No, not that,' I said. The Richters looked crestfallen. 'Vision. Wolfgang was a visionary.'

At this Frau Richter felt free to hug me again. 'It would have been his birthday next week,' she said, as if that somehow cemented the tragedy of the occasion, 'his twenty-eighth birthday.'

I moved away as swiftly and tactfully as I could, but not so far that I couldn't form a clear impression of what happened next. Theresa had made her way towards the Richters. I don't know if she knew them already, or if she had to introduce herself, but when I looked back again, she was standing before them, her hands clasped together in front of her, talking. I suppose she was offering her condolences. But then, without warning Frau Richter turned away, grabbing her husband's arm. She was angry. Then she thought of something to say. She leaned towards Theresa so as not to be overheard. I could tell from the fix of her gaze and the mean set of her lips that her words were not friendly. Then she and her husband took off smartly up the steps, leaving Theresa standing at the bottom, looking stunned.

Before I could go to her, the doors of the crematorium opened and we were all ushered inside.

Close to the cemetery gates was an old world *Konditorei* that did good business holding funeral wakes. I had spent many uncomfortable hours in one or other of its function rooms, which were decked out with faux-velvet wallpaper and artificial flowers that no one ever dusted. Nonetheless, given the short notice, the Richters had been lucky to get themselves a slot there, because it was not unknown (so I was told) for relatives to make a booking even while their loved one still breathed. The nearest alternative venue was a good distance away.

The Richter party, swollen by now to maybe sixteen, were trailing back down the avenue at a respectful pace. I left Schilling and dropped back until I was walking beside Theresa. I wondered if she would recognise me, so long was it since our one and only conversation.

'It's nice to see you again, Herr Krug,' she said, with a smile that was fleeting, but just warm enough to seem sincere.

'Bruno, please.'

'I'd no idea you actually knew Wolfgang.'

'I didn't really. I knew his work.'

'His scriptwriting?'

I hesitated. With Michael Schilling barely out of earshot, I didn't want to get into the whole business of the Richter novel.

'That's right, *Two on a Bicycle* is one of my favourite films.' Theresa looked puzzled. I chuckled by way of supporting evidence. 'That scene where the chickens get on the roof . . .'

'I haven't seen it.'

'Oh, good.'

'Good?'

'Good because . . . Because you still have that pleasure ahead of you. We could even . . .'

I just managed to stop myself from proposing we make it a date: she and I, watching her dead lover's film – if indeed they had been lovers. I wanted quite badly to ask, but, again, the circumstances were not propitious.

We walked on a few paces in silence. The mourner I had seen earlier, taking photographs among the graves, was still in evidence.

He had been outside the crematorium a few moments earlier; now he was just beyond the trees on the other side of the avenue, his camera round his neck, his hands buried inside the pockets of a sheepskin coat. His gaze met mine, then suddenly he became very interested in a stone angel praying at the foot of a yew. A moment later he had disappeared.

The head of the party was nearing the road. As she reached the kerb, Frau Richter looked back at us. Seeing Theresa, her mouth pinched and her nostrils flared, as if by now she had expected to find this particular mourner gone.

'I couldn't help overhearing . . .' I said. 'Frau Richter . . .'

Theresa looked down at her shoes. 'She thinks it's my fault. That's what she said.'

'She couldn't mean . . .'

'If I hadn't got my claws into him, Wolfgang would still be alive.'

'That's ridiculous. You heard how he died. It was meningitis.'

'Yes, I know.'

'The poor woman's still in shock,' I said, glad of the opportunity to offer support. 'When something like this happens – something so unexpected, so senseless – people often feel the need to blame someone, however irrational that is. It has nothing to do with you.'

'Maybe. Maybe not. Mothers have a way of knowing these things, don't they? An instinct? Maybe if he'd never met me, everything would have been different. Maybe Wolfgang would have stayed in Berlin. And none of this would have happened.'

'Now you're the one being irrational.'

Theresa looked at me. I felt sure she was going to tell me something, to confide in me. But then she changed her mind. 'I'm sorry,' she said. 'Forget what I said. It's not your problem.'

'So you and Wolfgang, you were close?' I was certain that with a little more probing she would tell me the whole story.

She sniffed and got busy pulling on a pair of hairy woollen gloves. 'I only met him a few weeks ago.'

'But still you came today. It looks like a lot of people didn't.'

'I wanted to say goodbye.' She dug her hands into her pockets. 'It all happened so suddenly.'

'Yes,' I said. 'It did.'

We stopped opposite the *Konditorei*. The Richters had already gone inside. A smell of baking pastry sweetened the chill air.

'I'll leave you here,' Theresa said.

'You aren't coming in?'

She shook her head.

'Then I won't either. I'll make my excuses and . . .'

She put her hand on my arm. 'No. You must stay. They'd be disappointed. It means something to them that you're here.'

Theresa was right. It would have been too selfish to disappear at that stage of the proceedings.

'I tell you what, though,' she said. 'I've got a mandatory performance in a few days. At the college; the Blochmannstrasse building. Part of my exams. Why don't you come along, if you can?'

'What are you playing?' I asked, as if that made any kind of difference.

'Brahms. The F minor sonata.'

She pulled a comical grimace, as if the prospect terrified her. I said I would be there, almost forgetting to ask for the exact time and place.

# 12

The night before Theresa's recital I did not sleep well. I woke often, impressions of unhappy dreams effervescing in my mind. In the last of these, I was on the set of a Wolfgang Richter film. This time he was in the director's chair – except that the chair was temporarily unoccupied. I stood waiting for him to return, while all around me technicians hurried about, trailing cables or adjusting lights. This being a dream, it goes without saying that I did not know my lines. I was not sure I *had* any lines, or if I had any business being there at all. I stood frozen in place, afraid to stray in case I was needed, but equally afraid to remain. I was sure to be humiliated when the director returned: either thrown off the set, or bawled out for not knowing my part. Even the part itself, I was vaguely aware, involved the humiliation of my character, who was about to be caught red-handed in some act of depravity. Meanwhile, somewhere beyond the glare of the lights, Theresa sat watching. Thematically similar visions, increasingly tortured and harsh, lay in my future; but for the present the notion of Richter as *auteur* of my life's drama was confined to the nebulous realm of dreams.

I got up early and went into the bathroom, where I discovered I had run out of toothpaste. Normally this would have been a minor inconvenience, but on this particular day, my date with Theresa only hours away, it had the potential to ruin everything. Intent on averting a halitocean disaster, I left at once for the nearest pharmacy, only to be told that their entire stock of ElkaDent had been withdrawn from sale.

'Haven't you heard?' the assistant whispered. 'It's contaminated.'

'With what?' I asked.

'Mercury,' she said. 'An accident at the factory.'

Accidents at the factory were not widely reported in the Workers' and Peasants' State, for fear of lowering morale and giving comfort to the enemy, who were known to keep their populations docile with a liberal provision of toiletries, among other things. But the lack of official reporting did not stop the rumours.

'I'll take my chances,' I said, but the assistant would not oblige.

'It's all gone back to the warehouse,' she insisted. 'We had some Putzi, but that's all gone too.'

It was the same story in the middle of town. The contamination scare had been around for a week or more, and the few alternative brands had vanished. Even the Intershop couldn't help me. Their limited supply of overpriced Colgate had been exhausted within hours.

Time was running out. I would have to resort to begging, but from whom? The obvious place to start was Ferdinandsplatz, which was a short tram ride away.

Schilling seemed glad to see me. No sooner had I got up the stairs than he thrust a cup of tea into my hand, apologising for the absence of coffee and solicitously clearing away piles of paper from the sofa.

'How are you feeling?' he said, as if my health were an issue.

'Frankly, a little unwashed. How about you?'

'Fine. Have you arranged for a test?'

'A test?'

'A blood test. You know, what with Wolfgang being . . . Just in case.'

As far as I was concerned, the only possible source of infection was Richter's manuscript. How long *could* a microbe survive on a sheet of paper? Perhaps long enough.

'No. What about you?'

'No, not yet. I suppose I should.'

Schilling looked out across the square. On the hoarding opposite the old slogan had been replaced by a new one:

## DON'T SHIRK! WALK TO WORK!

Had the previous campaign produced a sudden bicycle shortage, or an intolerable increase in road accidents? In all likelihood we would never be told.

'I don't suppose anyone's contacted you, have they, from the hospital?' Schilling asked.

'No, they haven't. You?'

'No.'

A faint electric drone marked the passing of a tram. Sparks flickered dully on the windowpane. The air felt thick, pressurised, as if held down by an invisible weight.

'Do you have Wolfgang's manuscript?' Schilling asked.

'With me? No. It's still at the apartment.'

'You finished it, then?'

'Yes, I did. It's a great book, really. I understand your excitement.'

Schilling's reflection smiled in the glass. 'I knew you would.'

'I almost felt now and then . . . that it was something *I'd* written, or might have written. In a good way. I recognised the voice, the voices. To tell the truth, it was a little spooky at times.'

I might have put it more harshly had Richter still been alive.

For a moment Schilling seemed lost in thought.

'Do you know what he said, Bruno? He said he wrote that book because you didn't, or wouldn't.'

'Which? Didn't or wouldn't?'

Schilling turned. 'I don't know.'

'You don't remember?'

He sat down behind his desk. 'No, that's what he said, Bruno: you didn't or wouldn't. I suppose he meant . . .'

'Meant what?'

'It was just a chance remark.'

'But what did he mean?'

Schilling took off his glasses and polished them on his shirt tails. 'I don't know. We'll never know, will we? Not now.'

The truth of this statement seemed to depress him once again. It came to me that this was how he had spent the whole morning: dwelling on Richter's untimely demise – Richter, the second great literary discovery of his career, cast into obscurity before he'd even been published. On the other hand a posthumous discovery was still a discovery. Having a recently dead author did no obvious harm to the success of a book.

Suddenly Schilling seemed to be avoiding my eye.

'You aren't planning to publish, are you?' I asked.

'I don't know.' Without his glasses, the heavy frames and heavy lenses, Schilling's face looked unnaturally naked. 'I'd planned to. I wanted to.'

'It's too risky.'

'You think so?'

'Yes.'

I told him what I had planned to tell him before Richter's death: that it would have been wise to make changes obscuring the political message of the story, ideally by setting it in the West. Even so, I knew my advice was now academic, because the only person who could have made those changes was Richter himself. Schilling knew this as well as I did.

'Do you think he would have agreed to a rewrite?' I asked.

Schilling sighed. 'I don't know. Maybe. Probably. He'd have found a way through. As it is, the book's a masterpiece of camouflage.

Everything's between the lines. It doesn't tell you what to think.'

'The best books never do.'

We were calling it Richter's book, but it was not a book in the physical sense and by now we both knew it was never going to be. It was only ever going to be a manuscript, written by one man and read by two more. Too small to be called a literary circle, ours was a literary triangle.

'Of course,' Schilling said with a fleeting smile, 'if there was one writer besides Wolfgang I'd trust with the job it would be you.'

I was flattered by this remark, but I didn't want to get Schilling's hopes up. 'What would be the point, Michael? It wouldn't be Richter's book any more. You'd only be taking it away from him.'

Schilling brought his fist down on the desk. 'But it should be published. It *deserves* to be published!'

He looked at me, appealing for support, for courage.

'Michael,' I said gently, '*Richter* deserves to be published. But Richter is dead. Publication won't help him now. His book's good, yes, very good. But it isn't *alive*. It's not going to be hurt if you don't put it into print. You, on the other hand . . .'

Schilling nodded, his mouth set in a grim line. I had given him the absolution he needed. It remained to be seen if he took advantage of it.

'Now,' I said, 'I need to ask you a favour. Do you have any toothpaste? I've a date later and I don't want to stink.'

Before Schilling could answer, the telephone rang.

'Not here,' he said. 'I tried to get some the other day, but there's this . . .'

'Contamination scare. Yes, I know.'

I got to my feet, determined to continue my search without delay.

'Try salt,' Schilling said, picking up the receiver.

'Salt?'

'Table salt. It's the next best thing. If all else fails.'

# 13

Three hours later, with coarse Halle salt still stinging my excoriated gums, I sat down in a recital room at the college of music. Four young musicians were to be assessed; a cellist, two violinists and Theresa. The audience, twenty-five people at most, was comprised of fellow students, except for a handful of much older people, whom I took to be members of the faculty. Three of these sat behind a table at the front, equipped with pencils and paper. Waiting for Theresa to appear, I had a strong sensation of being an outsider in this studious little world, a gatecrasher at a private rite of passage. Though I had attended concerts at the college before, it was not until I saw her smile at me – a brief, secretive smile, executed in the midst of tuning up – that I felt I had any business being there.

I wouldn't have admitted it, but my outlook had changed since our first flirtatious encounter at the Cultural Association: my ambitions had become inflated, my exposure (to borrow the language of capital) had deepened. Theresa herself had very little to do with it. Rather, it was the obstacles that stood in my way – the sheer difficulty of finding her; the absence of any obvious entrée into her social circle – these were what had raised the stakes, even as I struggled to overcome them. And then there was Wolfgang Richter, who (so I thought) had stolen Theresa from under my nose, as if to make a point. He had been the biggest obstacle of all. This is another way of saying that, in the two months since we met, Theresa had acquired the veneer of the unattainable, which few men can resist. No wonder, then, that desire had given way to what in romantic novels is called *longing*. Such mutations are subtle, but dangerous. Desire is an appetite, quickly sated. Longing is a wound, an opening in the heart or the spirit. Whatever the cause, whatever the duration, it almost always leaves a scar.

That night Theresa was accompanied on the piano by a young woman with short dark hair and a round face. I recognised her from the Kulturpalast concert. It was she who had told me, in a less than friendly tone, of Theresa's imminent departure for the holidays. At first, watching them play was like witnessing a conversation between two halves of the same spirit, between two voices in the same mind – the mind of the composer, I supposed, divided between keyboard and strings: a kind of intimacy like no other. But then, in the third movement, the strains began to appear. A frown of concentration formed itself on Theresa's face and never left it. In the faster passages she began to scuff the notes, producing dissonances that were clearly not intended. In the last movement she seemed to lose the tempo altogether, racing ahead of the piano part as if keen to get the performance over and done with as quickly as possible. Listening to her was quite nerve-racking. The possibility of complete collapse seemed real. I forgot my stinging gums, the lingering taste of chloride on my tongue. I even forgot why I was there, so afraid was I that she would fail.

The piece concluded. The audience of students clapped appreciatively (I with a sense of relief); then most of them headed into the dressing room, with me on their heels. The performers wanted to know how they had done; the audience, in a spirit of solidarity, was anxious to assure them that they had done very well. Theresa greeted me with a peck on the cheek. She seemed happy that the whole thing was over. I tried to think of something to say about her performance, something that a critic might say, but nothing unpretentious came to mind.

'Who was it on the piano?' I asked finally.

'My accompanist?'

'She was very good. The two of you were like . . . well, a perfect duo.'

'Did you hear the *Vivace*? It was like a bloody horserace. My fault, unfortunately.' She tapped someone on the shoulder. 'Claudia, did you hear that? We're a perfect duo, apparently.'

The pianist turned, a smile still on her lips. She saw me, recognised me. The smile vanished.

'Bruno, may I present Claudia Witt. Claudia, Bruno Krug, the writer.'

'We've met,' she said. 'Kind of.'

Fortunately I didn't have to explain the where and when; the sound of my name caused heads to turn all around the room. Among the student body, it turned out, *The Orphans of Neustadt* was still a favourite and I was soon fielding questions from several quarters. Theresa looked on, smiling but saying nothing. I performed for her as best I could, asking questions as well as answering them (questions designed to reflect my innate inquisitiveness and uniqueness of perspective), peppering my comments with as many humorous asides as possible. The students seemed delighted, all except the boyish Claudia, who stood staring at Theresa and fiddling with a cheap ring on her middle finger.

'So what are you working on now?' someone asked. 'Another novel?'

'Yes,' I said.

'What's it about?'

'Well, I don't like to . . .'

'Another one of the *Factory Gate Fables*?'

Theresa's brow momentarily furrowed. It was a reflex, over in a split second, but it told me something. Another one of my *Factory Gate Fables*? I would clearly have to do better than that.

'No,' I said. 'No, this is something on a grander scale. Something more like *The Orphans of Neustadt*, at least in tone.'

This was what everyone wanted to hear. The student body couldn't wait to get its hands on my new book.

'I heard you'd given up writing altogether,' one of the violinists said. 'So much for rumours.'

And everyone agreed that the rumours of my creative eclipse (rumours of which I had been hitherto unaware) were laughable and absurd – and quite possibly the work of rivals, jealous of my popularity and fearful of my inexhaustible talent.


Theresa and I left together for a café opposite the Volkspark. It was getting dark.

'I like your friends,' I said as we set off.

'I know what they're going to say,' she said. 'They're going to say I've got a thing about writers.'

I hoped her friends were right.

'Well, they seemed like a nice crowd.'

I didn't want her to know how out of place I'd felt among them: complicated, compromised, with so much more behind me and so much less ahead.

'They are nice, I think.'

'You only think?'

'I don't really know them all that well, except Claudia. They keep themselves apart a bit, you know, because I'm . . .'

'A Westerner?'

'I don't blame them. It's difficult, isn't it?' She looked over her shoulder at a solitary van parked by the kerb. Behind the wheel a tiny orange ball flared in the darkness, betraying the presence of a driver. 'I don't want to get anyone into trouble.'

A gathering wind shook rainwater from the trees.

'They wouldn't get into trouble,' I said. 'Where do you think you are? I expect they're jealous of you, that's all.'

Theresa shook her head. 'I don't think so. For one thing, most of them play much better than I do. Not just technically: they play with real passion. Music means so much to them. They give themselves to it completely. I can't do that.'

'Your playing seemed passionate to me.'

She shrugged. 'It's passionate music. You just have to get the notes right.'

I wondered if this was the reason she didn't play the violin: her passion deficiency would become too obvious. If so, there was something almost tragic about her predicament: to be committed to the life of an artist, only to find you lack the sensibilities an artist needs. I felt an urge to hold her. It was love she needed: reckless and raw.

'Have you always felt this way?'

She hugged her viola case against her chest. 'I always suspected it. The trouble was, people kept telling me I was the genuine article, when I was still learning. I could play all the notes, you see. But I knew it didn't mean anything. It was like tap-dancing on strings.'

Her fingernails rapped against the case. I was reminded instantly of a typewriter – and then of typing the *Factory Gate Fables*.

'Just give it time,' I said. 'You're young.'

'Not much younger than you were when you wrote *The Orphans of Neustadt*.' She smiled. 'It doesn't matter, really. Playing the right notes is all that's required of the viola, nine times out of ten. That's enough of a headache, as you may have noticed.'

I didn't believe her, as it happened, but at that moment a particularly strong gust of wind barrelled down the street, giving me an excuse to offer her my arm. After a moment's hesitation she took it.

We drank our coffee the Russian way. That is to say we had vodka before it and vodka afterwards. I could tell Theresa was not a seasoned drinker from the way she screwed up her face as each gulp went down. But that didn't stop her. Once the first shot was warming her insides, she was happy to accept the refills. As the hour wore on, I detected a touch of recklessness, an affected decadence, in the way she sat, leaning on one elbow, the glass dangling from her fingertips. I attributed this to the after-effects of nervous tension. Her performance had been an important event, as well as an exhausting one. It also occurred to me that perhaps she wanted to seem more worldly and despoiled than she felt, because that made her a more suitable companion for me.

She came from a small town near Linz. I asked her why she had chosen to study at the Carl Maria von Weber; why she hadn't completed her studies at a music school in the West.

'I couldn't get a place', she said simply. 'Too much competition.'

It was also a question of money. Everything cost less in the East.

'In the West I had to take a job to pay my way,' she said. 'Here I can study full time. That makes quite a difference. I'm never short of time to practise.'

She left it at that. What she'd said made some sense. Students from the non-socialist abroad were rare but not unknown. The dangers of ideological contamination were outweighed by the requirement for hard currency. All the same, I sensed in this brisk explanation a degree of brittleness. Perhaps the vetting procedure had been more rigorous than she implied.

'Your parents didn't mind?' I asked. 'Your being so far away?'

She shook her head. 'I'm twenty-five next birthday. Besides, my father works for the metal workers' union. He thinks it's good for me to see how the other half lives. He thinks I might *learn* something.'

This was credible too. Though Western labour unions had a long track record of collusion with the forces of capital, still there was always hope that they would one day rediscover their idealism and take up the cause of revolution. In the meantime their hard currency was as good as anyone else's.

An available place, a financial saving, paternal approval: why did I have the impression there was more to it than that?

'So what happens when you're done here?' I asked.

The table where we sat was very small. When we leaned on it, our arms touched. It meant we didn't have to shout.

'I feel happiest playing chamber music,' Theresa said, 'but I'll have to join an orchestra first. If I can find one that'll have me. It isn't going to be easy.'

I insisted she could have the pick of the orchestras, judging from what I'd just heard, but she scoffed at that.

'If only there were a viola players' convention somewhere. I could sneak in there and poison their food. Cyanide or something. If half of them dropped dead, *then* I could take my pick.'

'And what would your pick be?'

She didn't answer at once. She seemed suddenly lost in thought. Was it something I'd said – or something *she'd* said?

'Berlin. I'd like to play for the Berlin Phil. If we're talking pipe-dreams.'

I refilled her glass. Up until that point we hadn't mentioned Wolfgang Richter, but I knew we'd have to, at least once; if we didn't he would loom even larger in our thoughts than he did already. His memory was a boil that had to be lanced.

'Was that where you met?' I asked. 'In Berlin?'

'Met who?'

'Wolfgang.'

Theresa acknowledged my perspicacity with a faltering smile. 'Yes. Standing in front of the Pergamon Altar. I was being a tourist, seeing the sights.'

'And Wolfgang?'

'The same, I suppose. I remember the first thing he said to me. He said, "Take a good look. That's the last clean thing you'll see in this country." I had no idea what he was talking about. But then, when I started travelling around, all the soot . . .'

'The Berlin air is better than most,' I said. 'Up there, they keep all the factories at arm's length. I didn't know Wolfgang was an environmentalist.'

Theresa shrugged. 'Everyone complains about the pollution, don't they?'

'I don't know. Maybe they should. Complaining is certainly how we get things done around here. Although it only counts if it's in writing – ideally verse. A really good rhyme for lignite and it goes straight to Herr Honecker.'

Theresa laughed. She was, I sensed, eager to laugh, to stop the exhilaration of her recital giving way to melancholy. An actor I met once told me about the feelings of deflation that follow a public performance, when the hall is empty and the audience gone. He said it was not unlike the feeling of mourning. And, in Theresa's case, there was still real mourning to be done as well (for hadn't I seen her and Richter together? Hadn't I witnessed their secret embrace?).

'You know,' she said, 'you're not at all how I thought you'd be.'

'And how was that?'

'I don't know. You wrote a classic. You're a local hero – no, a *national* hero.'

'Not quite.'

'But you don't talk about it, not unless you're cornered. And even then you can't wait to get off the subject. All that beauty, all that achievement: it's as if it all came from someone else.'

'It was a long time ago. I just feel I've exhausted the subject.'

'That's all?'

'That's all.'

Theresa shook her head, still smiling. 'Is it true that one of your books has been turned into an opera in North Korea?'

The volume in question was allegedly the first of the *Factory Gate Fables;* the source of the rumour an unconfirmed report in an army newsletter, concerning an official visit to Pyongyang by a military delegation. If true, the North Koreans had proceeded without permission and without payment.

'North Korea?' I said. 'Now where did you hear that?'

'I'm not sure.'

'From Wolfgang, I suppose.'

'Probably. He talked about you a lot, you and your books.'

'Did he?' I tried to sound surprised, then reached for the vodka. 'Still, that doesn't mean we have to talk about *him*.' I handed her the glass. 'Or does it?'

She looked at the vodka for a few seconds, as if trying to make a decision. 'Maybe not tonight,' she said and took it. 'Tonight I don't want to be sad. Still, I thought it was very sweet of you to go to his funeral. I think it really made a difference, you know, to his parents.'

I clinked my glass against hers. 'To Wolfgang. And us.'

We drank, draining our glasses in one. As soon as we put them down again, as soon as I looked into her face, I knew that the next significant thing to pass between us would be a kiss.

# 14

She had a tiny bedsit apartment in a modern block, one street away from the college. It was sparse and bare like a hospital, but Theresa had done her best to make it homely. There were vases filled with dried flowers and a large ethnic blanket pinned up across the wall. A degree of intimacy was achieved by careful arrangement of two anglepoise lamps, one of which was trained on the space above the bed; so that from anywhere else in the room our bodies would have been seen in tasteful silhouette. We bustled into the room, laughing, my arm by now round Theresa's waist. If I am honest, I think she was a little drunk. I also think she was lonely. But neither of those considerations restrained me. I was puzzled and disturbed by the hold she had over me, by my own emotional incontinence.

I wanted her body and soul, but body first. I am speaking here chronologically. I saw no reason to put off carnal ecstasy until after our spirits had fused into some perfect ectoplasmic whole. I was already at an age when putting off anything was a bad idea. But that doesn't mean to say that the conventional accompaniments to sex – romance, companionship, shared recreation – were not also creeping on to my Theresian agenda. I had pictured them all, mentally trying them on for size. But elsewhere in my psyche was the under-standing that they would never materialise, or only fleetingly. Theresa was young and beautiful. I had nothing to offer her that she would want to keep, nothing real. You can only go so far on a reputation. But if I was not, in the end, to have Theresa's love, I thought, then the fact that I had once enjoyed her body might make the disappointment that much easier to bear.

I had bought a half-bottle of schnapps on the way there. The room was cold. Still in our coats, we sat side by side on the bed and drank the liquor out of coffee mugs, while a single-bar electric fire slowly warmed us from the feet up. Theresa switched on a tape recorder. The music was Bach: chorale preludes arranged for solo piano – hardly the conventional music of romance, let alone seduc-tion. But it seemed to have an effect on her. She put her head on my shoulder, humming the melody, allowing me to inhale the sweet, stirring scent of her hair. I imagined that during those first intoxi-cating (and intoxicated) minutes J. S. Bach and the musician playing

J. S. Bach and the author of *The Orphans of Neustadt* were fusing in Theresa's mind into a single creative entity: one mind, one spirit and one body – the body, as luck would have it, being mine. Still, didn't that mean it was Bruno Krug the artist to whom she was drawn, rather than Bruno Krug the man, the former being an intangible entity, a dream lover of infinite potency and immaculate breath?

By now any microscopic fauna still resident in my mouth were pickled, but still I wasn't confident that brushing with salt had done enough to sterilise the internal environment. The salt had been Michael Schilling's suggestion and he was anything but the Don Juan of the valley. I excused myself and went into the bathroom. Two toothbrushes stood in the tooth mug, but there was no sign of any toothpaste. Hastily I searched under the basin. Behind numerous bottles of shampoo and moisturiser and a roll of cotton wool, I found a wash bag. Inside, still in its cardboard box, was a fresh tube of something called Crest.

Running a tap to cover my act of larceny, I squeezed out an inch of Crest on to a toothbrush – except that it was not toothpaste as I knew it. Stripes, long, red and perfectly parallel, ran right through it. Seen end-on, they formed a Maltese cross, which impressed me greatly. I tasted it with my tongue. It *was* toothpaste. But what were the red stripes for? Were they supposed to improve the look of my gums? (Were red gums desirable, and not, as I had always assumed, a harbinger of gingivitis?) How was it possible to keep all these stripes in place as the paste was squeezed from the tube? Why didn't everything get mixed up, emerging as a smeary pink mess? And it occurred to me, even as I brushed, that the provision of innovative toiletries in maintaining a docile population must be even more important than I'd thought. For why else would a civilisation devote so much of its scientific and technical resources to meeting such a challenge?

I hurried out again. Theresa was lying down, one arm behind her head. I went and sat down on the bed. 'I expect you're tired,' I said.

That was when she reached up for me and our lovemaking began.

For the writer under Actually Existing Socialism describing sex is a simple matter: he simply does not do it (the describing, I mean, not the sex). All literature is serious literature, meaning literature with a clear social purpose. Although declining birth rates are a perennial problem in socialist countries, depictions of human coupling are not regarded as useful to the greater social project and are therefore discouraged. In Western literature, by contrast, the issue is beset with difficulty. In commercial fiction sex occurs in a story because sex is what the readers are thought to want. But in less mercenary forms of fiction, unless the story has no sexual dimension, the author is torn. Sex for the purposes of titillation is definitely out. But to leave the reader at the bedroom door can seem coy or old-fashioned. If sex is important to a character, the experience of sex should be conveyed as convincingly as possible. Sex is another lens through which the inner workings of a character may be revealed, which usually means (this being serious fiction) that the sex is awkward, troublesome and miserable. There is a great deal of silence and occasional weeping. Still, for my money this is preferable to the meltings and feelings of rightness that wash over characters in the grip of romanticised fiction, where sex can never be what it is; where metaphor and simile must work overtime to turn flesh into spirit and the human into the divine.

My memories of that first night with Theresa are, in any case, sketchy. Even those I have could not be called reliable. I am not being coy, or old-fashioned. But so much of what was good from that time was subsequently locked away, if only because to relive it would be to miss it more. I do remember that it was still chilly in the room, and that much of our lovemaking happened under sheets and blankets. At one point I wrapped them round myself like a Roman emperor, which made Theresa laugh. I remember the first sight of her naked: her skin paler, her breasts smaller, her lower ribs and pelvis more prominent than I'd expected. At one point I rolled her over and kissed her slowly from the nape of her neck to the base of her spine, pausing to massage the muscles between her shoulder blades.

As for the rest, I can reveal little in the way of objective truth. On other occasions, with other women, I had been in the habit of mentally replaying the carnal high points over the days that followed, retrospectively gloating on my sexual triumph. With Theresa it was different. Impressions of our night together – even things I couldn't recall noticing at the time – flashed before my eyes uninvited, and often: the gossamer-fine hair on the nape of her neck, the way she bit her lower lip at the approach of pleasure, the last deep sigh before she fell asleep. Such memories came to me at unguarded moments and I couldn't keep them out. This had happened with no other woman, with no other lover, and the experience was disquieting, because I didn't know what it meant.

I do remember the way Theresa felt as she lay asleep in my arms. The impression I remember clearly, as if it were yesterday: she felt vulnerable, like a lost child. And I wondered if she hadn't come here, to my smoky valley, not for any of the reasons she had given me; to save money or to please her socialistic father, but to escape from something in the West, something that could no longer be borne – something or someone. She had come for the same reason I had come: for shelter.

The bed was too narrow for sleep, but she fell asleep anyway. The recital and the alcohol and the sex had exhausted her. It was almost midnight. I decided it would be best to go. The morning to come would be awkward, hungover and malodorous – an unwelcome and premature antidote to romance. But I would leave behind a note, a charming and romantic note, one that she would press for ever between the leaves of a favourite book.

I got dressed and went over to the work table by the window, searching for pen and paper. There, to my surprise, I found a copy of *The Orphans of Neustadt*. It was a recent edition with a simple cover design: a skyline in silhouette, behind it a red sky split in two by the white beam of a searchlight. Theresa had told me she had taken my book from a library, but this was not a library book. The pages were clean and unread. It seemed she had bought herself a copy to keep.

I was about to put it back when I noticed something protruding from under the back flap of the jacket. It was a strip of black-and-white passport photographs inside a small greaseproof-paper envelope. I took the photographs out and found myself looking at three identical images of Wolfgang Richter. He was smiling.

# 15

I set off home on foot, along the wide empty avenues of Striesen (which even by day all looked the same: low-rise apartment blocks, grass, spindly trees). It wasn't too late for a tram or a taxi, but my mind was always clearer when my feet were in motion, and I needed clarity to rebalance myself and take stock. I didn't care that it was drizzling.

After my success with Theresa, I felt entitled to a period of calm. The long weeks of waiting and hoping, with the concomitant dangers of rejection and humiliation, were at last behind me. I had achieved my objective. The affirmation I'd craved was mine and it could not be taken back. If there was ever a moment to bathe in the afterglow, to breathe easy, it was now. In any event, I could not go on living as I had lived during the preceding two months: lurching from hope to disappointment and back again, working not at all, sleeping badly, wasting countless hours in draughty recital halls, hoping for a glimpse of my prize. As an interval, as a chance to re-experience the tunnel vision of the lovelorn youth, it was excusable, if not exactly edifying. As a way of life it was out of the question. From now on my dealings with Theresa would take place in a spirit of emotional and psychological equality, or not at all. Never again would there be quite so much at stake.

As for Wolfgang Richter, his memory would now bother me far less than it had. It was undeniable that his interest in Theresa had sharpened my desire for her. The thought of them as lovers had tormented me before his death and troubled me after it. But now I was her lover too. Romantically, sexually, the young screenwriter and I had arrived at an honourable draw, at which point the matter could be laid to rest. In the haven of my old life I would be safe again, with nothing to fear from either the living or the dead.

All this I told myself, even as the first memories – of words, of caresses, of flesh and hair, of scent and beauty and Theresa's smile – gatecrashed my thoughts, reminding me of what I had tasted but not yet won.

Could I make all of it mine, make Theresa mine, not for a night or a month of nights, but for ever? Hypothetically speaking, was such a thing possible? I decided it was. Obstacles remained, without doubt, but what love story was without them? Wasn't love tempered in the fire of adversity (in life just as in books and films)? Theresa might grow to love me, in spite of everything. She struck me as capable of loving – as made for it, in fact. She might go on loving me, even when she knew my secrets and my flaws. Maybe I, and I alone, could give her what she needed. How else had we come this far? Wasn't I more to her already than the author of a famous book?

Buoyed by this optimistic mantra, I found my pace picking up. Crossing the empty roads, it was hard not to break into a run. It wasn't until I was standing at the corner of the Neumarkt, the ruins of the Frauenkirche before me, that I realised I had been walking in completely the wrong direction.

In my note I told Theresa that I was going to be in town the following afternoon and that I would come by her apartment building on the off chance that she was free for an hour or so. It was a carefully balanced proposal: neither needy nor indifferent, solicitous but not presumptuous. Its one disadvantage was it left me in suspense for the rest of the day, not knowing if Theresa would be in when I called or not.

The only way to deal with this unpleasant interval of uncertainty, I decided, was to stay in bed, preferably asleep, for as long as possible. But my plan came to nothing. First, it was the morning the children came round collecting old newspapers for recycling. Next Michael Schilling telephoned. He was suddenly very anxious that I should return 'that manuscript' to him as soon as possible (the way he carefully avoided mentioning Richter's name struck me as comical). Finally, around nine o'clock, I was woken by a booming voice coming from the stairwell: the unmistakable voice of the swimming pool committee in the person of Frau Wiegmann. She was having a conversation with one of my elderly neighbours and did not sound in a good mood. I could guess why: weeks had gone by since our last meeting and so far I had not managed to come up with a single bag of cement, let alone machinery to mix it. She was, without a doubt, on her way to remind me of my obligations and of how the whole project was hanging by a thread.

I contemplated pretending to be out, but at the third peal of knocking I lost my nerve and sloped reluctantly to the door. 'Excuse me, Frau Wiegmann,' I said, trying to sound ill. 'I think I'm coming down with something. I think it's best you don't come in.'

Frau Wiegmann's face was a vision of motherly concern. She bustled into my kitchen and insisted on making me a cup of malt coffee, which she produced from her enormous handbag, along with a large slab of gingerbread, which I suspect had been left over from Christmas. I played the role of the invalid for all it was worth, hoping to lessen the scolding I knew I was in for.

Once installed in my best armchair, Frau Wiegmann went back to her handbag again and produced a piece of paper. 'I received this just yesterday,' she said, putting on her glasses, 'from a Herr Farber, assistant general supervisor of the construction department of the Fritz-Hecker Saxony *Kombinat*.'

I coughed as pathetically as I could, but Frau Wiegmann was not going to be put off any longer. 'It says: due to a temporary over-supply of construction materials and adjustments to our current planning objectives, we shall be able to offer you, at no charge, one thousand kilograms of cement suitable for the commendable restor-ation works you propose; additionally the use of cement-mixing equipment for the likely duration of said works.'

Frau Wiegmann took off her glasses and beamed at me. I had never seen her look so happy.

'Herr Krug,' she said. 'How can we ever thank you?'

I held up my hands. 'It's wonderful news, Frau Wiegmann, wonderful news. But I can assure you it has nothing to do with me.'

Frau Wiegmann put her head on one side and gave me another indulgent look. It was obvious that she interpreted my words as modesty and that nothing I could say, now or in the future, would make her believe them.

# 16

Later that day I made a second attempt to buy toothpaste. It was no more successful than the first. The only item I managed to procure was an antiseptic gargle that tasted powerfully of burnt rubber and stripped the lining clean off my tongue. It was on my way back from the pharmacy that I had a disturbing encounter with an old derelict who habitually wandered the eastern districts of our city.

In the Western world Gruna Willy, as he was known locally, would have been classified as 'long-term unemployed'. But not in the East. In the East no such designation existed, for the simple reason that unemployment, like prostitution, had been abolished by Party fiat and could no longer be said to exist. All citizens under Actually Existing Socialism were workers, regardless of whether they actually had work. In any case, Gruna Willy was not without employment. He was fully employed in poisoning himself, a task that demanded long hours and exemplary dedication. (Years later, after the Workers' and Peasants' State had ceased to exist, Willy took additional steps to fend off the West's undesirable nomenclature, which by that time applied to a fifth of the Saxon workforce. To the occupation of drinking he added that of urination – not the simple function, performed out of biological necessity, but public, premeditated and targeted urination. From somewhere he had acquired a bronze bust of Lenin, which he placed at a busy intersection south of the city centre. There, protected on every side by streams of traffic, he pissed at regular intervals on Comrade Ulyanov's bald head, grinning gleefully and shaking his Johnson for all it was worth. Proof that this amounted to self-employment was supplied by passing drivers, many of whom acknowledged Gruna Willy's performance by hurling their change at him. Whether the coins landed at his feet or struck him in the face, Willy's entrepreneurial response was always to bow low before scooping them up in his cap.)

Like many in his line of business, Gruna Willy had a number of proprietary catchphrases, which he used to distinguish himself from the competition. The most unnerving, which he would bellow at passers-by as evening fell, was '*Watch out for the death strip!*' This was a reference to the mine-sown no-man's-land that ran along our side of the inner German border, an undesirable stretch of real estate where the border guards (the *Grenzer*) were empowered to shoot more or less on sight. It was whispered – with what authority I cannot say – that Gruna Willy had been one of the *Grenzer* himself, and that he had shot someone on a night patrol, the guilt driving him into the arms of alcohol and madness. I even heard it said that his victim had been a young woman and that the young woman had been carrying an unborn child. These were fictional embellishments, I had no doubt, but they made Gruna Willy an object of dread and fascination, a spectre whose comings and goings were watched from behind the net curtains by young and old alike.

Blasewitz was not on Willy's regular mendicant circuit, but now and again he would show up like a bad conscience, reminding the local populace of his cautionary message and soliciting for funds. I had given him money on occasions, at other times food. Not only did I pity him; it struck me that the tenor of his message was essentially public-spirited. And there was something of the Old Testament prophet about his wild grey hair and deep oracular voice. Once I gave him a volume of my *Factory Gate Fables* (I had on that day's wanderings spotted it lying in a skip), an act of charity to which he responded with one of his deep, theatrical bows. This, I expect, is how he came to know my name.

The day of my second date with Theresa, I found Gruna Willy pacing the street outside my building, wearing a long military coat with a length of clothes line for a belt. Even from a distance he looked older and wilder than usual, his eyes red-rimmed, his lips twitching ceaselessly, as if muttering to an invisible companion, his breath making clouds in the freezing air. The kindergarten children were inside by this time, gas masks stowed, but I noticed several young faces pressed up against the glass, watching him open-mouthed.

To rehearse imaginary conversations on paper is called literature. To do so out loud is called madness. Sharing this common prejudice, I decided to avoid contact by crossing to the other side of the street. But no sooner had I reached the door than I was overcome with shame. What if Gruna Willy had made the journey to Blasewitz specifically in the hope of finding me? To survive in Willy's line of business it was important to keep a reliable mental record of where and from whom assistance has been received. I could imagine all too keenly his despair at seeing me turn my back.

Holding my shopping bag in one hand, I reached into my jacket for some money. I heard a vehicle pull up behind me and turned to see Gruna Willy hurrying across the street, uttering his usual warning, but with more than usual urgency.

'Don't worry,' I told him, producing a five-Ostmark note. 'I'm not going *near* the death strip.'

Willy's forward progress was abruptly halted by the appearance of two uniformed officers of the *Volkspolizei*, who unceremoniously seized him by the shoulders and dragged him towards a van that had stopped in the middle of the road.

'The dogs, Herr Krug! The dogs!' Willy cried, seemingly oblivious to his predicament. 'They've got your scent!'

The police officers threw him in the back, neither of them giving me so much as a glance. I lost sight of Willy at that point, the glass in the side windows being frosted, but even after they slammed the doors I could still hear him shouting – until quite suddenly the shouting stopped.

The human cerebrum produces strange visions when routinely pickled in alcohol. I did not take Gruna Willy's delusional outburst seriously, even if he had identified me by name (which I did find disturbing). Still, it must have made some impression, because when Theresa opened the door to me an hour later the first thing she said was: 'Are you all right?'

# 17

The temporary unavailability of toothpaste continued to dog the early days of my affair with Theresa Aden. Ordinarily it would have been a simple matter to borrow half a tube from a well-disposed neighbour, but the contamination scare had brought out the innate hoarding instincts of the valley dwellers. Even to make such a request would have been the height of presumption, like asking to borrow a selection of underwear or a litre of blood. The one person I could have turned to was Frau Wiegmann. She could not have been more kindly disposed towards me than she was at this time. But I found myself reluctant to approach her. To ask a favour of her would be to pretend that she was indeed in my debt and that I had, in spite of all my sincere protestations, been her saviour in cement. So instead of toothpaste I made do with salt and whatever I could steal from Theresa's bathroom – which I visited as soon as I could whenever we returned to her apartment, even though it must surely have left her with the impression that I suffered from a weak bladder, as older men often do.

Despite these oral inconveniences, those first few weeks brought me happiness. What's more, it was the kind of happiness men crave most: happiness that raises the pulse and dilates the pupils, happiness that fills the heart with hope. It was not an unwavering state, needless to say. Happiness, in my experience, never is – that breathless kind of happiness least of all. My continual state was, if anything, one of heightened anxiety, because when I wasn't with Theresa I worried that something would go wrong: her affection for me would fade, or she would find someone else she liked better.

Between these agitated states I did experience quieter pleasures. We talked a lot, mainly about music. A player's perspective, I discovered, is different from a collector's. The player sees the inner workings with greater clarity, the way an engineer sees a bridge. She sees the flaws, the devices, the cosmetic repairs, as well as instances of inventiveness and the innovation. Gradually I became familiar with her tastes and preferences, and not only when it came to music. She hated brushing her hair, to cite one example, which she was obliged to do often and always before bedtime; otherwise it would tangle spectacularly and self-knot during the night, leaving her looking like a warrior from some mythical tribe of savage blondes.

'Why don't you cut it short,' I suggested one time, as she fretted before the mirror, 'if it's so much trouble?'

'I did once,' she said. 'People started calling me "sonny".'

She would not eat beetroot or drink beer. Vodka, for reasons opaque to us both, frequently made her sneeze.

I remember a habit she had, when she sat down at the dining table, of spreading her fingers out in front of her and looking at them for a moment with an expression of confusion, as if unsure what should be done with them. I loved those moments of disengagement from the predictable continuum of life. It was as if she had glimpsed the strangeness of human existence, its arbitrary forms (ten fingers, not eight or eleven), and been able, if only for an instant, to perceive it from without, like a being from another world.

The way we passed our time together was not extraordinary. The valley, for all its history, was no recreational paradise. Yet every shared activity, no matter how mundane, was gilded with a sense of possession. We owned the streets we walked along, the parks we sat in, the cafés we frequented (or so it seemed to me); they were the backdrop for the drama in which we starred. I took photographs to prove it. Even a trip to the Hygiene Museum – her idea, not mine – with its giant glass bodies and luminous internal organs, its vivid recreations of bodily malformation and infectious disease, failed to put our romantic escapade in context, or to remind us that its days were numbered.

Not all my discoveries were happy. On my second visit to Theresa's apartment I asked her to play for me. She refused. Instead, she told a joke: 'Why do people take an instant dislike to the viola?'

'I don't know. Why?'

'Because it saves time.'

I assumed she was being modest and repeated my request, not because I was especially anxious for music, but because I liked the idea, in a depraved, sultanesque way, of her performing for me; and even though she would not, like an actual harem-dwelling concubine, be disrobing for my entertainment, I would still be able to enjoy a shameless perusal of her body, interpreted through the caress and cling of her clothes and the rhythmic shift of balance and weight.

Finally she played a transcription of Bach, a short piece, pure, timeless and impeccably mannered. I made her play some more. Then, sensing that time was moving on, I went to the bathroom and brushed my teeth; and when I returned I found that the viola was back in its case. I asked her to take it out again and play some more.

'The solo repertoire's very limited,' she said. 'I need an accompanist.'

'No you don't.' I lay down on the bed. 'What's the matter? You perform for strangers, but you won't perform for me?'

'It's not like that.'

'What is it like?'

Theresa blushed. 'What makes you think I like performing for *anyone*?'

'You mean you don't?'

She sat down on the bed with her back to me. 'As a matter of fact, no. Not recently. What I enjoy is playing for myself.'

'All alone?'

She said it was the only time she felt comfortable. 'The rest of the time I feel . . .' I remember how she brought a hand to her throat '. . . *constrained*. It's been that way since . . .'

'Since when?'

She shrugged. 'Since I got really good at it, I think. Since I started winning prizes at school. I'm sorry, I can't explain it.'

I was troubled by this revelation, though not as troubled as I should have been. The musician is a performer. She lives to be heard. Yet as Theresa's expertise had grown, so – apparently – had her inhibitions. But before I could question her on this paradox, she took out her viola again and knocked out a sweet, sentimental folk tune, moving round the room and doing circles as she played, like a gypsy violinist at a Hungarian restaurant. It was an insincere, kitsch performance, but having her dance for me, as well as play, was even more arousing than I'd hoped. I soon forgot her strange confession and the ardour with which I grasped her, pressing my mouth to hers, was genuine; likewise the hunger with which I pushed my hands beneath her clothes (both her hands were still occupied holding instrument and bow), uncovering her nipples with all the impatience of a teenager behind a sand dune. The coupling that followed I remember with almost as much affection as our first. It was breathless, hungry, impolite. And the look on Theresa's face (which I could see clearly, there having been no time for atmospherics) was mostly one of surprise, followed by breathless introspection, allowing me to imagine, if only for a minute or two, that she was experiencing revelatory levels of arousal.

I also recall distinctly, as we finally lay breathless and naked on the churned-up sheets, wondering for the first time what Theresa was doing about contraception. What if she was, in fact, doing the same as me, namely nothing? I considered this without the frisson of terror that such speculations usually engender in the male. Instead, I found myself thinking that it would be apt if such instinctive and primal lovemaking had a lasting effect; that for there *not* to be conception and birth (a bouncing baby boy, four kilos at least!) would be almost anticlimactic. These brief, post-coital reflections were, of course, almost adolescent in their selfishness. But, as I have said, so was the sex itself, on that day.

One afternoon we were walking through the Neumarkt. As we passed the towering ruins of the Frauenkirche I checked among the mounds of rubble and brambles for the bouquet I had left there to mark my mother's birthday. That was when Theresa, perhaps misinterpreting my interest, asked me if I believed in God 'by any chance'.

In spite of the obvious context, the question caught me by surprise. In the Workers' and Peasants' State the otherworldly was an important resource, not to be squandered promoting hollow observances and redundant moral strictures – *Thou shalt not covet thy neighbour's ox*, for example, oxen having been fully collectivised under the agricultural reforms of the 1950s. Visions and evocations of a Promised Land, although as fantastical as any vision of heaven in the Bible, had been brought down to earth and put to the service of society. Even under Actually Existing Socialism the halcyon prospect of a perfectly just world in which the coercive power of government was redundant, remained the official long-term goal. Churches, ministers and small congregations still existed. Among our hankering youth, religious gatherings were quite popular, providing both a frisson of countercultural danger and an opportunity to meet girls. But the rest of us saw no particular reason to get involved. The state had diligently supplanted religious rites of passage – marking birth, coming of age, marriage and death – with alternative, secular ceremonies. And since, just as in the West, this was all the use most people had for religion, the connections between Church and people had all but withered away.

'Why do you ask?' I said.

Theresa shook her head. 'That's what everyone says here. You ask them if they believe in God and they always say: "Why do you ask?"'

'And what do people say where *you* come from?'

Theresa glanced over her shoulder. It was a habit she had when we were out and about, a reflex. I had just begun to notice it. 'They usually say they're keeping an open mind.'

'They don't want to commit themselves.'

'I suppose not.'

'Isn't that the same thing?'

A pair of vertical creases appeared between Theresa's eyebrows. 'Not really. One lot of people are answering the question and the other lot are evading it.'

'It seems to me, calling yourself an agnostic is just another way of not answering the question.'

Theresa took my arm. 'You *really* can't see the difference?'

We walked on a few paces, going round the ruins now, although that hadn't been my intention when we entered the square. I suppose it must have been force of habit: to observe them from every angle, just in case.

'The difference lies in the motive,' I said. 'Both responses betray fear. But they're fear of different things – in the latter case, God.'

'And in the former case?'

'Man,' I said and left it at that, sensing no profit in any further discussion of divinity. Eventually we completed our circuit of the ruins and came to a halt at the exact spot where I had last seen my mother. Billows of mist blew across the scene, so that it was possible to believe the whole city was just as it was the day I lost her – except for the grass and the sign that read: KEEP OUT – DANGER OF COLLAPSE.

Theresa pointed at something among the fallen stones. 'I wonder who put that there?'

It was the remains of my bouquet: a brown bunch of twigs, camouflaged among the clumps of dying grass. The pale blue ribbon round it was the only trace of colour.

'I did,' I said. 'For my mother. It's the closest thing she has to a grave, you see.'

I had already told Theresa about the day of the disappearance. She had read about me growing up as an orphan and had winkled out the facts one morning as we lay in bed. But the birthday ritual was always something I had kept to myself.

'Don't tell anyone, will you?' I said. 'Technically, it's an offence. These ruins are supposed to be an object lesson, not a memorial.'

We carried on walking. Theresa fell silent, imagining perhaps the boy Krug abandoned in that wasteland. I noticed how she absently touched at her temple, at the faint depression below the hairline. It was something she did often when lost in thought.

'How did you come by that, by the way?' I asked, wanting to lighten the mood, expecting to hear some anecdote about a childhood mishap or an argument with a double bass. It was only then I noticed the tears in her eyes. I had never seen her cry before, not even at Richter's funeral. I suppose being here, at the scene of my tear-choked search, had made my story real for her.

'Come by what?'

'That,' I said, running my fingers over the spot. 'If you don't mind my asking.'

She sniffed and wrapped her arm round my waist. 'No, I don't mind.'

That was when I finally learned about her twin. It was a revelation she had been keeping back until the right moment, I realised, and the right moment had finally come.

'She was called Clara. She was born a few minutes after me and until she came out, nobody even knew she was there.'

I said Clara was a nice name.

'That's her right knee you can see up there. Her right knee made that impression.' Theresa touched her forehead again. 'It's all that's left of her now; the only living thing. She had heart problems, you see.'

The use of the past tense had already told me Clara was dead.

'Do you remember her?'

Therese shook her head. 'She only lived a few months, although . . .'

'Although . . . ?'

'I don't remember *her*. How could I? But I remember her presence. It's hard to explain. I remember the knowledge of her. When I close my eyes sometimes, I can feel the space she left behind, her absence.' Theresa sighed. 'I expect it's all in my head.'

We had left the Neumarkt and were heading down a narrow street beneath the shadow of the town hall. It was starting to get dark.

'My parents told me the story, years later when I was almost grown up – though I already knew it somehow. I must have overheard it, I suppose.'

I didn't have to ask what story she meant.

'My parents were woken up one night by the sound of crying – howling they said. They went into the room where we were sleeping, Clara and me, and I was the one making the ruckus. They thought I must have something really wrong with me. They picked me up and tried feeding me and burping me, and my father went to get a thermometer because he was convinced I had a fever. But nothing worked. I just howled and howled. It was only after a few minutes they thought to check on my sister. She hadn't made a sound, you see. That's when they discovered she was dead. I was crying because I knew I'd lost her, according to the story.'

We came out on to the main road. A tram sparked by, motor

droning, picking up speed as it headed towards the Hauptbahnhof. Another was approaching from the west.

'I'm sorry,' I said. 'That's awful.'

Theresa gave me a reassuring squeeze. 'Don't worry. It was twenty-five years ago, and it's not like I have any memory of it. All I have is' – she shrugged – '. . . no more than a feeling really.'

'A feeling of what?'

Of sorrow, I imagined. But it was Theresa's turn not to answer the question.

'Let's go home,' she said.

We hurried towards the tram stop and made it just in time. A man with a plump face and thinning blond hair jumped in behind us. I realised I had seen him before, a few minutes earlier, hanging around a corner of the Neumarkt. He looked at me with dull, unseeing eyes, then turned to face the window. I was just coming round to the idea that perhaps we *were* being followed when he got off again, at the next stop.

I didn't delve further into the question of Theresa's twin. We had shared enough history for one day, and – this came to me as we stood silent in the sullen crush, our bodies gently colliding, her hair ghosting against my cheek – the exchange had brought us closer. All the same, I couldn't help imagining what it must have been like for her, growing up a twinless twin, aware always of an absence, of her own unnatural singularity. Was it a burden to be always the lucky one, the one who got the chance to live? Was it this that had brought Theresa to the valley: the hope of lessening that burden, or laying it down altogether?

Perhaps, I thought, having an absent twin was not so very different from having a vanished mother, a woman who sets out to raise you and then is lost without explanation, leaving the job, like the child, incomplete.

# 18

The first time I took Theresa back to my apartment she wandered around the place as if it were a museum, her hands clasped together in front of her, in case she should inadvertently touch something. It was there that events took a fateful turn. 'So this is it: the writer's lair,' she said.

The building, once a private villa of brazenly plutocratic proportions, was now a labyrinth of subdivided flats. Mine was larger than most, with many of its original details in evidence, although not all in an ideal state of preservation: moulded ceilings, panelled doors, a parquet floor that I myself had repaired, bartering replacement blocks where necessary for all manner of hydrodynamical services. I even enjoyed the benefit of a turntable and a passable hi-fi system, the loudspeakers being Japanese.

'Where do you work?' Theresa asked. 'Where do you sit when you write?'

The desk and the typewriter, the only permanent accoutrements of my official occupation, were strategically situated in the bedroom. I had some days earlier dressed the surroundings so as to lend them an unmistakable air of ongoing artistic endeavour, the leading props being a copy of *The Magic Mountain* lying open and face down, a small stack of leather-bound notebooks, carefully disordered, a pewter mug full of freshly sharpened pencils, a photograph of Ernest Hemingway in a cable-knit sweater, two items of fan mail, dates necessarily obscured, a map of Budapest and an edition of *The Orphans of Neustadt* in Portuguese (which I had stopped short of annotating, for fear of tactical overreach). I let Theresa discover this cockpit of creativity on her own, busying myself in the kitchen making coffee and humming. I was pleased – in fact, relieved – that she seemed to take her time exploring it. I pictured her fingertips tentatively tracing the outlines of the landscape, checking the intentful sharpness of the pencils, flipping through a notebook, turning over the Thomas Mann to see for herself what I had supposedly just read: *'The ocean of time, rolling onwards in monotonous rhythm, bore the Easter-tide on its billows . . .'*

I was not simply showing off. This piece of theatre was a precaution. If Theresa's friends said she had 'a thing' about writers, that didn't mean they were wrong. Richter had been a writer. I was a writer. Viewed statistically, the case was cut and dried. But to qualify as a writer, was it enough to have written? Didn't you have to be writ*ing*: productive, fertile, creatively priapic? Where previous female conquests were concerned, this had not been an issue. They had been interested in the fruits of my labours (the modest perks and privileges my foreign royalties afforded me), not the labours themselves. But Theresa was different. She was an artist. Besides, she had no reason to be impressed by my Intershop lifestyle, having access to similar retail Elysia every time she went home. For all these reasons I preferred not to take any chances.

'So is this the work-in-progress?' Theresa called from the bedroom, after what must have been several minutes of silence.

I was in the kitchen by this time, waiting for the kettle to boil and contemplating which of my Russian LPs would put her most in the mood for sexual intercourse. 'Is what the work-in-progress?'

'This thing on the chair,' Theresa said. She sounded excited. 'Is it finished?'

With a jolt I understood what she was talking about. A few days earlier, tired of having it clog up the sitting room, I had moved Wolfgang Richter's manuscript to the one place where it would not be in the way: the chair in front of my desk. There it had stayed, unnoticed, even as I was carefully arranging my writerly camouflage around the desk itself.

I hurried towards the bedroom, scenes from a nightmare cascading through my mind like the visions of a drowning man: me telling Theresa about Richter's book; her asking why I'd kept quiet about it all this time; me making up some unconvincing excuse about it being a big secret (as if I couldn't trust her) or not wanting to upset her; her demanding to read the manuscript and discovering that it was very good; her discerning my jealousy and falling out of love with me even before she was in it.

I stopped in the doorway. Theresa was sitting on the end of the bed (clean sheets, new goose-down duvet) and was already glued to the manuscript. *They kept always to the edge of the road, where their shuffling, silent progress was hidden among the shadows of the trees.* I didn't know what to say. Deceit was dangerous, but the truth was suicidal.

Theresa looked up at me and smiled. If only she had known how that smile made my heart sink. 'So this is it,' she said. 'The book they've all been waiting for. For twenty years.'

At first, I didn't understand what she meant. Then it came to me:

she still thought the manuscript was mine. And why not? The first page was blank, revealing no author, no title. The relief left me momentarily unsteady.

'You know, I was starting to think . . .' Theresa said. 'I mean, you never talk about your work.'

'Starting to think what?' I sat beside her.

'That you weren't writing any more, that you'd given it up.'

'Like your friends said.'

Apparently the *Factory Gate Fables* didn't even count as writing.

Theresa put her head on my shoulder. I slid my arm round her waist. For the first time it felt awkward.

'But you were just being modest. I should have known.' She reached up and touched my face. 'That's one of the things I love about you, Bruno. You've got nothing to prove.'

To my knowledge, that was the first time she ever used the words 'love' and 'you' in the same sentence – an occurrence I would have liked to savour, had Richter's manuscript not been sitting there in her lap. I took it away from her and dumped it on the desk.

'You're going to let me read it, aren't you?' she said.

'Maybe. Some time. It isn't finished.'

'It looks wonderful.'

'It needs work.'

'Well, the opening's wonderful. You've just *got* to know what's round that corner.'

'Openings are easy. It's middles that are difficult.'

'I won't tell anyone about it, not if you don't want me to.'

'You can read it when it's ready, maybe. Some of it needs a complete rewrite.'

I tried to shove the manuscript in a drawer, but the drawer was already half full and refused to close. I had to take half the manuscript out again and find another drawer. Even then, I could feel the top sheets crumple as I rammed it home. All this Theresa watched in silence. When I turned back to her, I could see her cheeks burning.

I sat down. She stood up.

'I'm thirsty,' she said and went back to the sitting room.

It was the first time Theresa had been upset with me. Not that she didn't try to hide it. Over coffee (she declined the vodka) we conversed on a variety of neutral subjects, but I could see that it was an effort for her, that underneath she was disappointed. This was about more than missing a good read. I suppose she felt I had shut her out, that the openness we had shown towards each other was to be temporary and limited. I wanted to reassure her on that point, but that would have meant reopening the subject of the Richter manuscript, a book that confirmed not only the brilliance of the man she had lost, but also the creative sterility of the man who had replaced him. So I let the matter drop, hoping it would simply go away and never come up again. Years in the future, perhaps, Theresa would ask me what happened to that story of the people on the road and the boy with the revolver in his pocket; and I would say that I had thrown it away, because I simply couldn't make it work. 'It was just a genre piece anyway,' would be my final dismissive comment.

But that still left this evening: Theresa's first evening under my roof, our first night in a double bed (so I'd hoped) where, at last, sexual congress might be enjoyed without the accompanying hours of sleeplessness and cramp. When Theresa yawned – another first in my presence – I gave up on conversation and opted for abject service. Moving behind her, I started to massage her shoulders, which I declared (without evidence or authority) were terribly tense. Half an hour later my hands and fingers were pulsing with fatigue while Theresa lay sprawled out across the sofa in her underwear, sighing gratefully. It was then, at last, that she accepted the vodka, drinking it with her eyes shut and shivering as it went down.

'You know, Wolfgang was working on a book,' she said, out of nowhere.

'How do you know?'

'He told me. I was surprised, actually. I'd have thought movies were much more fun. Everyone likes movies. Books . . .'

'It's a question of creative freedom,' I said, from a seated position on the floor. 'The scriptwriter's not in control. Other people make the decisions. If you want to call the shots you write a book – even if they're shots that hardly anyone ever hears. What was Wolfgang's book about?'

'He didn't say. I'm not sure I asked him.'

'Or you don't remember the answer.'

'Either way . . .'

'Either way what?'

'Either way it doesn't matter, since he never got a chance to finish it.'

She rolled on to her front and wriggled her shoulder blades to indicate that more massage was required. I decided it would be best to comply, but not before I had put matters on a sexual basis by taking off the rest of her clothes.

'How long am I going to have to wait?' she said, as I slipped my thumbs into the elastic of her plain white knickers.

I hesitated. 'Wait?'

'To find out about Alex.'

She lifted her hips a fraction, enough to allow the undressing to be completed.

'Who's Alex?'

She looked back at me, frowning. 'The boy with the gun. In your book.'

I had taken care never to say it was *my* book. I had simply declined to correct Theresa's assumption that it was. I was reluctant to surrender that shred of deniability.

'Not long,' I said and slid both hands up her legs, forcefully kneading the muscles of her thighs so that she gasped with something between pleasure and pain.

The penis, I have discovered, presents particular difficulties of nomenclature to creators of English literature. The masters of previous eras, like their Continental counterparts, were prohibited by the mores of the day from mentioning its existence. Even when, between the world wars, indicative words began creeping on to the pages of respectable fiction, they were often placed in flashes of reported speech: vulgar slang placed in the mouths of vulgar characters. The modern artist felt at liberty to record this argot in the interests of verisimilitude. But coming up with a term that was not loaded with coarse or satirical connotations, that was merely honest without seeming technical, proved persistently problematic. In lovemaking scenes, one by one, *organs* began to rear their ugly heads; *tumescences*, *limbs* and *members* (some honourable, others not) soon followed in their wake – even the occasional *manhood*. *Penis* itself was too clinical for most writers; *cock* and *dick* smacked of smutty seaside postcards and bar-room jokes. The *sex*, long since discarded in the concrete nounal form, enjoyed a brief heyday during the 1930s, but eventually fell out of favour, being vague as well as inaccurate (would a man urinate with his *sex*?). The *pecker* and the *wang* made occasional post-war appearances in satirical Americana. My particular Anglo-Saxon favourite – useless for literary purposes – has always been *willy*. It seems familiar and affectionate, as well as being the name of choice for Saxon monarchs throughout history.

In any case these concerns, which apply as much to the female as to the male, merely betray a more fundamental ambivalence. Human genitals, most particularly our own, are a source of embarrassment and fear. We do not know what to call them (outside the bar room or the doctor's surgery) because we do not know how to feel about them. Will our genitals, with their strange shapes and their regrettable but structurally unavoidable tendency to wrinkle, be aesthetically pleasing to our sexual partners? Granted, they are necessary, both for reproduction and for pleasure, but what reassurance is that? When the thrill of the new has faded, will the only genitals our bed mates want to dwell upon be the imaginary genitals of imaginary lovers? We hope not. We hope our hirsute and swarthy privates will be objects of fascination and erotic delight, and remain so through the years. But few of us are naive enough to expect it. We expect to be turning the bedroom lights off sooner rather than later, even assuming we had them on in the first place, so that the imagination can sustain what reality would only weaken and destroy.

So that night in bed, when Theresa took hold of me without warning and started pumping with all the vigour of a milkmaid at an agricultural competition, I regarded it as a welcome sign. My attentions had been assiduous, by design. When it came to foreplay, I was determined that there should be no unfavourable comparisons between me and Richter. Theresa and I were, I thought, moments from a long-delayed and explosive coupling. My hands were already on the insides of her thighs, making ready to part them. But Theresa, moved to a new pitch of desire, it seemed, wanted something else, something more immediate. She wanted to *see*. I didn't protest. That she was interested in the appearance as well as the function, I took to be indicative of a deepening physical connection. I felt my anxieties melt away in this novel display of appetite and fascination.

It was only long afterwards, when Theresa lay asleep in my arms, that a different interpretation occurred to me: that she simply hadn't wanted to make love. Rather than expressing her reluctance, she had taken the necessary steps to defuse my desire, as quickly as possible. All my efforts at arousing her – my aching fingers, my swollen lips – had been for nothing.

I thought back to the moment that evening when it had all gone wrong: Theresa bright-eyed and beaming, clutching Richter's manuscript to her bosom. I should have let her read it, I thought. That was my mistake. I should have told her to help herself.

# 19

About a week later Theresa was gone. There was no explanation, no declaration, no note; only silence. She told me she had to spend the Wednesday practising and rehearsing. We were supposed to meet on Thursday, the time and place to be determined by telephone, she calling me from the phone booth in the hall of the college. In the event, no call came: neither on the Wednesday, as I'd expected, nor on Thursday. I didn't leap to conclusions. Student telephones were unreliable and Theresa was busy preparing for exams. Still, as the hours came and went without word, I couldn't exclude from my thoughts the possibility that I had, as the English euphemism has it, been 'let go'.

How well did I know Theresa Aden by this time? I was familiar with her bearing and her manner, and her sense of humour. Mentally I could map her body quite precisely in three dimensions, with the additional dimensions of texture, scent and temperature (her belly and breasts were always warm, her feet and earlobes always cool). I could recreate her voice in my head, her laughter, her smile, the scholarly way she tucked her hair behind her ears when she was paying special attention. But the desires and judgements that directed Theresa from within, how developed was my sense of them? When I imagined the world through her eyes, was my vision sharp and accurate? Or was my knowledge of my fugitive twin limited to how she made me feel?

It was the intensity of my fear, the fear of losing her, that brought the uncomfortable truth home to me. There was no point in denying it: I was in love. Not a steady, comforting love born of deep familiarity and shared experience, a love appropriate for middle age. I loved Theresa with all the blindness and ferocity of youth, though I was not young. I loved her in the here-and-now, without regard for my future needs or convenience. I loved her without calculation and in defiance of the dangers. If that was a mistake, it is a mistake I cannot bring myself to regret, even now.

In the face of impending disaster I did my best to keep busy and to carry on as normal. I refused to wait by the telephone like a lovelorn teenager. Writing was out of the question, since writing required reflection. Instead I decided it was time to free up some storage space in my cupboards, a job I had been putting off for years. This task took up all of Thursday, during which time the telephone was never actually out of earshot. I even emptied my bladder with the bathroom door open, in case I should fail to hear it ring. Still, I didn't mope. I wanted quite badly to drink, but the faint possibility that Theresa might show up unexpectedly to find me reeking and incoherent, kept me from the bottle (such are the tortures of hope). When someone finally did ring – it was Michael Schilling, sounding more anxious than ever, wanting me to come in again as soon as possible – I concluded the conversation quickly so as not to tie up the line. I ate from tins and jars rather than risk going out for fresh provisions. I looked out of the window a great deal, like a prisoner, hoping against hope for reprieve.

Finally there was nothing to do but get out, to walk and keep walking. A man who walks is occupied, even if it is only with putting one foot in front of the other. He has purpose and with purpose comes self-respect. I needed to walk until my feet hurt; so that I could then concentrate on dealing with the pain.

I had no particular route in mind. I found myself drawn towards the river. The river led me west into the Altstadt, and from there I turned south again towards the Volkspark and the building on Blochmannstrasse where Theresa had her lessons. It wasn't raining, so I circled the place a few times, on the off chance that Theresa might spot me and come running out. But that didn't happen. Instead I found myself face to face with Claudia Witt, the accompanist.

'Hello, Bruno. I suppose you're looking for Theresa.'

'I was just passing.'

'Twice?'

Actually I had passed by three times. She must have missed the first.

'Lost my bearings. Which way is the park?'

'Theresa's in Berlin.'

Berlin: where she had first met Wolfgang Richter. Who was she meeting now?

'What's she doing there?'

Claudia smiled, happy to know something I didn't know. 'She'll be back at the weekend, I expect. I'll tell her I ran into you, shall I?'

I said that would be very kind of her and took my leave. As I walked away, the possibility occurred to me that Theresa was watching this whole encounter from a window in the college – was watching me still, making sure I didn't return. I resisted the temptation to look back.

*

Then, on the Monday morning, I received a postcard from Berlin. On one side was a photograph of the Brandenburg Gate. On the other was written:

*Here for an audition. Tried to phone you a dozen times. What's wrong with your phone?*
    *Wish me luck! (I'll need it . . .)*
    *T*

A few hours later Theresa herself was on the phone. It appeared to be working perfectly, although it turned out she was only calling from a mile away. She sounded unhappy. 'I'm sorry I didn't tell you beforehand. It all happened so suddenly.'

One of her professors at the college had heard about an upcoming viola vacancy at an orchestra in Berlin. Theresa had raced up there to catch the tail end of the auditions.

'East Berlin or West Berlin?' I asked.

'West, of course. The Radio Symphony Orchestra. Have you ever heard of Riccardo Chailly? He's wonderful.'

As it happened, I'd heard Chailly conduct many times, on the radio. But it was the 'of course' that made the deepest impression.

'Didn't it go well?'

'That's just it: it went very well. At least, I thought so.'

I felt slightly sick. Had the countdown to the end of our affair begun already?

'Well, that's wonderful. Isn't it?'

'No, it's not. Because I didn't get the job. They let me know the same day: more experienced applicants, intense competition, blah blah blah. The thing is, I couldn't have played any better. They just saw through me.'

'There'll be other chances.'

'There's too much competition. Orchestras are going bust all round the world.'

'Not here,' I said.

'The symphony orchestra's a dinosaur. And it's slowly dying of neglect.'

'Not here.'

Theresa sighed. For a moment, I thought she was going to hang up.

'It's all very well for you, Bruno. You've got to where you want to be. I'm having trouble with the first step.'

'Why don't I make you supper?' I checked my watch. The Delikat would be closed in an hour. 'What you need now are calories and alcohol.'

'I have to work. I've got to hand a paper in tomorrow. Music theory. Dull as hell.'

'I *love* music theory. Bring your books and we'll write it together. You expound, I'll phrase.'

She seemed to like the sound of that. 'Just think: I'll be handing in an original Bruno Krug manuscript,' she said. 'And no one will know but me.'

I hurried to the Delikat and stocked up on a variety of expensive edibles and a superior brand of vodka. I also bought candles, a Vietnamese throw, some cushions and a brushed-steel reading light, the better to disguise the dingy furnishings in my apartment (for dingy they had begun to seem). Then I dashed off to a butcher, whom I bribed with Deutschmarks for a large salami sausage and a half-kilo of bratwurst. I wanted, I see now, to infuse the evening with cosiness; to make my home feel like her home. It was an unusual impulse for me, but all that talk of the future – of Theresa's ambitions, and mine – had left me uneasy.

The paper was about twentieth-century orchestration and Theresa had written most of it. All it needed were some extra references and a little editing. Regardless of this, I recomposed every sentence while we ate and drank, American jazz playing gently in the background; so that in the end it flowed with all the elegance of a prose poem, without a single rhythmic hiccup. There was nothing very clever about what I did, but Theresa seemed terribly impressed. It was at least a genuine piece of creative showing off, unsullied by pretence.

When it was over, we undertook a tour of the soft furnishings, lolling amorously on one after the other, in search always of greater comfort and horizontality. Still, I found it difficult for once to disregard the issue of our future and to concentrate on the delights of the present. It had always been very likely that Theresa would return to the West once her studies were over. Yet the fact that there had been no discussion of the matter – no discussion at all, in fact – was a cause for concern. Would Wolfgang Richter have encountered the same reticence at the prospect of parting? The same composure? He'd been daring; I was cautious. His glories had been in the future; mine were in the past. He'd had promise; I had history. In a fictional context, his was a better fit for the romantic lead.

None of which would matter if Theresa loved me, if our affair was more than an episode for her, an experience (of the kind students are supposed to have), a valued but temporary addition to the romantic curriculum vitae.

'What about an orchestra in this country?' I said, as we finally sprawled across the bed, still clutching our glasses. The geometry of the situation made it possible to converse without having to look at each other. 'That's where most of your classmates will end up, isn't it?'

Theresa was quiet. Her right hand, fingers splayed, moved mechanically back and forth across the covers. 'That would mean settling here, though. Permanently.'

'I just thought it might be an option. I mean, if things are really so tough in the West for serious musicians.'

'Bruno, my whole family are over there. And my friends. I don't really know anyone here.'

I considered reaching for her hand, but thought better of it. 'You know me. And then there's Claudia. You two make wonderful music together – even if she doesn't like me.'

Theresa laughed. 'Don't talk rubbish.'

'I didn't think I was.'

To my surprise, Theresa's hand found mine. But the intention, I sensed, was gently to curtail further discussion of our future. She turned on to her side, facing me. I remained looking at the ceiling. It made me look thinner and besides, it was easier that way to hide my disappointment.

'How's the rewrite going?' she asked.

With her finger she pushed a lock of hair from my forehead.

'The what?'

'The new book. Isn't that what you've been working on?'

'Yes. Yes, I have.' I was feeling reckless and not a little miffed. 'It's coming on well. You can read it if you want.'

Theresa jumped on top of me. Apparently this was just what she wanted to hear. I couldn't keep my hands from riding up under her dress. The future can always wait so long as the here-and-now is rapturous.

'This is turning into a good day after all,' she said and kissed me on the mouth.

I don't know how she did it, but her lips tasted of orange blossom. Her thighs tasted of honey without the sweetness.

# 20

I telephoned Michael Schilling the next morning. This time he wanted to meet in the Volkspark. I didn't question his choice of venue. I assumed it was a concession to me, as a keen walker, not a symptom of incipient paranoia. I found him pacing up and down outside the zoo, squinting at a newspaper while a crowd of Young Pioneers queued up to go in, their red scarves billowing in the breeze. The new raincoat lent him a veneer of elegance, but his shoes were muddy and his face was half hidden behind the peak of an ugly knitted cap that I had never seen before. We greeted each other with a nod and walked into the park without shaking hands.

'You still have Wolfgang's manuscript, don't you?' he said as soon as we were alone.

'You know I do.'

'I don't like the idea of it lying around. It's not that I don't trust you, Bruno, but I need to know it's safe.'

Rooks were gathering in the trees up ahead. Their noisy communion filled the air.

'We can go and fetch it now, if you like.'

I was confident Schilling wouldn't be so importunate as to take me up on my offer – which was just as well, because the manuscript was no longer in my possession. Theresa had taken it away with her. She had promised to be careful with it, but exactly where it lay at that precise moment, and how secure it was, I was in no position to say.

'I hope this doesn't mean you've decided to publish,' I said.

We were halfway along an avenue of maples. Spring was still months away, but some of the trees had retained a handful of their leaves. They dangled by their stalks, brown and lifeless, like scraps of prehistoric litter.

Schilling looked back the way we had come. 'Not any more. Not now.'

This was what I wanted to hear. If Richter's book was never published, Theresa would never have to know who wrote it. There would be no eventual need for a confession, no requirement for elaborate excuses. I would still have to explain why I was not submitting the new novel for publication, but that presented less of a challenge. I could profess endless dissatisfaction with content or form, stringing out the notional process of redrafting for years on end. And if all else failed, there was always the Ministry of Culture to fall back on. I might decline to submit the new book because I knew it would never get past the censors. The book *was* subversive, if you read between the lines. The excuse was built in.

I was relieved, at the intellectual level anyway: Richter's novel was dead, as dead as Richter himself. Strange, then, that the realisation coincided with a spasm of stomach pain so intense it doubled me over.

'What's the matter?'

I took a couple of deep breaths. 'Trapped wind.' The knot of pain loosened. 'What did you mean, not *now*?'

'Maybe we should sit down.'

There was nowhere to sit, except the ground.

'I'm fine. Has something happened?'

Schilling went on staring, as if afraid I would drop dead. No doubt he was thinking of Wolfgang Richter, who had pretty much done exactly that on a leafy street in Loschwitz, though it had taken Death a day or so to claim him finally.

Only when I had supported my self-diagnosis with a sonorous belch did my friend continue walking. 'I've started hearing things,' he said.

I glanced at his ridiculous knitted cap, an insane choice even given the prevailing fashions. 'Voices?' I asked.

'About Wolfgang. About his death, Bruno.'

'What about it?'

An elderly couple were walking towards us down the avenue. Schilling remained silent until they had passed.

'After that party he went to, someone saw him. On the street outside.'

'So? He was walking home, wasn't he, when . . .'

'He wasn't walking. He was getting into a car. The *back* of a car.'

'What are you talking about?'

'There were two other men inside.'

The blood drained from my face. I felt unwell again and not a little irritated. Didn't we both have enough regrets and fears to haunt us without conjuring up more?

'I expect they were giving him a lift,' I said.

'The police said he was found in the street.'

'Maybe they dropped him off, and then, after that he . . .'

The rooks were overhead now. They seemed to find my suggestion hilarious. They were lined up on the branches, like theatregoers in the front row, laughing. What Schilling had described was a typical encounter with the state security apparatus. Under Actually Existing Socialism, when the decision was taken to question an individual, he or she was often picked up off the street, using plainclothes officers and unmarked cars. This was no doubt considered more discreet than turning up at their place of work or their home and banging on the door. Ideally, the very fact of the interview would remain a secret, known only to those involved. That way, should the interviewee be inclined to cooperate by, for example, turning informer, his renewed commitment to the anti-fascist struggle would not be suspected by those around him. Likewise, if something went wrong, if the detainee had a seizure under interrogation, if he tripped or fell or hanged himself in his cell, the whole episode could be plausibly denied.

'Who told you all this?' I said.

'Does it matter?'

'Maybe it's just a rumour . . . You know how people like a good scare. Look what happened with the toothpaste.'

'The what?'

'The point is . . .'

'It was some other guests, from the party. They saw the whole thing.'

'You actually spoke to these people?'

'Well, no.'

'But the person you spoke to, he did?'

'I'm not sure. I had the impression . . . no, probably not directly.'

I began to breathe easier. Schilling's report wasn't just second-hand; it was at least third-hand – and possibly fourth-hand, fifth-hand or sixth-hand. As far as I was concerned that made it the very epitome of a rumour and therefore probably untrue. On the other hand I didn't want Schilling to change his mind about Richter's book. He was in danger of doing that anyway.

He was staring at the ground now, his head sunk on to his chest. 'Maybe the right thing to do is . . .'

'The right thing to do is what you *are* doing,' I said. 'You'd only be inviting trouble to publish now, rumour or no rumour. It's not going to help Wolfgang, is it?'

Schilling shook his head. 'I suppose it's too late for that.'

We walked on in silence. The park was very empty, the mist turning slowly to drizzle, but to me it didn't feel empty enough. I couldn't shake the irrational sensation of being watched. I pictured myself in a viewfinder, captured in the grainy vision of a telephoto lens.

'What are you going to do with the manuscript?' I asked.

'I don't know.'

I had a feeling he did know. He just wanted someone else to suggest it; part of his own private exercise in deniability.

'The safest thing would be to destroy it,' I said.

Schilling did his best to look shocked. 'Are you serious?'

'Just in case someone comes looking for it. In case questions are asked.'

'What sort of questions?'

'Why you didn't reject the book outright. Why you didn't let anyone see it except me. *Those* kinds of questions.'

Schilling stared intently at the ground. 'I suppose . . . I suppose that would be the safest thing.' He brought a hand to his face. 'My God, Bruno, what are we doing? It's the only copy. It'll be lost for ever. How can we . . . ? How *can* we . . . ?' He stopped. 'Maybe we could hide it?'

'Anything hidden can be found. And then there'd really be some explaining to do. Subversive literature must be reported, not concealed.'

Schilling seemed on the verge of tears. It came to me that he was actually incapable of destroying Richter's manuscript. Whatever the method and whatever the circumstances, when the moment came he would be unable to go through with it. For him, it would be a hundred times worse than torching a library. Books in a library could always be reprinted. This would be more like murder.

I put my hand on his shoulder. 'Why don't you leave it to me? And if anyone asks: you've never heard of *The Valley of Unknowing*. You never saw it and you never read it. Agreed?'

Schilling couldn't bring himself to look me in the eye. It was all he could do to nod.

# 21

Under Actually Existing Socialism the discreet destruction of compromising literature is not as straightforward as it is elsewhere. In the West, for instance, where mountains of printed matter accumulate daily on the doormat, uninvited and unloved, literary purges are built into the routine of every household. Sack loads of writing are collected and removed each week. Roomy suburban gardens provide ample opportunity for incineration if greater discretion is required.

None of these solutions was available to me. Garbage was not bagged up in the Workers' and Peasants' State, there being no ready supply of bags. Anything that could not be recycled was emptied in plain view into a communal skip. Ideally I would have burned Richter's manuscript – it was at least fitting that the created should share the same fate as the creator – but that was not an option: my stove ran on oil and any fire outside the building was bound to attract attention. I considered pulping. As a schoolchild I had spent many contented hours making papier-mâché masks and assorted wild animals. I mixed up some flour glue and attempted a trial run with an old set of page proofs. But the trial was not successful: the paper was too stiff, and after an hour of boiling and pounding, I had got through less than thirty pages' worth of *Factory Gate Fables*. There was always the river. I thought of drowning the manuscript the way people drown kittens, in a cloth sack weighed down with stones. But the bridges and quays were the most visible spaces in the city; I was almost certain to be observed. After much deliberation I decided that, just like a real murder victim, Richter's book was best buried in the woods.

As it happened, our city was blessed with sixty square kilometres of forest, the Heide, not half an hour's walk from Blasewitz. Nonetheless, planning was essential. I would need to establish a suitable location for the burial. I would need to get there without arousing suspicion. I would have to dig a hole – but with what? A man walking towards the woods carrying a spade might well have been deemed suspicious. The Heide was officially designated parkland. Digging there was a state prerogative.

I worked out the elements of my plan one by one. The key to it,

I realised, was to have an alternative explanation for every step, an explanation both innocent and credible. This required some creative thinking, but I was glad of the occupation, glad to focus on the how and not the why. The answer to why lay in the past, but the past could not be changed. Besides, I was taking a risk, for Schilling's sake more than my own. I was being strong for both of us, in case – only in case – the rumour he had heard about Richter's death was true.

Early one morning, a few days later, I set off on a bicycle towards the river. Theresa still had the manuscript, but that was fine. I had decided to make two trips: the first to find the spot and dig the hole; the second to carry out the burial. I was dressed in hiking clothes and carried on me, among other things, a pair of small binoculars and an ancient copy of *Native Birds of Central Europe* by Siegbert Pressler, borrowed from the library. I also had, tucked into my belt, a builder's trowel, with which I planned to do the digging. If challenged, I would say I had simply found it lying by the road.

The wind was strong and gusting as I passed beneath the pale blue girders of the Loschwitz Bridge. It was cold, but the smudges of sunlight that drifted over the rooftops and the woods and the flat grey waters of the river held out a promise of spring. I hadn't ridden my bicycle in a long time and it was badly in need of oil. Pedalling was difficult, especially when I reached the uphill slopes on the far side of the river. I broke into a sweat and my front wheel wobbled comically as my speed dropped to walking pace. A woman pushing a pram turned to look at me and laughed, revealing a missing front tooth. An old man stared at me from a window. The idea was to look like a birdwatcher on his way to watch birds. To this end I stopped to admire a pair of starlings perched on a telegraph wire. At the appearance of a sparrow, I paused to consult *Native Birds of Central Europe*. I tried not to look over my shoulder more than a birdwatcher would, though the approach of every car sent a pulse of effervescent terror up my spine.

Soon enough there were no cars and no pedestrians either. I climbed off my bicycle and wheeled it through an iron gate into the Albert Park, a landscaped corner of the Heide, mostly fallen into neglect – ponds rank with algae, rusty iron benches, paths pock-marked with molehills, moss and piles of undisguised dog shit. The place was named in honour of a nineteenth-century Saxon king and in its decayed condition there was the flavour of casual proletarian disdain. I soon felt better about my chosen location. It was empty, unregarded, unloved; the perfect final resting place for a stillborn work of art. My bicycle wheels made garlands of wet leaves as I struck out across an untended lawn.

I headed for King Albert's memorial, a plain granite monolith as devoid of originality as the man himself. The woods beyond were mainly birch, the trees bare and widely spaced, providing insufficient cover. I paused for some pantomime birdwatching (the birds themselves seemed to keep their distance, as if aware of the pretence) then continued, crossing a narrow potholed road, and pressing on into thicker and wilder woods.

The ground here was broken and uneven. It was impossible to maintain a straight line, especially with the bicycle. I tripped on roots and slithered down inclines, sinking in mud up to my shins. But at least no one was watching me, I was sure of that. What reason could anyone have for being out here, unless it was a reason like mine? I wished I'd had the manuscript with me. I could have got rid of it there and then.

In the lee of a slope I came across a trio of evergreens. The tidy symmetry reminded me of a pagan grove, as depicted in a neo-Gothic painting. It seemed like a good spot. I took out my trowel and began to dig. The ground was soft, but a couple of inches below the surface I hit a tangle of roots. Most were no fatter than my little finger, but the trowel was not an ideal tool to tackle them. I stopped digging and started stabbing, with one hand to begin with, then with both. Dirt flew into my face and into the folds of my clothes. Meanwhile the wind was growing stronger, kicking up leaves and spinning them across the hollow. I went on hacking into the ground, clearing the earth a handful at a time. I could have chosen a different place, but I was hidden here. I felt safe.

Then, over the hissing wind, I heard a sound, a deep animal sound, too faint and brief to identify – a dog perhaps, or something larger. The bears and wolves were long gone, but there were still wild boar and deer in the Heide. Barbara Jaeger once told me that shoots had been organised for visiting Party bigwigs from Berlin – Comrade Honecker was an ardent huntsman – though they had to freight in some extra livestock to make sure there was enough to kill. I went back to work. The hole wasn't as deep yet as the manuscript was thick. I picked up the pace, hacking at the stubborn ground and the stubborn roots.

It took me a moment to realise that I was not alone. It wasn't a sound that told me, or even a lack of sound, but a perceptible stillness behind me. I looked round and there she was, looking down at me from the lip of the hollow, still in that old brown coat I recognised, still holding that battered suitcase: my mother, older but still the same. The same brown eyes, the same dimpled chin, the same smear of dirt across her forehead. She was younger than me, of course: not thirty years old.

I got to my feet. In the distance I was dimly aware of dogs barking. They were coming closer, but I couldn't move. She should have held her arms out wide. After all this time, she should have been desperate to enfold me and hold me close. But she just stood there, my mother, neither smiling nor frowning.

'It's just a book,' I said. 'I'm burying a book.'

I knew then that I couldn't go through with it. I was no more capable of destroying the manuscript than Michael Schilling was.

My mother took a step back, turned and walked away. I threw down the trowel and hurried after her. The bank was steep. I slipped and fell. When I finally stood where she had stood moments before, everything had changed. I was no longer in the woods. I was back in the Neumarkt, a refugee among the mountains and valleys of rubble, with the dust clouds stinging my eyes and the tears rolling down my cheeks.

But the dogs were still there. I couldn't see them, but I could hear them. They had my scent. They were closing in. A voice came over a megaphone, screeching and bellowing. The only words I could make out were *stay where you are*.

When I opened my eyes I was in the middle of trying to scream. I'm not sure if I made any sound – that of a startled seal, perhaps – but in any case the effort was interrupted by the buzz of my doorbell. It was this that had woken me. Still shaky with fright, I climbed out of bed. The clock said half past nine. I went to the window and looked out, half expecting to see men in uniform and salivating wolfhounds, straining at the leash.

It was a girl wearing a black beret. She stepped back from the door and looked up: Theresa. I hadn't been expecting her. It had been my policy to avoid early morning encounters, except as an unavoidable coda to nocturnal ones.

I opened the window. She was holding something, a package, clutching it tight to her chest. Though the colour was different – she had wrapped it in a black plastic bag – I recognised the dimensions at once. It was Richter's manuscript. I had only given it to her a few days earlier, but here she was bringing it back.

'Sorry to show up like this,' she called up to me. 'Can I come in?'

I pressed the buzzer and spent the available sixty seconds throwing on a dressing gown, hastily rinsing my mouth and arranging my sleep-flattened hair so as not to look like Hitler. I also managed to drag some books from the shelves and leave them open around the sitting room, so as to give the impression of an intense creative stew.

'I woke you up, I'm sorry,' she said as soon as I opened the door. 'I tried to call, but the phone wasn't working.'

She was out of breath, and not just from the stairs. It occurred to me that she had hurried all the way, so impatient had she been to get here. All thoughts of my dream, its lingering aftermath of dread, were banished.

Theresa stumbled as I pulled her into an embrace. 'Let me get my coat off,' she said.

'Nothing's wrong, is it? Nothing's happened?'

'Your book.'

She handed me the package and wriggled off her coat. Her blonde hair tumbled out from under her beret with a crackle of static. A dizzying sensation in my loins told me I wanted her badly, and soon. If only I hadn't been standing there, unwashed and unshaved at half past nine in the morning.

I tossed the manuscript on to the hall table. 'I didn't think you'd like it.' She was going to say something but I held up my hand. 'Don't worry in the slightest. I told you it needs a lot of work.'

'You're right,' she said. 'I don't like it. I *love* it. It must be the best thing you've ever written. You seemed so unhappy with it last time, I just had to tell you how wonderful it is.'

She put her arms round me and squeezed.

'Thank you,' I said. 'I'm reassured.'

'It could only be you, Bruno. The voice is unmistakable.'

'You think so?'

'Of course. I just read *Orphans*, remember? Only this is even better. I'm so happy for you.'

'So am I.'

'And to think, if I hadn't found it here, I wouldn't even know the book existed.' Theresa looked up at me. I forced a rictal grin. 'How did you keep from boasting? From even talking about it?'

I shrugged. Words were beyond me.

'You're incredible.' She brought a hand to my unshaven cheek. 'Artists are meant to be egotistical. Most of them *are* egotistical, the ones I know. And vain. But not you.'

Theresa stepped back, the better to look me in the eye. I took a deep breath, struggling to rally.

'You really aren't in it for the glory, are you? What *are* you in it for?'

'The girls, obviously,' I said and dragged her towards the sitting room, just so she wouldn't look at me any more.


Theresa had felt compelled to come and see me that morning for another reason, besides the brilliance of Richter's novel: back in the West her mother had contrived to fracture her pelvis in a bicycling accident and was going to be wheelchair-bound for months.

'She says she can manage, but I can tell she's really struggling. She hates hanging around the house at the best of times.' Theresa was standing in the kitchen doorway by this time, watching me make coffee with my French cafetière. 'They've got her on all these painkillers. I think they're really dragging her down.'

'You've an aunt, don't you? Can't she help?'

'Astrid's got kids and she's three hours away. There's not much she can do.'

'I don't suppose your father . . .'

Theresa shook her head. Her parents had divorced when she was twelve years old (amicably, she maintained, which is to say the worst of the rage and bitterness had been hidden from her). As she saw it, she had no choice but to go home. A break from lectures was due in any case, and she could both study and practise perfectly well at her mother's house. All in all she could afford almost seven weeks away; enough time, she hoped, to see the maternal invalid through the worst.

'When do you leave?'

'The day after tomorrow. It's very soon, I know, but I think she really needs me.'

I needed Theresa too, but what was the point of saying so? I couldn't bind her to me with guilt. Guilt was an unreliable adhesive and notoriously corrosive. Still, her announcement brought one possible end to our affair a big step closer. When Theresa returned, it would be for her final term. Once her studies were complete, her visa would be revoked. From then on there would be a wall between us – not just any wall, but The Wall, an object which could in theory be negotiated (provided we both had the desire, the passion, the need), but which could no longer be ignored.

'In your place I'd do the same thing,' I said. 'You won't be happy if you stay.'

Theresa came over and gave me a hug. In spite of my unwashed condition, sex was now within reach: grateful sex, compensatory sex, anaesthetic sex. My right hand made mechanically for her breast, but after hovering briefly a nipple's length away, returned to the cups on the counter. The fizz in my loins was no more. It came to me that I no longer wanted to have sex with Theresa if I couldn't have Theresa herself; the inverse of my original feelings on the matter.

Theresa's embrace grew languid; then it was over. She slinked into the sitting room and threw herself down on the sofa. 'You know, I don't think I've ever been so stuck on a book,' she said, raising her voice over the rumble of the kettle. 'I *devoured* it. Why isn't there a title, by the way?'

'It's undecided.'

'You must have some idea. You can't work for years on a book and have no idea what it's called.'

She was right.

'*The Valley* . . .' I said, but the rest of the title stuck in my throat. For a moment I was back in the Heide of my dream, hacking away at the knotty earth as my mother's ghost looked on.

'*The Valley*,' Theresa repeated. '*The Valley*. Yes, that kind of works. Simple, profound, timeless. It brings out the book's, I don't know . . .'

'Mythic quality?'

'Yes, that's it exactly. *The Valley*. I wish I could read it again. It's exciting but it's deep. There are so many *layers*.'

'Like an onion,' I said.

Theresa couldn't hear me over the sound of the kettle.

'I wish I could reread it on the train,' she said. 'That'd be wonderful. If only I could take it home with me.'

With a hollow plop the kettle cut out and there in my head was an idea: bright, flawless and elegant, sparkling in the shadows of my worn-out cerebrum like a new star. I expect it had been coalescing in my subconscious for days. The human mind is rarely as spontaneously original as we like to think it is.

'Why don't you?' I said, walking into the sitting room, a cup of coffee in each hand. 'Why don't you take it?'

'Are you sure? You'd really . . . ?' Theresa sat up, eyes bright. I felt my desire return, like an old friend. 'You'd really trust me that much?'

# PART THREE

## 22

I was sure Theresa would accept my proposal, but I didn't come out with it right away. I suggested we go out in search of breakfast. There was a small, hopeless café on the far side of the Waldpark, best known for the rudeness of its staff, but it was the walking I wanted. Fictions unfold more naturally when accompanied by exercise. Blood flow invigorates the imagination, as well as the muscles.

When we were well on our way, I told her why I'd been so secretive about *The Valley*: because of what it was really about.

'I know it seems to be a story about the future, but it's really about the past and the present, here in this country.'

Which, of course, was true.

Theresa frowned. Several strands of hair had come out from under her beret and were now tickling her nose. 'It never struck me as political. I just loved the characters. That's what's so brilliant about it. They're so complex and so . . . *real.*'

'The political message is there, take my word for it – between the lines. In the white spaces. You have to be on the lookout for it.'

A certain stiffness in Theresa's demeanour told me she was troubled by this revelation. Strange as it will seem to those brought up in ideologically fragmented societies, I had made no serious attempt to fathom her political opinions, mainly because I didn't want her fathoming mine. Under Actually Existing Socialism political ideas are found in three forms and three forms only: public declaration, public acclamation and silence.

'It's funny,' she said. 'I never realised . . . I had the impression you stayed out of it.'

'Out of what?'

'Politics. The rights and wrongs. I actually heard someone say you must have . . .'

'What?'

'It doesn't matter.'

'Tell me.'

She sighed. 'Curvature of the spine.'

'From sticking my neck out?'

'From keeping your head down.' She shrugged apologetically. 'It just shows how wrong people can be, doesn't it?'

By 'people' I felt sure she meant Richter.

'I take it you don't disapprove, then. You aren't going to report me?'

She answered my question by putting her arm round my waist and holding me close. We walked on. I explained that the new book could, and probably would, be interpreted by the authorities as an attack on the history of our state, its founding principles and world view.

'You and I are the only people in the world who know that book exists,' I said.

'It's such a good story. Is it really so threatening?'

'In the East, yes. In the West, probably not.' We stopped to let a tram go by on the road to Loschwitz. I kept my eyes on the park up ahead. 'That's why I want you to take the manuscript with you when you go.'

The tram rumbled away down the street, but neither of us moved. It wasn't cold, but the sky felt heavy and close.

'You want me – what? – to smuggle it out?'

'Well, technically it wouldn't be smuggling,' I said. 'The transportation of unpublished novels isn't covered by the criminal code. The worst that could happen . . .' I began to imagine an unpleasant scene at the border, decided it was best not to. 'The worst that could happen is they confiscate it.'

'And once it's out of the country, what then?'

'I want you to find a publisher, if you can.'

Theresa stopped in her tracks. 'But you'd get into trouble. They'd arrest you.'

The alarm in her voice was gratifying. Apparently Theresa believed me capable of dashing and dangerous gestures, of self-sacrifice in the cause of freedom. Bruno Krug, literary martyr. The concept was novel and fleetingly appealing.

'That depends,' I said.

Writers who published without permission in the non-socialist abroad were usually sent to prison for tax evasion. Suggestive of selfishness and greed, the charge was preferable to that of slandering the state, which did not play well in the Western world, and which was associated with legitimate protest. Still, I explained, there might be a way of avoiding official retribution altogether.

'Suppose we put *your* name on the book? Suppose we tell the world that *you* wrote it? I can't be criticised for a book I didn't write. And as for you, frankly what a Westerner gets up to in her own country is of no interest to the authorities here. Western books aren't available here. They'd never even read it.'

This then was the plan: not a solution to my difficulties, but a useful accommodation with them; an improvised construction that, in the best traditions of Actually Existing Socialism, made the best of a bad job. I could not bring myself to destroy Richter's manuscript, but neither could I keep it. Getting it out of the country was the obvious alternative. Richter's novel could not be published in the East, for fear of retribution; nor could it be published under his name, even in the West, for the same reason. How had the work found its way across the border? Who was responsible? Who had been complicit? These questions would be asked – but not if the writer's identity and nationality were concealed.

And then there was Theresa. She already believed the book was mine. The discovery had thrilled her just as it had thrilled Michael Schilling. There was no going back on that score. Then why not take full advantage of the situation? Why not make her a part of the thing she loved? Her name on my book (to be accurate, her name on a book I had inspired): it would give us a common project; it would braid our hopes together like two strands of a single rope. She had been hurt when, as it seemed to her, I shut her out of my creative world. Now I was flinging the doors wide open.

We crossed the road and headed into the park. Theresa looked frightened. 'I don't know the first thing about publishing,' she said, 'or writing books. I wouldn't know what to do.'

'You look up some publishers; you send them the manuscript. It goes something like that.'

'But they might talk. How could we trust them?'

'We wouldn't have to. This has to be between you and me. No one else can know.'

As for the book's political dimension, I said she should keep quiet about it. I didn't want it spelled out, by the publishers or by her. I wanted it to emerge slowly, over time. 'Let people discover the deeper meaning for themselves,' I said, being confident they never would.

Theresa shook her head. 'I'd never get *away* with it, Bruno. I wouldn't fool anyone.'

'I know it's a lot to ask. I'll understand if you say no. It's just a book, after all, not a matter of life and death.'

I meant what I said, but I don't imagine Theresa thought so.

We walked on in silence. I suppose what troubled her were the lies she would have to tell: to the publishers, to a putative reading public, to people she knew. She was not a natural dissembler and there was no denying that the burden of dissembling fell all on her. The book might not be mine, but neither would the name on the cover.

'It wouldn't be for ever,' I said. 'One day, when thing's are different, we'll tell the truth.'

Like the rebuilding of the Frauenkirche, like the fall of the Workers' and Peasants' State, I assumed this would never happen in my lifetime and probably not in Theresa's either.

She shook her head. 'No one will believe I wrote that book. Would you?'

'Nearer the time you *could* put on some glasses. And maybe dye your hair an acceptable shade of mouse.'

'*Seriously.*'

'Seriously, seeing is believing. Besides, what you do already – your music – that's much more difficult than writing and more beautiful. I'd happily believe that writing was just a sideline.'

We could split the money, I added, if there was any money. A little hard currency might come in handy for both of us.

'Don't be silly,' she said. 'I couldn't take your money.'

'You could take a third of it,' I said, as we stopped beneath the branches of a dying cedar. 'A third, I insist. Anything less wouldn't be fair.'

She put her arm round me. For a minute or so we clung to each other, saying nothing, the smell of wet earth filling our nostrils.

'Wouldn't it be easier just to leave?' Theresa said at last. 'At least that way you could take the credit for your work.'

'I don't care about the credit. I thought we'd established that.'

We headed back to the road. I was elated at the efficiency of my improvised plan, the ease with which everything was already falling into place.

After a while Theresa said, 'I think you like living among all these ruins, Bruno Krug. I think in some strange way you need them.'

'Nonsense.'

'A lot of people in your position would have left a long time ago.'

'A lot of people did.'

'Then why not you?'

I shrugged. 'Someone had to stay. For the sake of the others. Besides, it's nice to be needed.'

I wasn't joking. To me, there had always been the element of desertion involved in the decision to flee. No matter who you were, someone was always left behind, someone whose life was harder for your absence. It was also the case that by the time I was in a position to defect, my reasons for doing so were fewer than ever; a grateful state had made sure of that.

'But you're not married,' Theresa said, as we reached the north edge of the park. 'You've no children, no family . . .'

'You're right. There isn't much keeping me here, not in that way.'

'And you could work just as well in the West, couldn't you?'

We were standing at a kerb, waiting for a signal to cross the road.

'I write about the world I know, which is right here.' I paused to recall a literary reference, one that would lend weight to my argument. 'You've heard of Isaac Babel?'

'Kind of. Wasn't he Russian?'

'Yes, and he went back to Russia, though he could have lived safely in exile in Paris. This was more than fifty years ago, in Stalin's time. "I am a Russian writer. If I did not live with the Russian people, I would cease being a writer." That's what he said. He couldn't write about a place where he was a stranger.' Opposite us the signal turned green. 'I don't think I could either.'

I crossed the road while the traffic stood waiting. Theresa remained motionless on the kerb for a moment, before setting off after me.

'So what became of Babel, back in Russia?'

'No one knows,' I said, which was true. It only came out later that he had been executed on orders from Stalin.

# 23

She left early on the Monday morning with her viola and a large suitcase. In the suitcase, besides clothes, were books, files and folders: hundreds of pages of lecture notes, study notes, sheet music and essays – material she needed to revise for her final exams. One of those files, an old ring binder with a grey cardboard cover, began with a series of photostat articles on counterpoint and fugue, continued with essays on Stockhausen and the Darmstadt School and concluded with an untitled manuscript, which I knew to be Wolfgang Richter's *The Valley of Unknowing*.

If there had been more time for conjecture I might have foreseen the dangers more clearly. I might have had second thoughts. Theresa might too. I didn't know it, but she had special reasons for caution, for going back on her promise. Yet she never flinched, never hesitated, never let me feel, even for a moment, that I was asking too much of her. When I recall her steadfastness at that time, it strikes me as the best and clearest evidence that she truly cared for me, that her love was real.

The night before, we had sat together carefully punching holes through the manuscript. It seemed to me then that *The Valley of Unknowing*, far from being destroyed at my hands as I'd promised, was now multiplying. From one identity, it now had three, each one distinct from the others; each one illuminated by a different authorial light (Richter's, Theresa's and mine), giving rise to different interpretations. Michael Schilling was not going to be pleased, if he ever found out. But at least there was no danger of his betraying us. Schilling was my friend and besides, he could not expose my ideological backsliding without exposing his own.

To leave the manuscript in plain sight had been Theresa's idea. Any hint of concealment ran the risk of arousing suspicion. In the unlikely event that a border guard got past the Stockhausen (the essays were as digestible as the music), she would claim that the novel was hers, that she had penned it at home during the holidays. There was nothing very suspicious about that.

We rehearsed the putative interrogation as best we could. This was my idea. If questioned further, she was to say her book was a work of science fiction. She was also to imply that it wasn't very good. She had already tried to find a publisher in the West, but none had been interested. She was disappointed, but not heart-broken. Writing was only a sideline, after all. Why had she taken the manuscript back to the East with her? Because she'd hoped to work on it. In the event she had never found the time.

The mock interrogation did not begin well. Theresa tended to blush when she was lying and that was not the only problem.

'Who gave this to you? Who wrote it?'

I played the role of the interrogator as sternly as I could, pacing up and down in my sitting room while she remained seated in an upright chair.

'I told you: I did. I wrote it.'

Not content with blushing, Theresa now nervously folded and unfolded her arms.

'Where's the machine you typed it on?'

'At home. It's my mother's typewriter.'

'Where did you get the paper?'

Her mouth opened, but no sound came out. This was an issue we had not discussed. In fact, that the origin of the paper might give us away had only just occurred to me. I suppose I hoped for some brilliant piece of improvisation.

'What do I say?' Desperation had crept into Theresa's voice. 'Where *did* you get the paper?'

The real question was: where had Richter got the paper?

'Say you bought it in East Berlin, the first time you went home. It was half the price of paper in the West.'

'Okay. So where was the shop exactly? What was the name?'

I had no idea.

'You've forgotten. Somewhere near Alexanderplatz. There are lots of shops near Alexanderplatz, aren't there?'

Theresa nodded. 'I think so.'

I cleared my throat, reassuming my role. 'You've been seen with Bruno Krug. Did he put you up to this?'

'Put me up to what?'

'Did he give you this manuscript? To smuggle out?'

'Of course not. Why would he do that?'

This was better. Theresa was looking me straight in the eye.

'You tell me.'

'I've no idea. I can't see what he would possibly gain.'

'What about money?'

'Bruno Krug has no need for money. He's perfectly content with what he has – which is a lot.'

No blushing now. The arms lying relaxed in the lap.

'Is he going to defect?'

Theresa shook her head, slowly. I was impressed by her cool. 'That will never happen.'

'What about Wolfgang Richter?'

A flicker of confusion this time; not unconvincing, though.

'What about him?'

'You were seen with him too.'

'We were acquaintances, nothing more.'

'You went to his funeral.'

'He seemed nice. I wanted to say goodbye.'

'You were seen kissing him.' I sat down in the armchair opposite. 'Do you kiss all your mere acquaintances?'

Theresa frowned, faltered, touched absently at the depression at her temple. 'What? I don't . . . What are you talking about?'

'Tell the truth. Were you lovers?'

'No. No, we weren't.'

'Are you doing this for him? Did *he* give you the book?'

I had to be sure. I had to probe a little, just in case she knew. I might never have another chance.

Theresa took a deep, steadying breath. 'No. No one gave me the book. *I* wrote it, for what it's worth.'

'Really? Then what's it called, this book you say you wrote?'

'It hasn't been . . .' Theresa checked herself. 'I haven't decided yet. I'm still thinking about it.'

I have to confess, absurd as it seems, that the ease with which she gave this answer momentarily unnerved me. *She* hadn't decided, she who now had the power of decision over the work and its fate – or would have, as soon as she was over the border. Of course, Theresa was only playing the part I'd asked her to play. Besides, the book was no more mine than hers anyway. All I can say, looking back, is that it *felt* more mine than hers; more mine, in fact, than anyone else's (that is, anyone living). The cuckoo's egg had been laid in *my* nest. I had inspired it, or provoked it. I had given rise to the itch that had given rise to the scratch, creatively speaking – Schilling had confirmed as much. That surely gave me some degree of precedence, a scintilla of entitlement.

'Is that it?' Theresa said, regarding me steadily. 'Am I free to go now?'

I dismissed these vain and petty thoughts, and smiled. It was good to see my lover play her part with confidence. It was exactly what the plan called for. It was an augury of success.

*

Two hours later Theresa was back in her apartment and I was alone in mine. We had decided she should go to the station on her own by taxi the next morning. Police were everywhere on the railway and, given Theresa's cargo, it was better if I didn't see her off. Theresa had also decided, unilaterally, against having me stay the night. It wasn't just the narrowness of the bed and the arduous journey that lay ahead of her. She wanted to have her wits about her the following day, she said, just in case.

This opportunity for a tender, valedictory bout of lovemaking was the first casualty of our scheme. An element of danger is an aphrodisiac for certain types of people, leading them in some cases to embark on sexual acts in semi-public places – department store changing rooms and municipal parks – where they risk discovery. On this evidence Theresa was not one of those types. Perhaps it was just a matter of degree, I thought. Perhaps, in her mind these risks, our risks, were too great to associate with pleasure. If so, I wondered that she was prepared to take them and whether she did so in the cause of truth, of art, or of love.

# 24

If the level of my anxiety over the following weeks were to be represented graphically, the resulting figure would be V-shaped. For the first days – days of steady, unceasing rain – I worried intensively, to the exclusion of all other activities. I worried that Theresa had been interrogated at the border and forced to reveal the truth. The lies with which I had equipped her seemed, in retrospect, inadequate. It was credible that Theresa had written the book, but when and where? She could not claim to have done the work in the East, because she could not produce the typewriter she had used; but the claim of Western provenance was almost equally vulnerable to disproof. For what if the authorities already knew what Theresa had brought into the country on previous visits? What if her effects had been examined and listed, there being no manuscript among them?

I did not walk, my usual antidote to stress. Instead, I stayed by my window, watching the street outside for the approach of arresting officers, struggling with a feline impulse to avoid being anywhere without an obvious means of escape (but where could I possibly run?). I worried that Theresa would have her visa revoked, permanently, making it impossible for her to return. In my darker moments I worried that she would simply disappear, because such things were rumoured to happen in the Workers' and Peasants' State, the way the toothpaste was rumoured to contain mercury. My one sustaining notion was that wherever Theresa was, whatever her predicament, I could not be far from her thoughts. My scheme would at least guarantee that. For better or worse, I had written myself into the story of her life – on to the jacket, on to the blurb – and nothing would ever write me out again. Even Wolfgang Richter could not say that (had he been alive to say anything). His role had been that of enabler, an involuntary Cupid, put to the service of my grimy, earth-bound Vulcan.

But the days passed and nothing happened. My neighbours came and went, hunched and hurrying to escape the weather. By now water was seeping in through a gap in the window frame, obliging me to place a towel along the sill. But the state security apparatus did not see fit to visit. No one visited me at all, in fact, nor I them.

I was in no mood for company, there being no one I could confide in. In the Workers' and Peasants' State, where the citizen's duty is always to report, the risk of official displeasure is like a disease: it spreads on contact.

Gradually my anxiety lifted. If something had gone seriously wrong, I would surely have heard before long. In the churning wake of relief came the spume of self-congratulation. The Richter manuscript – not just its disposal but its very quality – had been an embarrassment, a thorn in my side; but with a stroke of inventiveness I had turned it to my advantage. And gone unpunished. In such cleverness there is a special kind of delight. The impossible heist, the anonymous graffito, the perfect murder all impart to the perpetrator the same egotistical thrill.

After five or six days I felt calm enough to attempt some long overdue work. Awaiting me, half-finished, was a new *Factory Gate Fable* based on the struggles of Frau Wiegmann and the swimming pool committee. All the necessary ingredients were there: recognisable types, a worthy social purpose, obstacles both animate and inanimate, endless potential for conflict without recourse to serious social critique. But I found the subject, the whole, strangely unappealing. Instead I found myself digging out stories and sketches I had written years before: starker, bolder tales that a changed political climate had made it impossible to publish (Schilling himself had warned me off). The prose was rough and ready, but the voice was powerful. Was it too late, I wondered, to find that power again? I struggled with those stories late into the night, trying to re-enter their world, to write in the same vein.

As chance would have it, another meeting of the swimming pool committee was scheduled for the following week. I made my excuses and stayed away, but Frau Wiegmann was not so easily shaken off. She telephoned the next morning to inform me that a date had finally been set for the commencement of renovations and that there was to be a small ceremony at the site to mark the occasion.

'It would be a tragedy if you couldn't be there, Herr Krug,' she said, 'after all you've given for the project – a tragedy and an injustice.'

I didn't have the strength to make up another lie, so a few days later I found myself standing outside the mossy ruins of the Blasewitz municipal swimming pool, wielding a massive pair of bolt cutters. To cheers and applause from a crowd of local residents, I broke open the rusty iron chains that had held fast the main gates for forty years, the moment being recorded for posterity by a photographer from the local press. On cue, to even louder cheers, a small convoy of vehicles, bedecked with flags and pennants – a flatbed truck loaded with scaffolding, a mobile excavator, a cement mixer towed by a tractor – swept on to the site, the drivers in their shirtsleeves waving to the crowd like the youthful vanguard of a new Utopia.

By this time my anxieties regarding Theresa were on their upward leg. I had heard nothing for more than ten days. Ten days became two weeks; and two weeks became three. Spring arrived in the valley. On certain days the sky acquired a bluish tint, like galvanised steel, but still there came no word from the West. We had made no firm arrangements in this respect, but Theresa must have known of my concern. She must have wanted to set my mind at rest. I was reminded of her sudden disappearance to Berlin, but this time the wait was longer and more troubling. I worried about Theresa's incarceration, but also about her freedom and what she might do with it: return or not return, press on with our secret collaboration or abandon it and in the process abandon me. At any other time, in any other place, a phone call would have settled the matter; but it was a phone call I could not make.

After one especially unbearable Sunday I made my way back to the college of music. I knew it was foolish, but I couldn't help myself. In the night it had occurred to me that Theresa might have contacted one of her friends, especially now that the summer semester had officially begun. If it turned out that was true, if someone had heard from her, it would allay my earlier fears. On the other hand it would also intensify my new ones: because if Theresa could contact a fellow student, she could as easily contact me.

Theresa always had classes on Monday morning, ending at noon. I strolled up the steps at that exact hour, the bell ringing, the hall-ways slowly filling up with students on their way to the canteen. I searched for a face I knew, but reached the far end of the building without seeing one. I turned round and sauntered back again, maintaining a professorial air, then hung around near the noticeboard opposite the main doors. But my luck was no better. No one I recognised walked by, with the sole exception of an elderly member of the faculty whom I had seen at several student concerts. He gave me a vague smile as he passed.

With the last lecture room empty, there was nothing left but to go home again. I was back on Blochmannstrasse, about to turn on to the main avenue where the tram stop was located, when I saw out of the corner of my eye that someone was following me: a wiry-looking young man in a bomber jacket and jeans, with sunken cheeks and a feeble adolescent moustache. Though I didn't more than glance at him, I was sure I had seen him before.

Up ahead a tram heaved into view, sparks flickering dimly in the shadow of its belly. It struck me that I had seen the young man outside Theresa's apartment building one morning. He had been standing on the opposite side of the road, facing the entrance, looking as though he was about to cross. In the event he hadn't crossed, which had struck me as odd, hence the recollection. He had finished lighting a cigarette, then walked away along his side of the street.

I quickened my pace. The tram was drawing closer. The stop was two hundred yards from me, but no one was waiting there. I tried to wave down the driver, but he showed no sign of slowing down. I resisted the urge to look back, to see if the moustachioed stranger was still behind me. I was running away, but I didn't want to be *seen* to be running away; for implicit in such behaviour was the admission that I had something to run away from.

With an electro-mechanical groan and a squeal of brakes the tram pulled up: not to let me on, but to let a passenger off. I leapt aboard just as the pneumatic doors were closing. Looking back through the smeary glass, I saw the stranger come to halt on the other side. He had been running too, running after me – or maybe just running for the tram.

As we pulled away, I watched him through the back window, standing by the kerb, watching me.

# 25

I was afraid I would find someone waiting for me when I got home and so it proved. I turned the corner at the end of the street and there they were: two of them, standing opposite the front door – on the exact same spot where I had first seen my moustachioed pursuer a few weeks earlier. It had been stupid to run away. There was no hope of escape. All I had gained was a ten-minute tram ride with a knotted stomach. But again, I couldn't help myself. I spun on my heels and headed back the way I had come. I wasn't ready. I needed time to get my story straight. I needed time to shake off the clinging demeanour of guilt.

The street was full of noise. The youngest of the children from the local school were always in the playground at that hour, shrieking and squealing as if in full flight from a hilarious tornado. Perhaps it was just a routine enquiry, I told myself. Perhaps it had nothing to do with Theresa, or with Richter's book. I was *not* going to be arrested or interrogated. I was *not* going to disappear. What lay in store for me was probably no more than a harmless request for information, just like the last. As I walked slowly round the block, the children's innocent clamour made an unsettling counterpoint to these efforts at self-reassurance.

I approached the house again from the other direction, eyes on the ground, still turning over various forms of confession in my mind, my footsteps making no audible sound. I had my front door key in my hand when I heard them call my name. Reluctantly I turned. But the two people now hurrying across the road did not look like agents of the state security apparatus: the man was small and bald, the woman large and florid.

'Herr Krug, we were so hoping to catch you.'

Richter's parents. Having not seen them since the funeral, I'd failed to recognise them, although they seemed to be wearing the same clothes: the same pale blue trouser suit (she), the same ill-fitting jacket (he). The only thing that had changed was Frau Richter's home perm, which had been allowed partially to grow out, so that her hair was straight near the roots and curly at the ends, the unfortunate effect accentuated by the fact that the straight hair was grey and the curls a chemical yellow.

'We tried to call,' Herr Richter said. 'But I don't think we have the right number.'

'We were told you'd be here.'

I was greatly relieved at not being taken in for questioning, but my relief was short-lived.

'Is there something I can do for you?'

Frau Richter put her hand on my arm. I was struck by a smell of sweat and cheap perfume.

'We've had such difficulties, Herr Krug. Really it's awful.'

'Frieda, not here,' Herr Richter said, though with the noise from the playground we were in no danger of being overheard.

'We need your help,' his wife said. 'It's about Wolfgang.'

I tried to seem surprised. 'Your son?'

'I know what he meant to you. I felt sure we could count on you.'

Herr Richter gave me an apologetic look. 'We can come back another time. Any time that's convenient. We know how busy you are.'

I glanced up and down the street. A grey van was parked about forty yards away, opposite the kindergarten gates. Apart from that, everything was as normal.

'You'd better come in,' I said.

They refused coffee, tea and vodka, in spite of my repeated offers and their obvious fatigue. Eventually Frau Richter was persuaded to accept a glass of tap water, which she held on to with both hands, apparently terrified of spillage.

'I knew you'd help us, Herr Krug,' she said. 'You recognised our little Wolfgang's talent. You were his mentor.'

I insisted that I was no such thing. I had no experience of working in cinema. I had simply admired her son's work.

'And you should have heard how he idolised *you*. He wanted more than anything to follow in your footsteps. He told us he was going to write a novel, you know.'

'Really?' I said. 'I'd no idea.'

'Of course, he wouldn't give us any details. He didn't like to talk about his projects until they were finished. But he said he had it all worked out.'

'*Your* publisher and *your* editor, those were the ones he wanted,' Herr Richter said. 'I think that was the reason he came back here.'

'Yes, and that girl,' his wife said. 'Don't forget about her.'

This got my particular attention. 'A girl? What girl was that?'

'The student, the musician. She came to the funeral. What a cheek!'

'Now, Frieda, I'm sure Herr Krug doesn't want to hear about this. Herr Krug is a busy man.'

'No, no,' I said. 'I'm in no hurry. You were saying . . .'

'Theresa her name was. She played the violin. He said she was just a friend. He knew we'd worry, her being from the other side. Such liaisons aren't wise. You know what I mean, Herr Krug, don't you?'

I said I did.

'But then he said he was moving back here from Berlin, and we put two and two together. She'd obviously got her claws into him.'

'Frieda, I really think . . .'

'So I asked him straight: where's this going, Wolfgang? What'll happen in the end? You can't carry on for long with a border between you. In the end something's got to give.'

Herr Richter tapped his wife affectionately on the knee. If the idea was to silence her it didn't work.

'Of course, he didn't like it. He's always been very independent-minded. But do you know what he said? He said: maybe there won't always be a border between us, Mama. When people are in love they're prepared to make sacrifices. But he was kidding himself where she was concerned.'

'Sacrifices? You mean he thought Theresa would come and live here permanently? In the East?'

'Oh, yes,' Frau Richter said. 'That's what he thought. But look what happened. *He* came to *her*, he walked away from the Babelsberg studio to be near her. Not the other way round. If she hadn't turned his head he'd still be up there in Berlin and he'd still be . . .'

She fought back a sob. Touching though the spectacle was, I felt at that moment only disappointment, yawning and bleak. Theresa had been prepared to give up her life in the West for Wolfgang Richter, it seemed, but not for me. My mere mention of the possibility had been dismissed out of hand. But of course it had. How had I allowed myself to expect anything else? Theresa was from a different world and a different time. She was fond of me, no doubt. I was her comforter, her companion, her friend. But a partner for life? No objective observer would be foolish enough to bet money on that, let alone their heart.

'They promised us information, Herr Krug,' Frau Richter was saying. 'They promised to explain.'

I had lost the thread of the conversation. 'To explain . . . ?'

'The exact cause of death,' her husband said. 'Wolfgang's death.'

'Of course. I understood it was a type of meningitis.'

Herr Richter nodded. 'That's what they told us, on the telephone. I mean me. I was at work.'

He squeezed his hands together between his knees. Beneath his fingernails the flesh turned pink.

'He didn't get a name,' Frau Richter said.

'I didn't get a name. I was too . . . I'm not sure if they even gave me one.'

'A name?'

'The person who called. I tried to call back, for more information. Later. But I didn't know who to ask for.'

'No one would tell us anything,' Frau Richter said. 'They kept saying we would have to fill in a form. Even when we went to the hospital in Loschwitz, they wouldn't help us. We went back every day for a week.'

'We were hoping . . .' Herr Richter glanced at his wife. 'We were hoping to see him, before they . . . One last time, but the coffin was sealed, they said.'

'Sealed,' Frau Richter said, dabbing at her eye. 'We never saw him.'

'I'm sure that's standard procedure,' I said. 'One can't be too careful where infectious diseases are concerned. It would have been awful if . . .'

Outside, an electric bell summoned the children from their play. Slowly the squeals and shrieks died away. What I was left with was a picture, a picture Michael Schilling had drawn for me a few weeks earlier: of Wolfgang Richter being bundled into the back of an unmarked car.

But that was just a rumour.

Herr Richter reached into his jacket and took out an envelope. 'In the end they gave us this, as a special concession, they said.'

He took out a single sheet of paper from the envelope, and handed it to me. Beneath the heading PRELIMINARY REPORT OF DEATH were a few printed headings with information typed in: Richter's name, date and place of birth, and then the stark details of his demise, stamped and signed off by an 'attending clinician' by the name of V. H. Gatz. I supposed this was the information that would have been supplied to the state register office, where the beginning and end of each and every citizen was duly recorded.

'Under cause of death,' Herr Richter said. 'You see what it says?'

I read aloud the words: 'Cerebral atrophy'.

'That's not what they told us. They told us it was meningitis, an infection of the cerebral membrane.'

'Why would they change their mind, Herr Krug?' Frau Richter said. 'Why would they lie?'

'Frieda, please –'

'Do they take us for fools?'

Herr Richter put a restraining hand on his wife's arm.

'Are you by any chance a doctor, Herr Richter?' I asked.

My guest shook his head, his elfin ears turning a brighter shade of red. 'I work for the Post Office savings bank in Pirna. In the back office. I looked up meningitis in the library.'

'Well, isn't it possible that meningitis was the cause and this . . .'

'Cerebral atrophy.'

'Yes, this atrophy was the effect. An issue of terminology.'

Herr Richter put his head on one side. Neither he nor his wife said anything.

'Why don't you telephone this V. H. Gatz and ask him to explain?'

'I've tried many times,' Herr Richter said. 'He never takes my call. I've left messages, but he never responds.'

'That's a shame. Well, it's really the autopsy report one should rely on. Initial diagnoses are often mistaken.'

The Richters glanced at each other.

'Herr Krug,' Herr Richter said, almost apologetically, 'there has been no autopsy.'

I couldn't think of anything to say that wasn't glib or disingenuous. A healthy young man collapses and dies in forty-eight hours and the authorities don't hold a post mortem? I'd never heard of such a thing. But then, it was an unusual case. Perhaps the potential for infection was too great to risk an autopsy. Perhaps the morticians refused to hold one.

'We thought it was peculiar,' Frau Richter said. 'Don't you think there should have been an autopsy, Herr Krug? I don't understand it. Although the thought of . . .'

The thought of her son's body being cut open and systematically disembowelled on a mortician's table, the internal organs weighed on the scales one by one, as if to ascertain their retail value – yes, I could see how that would give rise to mixed feelings in a parent.

Frau Richter handed the glass of water to her husband and hastily pulled a handkerchief from her sleeve, the tears coming freely now, cascading down her pink cheeks.

For some reason I was starting to feel faint and a little nauseous.

'All we're asking for', Herr Richter said, 'is for someone to explain. But no one will talk to us. It's as if it's none of our business. As if we're being a nuisance.'

Frau Richter's voice was cracking. 'I just want to know what happened to my son.'

I managed to utter some soothing words, while her husband patted her on the arm. I had often wondered if, at some time or other, my mother had asked this exact same question.

'You're a man of influence,' Frau Richter said as she fretted at her wrinkled and snotty handkerchief. 'Would you put your name to a request, to an *Eingabe*? They couldn't ignore you, Herr Krug. They couldn't. You're a *decorated author*.'

The Richters had an inflated opinion of titular adornment and the influence it implied, but I could hardly refuse their request. 'I'll do what I can,' I said. By now I wanted the interview to be over. I had enquiries to make on my own behalf. 'The regional office of the Ministry of Health, I'll start there. I'm sure I can identify the relevant official.'

Frau Richter greeted this suggestion with an audible sob and a further seepage of tears. Then the thanks began – an insistent, pathetic chorus of thanks, that left me in no doubt that I had given her and her husband all they could have wished for. Not that it was going to do them much good. Wolfgang was gone and his body burned. Whatever the authorities settled upon as the final version of events, there was now no way it could be proven or disproven. Over the years I had been given several perfectly reasonable (and equally sickening) explanations for my mother's disappearance, but none of them had blunted my need to know. Only time had done that, and not convincingly.

Herr Richter got to his feet and helped his tearful wife to hers. He clearly regretted her indiscretions, which, as far as he was concerned, had no bearing on their current predicament. He handed me a piece of paper with their address and phone number on it, and, refusing all offers of further hospitality, escorted her to the door.

'It's the not knowing,' he said by way of mitigation. 'That's what makes it unbearable. I hope you can understand, Herr Krug. Not knowing is the worst part of all.'

As soon the Richters had gone I picked up the receiver and dialled Herr Andrich's number. My hands were shaking. At the other end the phone rang and rang – *where* it was ringing I had no idea, Andrich's office, like his job, being a notional entity, as far as I was concerned – but nobody answered. Grimly I hung on. I had questions. They had to be answered. I would stay on the line all afternoon if need be. What had Andrich and Zoch taken from our meeting before Christmas? When I'd given them Wolfgang Richter's name, when I'd described his work (truthfully!) as promising, had they taken me to mean something else? Had they been *stupid* enough to think I was labelling a potential defector? I had labelled Richter as *promising*, nothing more – and perhaps, in the context, arrogant (also true!), but nothing more dangerous than that. Had they imagined I was speaking to them in code? Had my words, grossly, obscenely misinterpreted, led to Richter's arrest? Because, if so . . .

The line clicked. 'Yes.'

A curt male voice, but not one I knew.

'Herr Andrich, please.'

'Who's calling?'

'I need to speak to him at once.'

'Who's calling, please?'

'It's urgent.'

'Your name.'

'What about Herr Zoch? Is he . . . ?'

'*What. Is. Your. Name.*'

It was then, just in time, that I saw where my putative interrogation of Herr Andrich would lead, where it was *certain* to lead: to the extraction of more names. I would learn nothing. The internal workings of the state security apparatus were not disclosed to anyone, not even Champions of Art and Culture. The flow of information was strictly one way, the information in this case being the identities of those who had slandered the state with their rumours of covert arrest, torture and death in custody. Where did you hear these rumours, Herr Krug? Who has been propagating these scandalous lies? Such were the questions that would be put to me, with ever increasing force. What would it cost me not to answer them, even assuming I had the strength?

'Hello?'

I put down the receiver. The vodka was still out on the table. I poured myself a shot, then another, then a third. It was the only thing I could think of to do.

# 26

The glass was still in my hand when the doorbell rang. The Richters had left behind their report from the hospital and I assumed this was what had brought them back, but when I looked out of the window it was not the Richters I saw. On the doorstep stood the man who had followed me from the college of music, his hands dug deep into the pockets of his bomber jacket, the butt of a cigarette protruding from his lips. For an agent of the state security apparatus his appearance was casual, even slovenly. But it came to me that this would be standard operational camouflage for agents of a certain type.

I had nothing to gain from being evasive. I buzzed the door open without demanding identification (as a man with no enemies might do) and settled into my armchair to wait. I also turned on the radio and hastily tuned it to Rundfunk der DDR, where a talk was under way on South Africa and the history of apartheid. I took deep breaths and mentally practised looking blameless, which I decided was best achieved with a show of contentedness and good humour – except where the situation in South Africa was concerned. Clearly no good citizen could be contented about that.

I waited a minute and another; then returned to the window. A black Wartburg crawled past the front of the building, but the stranger was no longer on the step, nor anywhere else that I could see. I sat down again for another minute, then went to listen at my door: sure enough, I heard footsteps – slow and laboured for such a young man – approaching from below. I sat down once more and waited for the knock, my stomach noisily imploding as if in response to the worsening South African situation. The footsteps in the stairwell grew louder and slower, then unexpectedly softer. I held my breath. Keys jangled – keys whose particular timbre I knew well: they were an old neighbour's keys, being readied for an old neighbour's door.

I went out on to the landing and peered over the rail. The lights were on but there was no sign of movement. What had become of my unannounced visitor? Why had he rung the doorbell if not to gain entry? Without putting my shoes back on, I went to investigate. As I reached the entrance hall – a tiled space, once grand, now scored, faded and smelling of fungus – the lights cut out with a clonk. Turning them on again, my eyes came to rest on an envelope propped up on the table by the door. On the front was written simply: *B.K.* I ripped it open. Inside was a letter in Theresa's tidy hand.

*Dearest Bruno,*

*I hope you received my postcard and haven't been worried. I have to write quickly now because there's someone who can take this letter to you and I think it's best to send it that way. I've some important things to tell you that I couldn't put on a postcard.*

At this point I stopped reading and climbed back up to my apartment, my footsteps heavy with the anticipation of a new disaster. When a young woman writes to her lover that she has *something important* to communicate it usually means one of two things: either she is breaking up with him or she is pregnant – rarely both, this being a mercy or a misfortune, depending on the lover's view of paternity. It did not immediately occur to me that the important something might be connected with Richter's book, because the book itself was not important, not to me. Theresa was what mattered.

I reinstalled myself in my old leather armchair and took a deep breath before reading on.

*I arrived back here without any problems, just the usual checks at the border. The guards took one suitcase away for a while – not the one that mattered – and when it came back it was missing a lipstick and, of all things, a tube of toothpaste! Otherwise, everything went fine.*

*Now I'm at home, looking after my mother and practising when I get the chance. At least I have no other distractions – although some of those distractions I could certainly do with. I expect you can guess the ones I'm talking about . . .*

*Now to my news. I've had some success regarding* The Valley. *I didn't know where to begin; so I went to a bookshop in Linz to see what was what. I wasn't ready to talk about the book, but when I was in there a sales rep turned up from a publishing company in Munich. We got chatting. He asked me what my book was about. I babbled hopelessly. It's about a lot of things and I hadn't rehearsed what I should say. The rep – his name was Matthias – said it* sounded 'interesting' and gave me the name of an editor. He said it would take months to get an answer, but that he would put in a good word. The company is called Bernheim Media Verlag. The man who worked in the bookshop said they were 'up and coming' and published a lot of science fiction. I went to a print shop and got the manuscript copied, and sent it off to Munich right away.

The one thing I almost forgot was to add a title page. I'd been putting this off, because I knew it would feel wrong. You know why. I managed it, though – after a few misaligned attempts – and, I must admit, I did get a guilty glow of satisfaction seeing my name on top of that pile of pages, which contain so much originality and life. It was the first time I felt able to imagine myself as an author. There is something liberating about being someone new, trying on a new persona. I imagine this is the thrill an actor gets, except that actors must play their parts as written. Maybe this is really the freedom of the writer, who makes up his charac- ters and lives inside them, in his mind. Is this why you do it, Bruno, because it gives you a special kind of freedom? If so, then perhaps I am closer to understanding you than ever.

A week went by and then, out of the blue, I got a tele- phone call from Konrad Falkner. He is the chief editor at Bernheim Media. He said he and his colleagues all agreed that the book was 'very powerful and very gripping'. I tried to sound surprised at this critical assessment, but once again, I don't think I made a good job of it – because, of course, I was not a bit surprised. I knew it was very powerful and gripping. I would have been surprised to hear anything else!

I think Herr Falkner was slightly disappointed at my reaction. He asked me if I'd had any offers for the book yet and I told him the truth: that his company was the first to see it. He then told me about all the successful books his company had published. I hadn't heard of them, but he did sound very enthusiastic. As agreed, I didn't tell him what the book is really about. I was a little surprised, though, that he didn't ask.

Herr Falkner finished by saying he was hopeful of being able to put together a 'pretty compelling' offer. His only reservation, he said, was that the title was too lyrical. Could I suggest an alternative? Something more 'gritty'? Of course,

*I couldn't. So I said I would think about it. Personally, I like*
The Valley. *Perhaps I should have said that, but I didn't
want to sound pretentious. What do you think? Can you
think of another title that might keep Herr Falkner happy?*

*I will try to get away to Linz again tomorrow so that I
can talk again to the man in the bookshop. How else will I
know whether or not to accept Herr Falkner's offer when it
comes? If only I could consult with you about it, but that's
impossible (I wonder what a 'pretty compelling' offer means
in the publishing world? Should one be compelled by a
thousand Deutschmarks? What about ten thousand?) How
long will it take them to get the book in the shops, I
wonder?*

*It is almost midnight and I'm exhausted. If only you knew
how much I miss you. I was sometimes a little lonely in the
East – before I met you – but I'm even lonelier here. Is it
possible I don't belong any more? How I wish I could curl
up with you right now and talk about everything. Even
when I'm scraping away on my viola, I'm so very often
thinking of you.*

*All my love,*
*Theresa*

*PS I may not be able to write another letter before I leave
here (on the 25th). There are risks involved in getting it to
you and I don't want to ask too many favours. If only for my
sake, please destroy this letter as soon as you've read it.
Promise?*

# 27

I never received the postcard Theresa had sent me, but on the afternoon she was due to return, I went down to the central railway
station to wait for her, carrying a bunch of white chrysanthemums
(the only fresh flowers I could find). I didn't know which train she
would be on. But the alternative – sitting in my apartment, waiting
for her to contact me – struck me as ungenerous and unnecessarily
cool. It was not enough to tell Theresa that I had missed her, that
her return mattered to me deeply. I wanted her to see it for herself.
By going to the station I was shrinking the time spent apart from
her to the smallest possible size.

The trains from Berlin came in about once an hour. The intervals
between them I spent in the waiting room, a rank and murky cell
full of litter and mouse droppings, or on a variety of benches, inside
or outside, depending on temperature and precipitation. In the end,
after the third empty train (not literally empty, but empty to me) I
took to touring the area on foot, pacing the stark expanse of Wiener
Platz and the surrounding streets, always returning in time to my
vantage point at the end of the relevant platform, where none could
pass without my seeing them. Between four o'clock and five there
were two trains from Berlin; another two between six o'clock and
seven. Theresa was not on any of them.

Hours went by. The shutters came down on the station café. The
waiting room emptied. The sky beyond the steel canopy went from
grey to pink to grimy blue. Lights went on high above the platforms.
I paced now to keep warm, multiple shadows wheeling around my
feet, ignoring the doubtful looks from station staff and the mice
darting brazenly back and forth. I had always liked the larger sort
of railway terminus. There is grandeur in the arrival of a train,
ceremony in its final approach: the stately pace, the declaratory hiss
of brakes. But this terminus held me prisoner. And, like a real prisoner, I had nothing to do but wait.

Of course, it was perfectly possible Theresa's travel plans had
changed. I knew that. Nothing could be reliably inferred from her
not appearing. As an episode it had neither drama nor consequence
– originality least of all. The lover, bearing flowers, waiting hopefully but in vain: it was a scene I would have hesitated to put into

a work of fiction. Characters in novels are not supposed to act like other characters in other novels; in so doing they show themselves as similarly fictional, which is something their creators generally seek to avoid. Characters do not come alive by conforming to type. Nothing can draw breath that is pressed from a mould – though some readers (I am told) prefer it that way, just as some people prefer their food from a tin. Yet here I was, bouquet symbolically wilting, the fallen petals inspiring rodent forays – likewise futile – from left and right, a cliché of the disappointed lover. Why had I taken on such an obvious role? Why, with night falling, had I not done the sensible thing, the painless thing, and gone home? The more I thought about it, the clearer it became that it was not my love for Theresa that had brought to me the station, but an older, more deeply rooted instinct, one which knew better than to believe in love stories with happy endings where Bruno Krug was concerned.

That evening I destroyed Theresa's letter, as requested.

She arrived the following afternoon and telephoned me from the music college. When I finally met her, at an outdoor café above the river, it struck me that she had already begun to change, though I never suspected that Richter's book was responsible. She reminded me now of a ballerina, fresh from the stage: she had lost a little weight; her eyes were puffy, her skin shiny, her hair pulled back and secured with an elastic band. The one dressed-up aspect of her appearance was a gold necklace from which hung a thumb-sized teardrop of amber – a leftover from her notional costume, whatever it was. As we held each other beneath the shade of a white plastic parasol, it struck me that she smelled different too: musky and sweet, like jasmine and vanilla ice cream. If I could have licked her without violating propriety, I would have.

Over coffee, as we held hands beneath the table, she updated me on her mother's convalescence and the upcoming crisis of her final exams, but it was not until we were walking away that she seemed content to tell me about the book.

'A lot's happened,' she said. 'I hope you'll be pleased. If I'd known, I'd have signed with an agent at the outset. It would have made things simpler.'

At the suggestion of the local bookseller, it transpired, Theresa had acquired the services of a literary agency in Zürich. Liebermann & Klaus AG were now handling the sale of all rights to *The Valley*, foreign and domestic.

'Martin thought we'd better stick . . .'

'Who's Martin?'

'Martin Klaus, my agent. I mean, *your* agent –'

'Though he doesn't know that.'

'Though he definitely doesn't know that, right. He said we were so far down the road with Bernheim that we'd . . .'

'Bernheim?'

'Bernheim Media. You did get my letter?'

My attention had been drifting to Theresa's mouth, to the prospect of the next long kiss.

'Yes, of course, sorry. The Munich people. Science fiction.'

'Mainly, but not exclusively. They're really spreading their wings. This is their ideal halfway house, Konrad said. It's just what they've been looking for.'

'Konrad, right.'

'So Martin thought we'd only hold out for an auction if Bernheim didn't come up with a decent offer, which they did. I let them know Martin was on board – he's very well known – and I think that got their attention, if you know what I mean.'

I didn't know what she meant, as a matter of fact. I was still wondering who Konrad was, and what the halfway house was halfway *towards* (Switzerland seemed the likeliest end point, with its bank vaults and bullion). Nevertheless, I was quietly impressed by Theresa's entrepreneurial zeal, which seemed to spring from nowhere, instinctively. She had been enjoying herself in the role I had carved out for her, which I saw as a good thing. Happiness, in whatever form, could only help keep us together.

'Anyway . . .' – Theresa took a deep breath and squeezed my arm with both hands – 'the offer, which I've verbally accepted, is for an advance of fifty thousand marks.'

In the Workers' and Peasants' State fifty thousand marks was roughly double an average salary: fair reward for two years of creative struggle – especially since they had not been mine.

'Well, that *will* come in handy,' I said. 'I'm impressed.'

'Bruno, I'm not talking *Ostmarks*,' Theresa said. 'I'm talking *Deutschmarks*.'

That was different. The official exchange rate between the two German currencies was one-to-one; the unofficial rate – the one everyone used, courtesy of the black market – was at least five-to-one; five Ost to one Deutsch. It was this that had made my foreign royalties from *The Orphans of Neustadt*, modest as they were by this time, so indispensable. At the Intershops, the Delikats and the

Exquisits, where all the best luxuries were to be found, the humble, fraudulent Ostmark was not even accepted.

'Fifty thousand Deutschmarks.' I found it necessary to repeat the sum.

'Less commission. But it may be just the beginning. Martin's very bullish about Frankfurt.'

'Frankfurt?'

'The book fair. There's the whole foreign market: England, France, America. Apparently there have been enquiries already from Holland and Italy. The word is definitely out.'

I felt a little dizzy. I tried to focus on Theresa, on the face I had been waiting so impatiently to see again, but everything was soon obscured behind a grainy red-brown mist.

'The last time I spoke to him,' she was saying, 'he said something about a strong possibility of pre-emptive bids.'

We were near the opera house, standing at the top of a flight of stone steps. I know this because I had to grab hold of the railing to keep from falling down them.

'Bruno, are you all right?'

It was the sudden stampede for Richter's book, the tidal wave of affirmation and expectation building behind it, carrying it upward (financially) and outward (geographically) at unstoppable speed – that was what unsteadied me.

My experience with *The Orphans of Neustadt* had been very different. After the publication of that pivotal volume, it had been nearly three years before Éditions du Seuil in Paris produced the first non-German edition. The book was translated into English a year later – badly and with several unauthorised cuts (a faithful edition, care of Faber & Faber, had to wait another four years). Other translations followed gradually, two or three each year for the rest of the decade and well into the next. Curious Koreans, Greeks and Indonesians were finally able to enjoy the work in their own language fourteen years after it was first published in mine. Perhaps this was because I had no agent in the West, the rights to the book being handled by Michael Schilling's firm; but from where I stood, it was as if *The Orphans of Neustadt* was being passed by hand, reader by reader, around the globe – a process that seemed to me quite natural, a true reflection of how books have always been experienced and weighed (that is, slowly and with the occasional pause for reflection). By contrast, *The Valley*, like the latest teen craze, was spreading round the globe like news of the Second Coming. Was it really that good? Was it really that much *better*? Had Richter been alive, I would have been jealous. But this was not jealousy, not exactly. It had more in common with fear.

'It's all a bit unexpected,' I managed to say.

'You are pleased?'

'Ecstatic.'

'It is what you wanted?'

A cool breeze blew off the river, carrying a hint of algae and burning tyres. Slowly my vision cleared.

'Of course. I just hadn't expected that kind of reaction. I pictured something a bit more discreet.'

Theresa took my hand as we walked down the steps. At the bottom she leaned closer, the better to whisper in my ear, lover to lover. There were still those 'distractions' she had mentioned in her letter. I assumed they were carnal and hoped she was anxious to make up for lost time. But it turned out love was not on her mind.

'Don't worry,' she whispered, 'I've been very careful. Not even my mother knows the truth yet. As they say in the theatre, I'm really growing into the role.'

It had been a worry to me that Theresa might find the burden of secrecy too much. I assumed that keeping secrets was something she wasn't used to. Had I been more cynical, or more shrewd, I might have been less concerned. People share secrets mainly to demonstrate that they have them. Secrets imply inclusion, influence and status – but not in this case. For Theresa to reveal that she was not the author of *The Valley* would have had the opposite effect. It would have revealed that she was not as talented, interesting or noteworthy as she seemed.

'What about your friends at the college?' I asked. 'You're happy to keep them in the dark?'

Theresa shrugged. 'I'll be done here before the book comes out. If anyone hears about it later, I'll say I wanted to keep it under wraps, in case it didn't amount to anything.' Her cheeks were pink and flushed, no doubt in marked contrast to mine. 'That makes sense, doesn't it?'

'Perfect sense.'

'It's what I'd do, if I actually wrote a book. I wouldn't tell a soul until the deal was done.'

I had exercised precisely the same caution when drafting *The Orphans of Neustadt*. I wrote it longhand in a series of notebooks bound in blue cardboard, working at night and whenever the chance came to be alone. When challenged, I claimed I was writing a journal of my dreams, which invariably had the effect of forestalling any further enquiries. Nobody knew what I was really up to. My motives for secrecy were complex. I was afraid of being mocked, yes. I was also concerned that my story might not meet with official approval; but more than these, I felt the fragility of the world I was creating. Like some rare fungus, it needed warmth and darkness to flourish and take shape. I had no thought of readers. If I addressed myself to anyone it was to my long-vanished mother, who I felt sure would take an interest in my imaginings, as being indicative of her son's interior world.

Those were my reasons. What were Theresa's? I assumed it was modesty that lay behind her instincts. Theresa played the viola. She didn't care for the limelight; she cared for music. It did not occur to me that to work in secret only because you dare not be seen to fail, that is not modesty. That is pride.

# 28

In the youngest northern summer there are portents of autumn. The fallen and trampled blossoms are forerunners of fallen and trampled leaves; clear summer skies usher in chilly summer nights; an unwavering sun bleaches colour from the land, anticipating the flat grey light of winter. But in the Workers' and Peasants' State this effect was accentuated by the hand of Man, by coal-fired production and the exigencies of the Five Year Plan. If autumn complemented the natural palette of the Workers' and Peasants' State, summer did the opposite: it worked against the prevailing ambience. Its character and its colours, like a badly chosen dress, rather than flattering the wearer, only accentuated her flaws. Mists and miasmas, intrinsic to autumn, were revealed as factory emissions (even the taste was stronger when warmed up). Leaves that should have been green were mildew green, skies that should have been blue were battleship blue. And when a rainstorm washed away the smoke and sulphur, bringing brief, unfamiliar clarity, the effect was far from harmonious: under a pure blue sky the streets of the city looked like rows of rotten teeth. Summer was a bikini on an unshapely woman. Summer in the Workers' and Peasants' State left too little to the imagination.

My summer was further compromised by the knowledge that Theresa would be done with the college of music before the season was over. What would happen after that was unclear. Creatively and financially we were now conjoined, thanks to *The Valley*. There was some satisfaction in that. But it was not enough. I wanted Theresa to come back to me, once and for all, and to stay – the way she had planned to stay for Wolfgang Richter, whom she now never spoke of, except in her sleep. Then I would know that she at least loved me as much.

We met often, but never for long. I saw nothing ominous in this. Theresa had missed many classes and tutorials during her weeks away and, with final exams looming, she had no time for recreation. Our encounters were always hurried, even brisk. Eating and sleeping took up most of them; lovemaking took care of the brief intervals in between. The rest of the time I was alone, the days empty.

In bed, though, I slowly began to notice other changes. The usual rites of seduction – rarely lengthy in our case – became abbreviated until they were little more than pre-coital semaphore. This, I am fairly certain, was not my doing. It was Theresa who was content to dispense with the preliminaries. I didn't see this as a bad thing either. I assumed that her impatience was indicative of a deep and abiding attraction. This change coincided with a novel preference for making love with her back to me. When it came to seizing the moment – in the kitchen, the bathroom, the sitting room – this was both convenient and easy, little in the way of furniture being required. There was the added advantage (valued, I suspect, by many) that it left both participants free to pull whatever grotesque and simian faces their lust inspired without eliciting laughter or disgust. It was brazen, lewd and playful – desirable attributes in any sex life, even that of the most sanctified and upright couple. Only much later did it occur to me that there might be deeper and less desirable undercurrents at work in this new preference; that the distance between man and woman left both freer to fill their heads with whatever they pleased: different places, different circumstances, different partners. Only later did I come to think of it as the coitus of betrayal.

'This position is ideologically unsound,' I said one night, when we were *in medias res*. 'Don't you care at all about female emancipation?'

'What are you talking about?'

'The male's posture is essentially upright; the female's submissive. This position reinforces patriarchal stereotypes. It's reactionary. You should really be on top.'

Theresa laughed. 'You just want me to do the work. Where's the emancipation in that?'

'The right to labour is inalienable from the socialist ideal.'

'You know, a lot of women give birth on all fours. It's well known to relieve stress.'

Not for the first time I was silenced by the thought of Theresa becoming pregnant. (Why do the English say *falling* pregnant, as if pregnancy were an illness, like influenza or shingles, properly eliciting sympathy? Is this a biblical reference to the fall of Adam? Is a pregnant woman a fallen woman to English sensibilities?) To me the notion of a Krug-Aden baby was wonderful and frightening, a window on a world of new priorities and new fears. Certainly it would have forced the issue where Theresa's future domicile was concerned. But it would also have clouded that issue, because now there would be a third party to consider; a child whose interests would be paramount. And I didn't want that. I didn't want Theresa to stay with me out of a sense of duty. I wanted the Krug-Aden offspring to be the natural outcome of our togetherness, not the cause of it. In any case, I assumed a child was a distant prospect. Theresa had once told me she'd taken the necessary precautions and I trusted her on that point without enquiring further. Perhaps this was rash, but like most men I preferred to keep the twin issues of female sexuality and female fertility as far apart as possible, with preferably a wall and a minefield in between them.

'I should have told you before,' Theresa said one morning, as she hurriedly got ready for another day of scraping and cramming. 'Martin says I need a few lines about the next book.'

Up until that moment I had been in bed, watching her dress, something that gave me an erotic pleasure that was all the more delicious for being subtle. I sat up. 'The *next* book?'

'Just a page. A couple of paragraphs. For Bernheim Media.' She picked up her brush and began the daily assault on her tangled hair. 'There will be a next book, won't there, at some point?'

'Yes, of course. I suppose.'

'Have you got some ideas?'

'Loads.'

'Martin says it's important they don't get the idea I'm a one-trick pony – I mean, *you're* a one-trick pony. Bernheim haven't paid all that much. So they'll be tempted to hold back on the marketing if they think there aren't more books to come. He said building authors is expensive. They need to see a payback going forward. Do you see?'

Once again, I didn't see. I was still struggling with the concept of an author being *built*, visions of a robot assembly line alternating with flashes of Frankenstein's monster.

'Apparently it's not unusual for people to write one book, even a very good book, and then pretty much dry up.'

I smoothed out the sheet with the flat of my hand, trying to appear both surprised and indifferent. 'Did Herr Klaus have anyone in mind?'

'He mentioned some names. I didn't know them. Of course, some of them soldier on, he said, but somehow they can never get back to where they started.' Theresa gave up on the hairbrush and began buttoning up her blouse. 'It must be dreadful. Imagine having all that technique and nothing at all to *say*. At least a musician never runs out of music.'

She got up and slung her bag over her shoulder. Reflective detours were a rarity in our conversations these days. I missed them.

'Anyway, the idea is to make it seem like *The Valley* is just the beginning. A début. Plenty more where that came from. Can you do that? It's not like it's a commitment. It just keeps your options open.'

Theresa must have read some concern in my face. She sat down on the bed. 'I'm sorry. It must be awful for you.'

'Must it? Why?'

'Everyone talking about your book as if it's the work of a novice, as if you've started from scratch. You can change your mind, you know. It isn't too late.'

I looked into her eyes and it was clear what she wanted me to say. Hadn't she told me she was really growing into the role? Hadn't she told me she felt liberated? I smiled and patted her on the hand.

'When's my deadline?'

# 29

If Wolfgang Richter had wanted to poison my happiness, if losing Theresa had made him jealous from the grave, if the way I had disposed of his work had angered his spirit, if he had sought revenge for any other reason, he could not have come up with a more ingenious plan than this. If he had wanted to punish or deride me (as he had often done in life), if he had wanted to highlight the tragedy of his demise and the joke of my continuing survival, what could have served his purpose better than the impossible task Theresa had just dropped into my lap? It was disconcerting the way Richter's book had been instantly taken up by the literary world. I feared unpredictable consequences, a raising of the stakes. But that was nothing. Now I had to *follow* it. I had to produce a new written work of my own, which – unlike *The Orphans of Neustadt* – would be explicitly and universally measured against *The Valley*. There was no escaping it: Richter's masterpiece was now the only point of reference that counted.

All comparisons are odious, but what could have been more odious than this? What could have revealed my creative eclipse more starkly? My inevitable failure didn't need to be public. It was enough that Theresa would witness it: because, as far as the world was concerned, that failure would be hers – my gift to her, long since turned sour. For some time I had been troubled by thoughts of decline, by my inability to write anything from the heart, anything that felt honest. Now Theresa, by extension, would be haunted too. I had wanted, I suppose, to be more like Richter in her eyes; I had succeeded only in making the difference more stark and disenchanting than ever.

The safest course in the short term was to do nothing and write nothing; to shrink into my shell, claiming a bad case of writer's block. People respected writer's block. In order to have writer's block you had at least to be a writer. But how long before an episode of writer's block evolved into something more embarrassing? How long before Theresa saw in my literary impotence a warning, a portent of the general impotence to come? Theresa had fallen in love with an artist. How could I bury that artist without burying her love alongside him?

You will say I should have seen this coming. Every success brings with it a burden of expectation. The question of what would follow *The Valley* was bound to have come up sooner or later. For the publishers *not* to have made enquiries might have been construed as indifference. Why then had I not been prepared?

Again, my own experience had been different. Enquiries about my second book had only surfaced well after *The Orphans of Neustadt* had been published. Nobody at the outset, not even Michael Schilling, had suggested I give up plumbing for a life in literature. We were both conscious less of what the enterprise promised than of what it threatened, namely censure and punishment. That had been enough to worry about.

A second explanation: I hadn't expected *The Valley* to be so warmly received, at least not by publishing professionals. It was far too easy for that. You could get through it in a handful of sittings; the sentences could be deciphered at the first attempt, and even its most reflective and analytical passages were hopelessly clear, inducing neither headaches nor dizziness nor rage. It was, in other words, the kind of literature I would have liked to write – which indeed I *had* written, once, a long time ago. Yes, *The Orphans of Neustadt* had been critically well received, but that had been due to its setting: a time and place that was both historically significant and fresh in the minds of millions. It was a book that spoke of (what turned out to be) a common experience. By contrast, Richter's setting was a world *nobody* had experienced, a future setting that existed only in his imagination. I had thought it possible *The Valley* might prove popular eventually. I had not expected it to be instantly acclaimed by the guardians of the literary high ground, right around the globe.

This was how I accounted for my blindness at the time. Looking back, I am not so sure I *was* blind. Perhaps a part of me – the part with no voice, the part that leaches into the consciousness via dreams – wanted me just where I was. I am speaking here of my conscience. Perhaps it wanted me comparing myself with Richter, day in and day out, judging my work against his. Perhaps it set me after Theresa too: so that I would be forced to measure her love for Richter against her love for me – its quality, its foundations, its strength. If so, I wonder if my conscience really had my best interests at heart; or whether what it really craved was a perverse form of martyrdom, an excoriating self-sacrifice in the wholly hopeless cause of truth.

Weighed down with this unwelcome challenge, troubled as never before by Richter's genius, I adopted my usual strategy: I walked. I walked all day and into the evenings, with pauses only for bread and beer, my path taking me (without the need for planning) in circles of varying diameter round the Altstadt. I went as far south as Mockritz, with its beleaguered little park, north to the wooded slopes of Hellerberge and the old streets of Pieschen. Occasionally I took a tram ride through the bleaker quarters of the city: Friedrichstadt, with its freight yards; Löbtau and Gorbitz, where the great housing projects had produced, together with certain material benefits, a landscape of arboreal deprivation reminiscent of the Russian steppe, only with less greenery and no horsemen. But in all these wanderings my mind remained fixed on the college of music. It was there that Theresa was hard at work, preparing for her future – a future in which I might or might not have a place. It was as if I were tied to her by an invisible force: no matter in what direction I set off, the college was always on my right or on my left. What I could not stand was to have it behind me. Resting at a tram stop in Plauen, I noticed a furry grey spider spinning a web in the uppermost corner of the shelter, moving in a precarious spiral round the centre of the structure. His motion was not unlike mine, but something about the sight disgusted me. I pulled down the web, sending the unfortunate arachnid clambering into a crevice for safety.

What would Richter have written after *The Valley of Unknowing*? What was the next step in his all-conquering career? If only I could have answered that question, I might have been safe. Theresa and her agent were demanding only a brief description. I could have strung out the actual writing for years. I thought of asking Michael Schilling about the Richter pipeline, but decided against it. There was no possible excuse for my curiosity and I didn't want to start arousing his. Besides, hadn't Richter's mother told me the boy was secretive about his work? *He didn't like to talk about his projects until they were finished.*

It was quite possible, of course, that Richter would have written nothing, or nothing good. Perhaps – this thought was perversely comforting – *The Valley of Unknowing* had sucked his creative well dry. Maybe the new star, celestially speaking, would have burned brightly and burned out, as the authors of so many promising débuts had done before him; as *I* had done, or so it was widely reported. Richter had confidence and swagger (in my memory he is always swaggering, hands sunk deep into his trouser pockets, a woman's petitioning arm looped through his), but success is a heavy mantle no matter how expensive the fabric. It suffocates the brightest artistic spark. Following *The Valley* might have proved as daunting a task for Richter as it was for me. In that event I imagined he would have opted for a quick literary death, rather than the long drawn-out one attributed to me.

All of which should have made my task easier. I was free, truth be told, to propose whatever story I liked. My anonymity afforded me protection – more protection than I had ever known. I had no censors to worry about, no ministry to please, no standing to protect, no reputation to defend. Fate had given me the rarest of luxuries: that of being able to ghostwrite my own book. What more freedom could a writer possibly ask for? But instead of opportunity, I saw only the multiple and conflicting requirements: for a story I *could* write, that Theresa *might* write, that Richter *would* write. I saw only the walls. It never occurred to me to look up at the sky.

I did not give up easily. I tried my best to imagine the kind of stories that might have entered Theresa's mind, if Theresa had been a writer; but all I could think of was her struggling to make music, and the twin she no longer had. I tried to become Wolfgang Richter as I strode through the Heide with the wind in my hair, but all I could think of were tales of petty jealousy and vengeance and clandestine betrayal – too confessional, too *close*: histories I wanted hidden from Theresa, not paraded before her. When at last we met again, I was exhausted and hollowed out from the fruitless hours of wandering.

I recall the occasion as being marked by a lack of conversation. It was a close, sticky night. Theresa had turned up late, downed the shot of iced vodka I had prepared for her, sneezed and disappeared into the shower, pulling her ribbed white sweater over her head as she went. In other circumstances I might have followed her, not in pursuit of arousal but to affirm my privileged position in her affections. But that night I did not follow. For once, I had neither the conversation nor the confidence. I lay waiting on the bed, nursing my blistered feet, listening to her wash away the grime of her day. Now and again I caught snatches of a tune, though it wasn't one I could place.

She came into the room wrapped in several towels and threw herself on to the bed beside me. 'So, what about your homework?' she said.

'Homework?'

'For Martin. The next book idea. Today's your deadline, remember?'

'Coming along nicely,' I said.

'And?'

'I'll write you something tomorrow.'

'Yes, but what? What's it going to be about?'

From somewhere in the building came the throaty roar of a flushing *Klo*. It was then that I remembered Frau Helwig.

'It'll be a sequel,' I said. 'Same setting, same characters, only five years on – no, make that ten years on.'

'Ten years on.'

'Yes. You get to find out what happened to everyone, in the end. It answers all the questions.'

Theresa was silent. I knew why. *The Valley of Knowing* was a perfectly complete work of fiction. Tacking on a sequel was the literary equivalent of regurgitating an excellent meal so as to enjoy it a second time, somewhat rearranged. It was bound to leave a bad taste in the mouth.

'A sequel. Great,' Theresa said.

She took off her towel and slipped beneath the sheets. By the time I was undressed and ready to join her, she was fast asleep.

## 30

Theresa's exams and assessments went on for several weeks, a period in which summer at last made a clammy and truculent appearance in the valley; the skies pregnant with veiled and distant cumuli, the river low and toxic, the streets ever more malodorous. It was a summer redolent with decay, a season that looked forward to its own demise – a summer of waiting and of uneasy calm, like the months before war.

Each day was hotter than the last. I gave up walking and stayed at home, burying my head in detective novels and *Robinson Crusoe*, until that too became unbearable. After that, I sought out churches and the larger, cooler public monuments, attaching myself to touristic troupes of Libyans and Bulgars, and corpulent, sweating Russians. I invariably peeled off at the ruins of the Frauenkirche – the star attraction, judging from the expenditure of photographic film – taking shelter in Tutti Frutti or one of the other *Eiscafés*, even when the only flavour of ice cream still available (seasonal variations in demand presenting a challenge to the central planning system) was a lurid green pistachio that tasted like deodorant.

The torpid days were made longer by Theresa's lengthy absences. These, she said, were unavoidable. She had to make up for the time she had spent away (time spent helping me, in part) and was dangerously ill prepared for her exams. Allegedly, an out-and-out fail was a real possibility. I never questioned these assertions, the memory of her unsteady Brahms performance being fresh in my mind. I didn't object when she filled her evenings with studying and practice rather than make the trip to Blasewitz; I didn't complain when she didn't call. The single telephone in her residence was often out of order, she had told me; and when it wasn't out of order, there was invariably a queue of students waiting to use it, making privacy impossible. When she did call, she sounded close to exhaustion.

Her explanations didn't stop me from worrying. I worried that my prowess, creatively speaking, had been deflated in her eyes on account of my recent capitulation. What was to follow the ingenuity and wisdom, the vitality and vigour of *The Valley*? A sequel. It didn't matter that Richter's book was a coded sequel to mine. The story of Thomas and Sonja was a story in two parts; it demanded two books. But a third? Thomas and Sonja in late middle age; what was that going to add? Even if Theresa was unaware of my capitulation, it would not be long before she was enlightened by her agent or her publishers in Munich. The same characters ten years on? Was that really the best she could do?

Then early one morning I found a letter waiting for me in my letter box. Like the last of Theresa's communications, it had not been entrusted to the postal service, the envelope having neither address nor stamp. It seemed she had access to some alternative delivery network, involving students and musicians – or so I assumed.

The letter was very short, the handwriting more untidy than usual. It assured me that the exams were going 'not too badly' and invited me to a party being thrown in the evening after the last test. *I hope you can come*, she wrote, the sentiment striking me as strangely formal. *I'm sorry I've been so wrapped up in myself. Things have become more complicated lately. It seems my whole life is in flux.*

I couldn't guess what she was talking about. For me it was only our circumstances that were complicated: challenges posed by geography, history and politics – nothing that actually mattered. One of the joys of being in love is that it clarifies your priorities. Complication arises from not knowing what you want.

Theresa signed off before adding the following *postscriptum*:

> *I passed on the sequel idea. To be honest, I wasn't sure about the response. The first book ends so beautifully. Is there any more that needs to be said? But guess what? Everyone's even more excited now than ever. Martin says a sequel is a masterstroke, because it gives everyone 'two bites at the cherry'. Konrad Falkner said it's just what he was hoping for and he's going to put more money on the table for the rights. I didn't know you could sell a book before it's even written, but apparently it's quite normal. (If the idea really caught on, bookshops would be funny places, wouldn't they? Lots of empty shelves . . .) Anyway what do you think? Should I sign on the dotted line? I think everyone is going to be very disappointed if I don't. Martin says it's vital to keep Bernheim 'fired up'.*

It was not in Theresa's nature to joke about my work, but even so, it took me a while to accept that my creative surrender really was deemed a masterstroke in the West; an idea so promising it could not be allowed to get away. Well, if repetitiveness and creative timidity were the order of the day, I had plenty more where that came from. As I wandered into town, crossing the Neumarkt on my way to my favourite bakery, it came to me that there was a simple explanation for this bizarre reaction. What if the pivotal entity here, the repository of value, was not the books, actual and putative, but the person of the author? What if Theresa herself was the key ingredient, the selling point par excellence? If so, then all this talk of a second book might simply be a way of extracting more money and of extracting it sooner. Why wait for the bubble to burst? Why take a chance on the difficult second novel being difficult for everyone; difficult to sell, difficult to enjoy, difficult to *read*? Success in this strange new world happened almost instantaneously. Maybe failure happened just as fast.

A humid summer wind blew through the ruins of the Frauenkirche, sending a plume of dust spiralling into the air. These were only speculations, but speculations were all I had. The little I knew of these negotiations and strategies, I knew from Theresa. My knowledge was limited to her perspective and her impressions – and to what she chose to reveal. The fact was, she could tell me whatever she liked. I was in no position to uncover her omissions, just as she was in no position to uncover mine. I had an inkling she could have told me more than she had; the way she spoke of her agent and publisher sometimes, it was as if they were old friends. What plans might they have made together? What futures might they have mapped out?

In spite of the hour, my shirt was soon sticking to my back. As I gingerly plucked the fabric from my flesh, it struck me that my thoughts were as grimy and sour as the city air. I had no reason to mistrust Theresa. If I envisaged duplicity or ambition on her part, this was merely a reflection of my own double-dealing and my own pride. A deceiver might be doomed to live in fear of deception, but only in fairy tales and fables (factory gate and otherwise) was he doomed to *be* deceived. Poetic justice was, as the term implies, a phenomenon confined to poetry and to lesser literary forms.

# 31

I had not been at the party more than a few minutes when a couple of Theresa's student friends – pale young men whose faces I recognised but whose names I could not remember – came up and asked me, in tones of wonder, if I had read her book.

'What book?' I stammered, being completely unprepared.

'Her novel. It's coming out this autumn, in the West.'

The festivities were being held outdoors, on the north side of the Blochmannstrasse building, a semi-rustic space compromised by tornadoes of small insects spinning hungrily beneath the shadows of the trees. Refreshments and sandwiches had been laid out on trestle tables, the white plastic tablecloths acting as a magnet for thunderflies, earwigs and various arthropodal detritus, which fell from the branches like rain.

I lowered my voice. 'I thought that was supposed to be a secret.'

'Not any more,' said one of the young men, a cellist, if I remembered right. 'Theresa's been telling everyone.'

'So what's it like?' asked the other young man. 'What's it all about?'

I said I didn't know, because Theresa had kept her book under wraps. Even I hadn't been allowed to see it.

The cellist smirked. I sensed that, beneath the smiles, Theresa's literary coup rankled – more even than her freedom of movement, or her idiosyncratic beauty. Perhaps the modest aspirations of the viola player had drawn the sting from these other advantages, rendering them less wounding to his self-esteem. But the status of *author*, that was a different matter. The author was a soloist, elbowing her way centre stage. The maker of fictions was an egotist, a romantic showman, congenitally disinclined to share (all characteristics that, upon reflection, made Theresa unsuited to the role).

'I expect she's afraid,' the cellist said. His breath smelled strongly of alcohol.

'Afraid? Of what?'

'Judgement. Your expert appraisal. She's afraid you'd see through her.' His friend gave him a censorious nudge. 'Well, anyone would be. This is the man who wrote *The Orphans of Neustadt*.'

I moved away. By now the gathering was around forty strong, but Theresa was nowhere to be seen. My insides began to gurgle and throb. The uncertainty that was intrinsic to our relationship, an inevitable consequence perhaps of its geopolitical instability, had a habit of resurfacing at times like these. Unexpected absences and casual farewells took on an ominous significance in retrospect. It was not the kind of uncertainty any normal man could tolerate for ever.

I was standing in the middle of the crowd, stifling nervous belches and feeling out of place, when it began to rain: a few spots on the back of my hand, a faint rumble in the distance, then a hissing downpour that sent everyone running for cover. The bravest revellers huddled around the trunks of the trees; the rest, myself included, headed inside the building where an unprepossessing common room was commandeered for festive use. There was still no sign of Theresa and it was not until I had emerged from the lavatories – the tension translating itself into an increased pressure on my bladder – that I spotted her sitting halfway up a flight of stairs, holding a glass between her knees. Next to her sat Claudia Witt. Before I could open my mouth, Claudia got up and left without a word, giving me a peremptory hello as she went by, but nothing that could be called a smile.

I took Claudia's place on the step. On the landing above us the wind hurled volleys of raindrops against a large window. Theresa looked tired. There were unfamiliar creases under her eyes, and a general puffiness that I could not help but associate with the aftermath of our longest and most voluptuous nights. Was this really the result of too much studying, or was some change in her health responsible? Was she falling sick?

She smiled and rested her head on my shoulder, forestalling my clumsy attempt to kiss her on the mouth.

'What are you drinking?' I said, peering into her half-empty glass.

'Lemonade.'

'Lemonade? I thought this was supposed to be a celebration.'

Theresa nodded towards the common room. 'The booze down there is awful. I think it's actually moonshine.'

Prepared for this eventuality, I pulled a small bottle of Stolichnaya from the pocket of my ancient linen jacket. But before I could pep up the contents of her glass, Theresa covered it with her hand. It really wasn't like her.

'My head hurts,' she said, placing a hand on her forehead, the gesture a touch too theatrical. 'I've been up since five.'

'You do look tired,' I said. 'Recently you've even been *sounding* tired.'

She sighed and said nothing, as if honouring a resolution not to expand on the subject.

'So how did it go today?' I asked at last.

'It could have been worse. No disasters anyway.'

Even expensive varieties of vodka are unpleasant when warm, but I took a slug before replacing the cap, if only to burn away the unsteady feeling in my innards. This reunion was ominously down-beat, ominously lackadaisical. In Theresa I saw none of the eagerness I felt, none of the need.

'I've a question,' I said. 'Have I read your book, or not?'

Theresa frowned. 'What?'

'Someone just asked me if I'd read your book. I didn't know what to say. No Party line on that particular issue.' Theresa continued frowning. 'You said you weren't going to tell anyone over here.'

'Oh.' She sighed. 'I told Claudia, that's all. She has a way of wink-ling things out of me. Sorry.'

'It doesn't matter.'

'It didn't seem natural keeping quiet about it. I thought if I said something now, there'd be fewer questions later, when the book comes out.'

'It won't come out here. Besides, you'll be gone before then, won't you?'

Theresa fell silent. It was clear to me that she had come to a decision, a decision about us. I wished I had a drink to sip, or a cigarette to light (though I've never smoked), anything to appear oblivious to the significance of the moment. With timing that verged on the ironic, a faint rumble of thunder rattled the window behind us.

'That depends,' Theresa said at last. 'There's a chance I could take a masters degree in musicology. At the Humboldt in Berlin. My professor here – Dr Thurman – says it could be arranged, for a fee. But I've the money now, thanks to you; so I can afford it.'

'Are you really interested in musicology? I thought you wanted to be a musician.'

'I do, but there are no jobs, are there? Not for a viola player.' Theresa began speaking rapidly. 'It's all right for you. You're a writer. You don't need anyone else. All you need is pen and paper. I need a whole orchestra.'

'You told me once that you felt sorry for writers. Remember? Because they have to make up their own material; whereas you musicians have always got other people's to fall back on.'

'Did I say that? I can't have been thinking. Anyway, if things worked out at the Humboldt, I could think about an orchestra here. In the East.' Theresa bit her lip as she looked up at me. (That tiny gesture made me drunk with joy.) 'What do you think?'

This time she let me kiss her. It was better news than any I had dared to hope for – better, in fact, than might have seemed credible to any objective observer. Yet I preferred not to examine my good fortune, the range of possible motives that might have brought it about.

I enfolded her in my arms and held her close, ignoring the tension in her body, the swiftness with which she broke away, even though, at another time, these would have suggested a degree of reluctance, as if she had reached her decision unwillingly, under some undeclared pressure. What I did reflect on later, when I was once more alone, was the compromise in Theresa's proposal. She had not decided to come and live with me for ever in the Workers' and Peasants' State; she had decided to remain within reach for another year, with a view to a final decision at a later date, contingent upon circumstances and the outlook for professional advancement. The moment of truth had merely been postponed.

'Of course, your being in Berlin,' I said, 'I suppose I won't see as much of you as I used to.'

Theresa put a hand on my knee. 'That's just as well. You've got a new book to write. A new masterpiece. It wouldn't be fair to distract you.'

With the mention of the book, anxiety sank a toecap into the lower reaches of my stomach wall.

'How long do you think it'll take you, as a matter of interest?' Theresa said, oblivious to my discomfort.

'I'm not sure. Does it matter?'

'I told Martin roughly a year. Is that all right? I didn't want to sound clueless.'

'A year is ambitious.'

'Is it?'

'For you certainly. You're supposed to be studying, remember?'

Theresa looked over her shoulder. Nobody was within earshot. 'But if I stay here, then it won't be so easy getting the manuscript out. You might have to use someone else. That's all I was thinking. It might be risky.'

This was true: as a conduit for the publication of unlicensed literature, Theresa was only of any use if she kept one foot in the East and one foot in the West, just as she was proposing to do. Once committed to one side or the other, her role as my alter ego was, in effect, redundant. But, of course, I had promised to write a sequel to *The Valley*; and a sequel has to have the same author as its precursor; otherwise it is not a sequel at all. It is at best *hommage*.

Did such considerations have anything to do with Theresa's decision? I dismissed the idea without a second thought. As we hurried across the road towards her apartment, my coat pulled over our heads, the storm around us growing wilder and darker, I was buoyed by the euphoria of undeserved success and a conviction that our road together, though haunted and treacherous, would lead us in the end to a place of truth, openness and clear-sighted love.

# PART FOUR

## 32

The following September a package arrived at my apartment building by the same mysterious means as Theresa's other communications. For the preceding two months she had been at home in the West. Her student visa had expired and her studies in East Berlin had not yet commenced. The package contained a hardback book with a glossy black dust jacket, on the front of which, in raised metallic type, was the title: *SURVIVORS*. Beneath the title was the silhouette of ruined buildings – skyscrapers and tower blocks – against an orange fireball of a sky. In the corner, in italics, was the solitary word: *Roman*; and along the bottom of the page, reversed out of the ruins in small, widely spaced capitals, was the author's name in arterial red: EVA ADEN.

*Eva* Aden? Who exactly was Eva Aden?

I stood in the dim light of the hallway, blinking at this strangely terrifying volume. I opened the book and scrabbled my way to the first page of the text: *They kept always to the edge of the road, where their shuffling, silent progress was hidden among the shadows of the trees.*

I flung open the door, just so I could examine the cover in daylight. The artwork was striking, but ineffably vulgar by the usual literary standards. The title was completely new to me. Theresa had once told me that 'the Bernheim people' weren't happy with *The Valley*, but the subject had never come up again. It seemed a decision had been made in my absence, but that wasn't what angered me. What angered me was the name underneath: Eva Aden. Eva was my mother's name, a fact Theresa knew very well. Without any thought of consulting me, she had stamped it on this fraudulent volume – a work, to all intents and purposes, stolen from the dead – where it would remain for ever, guilty by association. What right had she to do that? Had I *asked* her to intrude on my past, to play games with my mother's memory? I turned and hurled the book across the hallway. It smacked against the banisters and fell to the floor, the dust jacket flapping like a broken sail. Why couldn't Theresa have used her own name? Why the sudden need for anonymity?

On one of the floors above a door opened. The noise had made somebody curious. As I closed the front door, I noticed a piece of paper lying on the floor. I realised that it must have fallen out of the book when I opened it. It was a note from Theresa. It said only:

*Dear B,*

*By the time this book reaches you it'll be in all the shops. Survivors was Herr Falkner's idea. Should I have said no?*

*There's a lot I have to tell you, but now isn't the time. In the meantime, let's keep our fingers crossed.*

*I hope you're happy.*

*With love,*

*T*

*PS Eva Aden was my idea. I wanted there to be something of you in this book, some element of the Krug name. This was the only thing I could think of. I hope you don't mind.*

I went and picked up the book, carefully replacing the buckled dust jacket, smoothing out the creases. I sat down on the stairs and hugged it to my chest, feeling ashamed and not a little disgusted. *I wanted there to be something of you in this book, some element of the Krug name.* How could I have mistaken Theresa's act of tenderness for intrusion? Why was I so anxious to assume the worst? What was wrong with me?

I think I even asked the last of these questions out loud. For once, I didn't care who was listening.

# 33

A few days later I was riding a tram through the Altstadt. Evening sunlight was seeping through the dirty windows, gilding the static bodies and pallid faces of my fellow passengers, so that for a few seconds they looked like works of art. It was then that I spotted Claudia Witt sitting halfway down, a book open on her lap.

Until a copy of *Survivors* had turned up at my apartment, I had been taking the latest of Theresa's absences well. Her decision to study in the East for another year, together with the success of our literary collaboration, reassured me that I was on solid ground, that I had only to be patient and everything would fall into place. At a propitious moment, I had decided, I would ask Theresa to marry me, though this idea had less significance than might appear, divorce being quicker and easier to obtain in the Workers' and Peasants' State than almost anywhere else. I was in good spirits, which was why, in spite of previous chilly encounters, I went over to Claudia and said hello.

She had been reading with great concentration, furtively chewing a thumbnail as she frowned at the pages of a hardback book. Her hair was longer than before, collar-length but lank, and she was wearing a lot of eye make-up, which lent her a self-consciously mournful air, like the tragic clown in *Pagliacci*. She greeted me with a smile and an unusual absence of satire. Perhaps with Theresa gone (from her life, if not mine), I was no longer an irritation. I sat down on the opposite side of the aisle.

'What are you reading?'

Carefully replacing her bookmark, she handed me the volume. It turned out to be *Survivors*. I hadn't recognised the book without the dust jacket. But there was no mistaking the title and Theresa's half-pseudonym punched in gold letters on to the spine. Seeing this counterfeit out and about in the world – above all here, where Wolfgang Richter had lived and died – made me shudder.

'Where did you get this?'

'Where do you think?'

'Not a bookshop, I shouldn't think.'

'Look in the front.'

On the title page, where traders in first editions like them, was

Theresa's signature – or rather, her *new* signature – together with the following inscription: *To Claudia, my collaborator in art and life, with love and thanks!*

Theresa had left my copy unsigned and it was clear enough why. A signature, by its very nature, is a mark of authenticity. A signature says: *this book is mine.* But we both knew this book, whatever its title, was not hers. To send me a signed copy, then, would have been thoroughly inappropriate. The same considerations did not apply where third parties were concerned. Theresa had to maintain the masquerade for them, I reminded myself, and that included signing copies on request.

I felt a familiar unsteadiness in my belly, a gastro-intestinal inkling of trouble. How much did Claudia know, Theresa's *collaborator in art and life*? Was it more than I thought? The insouciance of the girl suggested a degree of secret knowledge.

'What do you think of it?' I asked.

'Amazing. She came up with all that. I still can't believe it.'

Reluctantly, I handed back the book. 'She's a very talented girl.'

'She certainly is. You're really impressed, though?'

'Very.'

'Jealous?'

'Exceedingly.'

Claudia laughed. 'I thought so. Writers can't help being jealous. It stems from their insecurity.'

'I didn't know that.'

'All writers are insecure, the male ones especially. It's well known. Why else would they spend so much time on make-believe? They're only happy in their imaginary worlds, because that's where they're in charge – where they're God. Did you know that Hemingway's mother dressed him as a girl until he was six years old?'

I was not offended by Claudia's glib psychological theory. Like many glib psychological theories, it struck me as fundamentally correct. But it wasn't me I wanted to talk about.

'If that's true of all writers, it must be true of Theresa,' I said. 'She must be insecure too.'

'She is.' Claudia opened up her book, her eyes returning to the page. 'She's basically uncomfortable with herself. Certainly she's uncomfortable with her talent – her musical talent.'

'She said something like that once.'

Claudia put her head on one side. 'It's like she doesn't really deserve it; as if she stole it from someone else. Maybe her dead twin or something.'

With a squealing of brakes the tram drew near a stop. The conversation was suspended for a minute as a procession of people nudged their way towards the door.

'Have you any plans to see her?' I asked. 'It would be a shame to lose touch.'

Claudia closed the book and placed it inside her denim handbag. 'I should be seeing her the day after tomorrow, with any luck. Though she won't be seeing me.'

'What do you mean?'

Claudia got to her feet, a look of amusement on her face. 'Didn't she tell you? She's doing an interview on ZDF. *Freizeit-Forum*, nine o'clock.' ZDF was a Western channel, impossible to pick up across most of the city. 'I'd invite you along, but I'm going out of town.'

The doors opened. Claudia gave me a childish little wave and stepped down on to the pavement.

Watching Western television had not been a crime in the Workers' and Peasants' State since 1972. The days were long gone when the Free German Youth would organise anti-propaganda sorties, noting the location and address of any aerial displaying a non-socialist orientation and passing the information to the police. But among my acquaintances in the valley there was only one who had no trouble picking up television transmissions from the other side of the inner German border, thanks to the hills that encircled us. Rudi Hartl was a printworks supervisor and aspiring artist, who spent most of his spare cash on paint and canvases, and experimented disastrously with abstractionism. An old friend of Michael Schilling's (in his youth, Schilling too had tried his hand at the graphic arts), he lived on the upper floor of an old farmhouse in the village of Elbersdorf, five miles east of the city. Elbersdorf and the surrounding hamlets were on high ground and enjoyed relatively good reception as well as good views, although in both cases atmospheric conditions regularly conspired to spoil them. This I knew because Schilling sometimes went out there to watch West German sports broadcasts, tennis being his particular fascination.

Hartl was a jovial man, whose boyish face wore a default expression of pleasant surprise. He was not clever, but his lack of acumen served him well. He believed what people told him – their excuses and evasions – and was therefore immune to the creeping affliction of cynicism. He even believed what he read in the newspapers, enough at any rate to sustain an optimistic view of life. I would happily have spent more time with him, but getting to Elbersdorf involved an inconvenient journey and his printworks were on the other side of town.

I telephoned him as soon as I could and proposed that we meet.

'I don't suppose you're free this Friday evening? I've been given some remarkable plum schnapps, which I'm eager to share.'

Understandably Hartl sounded surprised to hear from me after what must have been at least a year. 'How kind of you to think of me,' he said. 'And what a remarkable memory you have.'

The latter remark I did not understand.

He suggested meeting in town, but I objected. 'I was hoping to get a look at your latest work. I trust you've been hard at it.'

'Not as hard as I'd like. You know how it is. But I have been making progress with the studio. It's almost finished.'

'Well, that I have to see. I've always thought you needed a proper space to work – and to show your work.'

There was no need for further persuasion. Hartl agreed to pick me up after work and drive me out to Elbersdorf. 'I've a new car now,' he said. 'Well, a new *old* car. A gift from my uncle Rolf.'

It was then I remembered that the only thing worse than Rudi Hartl's painting was Rudi Hartl's driving. But to behold my beautiful Theresa on camera, to see her playing the role I had created for her, a role I had never yet been privileged to witness; to see her, in effect, playing me (though I, in turn, was playing Wolfgang Richter, authorially speaking), that was something I simply could not miss. That was a spectacle worth any amount of shredded nerves. The fact that Theresa had omitted to tell me about it, for whatever reason, had no bearing on the matter.

# 34

Hartl's new old car turned out to be an improvement on his previous vehicle in that the passenger door could be opened and closed, and was not attached to the rest of the chassis with twelve metres of duct tape. The chances of being trapped and incinerated in burning wreckage were therefore happily reduced. It also boasted a radio, which picked up the electrical discharges of the engine over frequent bursts of unintelligible short wave, and which could be neither tuned nor switched off. Our journey to Elbersdorf, during which Hartl enthusiastically updated me on his latest artistic direction, was accompanied by a frenzy of radiophonic wolf-whistling and electro-mechanical raspberries. My contribution was confined to pointing in mute terror at the oncoming traffic and occasionally smacking the radio with the heel of my shoe.

My intention was to converse with Rudi on cultural and aesthetic subjects for an hour, then casually bring up the subject of *Freizeit-Forum*, a segue natural enough not to seem premeditated. I could have come straight out and asked if we could watch the programme on his set. Perhaps no harm would have come of it. But a burning desire to watch broadcasts from over the anti-fascist frontier – even an innocuous arts programme – was not the kind of thing people willingly confessed to in the Workers' and Peasants' State. Watching Western television was, like masturbation, a strictly private activity, frequently done but rarely acknowledged, let alone discussed over the telephone.

It was dark by the time we left the road, turning on to a dirt track that snaked its way through woodland towards the house. We were far enough from the infernal glow of the city for stars to shine brightly through ragged tears in the cloud. Unlike their dim urban counterparts, these stars shimmered at immeasurable distance and in immeasurable numbers, so that the world beneath us seemed shrunken and solitary. As the beam of our headlamps swept round the last bend, I thought I glimpsed a spray of golden light among the trees, and I wondered idly if there were fireflies in those woods and if their season could really be this late in the year.

We pulled up outside the house, black and massive against the starry sky. It stood flanked on two sides by dilapidated outhouses that had once provided shelter for chickens and pigs, and which still tainted the air with a faint ammoniacal whiff. I was starting to get a sick, nervous feeling in my stomach. Theresa would soon be on air. What was she going to say? What was she going to reveal? Suppose she chose this moment to tell the truth? What then?

Hartl jangled his keys. 'Looks like Vera's gone to her mother's.'

This at least was good news. Frau Hartl, a plump and uneducated woman who, by common consent, did not deserve her husband, might easily have had her own viewing plans for the evening; and they were unlikely to have included anything devoted to the arts.

'What a shame. I was hoping to see her. Still,' – I gently clanked the schnapps bottles together – 'it's not like we're short of company.'

We reached the door. Waiting for Hartl to open it, I was struck by the depth of the silence. To a city dweller there is nothing so unnerving as the absence of ambient noise. It feels unnatural, as if the world all around is deliberately holding its breath. He waits instinctively for an exhalation, or for the trap to be sprung.

Hartl turned the lock and went inside. Stale kitchen smells greeted my nostrils, mingled with touches of old leather and old feet. Hartl flipped on a light switch. Nothing happened.

'We must have lost the power. I've a torch here somewhere.'

My heart sank. 'Does this happen often?'

'Just now and again. Not usually for long. An hour at the most. Ah, here we are.'

A sallow beam of light looped through the gloom and came to rest on a staircase at the far end of a tiled hallway. Along the left-hand side of the wall, beside the entrance to the downstairs apartment, was a line of creased and flattened footwear. I wondered if Hartl's neighbours – an old couple who allegedly put most of their remaining life force into growing vegetables and poisoning slugs – had gone to bed early, or if they were sitting there in the darkness, listening to us pass.

We crept upstairs, silenced by the enveloping darkness, the staircase creaking beneath us like an old hulk. I felt something stir above us, an almost imperceptible shift of weight. Perhaps Hartl heard it too, because he called out his wife's name.

Nobody answered.

'At her mother's,' he said again, as if repetition would make it true.

Beyond the door of the apartment was a tiny hallway where we left our shoes.

'Wait here,' Hartl said. 'We've some candles in the kitchen.'

Then I heard it: a squeak, like a stopper in a bottle, followed by a sigh of escaping air. It had come from the living room. I edged forward and pushed back the glass-panelled door, which squeaked on unoiled hinges. It was then that the lights came on.

'Surprise!'

I was staring at a room full of faces, none familiar, with the single exception of Vera's. A groan went up.

'Where's the birthday boy?'

Hartl appeared at my side, beaming and feigning a heart attack. The guests burst into a toneless rendition of 'Happy Birthday'. Glasses of punch were thrust into our hands. Someone put on a crackly Ina Martell record.

Hartl, still grinning, wagged a finger at me. 'I knew you were up to something, Bruno. All that nonsense about your plum schnapps. I knew there was something else on your agenda – like making sure I didn't get here too soon.'

'Guilty as charged,' I said. 'Happy birthday, Rudi.'

We drank a toast. The punch tasted like liniment. Still, I had the impression that many people present were already on their third or fourth glass. Hartl set off on a tour of the room, accepting from his wife a basket of sweets and Halloren chocolate wrapped in yellow cellophane. I wasted no time in locating the television: it stood in the corner by the window with a large doily draped over the top of it and a plate of meatballs on top of that. I looked at my watch: it was already after eight o'clock.

As a youth I was often frustrated by the collective nature of my encounters with the opposite sex. Such was the regimented nature of my existence – at the orphanage, in the army, at the *Berufsschule* where I was drilled in my ablutionary trade – that the only way of meeting girls was in large numbers: at rallies, sporting events or formal social gatherings. Females my age had visibility but not tangibility. In other words from an educational point of view, the typical experience had breadth, but not depth. And it was depth I craved, emotionally and physically. I wanted unfettered access, a free hand in every sense. I knew that only a complete demystification of the female sex and the female form would free me from destructive longing, leaving me to live as I wished. But for that I needed to escape the crowd and be alone with my chosen one, a requirement that proved hard to satisfy, private spaces and private time being hard to come by in the Workers' and Peasants' State.

Standing in the Hartls' dingy living room, my second empty glass in hand, listening to turgid conversation and atrocious music, I experienced a similar frustration. Once again I wished the crowd would disappear, so that I could be alone with my object of desire. All that had changed was the scale of my ambition. Instead of a woman, what I sought now was merely the image of a woman, electronically projected on to a cathode-ray tube; and whereas in the past my aim had been to demystify all women, now I was content to demystify one. It struck me how little I had learned since those boyhood days, in spite of the seductions and conquests and affairs that had followed. To know one woman – or even a hundred – no matter how intimately, was not, in fact, to know them all. The goal was unattainable and always would be. This reflection might have filled me with doubt, with a sense of time wasted and opportunities lost, had I not been so determined to see that night on Rudi Hartl's television the girl I was sure I had been waiting for all my life.

It was thanks to Rudi that I hit upon my disastrous plan, the consequences of which were long to outlast the night.

'Are you still keen to see the studio?' he asked me when everyone else had been greeted and thanked. 'I'd so value your opinion.'

I had just noticed that his television had wheels and that the cable connecting it to the rooftop aerial ran out through the window.

'Lead on,' I said.

We returned to the main landing. In one corner a flight of steps led up to a trapdoor. The attic above, though sizeable, was hopelessly unsuited to painting, having only two small circular windows, one at either end. Hartl had made up for this deficiency with a trio of neon lights fixed to the central beam and by painting everything white: the roof, the beams, the brickwork, the floorboards. The only things not white were Hartl's paintings: lurid, splashy creations, like the outpourings of a paint factory slewed over canvas, with here and there the suggestion of an eye socket or a mouthful of bared teeth.

'Remarkable,' I said, standing before one especially gruesome *oeuvre*. 'Brings to mind Edvard Munch.'

'Do you really think so?' Hartl said eagerly.

'Very much so. But never mind what I think. Let's consult the people.'

'The people?'

'The people downstairs.'

Hartl shook his head. 'Oh, no, I don't think they'd . . . My wife's friends . . . I don't think it's their thing at all.'

'Their *thing* being strictly figurative painting, I suppose.'

'I'm afraid so.'

I declared this to be an elitist and unproletarian sentiment (as only a Champion of the People can) and told Hartl to stay put. Before he could object further I went back down the stairs and into the apartment. There I turned off the music and made an announcement: Herr Hartl's latest creations – which, in my opinion, were extraordinary – were now on display in his studio. It would be the making of his birthday if the assembled company were to go and view them right away.

With some hesitation the assembled company did as it was told, taking its drinks with it. I followed as far as the landing, a schnapps bottle in each hand, topping up glasses as I went. To Frau Hartl (more flushed than usual and sweating through an excess of make-up), I bowed low before administering a triple shot and complimenting her extravagantly on her coiffure. Visibly flattered, she vanished up the steps, coyly pulling at the hem of her frock in a faux attempt to avoid showing me her underwear.

Alone at last, I checked my watch. *Freizeit-Forum* was due to start in two minutes. Heart pounding, caution blunted by alcohol, I disconnected the television and wheeled it into the bedroom, where a bedside light revealed an unsanitary landscape of crumpled bedding and discarded clothes. I never took Vera Hartl for a fastidious hausfrau, but these were the sleeping quarters of a sloven. Obscured behind a ball of used tissue, upon which a vision of her small mouth was imprinted in lipstick, I found the power socket. All that remained was to capture the end of the aerial cable, which now swung unattached from the edge of the roof. I found a wire coat hanger in the wardrobe, but that proved too short. I had better luck with a broom, which I found in the kitchen. I was leaning out of the window at a precarious angle, fishing in the darkness for my elusive catch, when it came to me – the realisation as striking as it was useless – that I had not seen fireflies on the drive up the hill, but the red and orange reflectors of motor cars and bicycles. Hartl's friends had left them out of sight among the trees, so as to maintain the element of surprise. A motorcycle was labouring its way up the hill now, its importunate roar muffled only by the surrounding foliage.

At the third or fourth attempt, I managed to snag the cable round the end of the broom head and pull it in. When everything was reconnected I turned on the set and sat down on a corner of the double bed, clearing the minimum space necessary of Frau Hartl's voluminous underthings. With a whump and a crackle of static a black-and-white picture bloomed on to the screen. Two cowboys were arguing in a saloon. They were smooth shaven and strangely clean. This was definitely not *Freizeit-Forum*.

I turned the dial.

A female newsreader was sitting in the middle of a snowstorm. Behind her was a photograph of a missile launcher in a forest. The signal strengthened. The newsreader wore sensible glasses and spoke like a recorded announcement.

I turned the dial

An image ghosted across the screen: a blonde girl, running across a meadow in slow motion, hair backlit by the sun. A shampoo bottle appeared in the corner.

I turned the dial.

Another newsreader, another missile launcher, this time with the missile captured mid-launch, the word PROTEST stamped diagonally across the screen. The newsreader wore a smart suit and looked grave.

I turned the dial. Nothing but white noise. Could it be the ZDF transmitter was out of range? Claudia had said she was going out of town. Maybe you *had* to go out of town – further than Elbersdorf – to pick up *Freizeit-Forum*. I turned the dial more slowly, trying to squeeze a signal out of the electro-magnetic storm. I caught hints of forms and faces, warped and muffled voices that seemed to emanate from a different world – and then *one* face, a face I knew. But it was not Theresa's.

I jumped, retreating across the bed. It was Wolfgang Richter. He drifted into focus and then out again, dissolving into white noise. I know I saw him on that screen. I can still recollect the image precisely: his long black coat, the tall windows of the Tolkewitz Crematorium behind him. Most clearly I remember his stare: neither reproachful nor accusing, but empty, as if he were simply observing me and waiting (for what I couldn't guess). At the same time I know I could not have seen him. No such image of Wolfgang Richter exists in the real world and, even if it does, why would anyone have been broadcasting it that night? I record the incident only as being indicative of my state of mind. For the truth is the memory of that vision, of Richter's terrible, hollow stare, came back to me often in the months that followed. I can picture it still.

Blaming the hallucinogenic powers of industrial alcohol and the hypnotic effects of television, I gathered myself and reached for the dial again. Before I could touch it, I found myself looking at Theresa – or rather at two Theresas. I was on the point of giving the set a thump when I realised there was nothing wrong with the picture.

The first Theresa was sitting on a sofa in a television studio. The second covered most of the back wall, where she appeared surrounded by the same smoking ruins that decorated the cover of *Survivors*. The creature in the studio I hardly recognised. She wore a shimmering dress that left her shoulders bare, the unsupported curve of her breasts discernable through the fabric. She sat with her legs folded under her, her golden hair partially woven into plaits, one plait circling the crown of her head. With black pearl earrings and a necklace made up of many fine strands – gold or silver, I supposed – she brought to mind a priestess or a sacrificial virgin. Here was my fantasy Theresa come to life. Here was the vision I had dreamed up that first night, while I waited to receive my medal. Even the little dent in her forehead, the subtle flaw left by her twin, was invisible. It seemed Eva Aden, novelist, had no twin.

The interviewer, a middle-aged man with a high forehead and an aquiline gaze, sat canted forward on his swivel chair.

'Since then, Eva, you've been called the most important new voice in German literature since Günter Grass. Others have described you as a feminist visionary. Is that how you would characterise your work, as essentially feminist in outlook?'

The director cut to a close-up. Theresa frowned. 'I made a promise that I wouldn't look at any reviews for *Survivors*. And so far I've kept that promise.'

'You don't agree with the critics?'

'I haven't read them.'

The interviewer leaned even closer, as if preparing to launch himself on to the sofa. I dug my fingers into the pungent bedding, amazed at Theresa's cool.

'That's extraordinary. Can you tell us your reasons?'

'I suppose you could say it's because I don't want anything to change. I want the next book to come about in the same way, in the same circumstances, as the last.'

'Do you mean in isolation?'

'I wouldn't call it isolation. Being a little apart, perhaps, yes. But maybe that's necessary for a sense of independence. And for perspective.'

For a moment the picture concertinaed, voices giving way to hiss. I smacked the top of the set.

'Chekhov once said that critics were like horseflies: they only prevented the horse from ploughing. Is that how you see them, as a distraction?'

Theresa shook her head. 'I find critics very useful when I'm trying to decide what to read. But as far as *Survivors* goes, and any other books that follow, I don't think my reading reviews would serve any useful purpose.'

It was a good answer; only she and I knew how good. And in that moment, in the confidence and cleverness of that answer – an answer that could never come back to haunt her when the truth was out, the way any other answer would have – it struck me: Theresa had done more than grow into the role. She had *become* the role. She was flourishing as she had never flourished with a viola in her hand, even under the glare of the lights, even with millions watching. This was the freedom she had talked of, the freedom that came with not being herself. For the first time in her life she was free from the ghost of her dead twin, free from the dread of self-celebration: because Eva Aden didn't *have* a twin. Her triumph was not a triumph over anyone, let alone a blameless infant sister.

'Some people,' – the interviewer's unctuous tone made it clear he was not among them – 'might say yours was an arrogant attitude for a newcomer.'

'I hope not. I don't think the purpose of reviews is to educate writers, to show them where they've gone wrong or gone right. Their purpose is to inform the public.'

'And what do you see as *your* purpose?'

Theresa looked down at her hands, as if not sure what they were doing there. I knew that gesture. It was the first thing in her whole performance I recognised.

'My purpose is to bring these stories into the world, so that they can be shared by whoever wants to share them.'

'You talk almost as if they weren't yours, as if you're no more than a midwife.'

Theresa smiled. 'Midwives are important people. Without them many of us wouldn't be here.'

The interviewer chose this moment to strike an especially pretentious pose, leaning far back in his chair with both index fingers tapping thoughtfully against his lips. 'You strike me as remarkably detached from your work – detached from its fate, at least. Is it that, for you, it's the *act* of writing that's important? Are you answering an inner need?'

Theresa took a moment to answer. The camera had her in close-up again, and profile, but now it zoomed out slowly, revealing throat, shoulders, lightly veiled breasts. At that moment, I felt certain, thousands of cultured men up and down the German *Länder* would be experiencing an involuntary rush of blood to their loins. No doubt some of them would find a way to reach her. No doubt some of them would call. Theresa had told me she was often lonely. She wasn't going to be lonely much longer.

'I'm doing what I want to do,' Theresa said. 'And yes, for me it is about need. Definitely. There are some stories that have to be told, whatever the consequences.'

From above my head came a loud thump and a peel of raucous laughter. Footsteps clunked down the steps from the attic, shaking the whole apartment.

'It looks like the consequences will be fame for you, perhaps enduring fame. Isn't that something you want?'

Theresa looked away from the interviewer, her mouth pinched as if unimpressed by the question. 'It's not something I can control,' she said. 'It's not in my hands.'

The interviewer moved on to the thorny issue of the sequel. What was next for Alex and Old Tilmann? What more was there to learn? Behind me a floorboard creaked. I turned to see Michael Schilling standing in the doorway of the bedroom, his raincoat draped over his arm, staring at the television. I guessed from his stunned expression that he had been there for some time.

I stood up. 'Michael, there are some things I need to tell you.'

'So, a sequel, is it?' he said, eyes still fixed on the flickering screen. 'The master follows the pupil follows the master. Very nice. Very incestuous.'

It was too late. He knew everything.

'Michael, you don't understand.'

'You're right, I don't.'

I tried to explain: how I'd had to publish under a false name, otherwise the whole project would have been traced back to its point of origin, to me and to him. Even dead East German writers needed help to be published in the West. It was an explanation I'd been rehearsing for months.

Schilling just stared at me, shaking his head.

'I was protecting Richter's family, too,' I said. 'They're still here.'

'So they know about this?'

'They will.'

'You're incredible.'

'It was either this or burn the manuscript. Which would you have done?'

The Hartl party had grown tired of the attic and were filing back into the apartment in search of further inebriation. I turned back to the television and flipped the dial back to DFF-1, where the General Secretary of the Central Committee was being applauded by a large roomful of people. By the time I turned back again Schilling had gone.

I went out into the living room and was relieved to see him greeting the Hartls just as if nothing had happened, apologising for his lateness and blaming a last-minute automotive failure. I looked for an opportunity to explain myself more fully to him, to apologise for keeping him in the dark, to plead for his discretion (which I never seriously doubted), but that opportunity never came.

At around eleven I heard Schilling's motorbike outside. I went to the window and watched him ride away down the hill, vanishing behind a funnel of dust. When it was my turn to leave I noticed that he had forgotten to take his raincoat with him.

# 35

There had always been two choices where Michael Schilling was concerned: tell him everything or tell him nothing. Anything else, any palatable halfway house, would have involved telling lies and I didn't want to do that.

Of the two choices, full disclosure was the safest. Michael was my friend. He knew what it was to be in love, how it could lead a person to do reckless things. His own marriage was a perfect example. Silence left him free to discover the fraud behind *Survivors* for himself, which in turn opened up the possibility that he might one day confront Theresa (somehow, somewhere) in the course of which encounter she would learn the truth about who really wrote it. Yet on this occasion I had not taken the safe option. I had pushed the issue to one side, rather than deal with it. Schilling did not have access to Western books. It was perfectly likely he would never hear about Eva Aden and her novel, let alone read it. (Had it not enjoyed instant success, he wouldn't have done.) But the truth is that I was embarrassed to admit to my deception. My work had apparently inspired Richter's; but to claim his work as mine – even to one person – there was something cannibalistic about that. Like cannibalism itself, it smacked of desperation, the abandonment of all that was civilised.

Be that as it may, *Freizeit-Forum* changed the equation. Now I had no choice but to tell Schilling the whole story. I set out for his apartment the following morning, armed with his coat, fully intending to apologise and make a clean breast of everything, but even as I sat waiting at the tram stop, trying to ignore a young couple ravenously kissing and groping each other in the corner of the shelter, I had to acknowledge the uncomfortable duality of my motives: I was acting to preserve a friendship, but I was also acting to prevent the spread of a dangerous secret. It was a duality that would be as obvious to Schilling as it was to me.

My friend lived opposite a disused cemetery in the southern district of Südvorstadt. The origins of the four-storey apartment building were pre-war. In its heyday it would have boasted a stucco façade, modelled to look like stone, but this had been replaced under Actually Existing Socialism with a soot-encrusted pebbledash that was now coming away in chunks, revealing patches of livid pink brickwork, like a leper's sores. It was a building whose hydrological entrails I knew well. Their age and disposition made them highly susceptible to blockage, and I had made several remedial visits over the years at Schilling's request, armed with caustic soda and drain rods.

I pressed Schilling's buzzer, but to no effect. I couldn't even be sure the buzzer was working. Finding the doorway unlocked, I decided to make my way up to the apartment. I was on the second-floor landing when the door opposite opened.

'He's not in.'

It was Schilling's neighbour, a garrulous and moon-faced widow by the name of Grabel, who smelled permanently of cats, her apartment being home to at least four felines of various ages and degrees of incontinence. As she spoke a tabby slipped between her legs and ran away down the stairs.

'Do you know when he'll be back?'

It was then Frau Grabel recognised me, after a fashion: 'Herr Klempner, she said, *Klempner* being German for plumber. 'What brings you here?'

'A social call.'

She looked relieved. Blockages in Schilling's building tended to produce unpredictable and malodorous side effects. No one was immune. 'He's gone to Berlin. Quite suddenly.'

'Berlin?' It occurred to me that the Ministry of Culture was in Berlin, and all the other ministries to whom a cultural scandal might be of interest. 'Did he say why?'

Frau Grabel hesitated. 'Well, it's not my business . . .' She sucked her teeth. 'Anyway, why don't you come in? Since you've come all this way.'

Normally I would have resisted Frau Grabel's pungent hospitality. I was still haunted by the memory of the banana cake she had served me during my last visit, which turned out to contain – I can still feel it catching on my tonsils – a large fur ball. But at that time any unexpected movement on Schilling's part was a cause for concern and would be until I knew where we stood.

No sooner was I inside than Frau Grabel began lamenting the state of her washers. Every tap in her apartment dripped, she said. Rust stains were playing havoc with her enamel. It soon became obvious that this was to be the price of her information, doubtless gleaned via the telephone line that she and Schilling were obliged to share. I protested that I did not have my tools, but it turned out that the late Herr Grabel had left his spouse a well-equipped toolbox, which she proudly extracted from under some cat litter. I found a few ancient but serviceable washers in a brown paper bag.

I turned off the water and set to work in the kitchen.

'So why the disappearing act?' I said. 'What's the big attraction in Berlin?'

Frau Grabel needed no further encouragement. The story of Schilling's recent past came tumbling out, sugared with phoney sympathy and spiced with anecdote. Chronology was largely lost in this outpouring, likewise any distinction between fact and supposition. Certain essentials were nonetheless discernible. In the early hours of the morning Schilling had received a phone call from his ex-wife, Magdalena, in Berlin. She was in what Frau Grabel described as 'a frightful state'. It seemed their son Paul had been taken into custody by the police – whether arrested or merely questioned was unclear. Magdalena seemed to think drugs were involved (at this point, I imagine, Frau Grabel had been obliged to hang up and was tiptoeing across the landing in her nylon fur slippers), although whether these directly prompted the police action was also unclear. Privately I suspected the worst. The last time I had seen Paul Schilling, I had been struck by his unhealthy appearance: the drawn cheeks, the lank hair, the bad skin. Of course, heroin addiction did not officially exist in the Workers' and Peasants' State, being a Western malaise arising from bourgeois capitalism and its constant need to subvert proletarian class consciousness. Under Actually Existing Socialism such addicts as existed were deemed to be mentally ill and locked up indefinitely in psychiatric hospitals. This, I imagined, was what had prompted Magdalena's desperate phone call.

Frau Grabel took a seat at the kitchen table, her back to the old tiled *Kachelofen* that kept the frost at bay. 'That boy's been nothing but a source of grief,' she said, manoeuvring an obese Persian on to her lap. 'And *so* unlike his father. It makes you wonder . . . well, that Magdalena, she was never what you'd call a good girl. Not in the least.'

I ignored these insinuations regarding Schilling's paternity, which I felt sure were unfounded. Either way, I preferred not to imagine what Paul's incarceration would do to my friend, the maelstrom of dread and guilt that was sure to engulf him. At the same time I couldn't help feeling relieved that the small matter of Wolfgang Richter's novel had nothing to do with his sudden dash to Berlin and that the former was unlikely, given his urgent family concerns, to occupy more than a fleeting place in his mind.

'I hope I can rely on you not to repeat what I've said, Herr Klempner,' Frau Grabel said, as I struggled with a heavily corroded headgear nut. 'It's just that I know how concerned you are about your friend.'

It dawned on me that the old woman thought Klempner was really my name. Herr Tailor, Herr Baker, Herr Plumber. She had no idea that I was also Herr Krug, the author of *The Orphans of Neu-stadt* and People's Champion of Art and Culture. A year earlier I would have enlightened her, but those days were already long gone.

I returned to Schilling's scabrous residence the next evening, like-wise unannounced, but again he was not home. It was not until the Monday night that I saw the lights on in his apartment. I walked up and banged on the door, but no one answered.

'Michael, it's me,' I said. 'Open up.'

From at least two places at once I heard a faint shuffling and a creaking of floorboards, as if the whole building were slowly coming alive.

'Michael, I've got your coat.'

Stillness descended again. I knocked one more time, but with the same result. There was nothing I could do but leave, taking the raincoat with me.

Reluctantly I resorted to the telephone, calling Schilling's office first thing Tuesday morning. I caught him just as he was arriving.

'Michael, I owe you an explanation. Can we meet somewhere?'

'You don't owe me anything, Bruno.' Schilling's tone was reassur-ingly breezy. 'If it's that book you're referring to, as far as I'm concerned it's history.'

'You seemed quite upset on Friday.'

'I was just surprised. Caught off guard. Seeing you there in the bedroom, hunched over that television. I've never seen you look so hunted.'

'Hunted?' I explained that, for all manner of reasons, I'd preferred to watch *Freizeit-Forum* unobserved.

'Anyway,' Schilling said, 'I'm sure you did the right thing, given the circumstances.'

'It was better than the alternative. Better than what we planned to do.'

'Absolutely.'

'Better than burning it. At least this way –'

'Nothing important is lost. I couldn't agree more.'

'But I should have told you. You were his editor, or would have been. I should have explained.'

Schilling's breath pushed against the mouthpiece. Maybe he was sighing, or maybe he thought what I'd just said was humorous. 'No, we agreed, didn't we? I never saw the book and I never read it. Better that way for everyone.'

'Well, in a way, yes.'

'The less you know, the less you're implicated.'

'So you're not unhappy?'

'Why should I be?'

This was going very well. I hadn't expected such an effortless absolution. But my friend had been so excited about his literary discovery; so horrified at the thought of losing it. Wasn't it unnatural that he should already feel divorced from its future, having no stake and no entitlement? On the other hand the mere possibility that handling Richter's work might incur official displeasure had sent him scurrying for cover. 'Safety First', in the Workers' and Peasants' State, was not a bad motto. I had lived by it myself very happily for as long as I could remember.

And then there was Paul. What were the needs of a dead writer – or, for that matter, a living one – next to those of your own flesh and blood?

'I heard you went up to Berlin,' I said. 'Is everything all right?'

Schilling took a moment to answer. If we hadn't been on the telephone I might have had some inkling as to why.

'Who told you?'

'Frau Grabel. Her cats are spying on you.'

Schilling didn't laugh.

'Everything's fine. Paul's got a new job. Right up in the north. He won't be visiting so much for a while. I wanted to see him before he left.'

There was a tightness in Schilling's delivery that told me this was not a matter he was keen to talk over.

'So what kind of job is it?'

'On the docks.'

'The docks? Are you kidding?'

'It's a clerical position. Magdalena pulled some strings.'

I said I was pleased. 'Let's hope he sticks with it this time.'

'I'm sure he will.'

I didn't interrogate Schilling further. I didn't ask about the heroin or the arrest, or if his ex-wife would really call him in the middle of the night to inform him of a filial change in career direction. After all Frau Grabel, from whom I had heard all this, was a mad old woman who smelled of cats' urine and who had nothing better to do all day but eavesdrop on her neighbours. Out of loyalty I would have relayed her shameless gossip to my friend, had I not felt instinctively that of the two accounts relating to his recent comings and goings, hers was the one that rang true.

# 36

It never occurred to me that the birth of Eva Aden, novelist and visionary, was the birth of what Westerners call a 'brand'. Brands in the Workers' and Peasants' State were blotchy trade names, stamped on to canned goods, bottles of alcohol and cameras manufactured for export. Their purpose was identification. They had no value of their own. For the same reason it didn't occur to me that there might be other parties involved in the shaping of this brand, other voices in Theresa's ear, instructing her on how to exploit her potential to the full. I was happy to witness the effects of her new-found freedom because I saw myself as its author. Seen in this way, the original deception regarding Richter's novel, though born out of fear, had worked out far better than I'd planned. Theresa was enjoying herself, finding new confidence, a new voice. Her talent as a musician had been real but inhibited, just as Claudia Witt had said; her talent as a writer was counterfeit, but natural and unconstrained. It was a puzzle, but one I thought I understood. The key to it, I reassured myself, was love.

If I had been cynical by nature, or perhaps familiar with Western ways, I might have worried more about the other side effects of our artistic collaboration: the money, for instance. I felt certain Theresa was not corruptible in that way, though she was susceptible to the occasional item of jewellery, the occasional French dress. Viola-playing was surely not a career of choice for those of a materialistic outlook. And then there was fame: a phenomenon notorious for its narcotic effect, especially on the young and the insecure. It engendered euphoria and, in many cases, the sensation of being loved. It could lead to dependence: fame as fix. Only now and again did I find myself imagining the secret dreams that might now be within Theresa's reach and asking myself if there was really a place in them for me.

I might not have worried at all if Theresa's plans had been settled, if the arrangements had been in place for another year of study in Berlin. But they were not in place, though months had gone by since the plan had been hatched. Approvals were awaited, payments were pending. That was all I knew. Was Theresa dragging her feet? Was she having second thoughts? Was it possible there was now someone else in her life?

Eva Aden, novelist and visionary, might not want me, but at least she still needed me. She needed someone, at any rate, capable of writing a sequel to *Survivors* (how I hated – on Richter's behalf – that popcorn-chasing sell-out of a title) and I was the obvious candidate. One night, lying sleepless in my still solitary bed, suddenly convinced of my imminent abandonment, I decided to remind her of this fact by writing a letter. I did it there and then, longhand. Then I went and posted it, so as to be sure of making the first collection. The relevant paragraph went something like this:

*I have been working on the new book. As you know, I hate to discuss my work before it's finished – I am not too happy discussing it even then – but I cannot stop myself from telling you how well it's going. For really the first time in my life I feel I have hit my stride. In the past I have often felt I was feeling my way through a fog. That anything clear or cogent came out of it seems miraculous. But now at last I see things clearly. The visions are so sharp they almost hurt, the passions so powerful they make me shake. How can I account for this sudden clarity? Maybe there comes a time in life when the mirror turns, when a writer can see the world other than through the prism of his own ambitions and his own fears. Or maybe I am happy because you are coming back to me. Either way, as long as my mind remains in its present hopeful state, I am certain that the new book will eclipse the last. It is a story of secrets within secrets and lies within lies, a story where the truth is no more than an idea in the mind of a child – but, for all that, a story about love. I feel certain that it will confound the publisher's expectations. Have a little patience and you will see for yourself.*

As soon as I woke the next morning I regretted what I had done. It was madness to raise such extravagant expectations. Worse, I had given way to my suspicions, which were based not on fact but on pessimism and self-doubt. Theresa loved me. If she was putting her heart and soul into the role of Eva Aden, that was for my benefit, not hers. She was doing it for me. My letter would make no difference. It certainly wouldn't bring her running to my side, like an obedient wolfhound.

Two weeks later I received a reply. In it Theresa told me that everything in Berlin was arranged, the fees paid, the visa granted, and that she had found lodgings with a retired professor and his wife in Prenzlauer Berg. I could expect to see her again before the end of the month.

# 37

One thing I knew about the novelist's task: when in doubt, write; when empty, write; when afraid, write. Nothing is more impenetrable than the blank page. The blank page is the void, the absence of sense and feeling, the white light of literary death. Having little hope of completing the task I had set myself, having despaired of my powers and my vision, having thought myself to a standstill and walked myself to exhaustion, I sat down to write. It was the only thing left to do.

I wrote many openings, taking the end of *Survivors* as my cue. Some of them were promising, many were bold. For days at a time things went better than expected, better than they had done for years. I began to sense that the clarity I had boasted of in my letter might not be so far away. I do not believe in Muses. Theresa was not my Muse, but she was my spur, she gave me back my appetite. I wanted to succeed for her as much as for myself, our interests being, so I believed, synonymous.

For all these hopeful signs, my openings never coalesced into a story. The snapshots never became a film. The characters were familiar to me, but I struggled to get inside their heads, to do the thinking for them. The reasons for this were clear: Alex, the reluctant warlord, Tilmann his nemesis, Tania his tragic bride, these were no longer my creations. Whatever their origins, they were Wolfgang Richter's offspring now. They reflected his mind and his imagination – entities I had no desire to reanimate or dwell in. Richter himself had shown me no such consideration when he wrote *The Valley of Unknowing*, but that made no difference. Irrational it may have been, but I wanted to keep out of Richter's domain the way sane men avoid Ouija boards, from an innate fear of trespass and a respect for the dead. It was to my detriment that I had no choice.

Sequels are supposed to be easy. So much that is in them has been imagined already. The willing readers stand ready. The hard work of seducing them has been done. It should certainly be easier than starting from nothing. But it wasn't for me. For weeks I slaved and drank, and paced and typed, my head filling up with plot lines and variations on plot lines, the mass of them growing and tangling like brambles in a wet summer, but without the promise of fruit. I went out only when at risk of starvation. I shaved rarely, sleeping only when exhaustion overcame me – at my desk, on the sofa, in the bath – my life resembling that of the archetypal artist more than it had ever done before. What I had to show for it was incipient diarrhoea and a mountain of screwed-up paper large enough to constitute a fire hazard. When Barbara Jaeger telephoned, inviting me to another of her soirées, I told her I thought I was dying and would be unable to attend. She gave me the name of a clinic in the suburb of Radeburg and told me to make an appointment, being sure to mention her name. In the meantime I was expected to attend her event.

'People say you've stopped going out. I hope you're not becoming a recluse, Bruno. That would be too boring.'

'I'm working,' I said, 'for the first time in years.'

'A Hero of the People can't be a recluse. A recluse only thinks of himself.'

'I'm not a Hero of the People, as you very well know.'

'An anti-social socialist is a contradiction in terms. Eight o'clock sharp, and whatever you do, don't *bring* anything.'

I asked her what she meant.

'That filthy moonshine you're always handing out. The schnapps or whatever. It's poisonous and much too powerful.'

Which was pretty much how I felt about Barbara.


That same night I dreamed of the Jaegers' soirée, the way people often dream about unavoidable engagements in their near future. The dream occasion was unusual only in that it stayed in my mind longer than the real thing. It remains there still.

At the beginning I was standing in a crowd, holding an empty glass. We were not in Barbara's flat, but in a large civic building, where spherical lights hung down from the ceiling on long wires. Barbara stood by the door, wearing a red cocktail dress and greeting guests as they arrived, throwing back her head as she laughed, exposing her pale throat and the golden fillings in her teeth. Having no one to talk to, I went looking for a refill. As I gently elbowed my way across the room, I became aware of another sound: a relentless, irregular tapping. It was coming from beneath my feet.

The other guests didn't notice. They were all too busy laughing and smoking American cigarettes. Despairing of refreshment I went in search of cleaner air, making my way out into the voluminous lobby. Absently I brought a hand to my stomach and was horrified to discover I was still wearing my medal. I had been wearing it all evening without knowing it.

I pulled off the medal and stuffed it my pocket, becoming aware once more of the tapping. It was louder, closer; an intermittent, mechanical sound, like Morse code. I followed the sound down a small flight of steps at the bottom of which stood a studded iron door. I looked for a handle, but there wasn't one. I found only a large vertical slot where a keyhole might have been. I reached into my pockets for coins, but found only my medal. It turned out to be exactly the right fit. I yanked it free of its ribbon and pushed it in. With a gentle click the door unlocked.

There was a long corridor in front of me, with more iron doors on either side, deeply recessed into the walls. There was a strong smell of earth, mingled inexplicably with a sickly aroma of cut flowers. The tapping sound was coming from the far end of the corridor. I knew what it was by this time: somebody was using a typewriter.

The sound of typing led me to a door that was different from the others. I recognised the grain of the wood, the pattern of cracks and flaking varnish: it was the door to my apartment. I understood then, as if it were something obvious that I had merely forgotten, that the corridors beneath the civic building where honours were conferred led beneath the city to the villa in Loschwitz. I peered through the spyhole. I saw the interior of my apartment shrunk to the size of a pea. A light was on in the bedroom, a band of brightness falling across the hallway.

I opened the door with my key. The smell of flowers was stronger on the other side. I tiptoed into the sitting room. My record player was on, the music gloomy and symphonic. I looked around for a weapon, some means of self-defence. What I found was a hammer, lying across the seat of my old leather armchair.

As soon as I saw him, sitting at the desk with his back to me, wearing a black velvet jacket, I knew it was Richter I had been expecting all along. This was because we were not in my bedroom, or my apartment, but in his. A glance around the room confirmed this, even though many of the objects and furnishings were identical to mine. It seemed that I was the intruder in this place and Richter his victim. But what was to be the crime?

I approached carefully. I wanted to turn and run, but I was on a mission and it was too late to turn back. Richter sensed my presence. He stopped typing and sat up, listening, his head turning just enough for me to make out the corner of his eyebrow, the waxy crescent of his cheekbone. The music covered the unsteady sibilance of my breathing and the pounding of my heart. Richter went back to typing, only the typing was different this time: much slower and regular, like the beat of a funeral march. It was, I realised, ironic typing, postmodern typing; typing that is aware of its own artificiality, its own intermediation – in short, typing that was aware of *me*.

I dropped the hammer. It landed on the floor without making a sound. Richter continued to type, faster now, swiping the carriage return lever as the bell sang out the completion of each freshly completed line. How I missed that sound: that clattering, pinging affirmation of fertility and achievement. And how I envied Richter for making it, even though it had cost him his life on earth (we were clearly not on earth now, but in some other world, where machinery and devices were plentiful, but communication was not).

By this time I was standing at his shoulder. I needed to know what he was writing. *That* was my purpose here. I had come as a spy, to discover Richter's next project, Richter the true author of *Survivors*. Only here, from him, could I find what I needed to satisfy Theresa, to bring her back to the valley and to me. The only unnatural aspect of the mission was that Richter seemed content to collaborate in this second literary theft, to give me at least a glimpse of his intentions; as if I were there at his direction instead of my own. Perhaps, I thought, he had no use for celebrity any more. Perhaps the voice I offered him was better than no voice at all.

I held my breath. My shoe leather creaked as I leaned over him. I could see the type, but my eyes refused to settle on it long enough to read it. They seemed to avoid contact the way one magnet repels another. Just a few sentences might be all I needed. One single line might reveal the nature of the book I was supposed to write. I forced myself to look again, to build the first line one letter at a time. And I saw this:

One November morning, while the schoolchildren outside
were going through their gas mask drill, the telephone rang.

I knew what came next: the phone call from Michael Schilling, the *Eiscafé* rendezvous, the handover of a manuscript – a manuscript without an author, without a title, awaiting my appraisal; a story set in the future, *a* future.

The beginning of that story played out in my head and when the memory was over I found that my dream was over too. I was in bed, awake. Richter had disappeared, likewise the scent of dead flowers and the sound of typing. A blind was tapping against the window frame. Around me lay the familiar chaos of my literary false starts, a room full of mutilated and discarded papers, gently shifting in the draught. The sight reminding me with sudden force of petals thrown over a grave, the grave being, of course, my mother's, since she had never had one, except for those I had provided for her in a thousand fearful imaginings.

It was still dark outside, but I didn't feel tired. I felt fragile and jumpy, like someone who has narrowly avoided a fatal collision. I climbed out of the bed and wrote down everything that had happened in my dream. By the time I had finished, I knew what it was the spectral Richter wanted me to write: not a sequel to his first novel, of course, but the story of that novel itself, its origins and its fate – which was, in part, my story, since I alone could tell it.

What he wanted, in short, was a confessional work. Creatively speaking, it was the one book I could write; in all other respects it was the one book I couldn't.

A few days later a letter arrived via Theresa's underground mail service, containing fifteen reviews of *Survivors*, cut from a variety of German newspapers and magazines. Hastily I skimmed through them, not out of concern with the general verdict (the book under examination was not mine, after all, but that of a man who was safely beyond critical range), but for fear of how the book would be interpreted. All the reviews were positive. Many were effusive. The longer reviews, in the more serious publications, detected weighty feministic themes and subtle intentions in the Aden début, upon which they expounded with miraculous confidence, as if they'd been eavesdropping on her mind. Thankfully none mentioned the Workers' and Peasants' State, or made any connection to its history. A couple pointed out in passing that the author had studied music 'behind the iron curtain'. Nevertheless, for safety's sake, I destroyed them, all except one, which appeared in a magazine hitherto unknown to me entitled *Die Berliner Literaturkritik*. The salient paragraph went like this:

Perhaps Miss Aden's greatest skill is in lending a timeless, universal significance to the smallest of human actions and the most private of human desires. It is not merely that we care about her characters and their fates. It is that in their struggles we sense the struggles of history, of whole societies and whole peoples. In this, and in the common themes of renewal, rebirth and betrayal, her work is strongly reminiscent of –

perhaps even a subtle *hommage* to – *The Orphans of Neustadt*, the 1960s classic by the late Bruno Krug.

My first reaction on seeing myself described in this way (as recently deceased) was one of indignation, tinged, I must admit, with a frisson of doubt. Foolish as it may seem, I did go into the bathroom and look in the mirror and splash water on my face, just to reassure myself. Only when fully satisfied that my existence was still corporeal did I examine the cutting again. This time, instead of indignation, what I felt was a haunting and inexplicable sorrow, as if at the passing of an old friend. The critic had made a factual error (how telling that the editors had failed to spot it). At the same time his manner of describing me was, as far as Bruno Krug the writer was concerned, nothing less than a statement of fact.

# 38

'Hello, Bruno? It's me.'

Theresa's voice was faint and distant, masked by pings and rattles and a swelling ocean of hiss, as if she were calling from another world.

'Hello, you.'

'Darling.'

*Darling* was a first from Theresa, a little touch of theatre.

'Where are you?'

'Berlin. East Berlin. I just got in this afternoon. I'm using a neighbour's phone, so I can't . . . Is everything all right?'

In my hand the receiver creaked. I was holding it so tightly I was in danger of rupturing the plastic. 'Of course. Never better. I thought you were coming over last week.'

'I meant to. Something came up. Martin said it was . . . I couldn't really get out of it.'

'When am I going to see you?'

'Soon. I have to sort things out here first. I can't just dump my suitcase with Professor Ebert and vanish – though I wish I could. I'm supposed to be studying here.'

Even through the noise I could tell that she was nervous, troubled. But about what?

'I was thinking I should come to you for a change? They have hotels in Berlin, after all.' I attempted unsuccessfully to make the suggestion sound breezy, compounding my failure with a demented chuckle.

'Another time, Bruno. I need to get dug in here first. I just need a week or so. Then I'll come.'

It was important, I felt, not to beg.

'Are you getting time to practise?' I asked.

Theresa sighed. 'I'm not sure there's much point in practising any more. I've no performances coming up.'

Down the line I heard a door close. Theresa was not alone. It made little difference either way. Theresa never told me anything sensitive over the telephone. She was convinced that the telephones in the Workers' and Peasants' State were all bugged, though I assured her the idea was ridiculous.

'Did you see the reviews?' she said.

'Yes, I did.'

'What did you think?'

'Very generous. Very perceptive.'

'Weren't they the best reviews you've ever seen?'

'Generous to a fault, I'd say.'

'There's a whole lot more to come. That was just the first batch. Konrad's promised to send them over.'

I couldn't help recalling that on *Freizeit-Forum* Theresa had maintained that she had not read the reviews of *Survivors* and had no plans to do so. It seemed that wasn't true. Or was I mixing up Eva Aden with Theresa Aden? Was it only the notional writer who turned her back on the critics, while the actual musician hung on their every word? It was confusing, but I didn't mind being confused, as long as it didn't stop me seeing my golden girl again.

'So what came up?' I asked. Theresa didn't answer. 'What couldn't you get out of?'

'Just another bit of publicity.'

'Another TV appearance?'

'No, no. Just a page in *Stern*, this weekly magazine we have.'

Even I had heard of *Stern*.

'An interview?'

'They called it a profile. There was a photographer and a journalist. It took for ever. But it could really help the sales, Martin says. It could really put *Survivors* on the map.'

'I thought it was already on the map. I thought it was all round the world.'

'Yes, but that's just the literary world, Bruno: publishers and bookshops, intellectuals. *Stern* keeps you in the public eye, the general public. Mass media, that's what really empties the warehouses, Martin says.'

'When's it coming out?'

'Next weekend, I think. My mother's bound to keep a copy. She's already started a scrapbook.'

Theresa laughed. Had she mentioned her mother to remind me of the price she was paying for our arrangement, a price that included making dupes of her family? How proud she must have made them, how dazzled and delighted (*We knew she was musical, but this!*): uncles and aunts, cousins and second cousins, friends and acquaintances, old and new – all of it built on a lie.

'So when . . . ? When can you . . . ?'

'Soon. I promise. As soon as I can.'

'All right. Fine. I'll wait.'

I heard her exhale. Was she laughing or sighing? I couldn't tell.

'So, Bruno, tell me: how's your wonderful new book coming along?'

'I'm having some second thoughts about it, to be honest.'

'Oh?'

'It's nothing serious.'

'I'm glad. I know what it means to you, your work. It's funny, but I understand now, better than ever.'

'That's good.'

Another benefit of growing into the authorial role, I assumed.

'You'd be lost without it, wouldn't you?'

'Quite possibly.'

'Your work tells you who you are.'

# 39

Before I fell in love with Theresa Aden my relationship with the wider world was, in a word, declamatory. I spoke, but I had no desire to listen and little need to do so. I was a transmitter, weak, distant and increasingly prone to interruption, but content to carry traffic in one direction only. The responses and opinions of my local readership, the fellow citizens who asked me to sign their battered copies of *The Orphans of Neustadt*, who expressed their admiration in gifts of home-grown vegetables and lardy patisserie, these were of some concern to me, and I was careful to participate in official masquerades of dialogue and constructive criticism when invited to do so. But when it came to readers in the non-socialist abroad, I was pleased to note the fact of their existence and (occasionally) their numbers, for reasons of vanity and financial advantage; but even if their comments had been audible, I doubt if I would have paid them much attention. I saw no benefit in subjecting myself to the judgement of strangers, let alone strangers in a foreign land. I was not a true participant in their cultural marketplace, where cash was king and the customer was always right. As I had often asked Theresa (rhetorically, of course) during the early, carefree days of our affair: how could an artist remain true to his own vision – in effect, honest – if he allowed his idea of beauty to be dictated by others? This indifference to Western opinion played well with my ideological overseers, who took it as indicative of loyalty. The truth is that I was afraid of what I might hear.

With the publication of *Survivors*, with the miraculous birth of Eva Aden, I experienced a disturbing reorientation. The transmitter was finally silent. Now I wanted only to receive. The knowledge that things were being written and said about the woman I loved, that her image was being captured and pasted and reproduced all over the world, giving rise to all manner of lust and speculation, left me burning with curiosity. The fact that Theresa's disclosure was evidently incomplete made my hunger all the greater. That is why, despite my dangerous proximity to the Richter affair, I began to take risks.

After Theresa's phone call, all I could think about was the profile in *Stern* magazine and how I could get hold of a copy. The challenge was daunting. Of the day-to-day items produced in wasteful abundance by the capitalist West, newspapers and magazines were the hardest to come by in the East. They were not carried in the Intershops for ideological reasons and even women's magazines, glossy publications whose principal subject matters were dieting, clothes, make-up and sex, were eschewed as a source of unfavourable lifestyle comparisons (*Pramo*, our own most popular women's magazine, necessarily adopted a practical approach to fashion, invariably including pattern charts for do-it-yourself couture). The safest way of seeing for myself what Theresa's agent considered so significant would have been to exploit my official contacts. A suitably framed request to the Cultural Association might have borne fruit eventually. But I was in too much of a hurry for that. Instead I turned to Frau Helwig, the timid spinster of the lachrymose lavatory, who I had some reason to hope could be bullied.

Besides tending her allotment, Frau Helwig's other lurid passion was needlework. She knitted prodigiously and when she wasn't knitting she was embroidering or crocheting. Most of the moveable objects in her draughty flat had been fitted with some kind of decorative cosy; not just the obvious candidates – teapots, cushions, hot-water bottles – but mugs, door handles (to impede the draughts whistling through the keyholes), plant pots, photograph albums, the arms of her armchairs and the headrest of her bed. Many of the patterns – ducks aloft were a favoured pictorial theme – came from magazines and it was here that I saw my chance: the magazines in question were Western and came in the post from an elderly cousin outside Hamburg. This much Frau Helwig had confessed to me when I came across them on one of my reparative visits, carefully stacked inside a hollow bath stool.

*Crochet Today*, *Needlepoint*, *World of Yarn*, *The Knitter*, these publications could hardly have been more innocuous, politically speaking. If anything, the subliminal message of textile self-sufficiency had a Marxian flavour, harking back to a pre-capitalist golden age, when the slavery of industrial mass production had not yet parted the working man from the fruits his labour. But what was to stop Frau Helwig's cousin slipping in a few pages from *Stern* among the usual patterns and handy hints – apart, that is, from Frau Helwig's terror of official displeasure and the faint possibility of arrest?

'*Stern*?' the old woman said, as she shut the door behind us. I had caught up with her as she was returning from the shops and was at that moment carrying her shopping bag. 'I've never heard of that magazine. Is it about astronomy?'

*Stern* in German means 'star'. Perhaps in Frau Helwig's utilitarian world – the world of *The Knitter* and *Crochet Today* – magazine titles were only ever literal and descriptive. Either that, or she was sounding me out.

'Not exclusively,' I said. 'It's more what they call general interest.'

The old lady frowned. She was, as ever, anxious to be obliging. In the time it had taken us to get up the stairs she had recounted a long list of plumbing and heating irregularities, menaces that worried her no end 'what with winter on its way'. I could sympathise: her flat was cold and draughty at the best of times.

'The thing is, Helga lives in quite a small town,' she said, watching me as I placed an investigatory ear against the old iron radiator in the hallway. 'I doubt if they'd have much of a selection in the local shop.'

I assured her that *Stern* enjoyed a wide circulation. 'I'm only really interested in one particular article. It should be in the next edition. A profile. An old acquaintance of mine, by the name of Aden. She writes on cultural matters.'

'Well. How interesting.'

'I think so. If you write to your cousin now, she'll be sure not to miss the next edition. I can post the letter for you. I hate to beg a favour, but I've nowhere else to turn.' I handed Frau Helwig a scrap of paper upon which the details had already been written. 'Tell your cousin it would be best to cut the article out. I really don't want the rest of the magazine and it'll reduce the cost of postage.'

I insisted on this rudimentary precaution, not to protect Frau Helwig, but to increase the chances that the item would actually arrive. Ideologically dubious correspondence had a habit of going missing, especially when sent from abroad. Superior brands of chocolate fared little better.

Unfortunately Frau Helwig, for all her years, was not stupid. She squinted at the paper in her hand, eyes narrowing. 'Shall I tell Helga that the article's for you?' she said. 'She'll be sure to pull her finger out if she hears that. She's always been a fan of yours, Herr Krug.'

The purpose of this suggestion, I realised, was to ensure that any blame arising from her request could be credibly directed at me.

'Of course,' I said. 'If you think it'll help.'

'Oh, I'm sure it will.'

I took an adjustable spanner from my jacket and tapped the in-pipe, like a doctor testing for reflexes. 'Your system needs flushing out. It's in danger of seizing up. I'd better go and get my tools.'

In this way a transaction was completed, the true nature of which remained implicit, neither party having openly acknowledged it. In that sense it was no different from many thousands of transactions taking place every day in the Workers' and Peasants' State, where the more weighty and significant a need, the more it touched upon the innermost desires and the deepest fears, the more likely it was to remain unspecified.

# 40

In the interval that followed Frau Helwig's domestic heating arrangements received the kind of pastoral care normally reserved for sick and dying relatives. I visited every day, ostensibly to check up on the health of the boiler and the circulatory flow of the radiative system; in reality to see whether cousin Helga the Hamburger had done as she was asked and mailed the profile in *Stern*. After a week or so of pointless plumbing my persistence was rewarded. The day before Theresa was due to visit from Berlin a letter arrived. I was too impatient to wait until I got home. I examined the contents in the privacy of Frau Helwig's dingy lavatory, on the pretext of inspecting the cistern, my heavy toolbox blocking the door.

Frau Helwig's cousin had not sent what you would normally call a cutting. A typical cutting is not five pages long, and does not open with a photographic double-page spread across which is written the headline: *PROFITS OF DOOM*. It is also customary to preserve, where possible, the name and date of the publication, which typically appears in small type at the bottom of each page. In this case all the folios had been trimmed off. A large panel on the last page had also been excised, doubtless because an advertisement had been displayed there, Western advertisements being regarded as more or less politically corrosive depending on the product, and whether an equivalent was available in the East. It seemed cousin Helga was not naive when it came to sending printed matter across the inner German border. Stripped of contextual orientation, the article could have been mistaken, at least by a casual observer, for one in *Needlepoint* or *World of Yarn*.

The photographs revealed a startlingly modern and spacious house: polished wooden flooring, a raised fireplace with logs blazing, white walls decorated with tasteful abstract art (bold yet balanced, striking but never garish). The furniture was bound in what looked like suede, perpendicular in form and low, as if to avoid cluttering up the sight lines. One wall was made entirely of glass. Beyond it lay immature autumnal woodland and a stretch of sunlit water. In one corner of the room, on a marble plinth, stood a bronze statuette of a female nude with outstretched wings.

This, it transpired, was not the Aden dwelling. It belonged to

Martin Klaus, whom the article described as 'one of a new breed of super-agent'. (The article did not reveal where or how the breeding took place; I assumed in secret laboratories at the Swiss Ministry of Culture.) It was located on the north shore of the Zürichsee in a place called Erlenbach. Reportedly Erlenbach was 'exclusive'.

> Aden's is a beguiling but strangely unsettling presence. Demure but watchful, engaging but reticent, there is always a sense that she is holding something back, that her soul perhaps abides elsewhere.
>
> '*Survivors* is a haunted, traumatised novel, a dark vision, a lament,' says Klaus. 'When I first met Eva, I thought there had been a mistake. How could someone so delightful have written something so traumatic? It's only as I've got to know her that I've begun to perceive the complexity within.'

Klaus was older than I'd expected – possibly my age, within a year or two – but unbookishly tanned and heavily built. In the opening spread he sat perched on the back of a sofa, dressed in a blue suit and an unbuttoned shirt, over which peeped a curl of manly thoracic hair. He wasn't looking at the camera, but at Theresa, who stood a few feet away beside the fireplace. She wore jeans and a flowing purple blouse that left one shoulder bare (no bra strap in evidence, I noted). The agent looked at the writer, the writer looked at us. He sat, she stood, her hands hidden behind her, as if bound. At first glance the geometry of the scene was unambiguous: Theresa was the performer, the centre of interest; Klaus, like us, was in the audience, a mere advocate. But on closer inspection, other connotations suggested themselves: the advocate was also a connoisseur; and that made the writer an *objet d'art*, a creation just as much as a creator. She added lustre to his already impressive collection.

I had never much liked the sound of Martin Klaus. The way Theresa quoted him in every conversation – Martin says this, Martin says that – suggested she saw him more as a mentor than a business associate. And his utterances seemed obsessively focused on the market; how to please it, tame it, exploit it, as if that were a writer's only possible concern. That the man was successful, at least in his own terms, was undeniable. His lakeside villa alone established that fact. But he was also an interloper and a fool. For hadn't he been taken in like everyone else?

I turned the pages, squinting at the text as I perched on the seat of Frau Helwig's ancient *Klo*, absorbing the moneyed ambience of Switzerland, drinking in the story. Apparently, before Klaus had even finished reading *Survivors,* he had jumped into his vintage Alfa Romeo and raced down the Autobahn to Linz, arriving unannounced outside the Aden household, Theresa having omitted to include her telephone number in the covering letter.

> Dinner followed at a nearby *schloss.* Within half an hour Klaus had, in his own words, 'proposed'.
>
> 'I went down on one knee — quite literally — and begged Eva to be my client,' he recalls.
>
> 'It was flattering and actually rather romantic,' Aden says, 'in a funny kind of way. Everyone in the restaurant was looking at us. When I said yes, the waiters brought us complimentary champagne.'
>
> Since that day the happy creative couple have enjoyed a fairy tale honeymoon. In the publishing world, *Survivors* was one of the season's most hotly contested titles, Aden herself appearing prominently in the advance publicity. Early sales have lived up to expectations. Though US publication is still some months away, the calls from Hollywood have already begun.

On the third page was another photograph, shot outdoors in black and white. It had been taken on a different occasion. Klaus was sitting on the grass wearing a polo shirt and sunglasses, holding papers in one hand, gesticulating with the other. Theresa lay opposite him on her stomach, holding a wine glass.

> 'Success and fame can suffocate a young talent,' Klaus explains. 'Everywhere there are siren voices and unhelpful distractions. Part of my role in Eva's life is to act as a confidant, a father-confessor and a sounding board. If ever Eva has questions or doubts, I want her to come to me first.'

Part of his role. *Part.* What about the rest of it? And why was there never any mention of a Frau Klaus? The agent was apparently unattached. If so, why? Was he impotent? Was he homosexual? Worse, was he an habitual playboy, a man for whom the comforts of marriage were a poor substitute for unbridled promiscuity?

> Where Eva Aden goes from here is a subject of the utmost delicacy, creatively and commercially. There are rumours of a sequel to *Survivors,* which neither Aden nor Klaus was prepared to confirm. 'Eva has more great novels in her — I'm sure of that,' Klaus says. 'But I don't want her embarking on another major work just because everyone is egging her

on, or because there's money to be made. She needs to work at her own pace and in her own time. Right now she's experimenting with the short story form and I'm encouraging her in that.'

The short story form? I had to laugh. There wasn't much money in short stories – the experimental kind least of all. Short stories were written for love and for practice. Short stories were where writers began. But as a presentational ploy, I had to admit it was ingenious. It projected seriousness and long-term ambition, while defusing the charge of exploitation that was bound to accompany a sequel. Where had my sweet Theresa acquired such casual, skilful mendacity? And from whom?

A new thought, disturbing but seductive, occurred to me: what if it wasn't a lie? What if Theresa *was* experimenting with the short story form because she planned to become a writer for real? What if the life of the viola player – the difficulty, the obscurity, the scant reward – was no longer enough? How many times had I heard her complain about it? How many times had she seemed on the verge of giving up? I remembered the last time we spoke: *I'm not sure there's much point in practising any more.*

I stood up, banging my skull on the overhead light. Once established in her own right, she would have no further need of me. No more keeping Bruno happy; no more tedious sojourns in the suffering East. I would have given her what she needed, what every new writer needs: an audience. The freshly liberated Eva Aden, feminist visionary, could manage the rest for herself.

I took deep breaths to slow my racing heart. The scenario was fantastical. It couldn't possibly be true. To give Eva Aden her own literary career would mean appropriating *Survivors* for ever, safe in the knowledge that I would never be in a position to reclaim it. Theresa, my Theresa, would never have done that to me – even if, through some unimaginable chance, she had discovered that the book had never been mine in the first place.

There was one more photograph, smaller than the others, hidden away on the last page. Theresa was at a signing, stationed behind a table, either side of her copies of *Survivors* piled shoulder high. She sat, pen in hand, sandwiched between the two towering manifestations of her deception – themselves a fraction of the warehousefuls of fraud already fanning out across the globe. The camera had caught her looking daunted, bewildered. I expect she was thinking: *what have I done?* Klaus was standing behind her, stooping solicitously, as if he too had noticed something wrong. A steadying hand, blurred by motion, was on its way to Theresa's left deltoid. The other hand was already resting on the opposite shoulder, close enough to her neck for the thumb to be invisible beneath her hair. How long had it been there, I wondered, that proprietorial digit? How natural had such caresses become?

I stared at the picture and it was if the editors at *Stern* were sending me a covert message. *Look at her, look at him. What is the relationship here? What do you think?*

I sat down again. Did Klaus know everything? Of course he did. Either Theresa had told him, or he had guessed. Either way, he was not the fool in this equation. *I* was the fool. I had sent Theresa out into a world I didn't understand, a world where Klaus and his kind were in charge; and they *had* taken charge – of her. They had done more than give her a new name. They had remade her from the heart up.

Above my head the light bulb fizzled and went out. I was in darkness.

After I don't know how long, Frau Helwig rapped on the door. 'Is everything all right, Herr Krug?'

She sounded scared.

# 41

The wind was in the west the day she returned, a strong wind that purged the air of smoke and dust, and sent the arboreal debris of the late departed summer spiralling down the streets. The tramway power lines bucked and swayed, sending showers of sparks through the air. On my way to the central railway station I saw men at a restoration site scurrying for cover as a tarpaulin broke free from the scaffolding, loose ropes flailing like whips. I went to the bridge on Budapester Strasse, which crosses over the tracks, and watched the trains trundle in and out of the terminal building, their clatter and screech barely audible over the gusting wind. I was afraid they might close the line. I was afraid Theresa wouldn't come. If the weather was wild down here, what would it be like up on the hills? In the event the line stayed open. Theresa did come. But it was to be her last visit. The valley was never to see her again.

I waited hopefully. I still believed that the business with Richter's fiction would not trouble us for long. Books are ephemeral. In all but the rarest of cases their season is brief. *Survivors* would be forgotten soon enough, and so would its author and all questions relating to its authorship. Theresa and I would look back on it as an amusing detour in the shared journey of our lives. With this in mind, I had decided to waste no more time in proposing marriage. This, it seemed to me, was one thing I could offer her that Martin Klaus never would. Klaus was a collector of beautiful things, but the last thing a collector wanted was to be collected. For him the exclusivity inherent in marriage was repellent, a limitation on the very basis of his self-expression. Whatever the current status of the Klaus-Aden alliance, my proposal would expose its limitations and its weakness. So it was that in compliance with the inverted logic of love, I set out to make Theresa Aden my wife at the very time when I was least assured of her affection.

The Berlin train arrived ten minutes late. The wind funnelled down the covered platform, jostling the passengers and tearing at their clothes. A woman's scarf whipped by overhead, somersaulting as if intoxicated by the sudden taste of freedom. A sheet of newspaper followed. I spotted Theresa and fought my way over, my spirits lifted by the sight of her smile (the smile is what I remember still, her smiling and her tears, her whole being reflected in those fragments). The train must have been full, because it took us several minutes to get clear of the crowd.

Outside, the gale made communication difficult. Theresa said something about my looking exhausted. I thought the same about her: she struck me as paler and thinner than usual, as if recently recovered from an illness. I hung on to her suitcase and Theresa hung on to me, but it was not until we were safely installed at Tutti Frutti that we had a chance to talk.

I remember little of the early conversation, which covered breathlessly Theresa's arrangements in Berlin, the kind old couple she lodged with and her initial contacts with the Humboldt faculty. I was too wound up to pay attention, intent as I was upon my proposal and the question of how I should frame it. The *Eiscafé* had been almost empty when we first arrived, which seemed propitious, but no sooner had I embarked upon my declaration than a gang of insolent youths barged their way inside, leapfrogging the stools and upsetting a huddle of pensioners in the far corner.

'What is it, Bruno? What did you want to ask me?'

We had both put down our coffee cups.

'Nothing. Nothing much. Have you seen the piece in *Stern*? The profile?'

Besides the proposal, it was the only thing I could think of.

'Not yet. I've tried to get hold of a copy, but no luck so far, not even at the university.'

This struck me as incredible: not that *Stern* should be unavailable in East Berlin, but that a young woman profiled in such a magazine wouldn't make the time for a day trip to the West, where it would be for sale on every street corner – a day trip being all it would have taken.

'Then I'm ahead of you. They gave you five pages. Quite a spread.'

The first hint of colour returned to Theresa's cheeks.

'Five pages? How on earth did they fill five pages?'

'Photographs mainly. There are a lot of photographs. Klaus's luxury villa takes up most of them.'

'I expect they didn't show the damp patches. The whole place smelled of mould.'

'He said something about short stories. You were going to write some short stories before tackling another novel. Is that true?'

Theresa shook her head. Her cheeks were pinker than ever.

'No. I mean, one day maybe. Not now.' She pushed her fingers

197

through her hair. I caught the comforting, musky scent. 'It's something Martin's been going on about. He says short stories are a good way to build up stamina. He says a second book is always more pressure than a first. Nobody's waiting for your first book.' She lowered her voice. 'I'd like to tell him his advice doesn't actually apply, but how can I?'

'I thought he wanted a sequel as soon as possible. The one-trick pony issue, remember?'

'That was before.'

'Before what?'

'Before I showed him what you wrote, about the next book.' On her last visit, I had penned a skeleton plot for her in two paragraphs, as requested. '*I* thought it sounded great, but he said . . .'

'What? What did he say?'

'Nothing bad. Just that, on reflection, it was a bit . . . unformed.'

'That's what he said? *Unformed*?'

'Unformed. Predictable. Don't get me wrong: the publishers are happy. Everyone's happy. It's just that when it comes to Martin, I haven't been able to fill in the blanks. He asks me things about the next book and I can't answer. I've tried to reassure him that everything's under control, but I'm sure he thinks I'm hiding something.'

'You are.'

'Yes, but he thinks what I'm hiding is writer's block. That's why he's been lavishing so much time on me. He thinks I'm having problems and I'm afraid to tell him. He's no fool, you know.'

Theresa's handbag was resting by her feet. A paperback with a black spine was peeping out of the top.

'You said, *one day*. How soon did you have in mind?' Theresa frowned. 'These short stories you might write.'

'For God's sake, Bruno, I told you: all that was just Martin buying time. Managing expectations, he called it.'

Theresa picked up her bag and began unpacking it.

'So *one day* actually means never.'

She pulled out a tissue, shaking her head in despair. 'Probably. Yes, never. I'm a musician. I can't write short stories. I wouldn't know where to begin.'

'With reading some maybe?'

Theresa's gaze followed mine, coming to rest on the book that now lay on the table between us. On the cover was printed: *Anton Chekhov – Short Stories*.

The noisy youths had gone and the pensioners in the corner had returned to their usual discourse of complaint. Once again the coast was clear for a proposal, but my line of questioning had spoiled the mood. I decided, all things considered, that it would be better to make my declarations outdoors.

'Anyway, something we have to talk about is the money,' Theresa said. She was definitely blushing. 'It's started coming in. You're going to have to tell me what to do with it.'

We left the *Eiscafé* and headed east towards the Volkspark, the wind shoving us along as if impatient for the matrimonial question to be settled one way or the other. Theresa seemed in no hurry to adjourn to my flat and I wasn't in my usual hurry to take her there. I knew it would look mean and tatty after the modernist grandeur of Klaus's lakeside palace. Nature, on the other hand, was not so easily upstaged. The valley might lack a mountain backdrop. Its waters might be muddy and poisonous, but it had trees in abundance – stately, ancient trees whose foliage of russet and muted gold spoke to me of patience, steadfastness and forbearance. How different from Klaus's realm, where the only gold that mattered lay hidden in vaults.

Except for a few dog walkers, slaves to canine bowels for whom being caught in a gale was a minor inconvenience, the park was empty. Along the avenues we found some shelter, though the air was still full of spinning leaves. I was glad to be where no one could overhear us, though it was hard restarting the conversation. A proposal of marriage requires a context, a gloss of spontaneity. I had to do better than: *Theresa, you know I've been thinking* . . .

'You're not happy, are you?' she said. 'You think I've done this all wrong.'

'What are you talking about?'

'Is it the pen name? Eva Aden? Is that what's bothering you?'

'No. That was thoughtful of you, a nice thing.'

'Well, it wasn't completely selfless.'

'No?'

She dug her hands into her pockets. 'I wanted to be able to disappear again once it was all over. You can understand that, can't you? I didn't want to spend the rest of my life being the woman who *didn't* write *Survivors*.'

'I was touched all the same.'

'Then it must be Martin. You think I shouldn't have signed with him.' Before I could deny this she went on, 'Honestly, I don't know how I'd have managed without him. I'd probably have given myself away and I'm sure we wouldn't have got anything like as much money.'

I told her I thought Klaus was an excellent choice. 'Why have an agent when you can have a super-agent?'

'So, what is it? You just don't like his *villa*?'

A bullish insistence coloured these questions, as if Theresa was determined to bury the issue of Klaus's suitability once and for all.

'I described the place as luxurious. You were the one who said it smelled of mould.'

Theresa looked at me closely, then laughed and took my arm. 'Well, it did a little, here and there. And it is a bit like a museum, or an art gallery. Not what you'd call homely.'

'Lacks a woman's touch, perhaps.'

'That's what I said.'

'So where's Frau Klaus in all this?'

'Didn't it say in the article?'

'Why should it? It was supposed to be a profile of you.'

Theresa looked at the ground. 'Martin was married for five years, then divorced. That was ages ago. Now he's married to his work, he says.' She gave me a little nudge, though I hadn't said a word. 'You needn't look so dubious. It's not as if you're anyone to talk. There's no Frau Krug, is there?'

This was the moment: the mood light, the topic of conversation matrimonial, my sense of urgency reignited by the thought of Martin Klaus making the natural (even logical) transition from marrying his work to marrying his client.

'I've just been waiting, that's all,' I said.

'For the right woman?'

'Yes.'

'What made you think there'd ever be one?'

By this time we were close to the willowy oasis of the Carolasee. A flight of mallards took off from the water, furious wing beats battling the wind.

'It was a risky strategy, I admit. But I know there's a right woman now.'

'Really? How?'

'Because I'm looking at her. Unfortunately the strategy won't be vindicated unless she agrees to marry me.' I took her hand. 'What do you think, Theresa? Will she?'

Just at that moment a violent gust bore down on the willow tree above us. Instinctively we ducked to avoid its flailing limbs.

'I think we should go home,' Theresa said, once we'd hurried to safety. 'It's starting to rain.'

The nearest available shelter was the Carolaschlösschen, a grand, boxy villa on the near side of the lake that served as a café and occasional wedding venue during the summer months. Unfortunately the season was already over and there were no signs of life. Had Theresa heard my question? If so, she was taking an ominously long time to frame a reply. Beneath the shadow of a partially retracted awning, I turned to her again.

'Theresa, what I was trying to ask you was –'

'I know, Bruno, I know.'

She put an arm round my neck and buried her head beneath my chin. I held her close with my one free hand (the other held her suitcase), aware, even as the warmth of affection flowed through me, that this was the one position in which it was impossible to see her face.

'The answer is . . . one day.'

'One day? You mean, *yes* one day?'

'I think so. When it's . . . So much has been going on, Bruno. You don't know . . . You don't know all of it.'

'Then tell me.'

'I need to think, Bruno. I need to think. I've just got here and suddenly you're all . . .'

*Desperate* was the word she was probably trying to avoid.

'I missed you,' I said. 'I always miss you.'

'I missed you too.' This would have been a good moment for her to look at me. She didn't. She was silent for a few moments, then I felt her sigh, as if facing a truth she didn't want to face. 'I know why you're asking me, Bruno.'

'Why am I asking you?'

'Because you think it's what I need to hear. A proof of love.' She looked up at me then. 'You think otherwise I'll leave.'

She was right. Still, I was startled by her insight. 'It's what I want,' I managed to say. 'It's as simple as that.'

She shook her head. 'But it isn't simple, is it? Because of your work.'

'What do you mean?'

'If I'm over here, permanently, I can't help you over there. You'd need someone else. Besides, nobody knows about us in the West, not now. But they *would* know if I became your wife. There'd be stories in all the newspapers – about who really wrote the book and how it was smuggled out – and then everyone here would know too. The fact is you need me exactly where I am.'

From a practical point of view this was also true. One consequence of the splashy, publicity-soaked publication that Martin Klaus had engineered for *Survivors* was that its fate and history were potentially newsworthy, something I had never anticipated. The obvious solution to the problem – a solution Theresa was reluctant to propose – was that I should leave the valley for ever, leave the faulty plumbing and the bad air, the uncritical readers and everything I had ever known, and go to live in her world; in a museum, perhaps, beside a Swiss lake, assuming I could afford one. This was, of course, easier said than done. The very act of applying for a travel permit was likely to invite scrutiny and arouse suspicion. As Herr Andrich and Herr Zoch had made clear, artistic defections had, in recent months, become a matter of the utmost sensitivity.

And there was the other difficulty, the one Theresa didn't know about: once outside the Workers' and Peasants' State, I would have no justification in maintaining the Eva Aden front. Full disclosure would have been unavoidable and that would mean revealing Wolfgang Richter as the author of *Survivors*. Certainly I could not claim the book as mine. That would change a discreet, interpersonal lie that was all about love into a monumental public lie that was all about profit. Whatever else might be said of me, I was not yet ready to go down in literary history as an out-and-out thief.

Theresa was watching me closely. Perhaps if I had told her to forget the books, that they didn't matter to me, that I had no plans to write anything because I had nothing to say – if I had told her all that she might have offered no further resistance. But instead I said nothing. I was still afraid to let her see what I had become.

'Besides, it's a big step, becoming a citizen.' That was what she said next. 'I'd be leaving my family. How often would I get to see them?'

'Trips to the West aren't unknown. And your family could visit here.'

'Maybe. If the authorities allow it. If they grant permission.'

'You're here by permission right now.'

'It's not the same. I want to be here by right.'

'As Frau Krug, you would be.'

Theresa shook her head. Across the empty terrace puddles were forming among the wet sand. My heart was already sinking. I could see *yes, one day* slowly but surely evolving into *no, never*, the former being no more than a panacea of temporary worth.

'People say things will get better here,' Theresa said. 'It'll get better. My father says that. It's a transitional phase. But it doesn't change. Everything stays the same.'

She was wrong. In recent years things had actually been getting steadily worse: the cities more decayed, the shortages more wide-spread, the Party rhetoric more belligerent. Fortunately, as a recent visitor, Theresa lacked a basis for comparison.

She shook her head. 'It's different where I come from. I wish I could make you understand.'

'Don't worry. The *Stern* piece was most illuminating. Erlenbach looks charming.'

'I'm not from Erlenbach. I'm from Linz. Industrial Linz. They're very different.'

'That's a shame. I've heard Erlenbach's quite exclusive.'

'You're not being fair.' She pushed back, hanging on to me by my lapels, but her eyes remained fixed on my chest, as if addressing an intelligence located somewhere behind my sternum. 'All I'm saying is what's the rush? I'm here, aren't I? I'll be here for another year, maybe more. And you have a book to write. Your best book ever.'

There were tears in my eyes, but Theresa's grip on my coat made it impossible to turn away. It struck me that I was being kept in place, metaphorically as well as literally. Why was this so hard to bear? I had been in the same place most of my life. Why did the prospect of being there a little longer fill me with despair? Because, in that moment, I could not rid myself of the notion that the main beneficiary of the status quo was Eva Aden, novelist, feminist visionary and cash cow. And if this was no accident, it meant that everything we had, Theresa and I, even her presence that very day, was all for Eva, for Martin Klaus, for Bernheim Media. It meant that Theresa had already left me and was never coming back. It would mean, in effect, that she was dead – if indeed she had ever really lived. For as my hopes faded of a happy ever after, I began to wonder if the girl I thought I knew (modest, loving, loyal) was anything more than a character in a story I had told myself.

Despair is a dangerous state of mind. Anger is much safer. Anger is outward-looking. It conjures up enemies, identifies the blameworthy and holds out the invigorating prospect of revenge. Despair turns to anger out of nothing more than an instinct for self-preservation.

'So why have you changed your mind?' I said. 'Barely a year ago you were ready to settle here.'

Finally Theresa looked me in the face. 'I never said that.'

'Not to me, no. You said it to Wolfgang Richter. I have it on very good authority.'

'What authority?'

'He was in love with you. And you loved him back. I can't blame you. Lots of women loved him. He was talented, dashing and hand-some. What more could you wish for?'

Theresa's frown turned to nervous laughter. 'Are you serious?'

'Deadly.'

She let go of me. 'Well, your good authority stinks. For your information, Wolfgang wasn't my type.' Her blushes gave the lie to her words – unless she was angry too.

'It's nothing to be ashamed of.'

Theresa did an impression of someone who can't believe what she is hearing. 'Look, Wolfgang *was* handsome, yes. And witty. And he had a lot of confidence.'

'Don't forget talent.'

'But he was also arrogant and unfeeling and, if you really want my opinion, selfish.' Theresa took a couple of paces, then turned round again. 'Do you know what I really didn't like about him? He thought everyone was a bit of a joke – everyone except himself. He made fun of people and the worst of it was he was *good* at it. He *enjoyed* it.' Theresa's voice hardened. 'He was fun to be with. I will say that. But he wasn't nice. He wasn't kind.'

I didn't know what to say. I didn't know what to believe.

'I'm sorry to shatter your illusions, Bruno. I'm sorry to speak ill of the dead, but that's the truth.'

'He came back here because of you,' I said. 'If you two hadn't been an item, he'd still be in Berlin.'

'Did he tell you that?' Theresa's eyes narrowed. 'Or was it his mother?'

'It's true, isn't it?'

'In a way, yes. But not in the way you think.'

'I saw you together. I saw you kiss him, outside the Kulturpalast – the night of the Christmas concert. I went looking for you.'

'Wolfgang might have kissed me. He was like that. I never kissed him back.'

'So he was in love with you, but not the other way round.'

'He wasn't *in love* with me. He tried it on with every girl he met.'

Jealousy, I thought. Now it made sense: she had loved him, but he had been unfaithful. Her anger was born of humiliation. *That* I could understand.

'What's the point of pretending? It's over now.'

'What makes you think I'm pretending? He wasn't irresistible, you know.'

'Then why did you keep his photograph? Why did you *have* his photograph? I found it in a copy of my book. Admit it: you were smitten.'

The rain had stopped. Theresa picked up her suitcase, stepped out from under the awning and walked stiffly across the terrace. At the top of some steps she stopped to steady herself against the railings. I hurried to her side. For a moment I thought she was going to faint.

'Why didn't you say something? All this time, Bruno . . . You actually thought I was in love with someone else.'

'*Were* in love. Had been. Pluperfect tense.' I reached for her shoulder, but she pushed my hand away. 'An infatuation. I didn't think –'

'You thought I lied to you. I was pretending to have feelings I didn't really have.'

As if there was anything unusual about that.

'No.'

'You were jealous.'

'How could I be jealous of a dead man?'

'I don't know. It seems you found a way.'

Theresa kept her face from me, and that was how I knew she was crying. They were tears for Wolfgang Richter, tears that could no longer be hidden.

'You dreamed about him,' I said gently. 'You talked to him in your sleep.'

Theresa didn't respond. Why did she keep these feelings a secret? She and Wolfgang had been ideally suited and unattached. What was there to hide?

'Why would you dream about him, if you never liked him? Why would you go to his funeral?'

Theresa sighed. It was the sound of a burden being put down, a pretence abandoned. 'I expect it was guilt,' she said.

# PART FIVE

## 42

This is the story she told me as we walked back across the Volkspark. In spite of what happened later I have always believed it to be true. Fictional stories, if they are to be consistent and credible, need advance preparation; and I had not given Theresa time for that. In any case I wanted to believe her. I had always sensed that she kept things from me. I sensed it in her reticence and in those moments of stillness when I would catch her staring out of the window or at the ceiling as we lay in bed. I would ask her what she was thinking about and the reply was always 'nothing'. On these occasions her thoughts were her own and I could never prise them out of her.

A few weeks before she first came to study in the East she had been approached by a stranger. Theresa was doing a summer job at the time, waitressing at a café in Linz, and it was there that the stranger appeared. After eating a sandwich he had followed Theresa out at the end of her lunchtime shift. On the street he addressed her by name, said he had heard about her from some mutual acquaintances and asked if they could have a chat about her upcoming trip. He said it was important.

'I think I had a good idea what he wanted me to do,' Theresa said. 'Because when he asked me, I wasn't really surprised.'

The stranger started by asking Theresa if she thought people in the East should enjoy the same freedoms as people in the West. Theresa said yes, they should. Then the stranger asked what she thought about the travel restrictions in the East, and if people should be forced to stay there if they didn't want to. Theresa agreed that they shouldn't. Perhaps she didn't agree forcefully enough, because the stranger then produced a small stack of photographs. They were mostly of young people, men and women posing for studio portraits or official documents. The stranger said what they had in common was that they had all been killed trying to cross the inner German border, blown up by landmines or booby-traps, or shot by the guards. Then there were more photographs, grainy, blurred photographs:

bodies left hanging on barbed wire, being dragged out of the water by men in uniform, or simply lying out in the open with the blood spilling out of them. The stranger knew the place and date of every picture; the names and histories of every victim, information he recited without hesitation or emotion until he came to the last picture. This was of a pretty young woman from Leipzig, apparently; a student of medicine and a keen amateur musician. She had been shot through the neck before she even reached the border and had bled to death where she lay. She had been twenty-four years old, the same age as Theresa.

When the stranger was finished with the photographs, he asked if Theresa would be willing to help a few young people get across the border without being killed, if she could do it with very little risk to herself. Theresa had said she was.

'He wanted me to take photographs out of the country, passport photographs. Somebody at the college would contact me and I'd get the prints from them. I'd never come into contact with the escapees. I'd never even know their names, because it was safer that way. All I had to do was take their photographs to the West when I left for the holidays, or for any other reason. He said it was easy to conceal something that small if you knew what you were doing. He showed me some techniques. He said in many ways it was easier for women.'

Theresa visibly tensed at the recollection.

'And these passport photographs, they were for . . .'

'Passports, I would think. What else? West German passports.'

At last I understood: the best and safest way for a citizen of the East to cross the inner German border was to become a citizen of the West, at least temporarily. He would need a day visa too, but that was just a pair of rubber stamps, relatively easy to forge.

'But you'd have to take the passports back again, back here. Did you do that too?'

'No. I don't know how they arranged that. Some other way. I was more useful on the outbound leg and that's all I did. Except once, about a year ago. They gave me a passport to bring in.'

'Why that time?'

'Does it matter?'

'I'm curious.'

Theresa stared at the ground. It was getting a little late to be discreet. 'I think he was important. I recognised him from his picture. Famous people were a priority. They never said that, but it was obvious.'

'And this man was famous?'

'He was an artist.'

Mentally I flipped through my record of significant defections. When it came to the previous autumn only one sprang to mind: that of the sculptor Manfred Dressler, the last People's Hero of Art and Culture, he whose unsanctioned bunk from Yugoslavia had sent shock waves through the local state security apparatus and (incidentally) reduced my own status to that of People's Champion. The thought that Theresa had played a role in the affair made me shudder. I had set out to change her life, but it seemed she had changed mine before we even met.

'What about Wolfgang. Where did he come into it?'

On a stretch of open ground a flock of black-and-white birds had appeared from nowhere, grounded by the gusting wind. Some huddled together, others scurried about in confusion, as if caught out by the early onset of winter. For the first time that day I felt cold.

'Wolfgang was my idea,' Theresa said. 'I proposed him. It was the one time I did that.'

'So you really did meet him in Berlin, at the Pergamon Altar?'

'I didn't lie to you, Bruno.'

I didn't reply. I was running through my memories, trying to work out if that was true.

'I got to know him,' Theresa went on, 'and some of his friends. He told me he planned to leave here one day, if he got the chance, if he could make a name for himself.'

'I would have thought being able to make a name for yourself was a reason to stay.'

'Not for him. He said he knew . . .' Theresa bit her lip.

'Knew what?'

She sighed. 'He said he knew what would happen to him, as a writer, if he stayed. He said he'd end up –'

'Like me?'

'I think he only meant . . .'

'Don't worry.' I shrugged with all the nonchalance I could muster, which, in all likelihood, wasn't much. 'I've always known he wasn't a fan. He made that very plain.'

'But he *was* a fan.'

'You're beginning to sound like his mother.'

'It's true. Why do you think I was reading your book when we met?'

'I assumed it was a coincidence.'

'Because he *gave* it to me. He said I *had* to read it. In fact, he said he found it impossible to have a conversation with anyone who hadn't.' Theresa shook her head. 'Typical Wolfgang.'

I suppose I should have felt flattered. Strangely, I didn't. 'So what happened?'

'I went to my contact here and I asked if we could help him. That's why I had Wolfgang's photographs, Bruno: they were for a passport. He gave them to me the night of the Christmas concert. They were inside a copy of a book.'

I recalled the moment outside the Kulturpalast: the swirling snow, Richter handing something over, the spontaneous embrace.

'What book was it?'

Theresa looked at me. 'You have to ask? The same book you found them in: *your* book. Like I said, Wolfgang was a fan.'

A clammy, distasteful irony occurred me. If I had unwittingly identified Wolfgang Richter as a likely defector, my tip would have turned out to be spot on. I would have given Herr Andrich and Herr Zoch exactly what they were looking for. And they would have been grateful: grateful enough for a truckload of cement, at least.

'I took his photographs home at Christmas,' Theresa said, 'but when I went to hand them over, they told me it was too late. Wolfgang was already dead.'

I felt faint: too many nerves, not enough food. I sat down on a bench. Theresa sat down beside me. I reminded myself that there was still an innocent explanation for what had happened. The evidence of a crime was circumstantial and inconclusive: bureaucratic inconsistencies, administrative corner-cutting, gossip.

'Guilty. You said you felt guilty. Why?' I asked.

'Because at first he wasn't keen. He had something in the works, he said, something he'd written – another screenplay, I suppose. He had high hopes for it, whatever it was.'

'But you persuaded him . . .'

'I told him if he passed up the chance to go now, there might not be another. I was due to leave, you see, and Anton – I mean, my contact – he took a bit of persuading. I don't know why, but they had doubts about Wolfgang. Maybe they thought he was indiscreet.'

The moment Theresa said the word 'Anton', I was reminded of the skinny young man in the bomber jacket who had followed me from the school of music the day I went there hoping for word of Theresa. From his shifty demeanour I had taken him for a secret policeman, but it was he who had delivered her letter, he who had been trusted where the state postal service was not.

'So you pushed Wolfgang into leaving, before he was ready.'

'Yes.'

'But he didn't leave.'

'He never got the chance.'

'Exactly. He never left.'

'So?'

'So there was no harm done, no risks taken. Why should you feel guilty when the plan came to nothing?'

'You haven't heard the rumours, then,' Theresa said. 'Wolfgang was arrested before he . . . before he died.'

'You shouldn't listen to rumours.'

'There were witnesses.'

'To what? Wolfgang getting into a car.'

'So you *have* heard the rumours.'

'Even if they're true, they don't mean anything. If the police knew enough to question him they'd have arrested you too, sooner or later.'

'How do you know that?'

'Because he'd have given you away. Why wouldn't he? You'd only be deported, whereas he . . . For all you know, they might have picked him up for pissing in the street.'

'Is that what you think happened?'

'I don't know what happened. I just don't automatically assume the worst.'

'Except where I'm concerned. Then you do.'

I told her that was nonsense. In the past, I had sensed that she was keeping things back about Wolfgang Richter. It turned out I was correct.

'You're quite the secret agent,' I said, trying to put things on a less confrontational footing.

'I was never that. Anyway, I've quit now.' Theresa's hands gripped the far edge of her suitcase. She looked glum. 'A secret agent keeps her secrets. I've told you mine.'

'You could have told me before.'

'There was no *need* to tell you before.'

'You wouldn't have had to lie.'

'I *didn't* lie, Bruno. I kept quiet. It isn't the same thing. If it were the same thing, you'd be the biggest liar on earth.'

I didn't reply to this. I didn't try to defend myself. I needed to know if Theresa's words arose from momentary anger or something more deep-seated.

'I'm sorry, Bruno,' she said at last. 'That wasn't fair. I know you do what you can. Your book's out there after all, isn't it?'

I took her hand. In the ensuing silence it occurred to me that in describing her covert activities it was possible she wasn't simply dispelling my jealousy. She might also be telling me that if I felt the need to abandon the East, as Manfred Dressler had done, as Wolfgang Richter had planned to, the means were there. And if she had asked me, there and then, to take that step, to come and live with her in the West, openly and without the need for secrets, then I would have said yes. I would have abandoned the safety and familiarity of the shadows and braved the harsh light of a new world, however exposed it might leave me. All I needed was to be sure of my welcome.

Theresa got to her feet. It would soon be getting dark.

'I promised to visit Claudia,' she said. 'If it's all right, I think I'll do that now.'

'You aren't coming back with me?'

'Later. I'll come later.' She dragged me to my feet. In the greying light she looked older: not quite young. 'You'll have to be a little patient with me, Bruno. What with everything that's been going on, I'm not really myself.'

# 43

The rest of Theresa's visit passed in an opiate fog of reassurance and hope. We talked no more about marriage or about our future together. Those issues, we had agreed, could wait a while. In the meantime I would remain in place, working on the sequel to *Survivors*, the book that would establish Eva Aden as a durable presence on the global cultural scene; not a passing sensation, but a writer of intensity and depth. Theresa's mood lightened. She hadn't explicitly accepted my proposal of marriage, but the fact that it was now on the record seemed to make her happy, and this made me happy in turn. At least there was no awkwardness about the matter. I was not obliged to pretend it had never happened, like some embarrassing indiscretion. By the evening of the second day – a Saturday – we were able to joke about it (more accurately, Theresa joked; I laughed obligingly). This reassured me that our eventual union, though still unscheduled, was a likely prospect in both our minds. At certain moments it even took on the tentative aspect of a plan.

I detected no insincerity in Theresa's warmth, no hidden motive. I wanted to believe more than anything that she still loved me. With each hour that passed in her company, each smile, each caress, with the scent of her hair and the taste of her skin (sensual pleasures I had missed more than I knew) my doubts faded. The West grew distant in my mind, its powers of seduction weaker. I worried less about Martin Klaus and about Eva Aden, a being I had glimpsed only in a magazine and on a screen. She was a fiction, after all, an act. Theresa Aden was real and she was here. Nor was she so very different from the girl I had first met a year before.

In my more serene moments, when tipsy and amorous, I was tempted to confess everything. Theresa had made a confession of sorts and I felt an urge to reciprocate. If I was ever to make a clean breast of the Richter affair – by which I mean his authorship of *Survivors* – this was surely a good time to do it. Theresa would have to forgive my deception, since I had already forgiven hers. What held me back was a nagging sense of moral asymmetry. It wasn't that Theresa's deception had involved only silence, as she maintained; for so had mine, technically. The difference lay in motivation.

Theresa's deception was undertaken for what she considered a noble cause. She herself stood to gain nothing. I, on the other hand, had been concerned exclusively with my own interests, specifically Theresa's interest in me. She emerged looking courageous and self-less from her confession; I would emerge looking selfish and cowardly from mine. My love for Theresa herself had inspired this ethical abasement, but was that excuse enough? Were my creative powers irrelevant to her feelings? Would she see me in the same light, knowing that I had not, in fact, written the book that she loved even more than she loved *The Orphans of Neustadt*?

In the end I decided that openness on such questions of character was a luxury I could not yet afford. When Theresa and I were together for good, when the manoeuvrings of our courtship had faded into distant memory, when our love for each other had been cemented in place by shared circumstance and habit, when Wolfgang Richter had been quite forgotten, *that* would be the time. Theresa would know who I was by then, through and through; and no amount of skeletons unearthed would have the power to undermine her confidence in that knowledge.

But for the time being Richter was still with us. Or rather, he was with me, an ever-present fly in the ointment of love – ever-present but not unchanged. He had failed in his pursuit of Theresa; perhaps that was part of it. But there was also the way she had described him. I couldn't help thinking of his mother and father, that sad, devoted couple. Had he planned to abandon them without saying a word? I could picture their bewilderment and despair all too well. Perhaps they had embarrassed him once too often with their dearth of sophistication, their complete absence of style.

Now when I pictured him, it was always as I had seen him outside the Kulturpalast, standing beneath that solitary street light, the snowflakes swirling around us, obscuring my view, catching on my eyelashes. It is how I picture him still. He is handing over a copy of *The Orphans of Neustadt*, inside which lie hidden the photographs he will need to begin a new life. Arrogant it may have been, but the young writer did not think of himself as my rival. He thought of himself as my heir, creatively speaking, as my self-adopted son.

This was what had inspired his attacks on me, his sniping and his satire: I had disappointed him. I was not the hero he had grown up believing me to be (nor even, it seemed, the champion). Courage had given way to convenience, honesty to evasion. According to Michael Schilling, Wolfgang had written *The Valley of Unknowing* because I couldn't or wouldn't; and that was why I'd been afraid of him. He had written what I could have written, but hadn't. He was everything I had been and would never be again. I was the ghost of an artist; he was the flesh and blood – or rather, had been. As luck would have it, it was the ghost who still lived.

These thoughts disturbed my sleep and upset my stomach. During the last night of Theresa's visit the discomfort, shifting and dyspeptic, was such that the anticipated sexual foray had to be abandoned. Only in a foetal position, with my stretched and bloated abdomen released from all tension, did I manage to fall asleep. In the morning, though the pain had receded, my guts felt tender, as if bruised. I drank black tea for breakfast and avoided any sudden movements.

Theresa must have noticed this. As we held each other on the railway station platform, the shriek of whistles and the clatter of doors echoing beneath the great canopy, she placed her hand on the flat of my stomach and said, 'Bruno, you have to do something about that. You have to get it checked out.'

I said it was probably indigestion and nothing at all to worry about.

'You've had trouble down there all the time I've known you. Go to a doctor. Get it seen to, please.'

I said I would, if it made her feel better.

'You never know, Bruno, it might actually be something serious.'

Apart from some conventional words of parting, which I can no longer recall, that was the last thing she said to me.

# 44

The next day I telephoned the clinic in Radeburg that Barbara Jaeger had recommended and asked for an appointment with Dr Engell, her preferred physician. A woman took down my details, including the source of the recommendation, and said she would have to call me back. Several hours later she did so, informing me that Dr Engell would see me at ten o'clock the following morning. She then proceeded to give me very precise directions, as if I were in serious danger of getting lost on the way.

The Radeburg district lay on the other side of the river, close by the southernmost tip of the Heide where, in my dreams, I had attempted to bury Wolfgang Richter's manuscript. It also neighboured Loschwitz, where my would-be protégé had last been seen alive, a fact to which I attached no great significance as I made the journey the next day on a succession of trams, finally getting off, as directed, at the corner of Bautzner Strasse. A few yards behind me stood a large, blank building clad in pale stone, which I recognised as the regional headquarters of the secret police. I wondered if this was where Herr Jaeger worked when he was not away spying somewhere, or if Herr Andrich and Herr Zoch came here to lodge their reports; but the geographical proximity of these various landmarks did not suggest to me a narrative, a chain of events, until later that day.

Angelikastrasse was a quiet street. Nobody passed me as I walked along its well-swept pavements. No cars or trucks trundled past. Large villas in spacious lots stood on either side, partially hidden from each other by stone walls and tall trees. The layout was not so different from Blasewitz, but the houses here were in a much better state of repair. Many of them appeared to be almost new. Even the grounds were neat and tidy, although strangely uniform, as if planted and maintained in concert. For a while the Jaegers had lived in a street not far away, until Barbara had insisted on a more bohemian address in the smartest quarter of the Altstadt. Russians were rumoured to live in this part of the city, KGB men and generals. Looking at the clusters of antennae sprouting from the chimneys, I could believe it.

My instructions told me to turn right at the top of the road and to count the houses on the far side. I soon realised the reason for this precision: there were neither numbers nor names on any of the buildings. If you didn't know where you were going, I supposed, you had no business being there. I knew my destination was not a facility open to the general public. I began to suspect that it was not generally available to rank-and-file Party members either. Otherwise, why would I need an introduction from Barbara Jaeger?

The clinic was easily missed. I walked past it the first time without registering its existence. It was set well back from the road, hidden behind a line of yews and a chain-link fence. A curved driveway led up to the front of the building, which itself lay at an angle to the road, as if anxious to hide its face. A white L-shaped structure, with an exterior of prefabricated concrete panels, it was much bigger than it first appeared, one long wing extending behind. Like the houses round about, it bore no form of identification whatsoever. As I approached the front entrance, still unsure if I was in the right place, I realised that I was being watched. A large and well-groomed Alsatian was chained to a post a few yards away. It sat motionless, staring at me with its tongue out. It was the type of animal kept by policemen and border guards, and when I saw it I thought instantly of Gruna Willy, the old derelict, screaming at me about the death strip as they dragged him away. I was just at the door when a man in a khaki uniform came walking round the corner of the building.

The interior ambience was more recognisably medical. The air was tainted with the smell of antiseptic. The female staff wore nurses' uniforms and the males wore white coats. A sprawling cheese plant squatted in the corner of a small waiting area, where a woman with a voluminous head of white-blonde hair sat reading a magazine. Opposite her dozed an old gentleman with a medal on his lapel. I identified myself to one of two nurses at the front desk and was immediately directed down an adjacent corridor. This was where the resident doctors had their consulting rooms. I counted six of them, proprietorial names displayed on brass plaques outside. Searching for Dr Engell's room, I came across a name that seemed familiar: *Dr V. H. Gatz*. I knew I had seen it before, but I couldn't remember where. I assumed I had consulted him somewhere else, in the distant past.

My consultation with Dr Engell, a small bald man with glasses and watchful grey eyes, was brisk but thorough. I was told to describe my symptoms and then my daily diet in detail – which provoked no reaction except the occasional raised eyebrow. I was then examined wearing nothing but my underpants and my socks, my belly and intestines being poked and prodded until they were sore.

'So what's the matter with me?' I asked, when finally I was given permission to dress.

Dr Engell said it was hard to tell. Peptic ulcer, duodenal ulcer, kidney stones, gallstones, appendicitis; these were just some of the possibilities. And then there was stress.

'Have you experienced an untypical degree of stress recently?' he asked, his pen hovering over his notebook.

I said I had not.

'Stress isn't always obvious, even to those who have it. It creeps up, especially at times of change: marriage, divorce, bereavement, relocation.' The doctor paused. I sensed that 'relocation' was what interested him most. 'Have any of these been . . . on your mind?'

I shrugged and said no.

'Travel plans?'

'None.'

After several seconds of incredulous staring, Dr Engell made a note on his pad. 'I shall need a stool sample,' he said.

'What, now?'

'The nurse will give you a container. Ask at the front desk.'

'I can't *now*,' I said. 'I don't think I have it in me.'

The doctor showed no sign of being amused. 'You can bring it back tomorrow, or whenever you feel able.' He handed me a slip of paper. 'I'm also prescribing this. Tell me if it helps.'

I returned to the waiting area, handed over the prescription to one of the nurses and requested my container, fleetingly wondering if they came in different sizes. The nurse disappeared into a room behind the desk, where I glimpsed rows of shelves piled high with packages and bottles of pills.

A moment later a man in a white coat appeared at my side. He was taller and older than Dr Engell, with tidy grey hair and a long, lined face. A trio of gold fountain pens in his top pocket added further to the general air of rank. At the same time he was sucking a lozenge, which imbued his breath with an incongruous smell of cherry syrup. He slapped down a handful of cardboard folders. 'File these, would you, Frau Pitmann?' he said, his tone imperious and weary.

The other nurse, a pale, middle-aged woman with raven hair and painted eyebrows, rose to her feet. 'Right away, Dr Gatz.'

The man was a stranger, but I knew now where I had seen his name before: V. H. Gatz had signed Wolfgang Richter's 'Preliminary

Report of Death'. V. H. Gatz was the attending clinician. It was he whom Richter's desperate parents had tried time and again to contact, without success; he who had ignored their messages and refused their calls. I had promised to help the Richters, to wrest from the authorities a definitive account of their son's death. They had been counting on me, but so far I had not mustered the courage to turn over that particular stone. My *Eingaben* to the Ministry of Health had never been completed, let alone sent.

Dr Gatz sauntered off. Nurse Pitmann gathered up the files and walked away in the opposite direction, leaving me alone. I watched her disappear round a corner, her rubber soles squeaking on the flecked grey linoleum; and before I could stop myself, before I could think through the consequences or work out a strategy, I had set off after her.

I had only gone a few yards when the squeaking abruptly stopped. Peering round the corner, I caught sight of a shiny bun descending via a staircase to the floor below. This turned out to be a basement, an area lit by strips of neon, which flipped lazily on and off, revealing my surroundings in a drab, slow-motion stroboscope of brightness and shade. The smell down here was not of antiseptic, but of wet cement mingled with disinfectant and sewage. Galvanised pipes ran along the ceiling, emitting a faint trickling sound.

The smell led to the staff lavatories. Nurse Pitmann walked past them and stopped in front of a grey metal door with a glass panel near the top. Edging closer, I watched her push it open and turn on the lights. Inside were rows of filing cabinets reaching halfway to the ceiling. This had to be where the patients' medical records were kept, where, in due course, my records would be kept; where, perhaps, Wolfgang Richter's records were kept still.

The door swung shut. I took a few steps closer. Through the glass panel I could see Nurse Pitmann's head, partially silhouetted against the naked breeze blocks of the far wall. The filing took a long time. I heard heavy metal drawers rolling back and forth, a single impatient sigh. Either the files were not well organised, or Nurse Pitmann was bad at filing. At last the light went out again. I took cover in the nearest lavatory, which turned out to be the women's. This was a mistake. Nurse Pitmann's footsteps came back down the passage, slowed, then stopped. With a rush of panic it came to me that she planned to make use of the facilities before returning to her post.

I dived into one of the cubicles and locked myself in, jumping on to the seat so as to hide my conspicuously unfeminine footwear. Nurse Pitmann was already in the room. Her shadow drifted across the floor. She was sure to have heard me, but had she seen me too? If so, how would she react? What was the established procedure regarding such instances of cross-gender intrusion?

After half a minute of chilling stillness, followed by several further sighs (it was her reflection that displeased her, I suspect), Nurse Pitmann went into the adjoining cubicle and sat down. It was then, as I crouched on the slippery black toilet seat, listening to my neighbour's sibilant and lengthy evacuation, that I hit upon a plan. It was a naive and reckless plan, one better suited to the *Factory Gate Fables* or *Two on a Bicycle* than a work of greater seriousness. I knew if I stopped to think about the risks, I wouldn't go through with it. So, once again, I didn't think. I pondered neither the dangers nor the literary/aesthetic shortcomings. I used the little time available to study the cistern above my head, the type and model, calculating approximate volumes and rates of flow. Could I make sabotage look like a natural systemic failure? Could I cause inconvenience that fell short of disaster?

As soon as Nurse Pitmann had completed her ablutions, I rolled up a sleeve and set to work. There were three lavatories in the room, three cistern lids to lift, three floats to unscrew so that the fill valves no longer fully closed. Fortunately I could make these adjustments with my eyes shut, the mechanisms being of the standard *Kombinat* variety. Less than two minutes later I was on my way up the stairs again.

I arrived back at the waiting area just as the first nurse emerged from the pharmaceutical store behind the desk. She handed me my prescription and a small glass jar with a plastic lid. My heart was beating so fast that I found it difficult to breathe. 'Sign here,' she said.

An hour later I returned wearing blue overalls, a cap and a pair of reading glasses that a myopic sleeping partner had left in my apartment years before and never returned to collect. With me I carried my tools in their heavy metal box and the air of insouciance common to those who clean up messes their supposed betters can't clean up for themselves. By that time, if things had gone to plan, a minor flood should have been in progress in the lower quarters of the building.

Nurse Pitmann was on the telephone at the front desk.

'Someone call a plumber?' I said without waiting for her to finish.

Nurse Pitmann looked confused. Maybe there was no flood. Maybe they had a plumber in house. Or maybe, like citizens generally in the Workers' and Peasants' State, she hadn't expected anyone to turn up for a fortnight.

'It doesn't matter,' she said down the phone. 'Someone's here already.' She replaced the receiver and turned back to me. 'Women's toilets. End of the corridor, down the steps. The janitor just went to shut off the water.'

'Did he now?' I said as I walked away, feigning mild resentment at this lack of respect for professional boundaries.

In the basement the janitor was nowhere to be seen, but someone had been busy. A sign on the door of the women's lavatory read OUT OF ORDER, and a heap of towels and old newspapers had been arranged across the threshold. Even so, a pool of water occupied most of the passage. I went inside and checked the cubicles. All three cisterns were still gently but noisily overflowing, the floor now being completely submerged to a depth of half an inch. I didn't waste time correcting the problem but went straight away to the records room, which was unlocked just as it had been earlier. Rather than turn on the lights, I took a torch from my toolbox and began the search.

It was just as I'd feared: the drawers were not labelled alphabetically. Instead, some opaque system of numerical classification had been deployed. I began with the nearest drawer, pulling out file after file, trying to work out the system, the principle of organisation. It took me a moment to realise that the patients I was looking at were all women. I moved to the next row of cabinets, opened another drawer. Here the files all referred to men. I was getting somewhere. I examined the data more closely, found immediately another connection: all the patients in this drawer were born in the same year: 1949. I pulled out another stack. The order was clearly chronological: the eldest were at the back of the drawer, the youngest at the front. To find Richter's file, all I needed was to know when he'd been born.

But I didn't know. I knew that he was young. I could narrow down the date of his birth to maybe three or four years. But that still meant a lot of searching.

To make matter worse, I dropped the torch. It hit the cement floor with a loud crack and went out. I stooped down to recover it, aware now that something in the audible environment had changed. I held my breath and listened: the noise of dripping water, previously constant, had stopped. The water had been turned off. The janitor had accomplished that task. In which case, where was he now?

I found the torch, batted it against the palm of my hand. The bulb flickered and came back on. At the same moment, as loud and clear as if she were standing beside me, hugging me as she had at the Tolkewitz Crematorium, I heard Frau Richter's voice: *It would have been his birthday next week. His twenty-eighth birthday.*

The funeral had been in early January. It was a simple matter to work out Wolfgang's date of birth to within a few days.

The 1959 files shared a drawer along with the 1957, 1958 and 1960 files. The medical requirements of men in their twenties, it seemed, were few and far between. Even so, the drawer was packed tight and, with the torch now clenched between my jaws, it took time to locate the period I was after. Finally I found what I was looking for, written in fountain pen along the vertical tab: *Richter, W. F.*

I was about to open the file when I heard footsteps splashing along the corridor. They were coming closer. I switched off the torch and hurried to the door. Through the glass panel I caught sight of a burly man in overalls carrying a bucket and a mop. Muttering to himself, he set down the bucket and got to work. There was nothing I could do, no alternative way out. I was a prisoner among the filing cabinets until he was done.

I slipped Richter's file into my toolbox and crouched down in the darkness to wait. No sooner was I down on my haunches when I heard someone else outside, their approach marked by the familiar rubbery footfalls of institutional footwear. Again I peered out through the glass. Nurse Pitmann, alternately silhouetted and starkly lit, was making her way gingerly down the swampy corridor. I hoped she had come to check on the progress of the clean-up, but then I saw what she was carrying under her matronly arm: *another stack of files.*

I was certain to be discovered. Frantically I tried to think of an excuse, an explanation for my presence in a room full of confidential records. Nothing sprang to mind. But then it was suddenly clear to me what I had to do. With an agility that surprises me even now, I raised myself towards the ceiling, planting my feet on the handles of the filing cabinets on either side of me. I reached up and with a single motion yanked the fuse out of the neon light fitting. All this must have made some noise, but I suppose the janitor's mopping and splashing made even more. I jumped down again and scurried into the far corner just as the door opened.

Nurse Pitmann threw the light switch. Nothing happened. She repeated the action twice more, with the same result.

'Unbelievable,' she said under her breath.

I heard her footsteps squeak and splash down the corridor.

'The bulb in there's gone again,' she said. 'We'll need a new one right away.'

'Can't it wait?' the janitor said.

'No, it can't.'

The janitor squeezed out his mop and walked away towards the stairs. I got up and crept back to the door, just in time to see Nurse Pitmann disappear into the men's lavatory. Whatever the reason for such an early return visit, it gave me my one chance to make a clean getaway. I didn't need a second.

# 45

The journey back to Blasewitz was a journey across a city I no longer knew and where I did not belong. After my escape from the clinic, when finally the building disappeared from view round the corner of Angelikastrasse, I had experienced a moment of elation – relief, mixed with pleasure at my own decisiveness and guile – but that moment had been all too brief. By the time I was standing at the tram stop, standing in plain view of Stasi regional head-quarters, its rows of blank windows like a blind man's eyes, I was in the grip of different emotions. I had committed a criminal act. I was now a renegade, a saboteur. My actions were that of a man who had changed sides. But fear of detection was only part of it. I was afraid of what I was about to discover, afraid of the slender file concealed in my toolbox. That file would answer questions I had spent a year trying not to ask. (A year? Or was it much longer than that?) I climbed aboard a tram, stared through the cloudy windows at streets and skylines that were simultaneously familiar and strange, homely and hostile. I searched for reassurance in the faces of passengers and passers-by. Their expressions revealed nothing but a determination to keep their thoughts to themselves. And it came to me then, their very silence told me, that they all knew the answers to my questions. They had known them all along.

I was sure police officers couldn't be waiting for me at my apart-ment, not yet. Whatever detective powers had been brought to bear on the mystery of the unidentified plumber, they were unlikely to have produced results in under forty minutes. Even so, the sweat was trickling down my face as I turned the final corner. What if the file was snatched away from me before I had a chance to read it? I might be forced to spend the rest of my life in a state of suspense, able neither to begin a new life, nor return to my old one. Nor, I might add, did the prospect of imprisonment hold any kind of appeal.

In the event I found the street empty. The schoolchildren were playing outside, filling the air with their innocent screams, but otherwise everything seemed normal. Slowly I climbed the stairs to my apartment – slowly, because I was still unprepared for the possible verdict of *guilty* that awaited me upon arrival. When at last I turned my key in the lock, a voice in my head told me to stop what I was doing before it was too late, to destroy the file instead of reading it. My old life could still be salvaged. Nothing had to change. The years of waiting might still be rewarded. It was like the voices in my dreams that said *stay where you are*; only this time I wasn't going to listen. There was another voice now, Richter's voice, my literary son and heir. I couldn't bring myself to ignore it any longer.

I gulped down a glass of water and went to sit down in my leather armchair. Less than a year had gone by since I first read Richter's untitled manuscript – read it sitting in that same chair, opposite that same window with that same rooftop view – but recalling the occasion now was like recalling an event from adolescence. I couldn't disown the individual who had sat in that chair, but neither could I be proud of him. The Bruno Krug I saw was the one Wolfgang Richter saw, and probably many others besides. I didn't want to be in his company for longer than necessary.

I turned away from the armchair and sat down instead at the dining table. I opened the toolbox. I took out the file. I allowed myself two deep breaths, then opened it.

The file held just one sheet: a form, printed on thin white paper. At the top were the words: *PATIENT ADMISSION (Emergencies)*. Underneath were sections for name, date of birth, identification number, time of admission, the name of the attending physician and other administrative details. These had all been filled in by hand. The blood group was stated as O. Finally I saw a number of tick boxes relating to medical conditions that, I assumed, might affect the range of possible treatment: allergy to penicillin, morphine and cortisone, haemophilia, asthma, hepatitis. All of these were blank, but for a smear of blue ink across the bottom of the page.

I turned the form over. The back too was blank. Nothing more had been written, not so much as a line about the patient's actual condition. Richter's file was a non-file. It recorded his arrival at the clinic – at 4.14 a.m. on a Saturday in December – but nothing more, as if the clinic were a cemetery, a final resting place from which new arrivals were not expected to progress. I saw then that I had been naive. Richter's death had been unusual and unexpected. There had been a risk of contagion, allegedly, perhaps of an epidemic. If that were true, the proper medical records were most likely under study at the Ministry of Health – either that, or they were still in the basement of the clinic, still in that same drawer, where I, in my haste, had failed to notice them.

I stared at the form, at Dr Gatz's handwriting (tidy but blot-prone on account of the inferior grade of paper), and something struck me as peculiar. Near the top left-hand corner was a paper clip, one easily large and robust enough to hold twenty sheets of paper. But it was holding only one. One sheet of paper does not need a paper clip. It is in no danger of becoming detached from itself. At one point there had to have been at least one other page, perhaps several. But they had been removed, the top sheet retained perhaps out of respect for bureaucratic tidiness.

My stomach began a slow-motion capsize. I turned the form over again. In several places the ink from Dr Gatz's fountain pen had seeped all the way through. Letters and traces of words appeared in mirror-image, slanting backwards. Here again, something wasn't right. I flipped the paper over and back again, to make sure I wasn't deceiving myself. But I was not mistaken: the mirror images of Dr Gatz's writing outnumbered the originals. The explanation was instantly clear: ink from a second sheet of paper had leached into the one on top.

Examination with a magnifying glass revealed that there had been several lines of writing. Full stops, commas and dotted 'i's came through clearly. But as far as the words were concerned, I could make out next to nothing. Only one fragment held out a promise of meaning, but no matter how long I stared at it, that meaning eluded me:

*Fr  t r de li k  Schlä  nl p  ns,*

I needed more light. I needed a reflection.

I went into the bathroom and stood before the mirror, holding the form in one hand and the magnifying glass in the other. Somewhere in the building water was emptying from a sink, temporary airlocks popping and belching as the pressure slowly re-equalised in the system. As if approaching through a mist, the letters became words and the words a phrase:

*Fraktur des linken Schläfenlappens,*

which roughly translates into English as: *Fracture to the left temporal lobe.*

The words pulsed before my eyes, black on white, white on black. Then my vision clouded over and I vomited into the sink.

# 46

This was not the easiest time. I prefer, if I am truthful, not to discuss it. In any case my recollection is unclear. I stayed a while in the bathroom. I'm not sure how long. At some point I wandered into the sitting room, the familiarity of which brought me the opposite of comfort (something like revulsion). Again, I cannot say why. I went to the window and looked out over the city, at the low rolling sky, at the ragged clouds, indistinguishable from smoke, at the children in the playground, obscured behind a veil of leafless trees. I must have stood for some time, because it was almost dark when I turned away and the children had gone. I cannot report on my thoughts. I am not sure if thought was what went through my head in any case. I saw pictures and heard voices, some from the past, others from a past that might have been (if I had done things differently, if only I had known), others from a future that was now lost and could never be recovered. Their effect was like – if it was *like* anything, if metaphorical treatment is what the occasion requires – it was like music, except that music has the power to soothe and purify; and these visions did neither. I did not eat. That much I can say. I had no appetite, and no pain either, of the physical sort. I was, I suppose, simply waiting: waiting for that state of being to pass, waiting to feel something – anything – other than what I did feel. Because sooner or later I would feel something else. It is in the prosaic nature of life that it continues to demand maintenance, attention to physical necessities, the endless rekindling of purpose. In the West this blessing, or this burden, is called simply 'carrying on'. And, much like the Workers' and Peasants' State, there is very little hope of escaping it, this side of death.

In my case what rescued me, the lifeline that I clung to, was anger: anger that burned with a righteous heat and grew with each passing hour. Such is the utility of outrages and atrocities for those who survive them: they simplify matters. Moral ambiguities, paralysing complexity, divided loyalties, all of them are swept away. My anger left me clear about what to do next, which was no less than what Richter had always wanted me to do (the Richter of my thoughts and dreams, and the occasional fleeting vision): I had to speak out. What had *really* become of Sonja and Thomas, the hopeful young lovers in *The Orphans of Neustadt*? What had become of us all, who had put our faith in that dream of a better world, a world of justice and common purpose? Richter had been waiting for me to answer that question all his life and half of mine.

But I could do nothing where I was, there in the suffocating bosom of the Workers' and Peasants' State. To speak out there would have been suicidal and impracticable, there being no means to disseminate my words. First I had to leave, to brave the death strip, to vault the inner German border, and the sooner the better. Every day of silence would be another day of falsehood, another drop of poison.

Theresa was still in East Berlin. My first thought was to go to her and beg her to set the fugitive wheels in motion (phone calls and letters were out of the question). Her network had helped Manfred Dressler; they had agreed to help Wolfgang Richter. Surely they would help me. But Theresa had said she was done with the artist smuggling business and besides, if we talked it over beforehand the matter was sure to become entangled with the issue of our future together. She might think I was trying to force her hand, to crush her doubts beneath a weight of obligation: changing my life, leaving everything I knew, just for her. In short, I was afraid that to escape such an obligation she might decide to leave me once and for all.

No, I would not go cap in hand to Theresa. I would approach the network myself, on my own behalf. I knew the name of her contact. His name was Anton. All I had to do was find him.

# 47

I went up to the college of music the very next day, in time for the start of morning classes. I didn't see the young man in the bomber jacket, nor anyone else I recognised. The next day I returned, carrying a stack of books under my arm so as to appear professorial. I paced up and down the corridors, attracting occasional nods of recognition from pupils and staff, but with nothing to show for it. If Anton was a student it was possible he had graduated by this time and left. Nevertheless I decided to widen my search before giving up. I began to patrol a number of student haunts: a scruffy cellar bar on the corner of Pillnitzer Strasse, a hall of residence near the medical school in Johannstadt, a café on Seitenstrasse that Theresa had always liked, though it was a good twenty-minute walk from her apartment. On my second visit to the cellar bar – it was a dank and drizzling Friday night – I ran into Claudia Witt.

She was sitting at a corner table with three friends, two female, one male, none of whom I knew. A celebration was under way, judging from the accumulation of glasses, bottles and cigarette ends on the table. Claudia's hair was messier and more voluminous than at our last encounter, and she had acquired a pair of large looped earrings that visibly weighed on her lobes.

'Well, if it isn't the orphan of Neustadt,' she said when she saw me. 'What are you doing here?'

The bar was crowded and noisy. I elbowed my way over.

'Whose birthday is it?' I asked.

One of the females in the party pointed an unsteady finger at Claudia and shouted, 'Guilty!'

The party, it seemed, was well under way.

'Happy birthday,' I said and went to fetch a round of drinks.

Upon my return Claudia grudgingly introduced me. Her female friends did not react to my name, but the young man seemed to know who I was. A plump individual with thinning hair and gold-rimmed spectacles – Johann or Johannes or Jürgen – he stared, then stumbled to his feet and offered me his chair. I declined it and pulled up my own.

Not wishing to seem too eager, I asked Claudia a series of avuncular questions concerning her plans for the future. In tones heavy with forbearance she described how she was training to become a music teacher and filling in as a cleaner at the main city hospital.

'But you're still playing in the meantime? Keeping your hand in?'

She said something about forming an ensemble with some other music graduates, who were likewise short of employment. I made encouraging noises and said I would certainly be in the audience whenever her plan bore fruit. After the conversation had meandered through a melancholy discussion of career opportunities generally, I leaned closer and asked Claudia if she could help me.

'I wanted to look up a friend of Theresa's, but I don't know how to find him. His name's Anton.'

Claudia shrugged. 'I've no idea who that is.'

'Are you sure?'

'Unless you mean spotty Arnold. I wouldn't call him a friend.'

'Who's that?' one of the other girls asked.

'Arnold Seybert. Campus secretary of the Free German Youth.'

The girl wrinkled her nose. 'Oh, him.'

'Otherwise known as Arni Sebum.'

'The name was definitely Anton,' I said.

At that, Johann or Johannes or Jürgen looked up at me and then, just as tellingly, looked away again.

'I don't know anyone called Anton,' Claudia said. 'What do you want him for?'

Johann or Johannes or Jürgen had turned away from us. He was stroking his chin and pretending to be interested in the street outside. He knew who Anton was, I felt sure. Maybe they all did.

'I've got some photographs for him,' I said. Not wanting to explain further, I got to my feet. 'If something comes to you, Claudia, could you give me a call? I'd really appreciate it.'

I told her my phone number twice, slowly and clearly.

Claudia and her girlfriends looked at me as if I were crazy. By contrast, Johann or Johannes or Jürgen hardly looked at me at all. When I looked back over my shoulder, I saw his lips twitching, as if he were committing something to memory.

A week went by and nothing happened. I continued my searching, but Anton was nowhere to be found. I grew impatient. The decision had been made. The path was now clear, but I was unable to take the first step. Had Anton really left? Was I looking for him in the wrong places? Or was he – the most troubling explanation – eluding me on purpose? According to Theresa, he had been reluctant to help Wolfgang Richter with his escape because he hadn't trusted him. Maybe he didn't trust me either. And why should he, given my ambiguous history? Perhaps the chances were too great that I was the bait in a trap, a covert servant of the secret police, acting under direction. If that was Anton's thinking, I would have to find my own way across the death strip, because he was not going to help me, not even with Theresa pleading my case.

Had I been weighed and found wanting? With each passing day it seemed more likely. I began to resent this Anton, whoever he was, for refusing to manifest himself in my presence, for forcing me to live in limbo, my heart and ambition in one place, my flesh and bones in another. I didn't deserve to be shut out of the West, any more than I deserved to be shut in the East – and I *was* shut in. Every day the valley, which is to say my whole world, felt smaller and more confined. I swear that at times I found it physically difficult to draw breath. I paced the city perimeter in those darkening days, not for relaxation or inspiration, but like a caged animal hungry for the wild. I slept badly or not at all. Gruna Willy's prophecy (for so it now seemed) was coming true. The death strip *was* all around me, slowly contracting like a barbed-wire noose.

Then early one morning I found a small brown parcel waiting for me in my letter box. There were no stamps on the front, only my name and address. These had been written in a childish hand, the letters circular, the 'i's dotted with swirls. Round the address a square had been drawn, the perimeter decorated with a succession of semicircles, like the edge of a pelmet or a bedspread. In each of the four corners a flower had been drawn in red ballpoint. It was unmistakably a gift from a juvenile relative, a niece or a very young nephew; except that I had neither. I must have stood for a minute or more with that parcel in my hand, wondering if I was not in fact dreaming, and waiting for the realisation to wake me.

Inside the parcel I discovered a book, an old edition of a novel I knew well: *The Orphans of Neustadt* by Bruno Krug. In my sleep-deprived state this did not strike me as strange. Given the nature of my mission, in fact, it seemed quite natural. A glance inside the front cover revealed that this particular copy was the property of the Johannstadt District Library and was due back in two weeks' time. Attached with masking tape to the inside cover, just to the right of the reinforced jacket flap, was a small note. It read:

**Your photograph here**
**(35mm x 45mm)**

**Happy Christmas**
**Anton**

# 48

Unfortunately for me, the coin-operated photographic booth, a commonplace facility in Western railway stations and shopping malls, had yet to arrive in the Workers' and Peasants' State. Citizens had their official photographs taken in studios by state-licensed photographers, whose task routinely included seeing to their subjects' hair, dress and facial blemishes, as well as to lighting and composition. Days later, names and addresses duly recorded (and shared, so it was rumoured, with the police), the resulting prints would be ready for collection, prints in which every citizen was rendered wholesome: sober, tidy, bright-eyed, spotless morally and dermatologically, in accordance with Party ideals. This was in marked contrast to common practice in the West, where citizens procured their own pictures and where an outsider might be forgiven for thinking passports were granted only to vagrants, idiots or carriers of the plague – doubtless as a prelude to exporting them on a permanent basis. The contrast might have provided a shred of ideological comfort to the Actually Existing Socialists who guided our ship of state, but it was of no use to me. I needed convincing passport photographs quickly and, above all, discreetly. But where could I get them? I did not have access to a darkroom. I did not know a reliable photographer. Even if I took the pictures myself – a considerable technical challenge – I might have to wait weeks for the resulting images, which I felt sure would end up being the wrong size. What I needed was Anton's guidance, but Anton, for the time being, was little better than a name.

I owned an expensive camera, a largely symbolic purchase made twenty years earlier in the afterglow of my one literary triumph, but I had used it less and less over the years. A brief wave of enthusiasm for urban landscapes had given way to a sporadic flirtation with portraiture and a more enduring (largely prurient) interest in the female nude. Now I took down my boxes and my albums and scrambled through them in search of my own image, my progress dogged by the knowledge that I would soon have to abandon this record of my past, mute and patchy as it was, for ever. Though I was in a hurry, I couldn't stop myself from pausing now and then to reflect on the image of a friend or a lover, people whose names

I could recall only with difficulty, or not at all. How young they all seemed and how different. It struck me as a waste, an emotional inefficiency, that I had squandered so much of my life among people who were destined to become strangers: people to whom I had no ultimate significance, and who were ultimately insignificant to me. Had anything worthwhile come of those ephemeral affairs, those temporary bonds? Had the experience, most of it forgotten, been valuable? Should I have been more productive, more probing in my choice of companions? Should I have been more concerned about the long term? Then I found some pictures of myself, twenty-five years younger, and it struck me that I was just another of those strangers in the frame (with their abundant hair, narrow hips, angular jaws). I knew almost as little about him, the young Bruno Krug, as he knew about me. Our connection was one of common ancestry and not much more than that.

The boxes yielded nothing usable, the albums a solitary self-portrait: Krug, mid-thirties, leaning against a white wall, arms folded, still discernibly pleased with himself, despite the descent into creative timidity, by then already well under way. I cut the photograph from the page and held it up to the mirror so that I could compare it with my own reflection. After an uncomfortable minute or so, I was forced to acknowledge that there was no real resemblance at all.

I decided I would have to take my own photograph after all and was on the way to buy film when I hit on a better plan: my publishers kept authorial pictures. I had been photographed on several occasions, the last about seven or eight years earlier. In the shot used most frequently I was pictured with the fingers of one hand curled thoughtfully under my chin – no good at all for a passport – but I recalled adopting other, less pretentious poses during that sweaty half-hour under lights. With any luck, those pictures would still be in the file.

I changed course and went straight to Ferdinandsplatz. I found Michael Schilling alone in his office, staring out of the window. We hadn't seen each other for months, but his expression upon seeing me was not one of surprise or pleasure, but of confusion, as if I had just stepped out of his thoughts, as Wolfgang Richter was apt to step out of mine.

'Sorry to show up unannounced,' I said, closing the door behind me. 'I hope you're not busy.'

Absently Schilling surveyed his desk, presumably to see if he was busy or not. (It was piled high with papers, messier and more over-crowded than usual.) Then, with a shake of the head, he was back to his old self.

'Not at all, not at all,' he said, getting to his feet. 'Pull up a chair. How have you been, Bruno? How's the work going?'

To these rhetorical questions I responded with equally rhetorical replies. We both sat down again. Schilling laced his fingers together and smiled at me jovially, the intention, no doubt, being to reassure me that all was well; the effect being exactly the opposite. Schilling had never been a jovial man.

I came straight to the point: I needed my photographs. Were they still on the premises?

'I expect so,' Schilling said. 'Technically they belong to the company. We'd have to have them back.'

'Not a problem,' I said.

'What's the occasion? Why the sudden attack of vanity?' Schilling frowned. 'You look awful, by the way. Have you been ill?'

'It's for a present,' I said, ignoring the observation. 'I promised my girlfriend. Her birthday's coming up and I forgot about it. You know how women are with these things. One little oversight and it's as if you don't care.'

'I thought you didn't like our pictures. You said they made you look . . .'

'Pretentious. I know. But it doesn't matter. I just need a mugshot for her purse. Can we take a look?'

Schilling was looking at me, lips pursed. 'Bruno, what's going on? What do you really want the pictures for?'

I'm not sure why, but faced with this simple question, my powers of deception, like my powers of narrative invention, evaporated. Self-camouflage, instinctive to the point of second nature, was suddenly beyond me. Perhaps at the back of my mind was the thought that this might be the last time Schilling and I ever saw each other, that we were destined to join the ranks of barely identifiable strangers in each other's yellowing albums. How sad, how hopeless it would be to conclude twenty years of friendship with a lie.

'Michael, I'm leaving.'

An awful stillness came over him, presaging, I felt sure, an outburst of some kind. But when the stillness was over, all Schilling did was nod to himself, as if my abandoning the valley was some-thing he had long anticipated. Not for the first time I had the sensation of living down to expectations.

'When?'

'I'm not sure. Some time around Christmas, I think.'

'It's all arranged?'

'It will be.'

'You do know what you're doing? You're not just heading for the border with forged papers?'

'I expect the papers will be genuine, except for the photograph.'

'Your photograph?' Schilling frowned. 'Aren't you afraid you'll be recognised?'

'No one recognises me any more, Michael. Twenty years of mediocrity turns out to have compensations.'

Schilling folded his arms. He'd worked on the *Factory Gate Fables* too. I tended to forget that.

'So,' he said. 'Are you going to tell me why?'

'My reasons are the same as everyone's. I make no claims to originality.'

'Why *now*?'

This question was harder. I could have explained the business with Richter, my suspicions regarding his death – suspicions Schilling had once shared – that I would not be silent or complicit in the murder of a fellow artist, that I needed to leave in order to tell the world what had happened. But when the moment came I said none of this. It wasn't that I didn't trust my friend. Nor was I concerned to shield him from knowledge that might bring him harm. The fact is I didn't think he would believe me.

'It's Theresa. I thought she might come and settle here with me. But that isn't going to happen. So I've no choice but to settle over there.'

'You two . . . it's really that serious?'

I shrugged. 'You know how it is.'

Schilling's expression betrayed neither affirmation nor denial. Yes, he knew how it was; and he knew how it ended too.

'So, when you're over there,' he said, 'are you going to tell everyone the truth?'

'About what?'

'About Wolfgang's book.'

'Of course.'

'That your girlfriend didn't write it?'

'Why not? What'd be the point of keeping up the pretence?'

Schilling shrugged. 'I'm not sure why you pretended in the first place. You said something about protecting everybody, making sure they didn't get into trouble.'

I'd forgotten about that.

'It'll be different once I'm on the other side. I'll tell everyone that Richter gave his manuscript to me. No one else was involved.'

'So not the *whole* truth, then?'

'Almost the whole truth.'

'What about Richter's parents? They could suffer too.'

I hadn't considered this. I hadn't considered anything very much. I just knew I had to get out and that this might be my only chance.

'I'm sure they'd want their son to get the recognition he deserves, even posthumously, whatever the cost. They were very proud of him. He meant the world to them.'

Schilling's bespectacled eyes remained fixed on me for a moment, then he pushed back from the desk. 'I expect you're right. I'd probably feel the same way. Still . . .'

'Still?'

'Are you sure she'll go along with it?'

'Who?'

'Your girlfriend, Eva.'

'Theresa. Eva's a nom de plume.'

'Was that your idea?'

'I can't remember.'

'And she's happy for you to spoil the party?'

'It's not a party, Michael. It's been an exercise in literary preservation, necessarily disguised.'

'You've told her. She knows what you're planning?'

'In principle.'

'What about in practice?'

'She will soon. Very soon.'

'And she'll be happy to bow out?'

'More than happy. You've got it all wrong, Michael. She was doing it all for me, not for herself.'

Said out loud, this contention sounded somehow less convincing.

Schilling sucked his greying incisors. Magdalena, his one great love, had betrayed and abandoned him. The experience had made him cynical.

'Anyway, there's not much she could do to stop me, is there?' I said. 'Even if she wanted to.'

At that moment the telephone rang. Schilling picked up, promised someone he'd call back in ten minutes, then hung up again. Looking back, I suppose the ensuing pause was the ideal moment to express our feelings at what was almost certain to be a final parting, to set down for the record what it meant to us and what we had meant to each other. I suppose I owed him that. But all I could think of was getting my photograph to Anton. Only when that was done could my life begin again.

'All right, Bruno,' Schilling said, finally. 'Let's see what we've got, shall we?'

In an annexe to the main office, where several people were at work, was a storage room, home to a meagre stock of stationery, a pair of overcrowded bookshelves and various items of redundant office equipment. A filing cabinet stood in the far corner. The top drawer sported a torn label that read: AUTHORS A – .

Schilling opened the drawer beneath it. 'Should be in here somewhere.'

I stood watching while his bony fingers riffled through the contents. I knew what he must be thinking: that I had planned to go without saying goodbye, that I was only here, now, because I needed a favour. I wanted to explain myself further, to offer some appropriate valedictory sentiments, but we were in too much danger of being overheard. I was relieved when he pulled out a fat file with the word KRUG on the flap.

Among the papers were contact prints, negatives and enlargements in various shapes and sizes. In all of them I appeared unnaturally fit and virile, which was not what I thought at the time they were taken. But none of that mattered now.

'What are you looking for exactly?' Schilling asked.

From the main office came a regular tap-tap-tap of inexpert typing.

'White background, full face, thirty-five by forty-five millimetres.'

Schilling turned to one of the bookshelves and extracted a volume. 'Something like this?'

It was an English paperback edition of *The Orphans of Neustadt*, a recent one, judging from the deconstructionist artwork and the *Modern Classics* label. On the back cover there was not one photograph of me, but three, arranged as on a roll of thirty-five-millimetre film, complete with sprocket holes and frame numbers down the sides. In keeping with the no-frills design, the chosen images had me staring at the camera, my face registering a numbness normally characteristic of the recently arrested.

'These are perfect,' I said.

'You look younger. Not so grey for one thing.'

'So? I could say I dyed my hair. People do. Have you another copy?'

'That's the only one they sent.'

'I guess I need a sharp knife.'

'I keep a scalpel in my office, for cut-and-paste purposes.'

We went back there and closed the door behind us. Schilling cleared a space on his desk and we got busy surgically extracting my image from the back of the British edition. In the end I let my friend use the blade. When I rested the scalpel against the metal ruler, it made a faint rattling sound, like a tiny telegraph machine. I couldn't afford a slip.

Schilling worked in silence. I had never thought of him as remotely dextrous, but hunched over the book, the desk lamp pulled down low, each of his blue eyes enormous behind its Cyclopean lens, he resembled a watchmaker, the intricacy of his craft commanding absolute concentration. Had he laboured over my texts, and the texts of others, with the same heroic attention? Of course he had. And the excitement he exhibited at each new literary discovery, Richter's being one, the way it electrified him; it moved me to be reminded of it. Nobody else in my experience was capable of such unselfish devotion to the written word. Was love too strong a term for it? If so, it was the purest kind of love, unacknowledged and unrequited. This, I saw, was the reason I felt so disloyal: my sudden departure was the embodiment, the epitome of that tragic asymmetry.

Four cuts made a rectangle around the uppermost of my three disconsolate visages. Schilling placed a finger inside the book's back cover and prepared to ease the picture free.

'Listen, Michael,' I said, 'why don't you come with me?'

Schilling didn't look at me, but my image remained in place.

'Are you serious?'

'If I can arrange it. And I think I can. You're my editor. We're a team.'

'Don't these things cost money?'

'Not this time. Anyway, I've got money. It's all waiting for me on the other side.'

'Western money?' Schilling looked up at that point. 'How come?'

'From the book, of course,' I whispered. 'Richter's book. You wouldn't believe how much.'

'You mean, *she* has the money. Your girlfriend. Are you sure that's the same thing?'

'I told you, Michael: we have an agreement. She'll do what she's told. So, what do you say? Are you going to come with me?'

Schilling went back to work, pushing at the back of my picture with his thumb. The cardboard buckled but refused to separate.

'I can't.'

'Why? What's keeping you here?'

'You have to ask? My son.'

'Paul? You know, I think he'd understand. In fact, he'd probably urge you to go while you can. It doesn't sound like he's exactly an enthusiast for the system.'

Schilling shook his head. 'You don't know what you're talking about.'

'Well, why don't you ask him? Let him speak for himself. You might be surprised.' Hearing no response to this suggestion, I pressed home my advantage, in the process casting sincerity to the winds. 'You know, Michael, maybe you've underestimated him. Maybe Paul's got more maturity than you give him credit for. People can change.' I put my elbows on the desk and leaned closer. 'We'd probably cross the border in Berlin. You could arrange to meet him there before-hand. You wouldn't have to leave without saying goodbye.'

Schilling was staring at the book in front of him. After a moment of stillness he deliberately picked up the scalpel and sliced off the back cover. I supposed it was easier to work that way.

'Bruno, I want you to understand something.' I feared I'd gone too far in my efforts to persuade him, but Schilling wasn't angry. His voice was calm. 'I know Paul has his problems, but he's every-thing to me. I loved him from the moment he was born and I'm certain I'll never love anyone that much again. If you had children – and maybe you will some day – you would understand that; you would understand that there's nothing you wouldn't do to protect them.' Once again my image found itself sandwiched between Schill-ing's finger and thumb. 'What you're asking me to do is abandon my son; and that's the last thing I could ever do.'

The subject of child abandonment had always been a difficult one for me. I couldn't hear it mentioned without a conflict of emotions erupting inside me. These feelings had been at their most intense when I was a child, but even forty years later, when the hope of seeing my mother again had dwindled to the status of a pipedream, I still felt the tug of war within. I wanted to believe that I had not been abandoned (even by a young widow traumatised by grief and the privations of war); but I also wanted to believe that my mother was still alive and might one day return. These two hopes were, of course, incompatible: if my mother had never planned to abandon me, I had to assume she had died somewhere in the ruins of the city, at the hands of soldiers or looters or boys with guns; if she had abandoned me out of choice, it meant there was no point in seeking a reunion, because, put in simple, childish terms, she didn't love me and wouldn't want me back in any case.

At my uncle's house in Halle, and at the orphanage, I kept these equally unwelcome possibilities at bay by inventing others: my mother had been kidnapped (that was a favourite, one that served as the basis for a wealth of variations); my mother had been struck down with amnesia; my mother had been hit on the head by a piece of falling masonry and lay in a coma for many months. That I was later drawn to storytelling of the formal, literary variety, I trace back to those endless imaginings; but with time they had lost their power, their credibility eroding gradually, the way fairy tales do.

All this is to explain why I didn't argue further. I resented the way Schilling evoked the sacred bonds of parenthood, as if the subject meant nothing at all to me. Besides, his son was a grown man, demonstrably quite beyond the range of his father's power or protection. No, Schilling's declaration was a proxy, I realised, a barbed metaphor: I was supposed to feel about leaving my friends in the East the way he would feel about abandoning his son.

Schilling pushed my photograph across the desk. 'Will that do?'

The quality of the image was, if anything, a little too good, the contrast strong, the definition sharp.

'It'll have to.' I tucked it inside my wallet. 'Better let me have the other two, just in case.'

Schilling picked up the scalpel again. Silence resumed, a bleak, manly void that I knew should be filled with words. But I could think of none – none that wouldn't sound flimsy and false. Emotional improvisation was not my strong point. I expect Schilling felt the same way. The written word was his medium, just as it was mine, the empty page his natural intimate.

'Of course you could just emigrate,' he said out of the blue.

'Emigrate?'

'Yes. Put in a formal request, through the Foreign Ministry. You're famous enough. They'd probably let you go.'

'What if they didn't? I'd have only drawn attention to myself, in the worst way possible. I'd *never* get out then. Besides . . .'

Besides what? I might have confessed, but didn't, that I had become attached to the idea of an unannounced departure, of slipping away under an assumed name, leaving others to make sense of my disappearance. It was in keeping with the spirit of the venture: risky but bold. It was what Wolfgang Richter had planned for himself. Theresa would appreciate that, even if nobody else did. She would make the connection.

'Besides?'

'I don't think I can wait any longer. I told you, I'm in love.'

Schilling peered at me over his spectacles. 'Yes, you must be. Only love could turn you into a fool.' I thought he was joking, but I waited in vain for a smile. 'My advice remains the same: don't go, not like this. It's a risk you don't have to take.'

The other two pictures were ready. I got to my feet and offered Schilling my hand. 'We'll talk again,' I said. 'There'll be time enough yet.'

As it turned out, there wasn't.

# 49

Instructions were superfluous. I knew what Anton wanted me to do. My photograph was to be concealed inside the jacket flap of the book he had sent me (*The Orphans of Neustadt*, my means of salvation, now as before). The book was then to be taken back to the Johannstadt District Library, I assumed before the due date of return. Less clear was what happened after that. Would Anton be at the library to meet me? Would I have to wait to be contacted? If so, for how long? A week? A month? A year? All the while Theresa was in Berlin, oblivious to my plans – plans I had no way of safely sharing with her.

Concealing the photographs was easy. The sticky tape securing the jacket flap had come away near the bottom. It was a simple matter to slip the pictures inside (I used two, keeping one back for emergencies) and reseal the gap. This task completed, I rode the tram to Johannstadt, only to find the library shut. I returned the next morning and joined a queue of people handing in their books at the front desk. I lingered a while among the book stacks to see what became of mine, expecting it would swiftly and silently disappear, finding its way to Anton via secret means. I was wrong. Like all the other itinerant literature, it was logged in by means of an index card and placed on a trolley. Half an hour later an adenoidal young woman with a pudding-basin haircut began wheeling the trolley around the shelves, replacing books one at a time. I watched her from a distance, but nothing out of the ordinary happened. *The Orphans of Neustadt* was duly returned to Fiction J–L, where it nestled between an older, more battered edition and a novel by Siegfried Lenz.

Spy fiction, a staple of Western literature, was almost unknown inside the Workers' and Peasants' State. This explains my unfamiliarity with the world of covert operations. Had I been exposed to a wider range of popular fiction, I might have understood that the Fiction J–L section of the Johannstadt public library was serving on this occasion as a 'dead letter box', one of the principal requirements of a dead letter box being that it should attract as little attention as possible. As it was, I couldn't help feeling the whole library procedure was lackadaisical. My book, with its precious and incriminating cargo, could now be taken out by anyone. They might borrow it for six weeks, or even longer. What if they found the photographs? What if they recognised my face? What would happen then?

To forestall this alarming possibility, I decided to occupy the vicinity of Fiction J–L, deterring potential readers by whatever means I could (unaccountable smiling in the first instance, lechery in the second). But how long could I keep that up? How long before someone complained? Only when the best part of an hour had gone by, during which nobody had shown the slightest interest in *The Orphans of Neustadt*, the favoured titles being children's fiction, romances and books about sport, did I muster the courage to leave the building.

Three long weeks went by. Christmas drew near. I received two letters from Theresa via the regular post – pleasant, cheerful letters full of details about her life in Berlin and enquiries as to my creative productivity – but even these did not make the waiting more bearable. I was forced to reply in the same vein, the difference being that while her words were incomplete and rigorously self-censored, mine were wholly fictitious. My daily life consisted of waiting for a sign from Anton and nothing more. My creative productivity was non-existent. I planned to write again; I planned to live again – Wolfgang had given me my subject and my purpose – but there was no prospect of those plans being realised until I was free.

In her second letter Theresa told me she wanted to go home early for Christmas, on the 14th, but would return early too, giving us the chance to spend the rest of the holidays together. *Maybe we can go somewhere*, she said, a suggestion I thought dangerously open to misinterpretation. I replied in haste that I had an old school friend we could visit in Weimar, a pretty town of great cultural significance, unequivocally my side of the inner German border. As an additional precaution I wrote to the friend in question, a man I hadn't seen for at least a decade, and told him I planned to renew our acquaintance. It was not until some time later that I learned from his widow that he had died of lung disease some seven years earlier. *I had no idea you and Arno were friends*, she wrote. *We have all your books, but to my knowledge, he never mentioned you once.*

# 50

Late one night, unable to stand the silence any longer, I rose from the twisted ruin of my bed and sat down to write. What took form upon the page – the original impulse was unfocused – was a letter to Theresa. I can't recall the exact contents of that early draft. I'm sure it was rambling and emotionally incontinent. I know it described my deception in detail, the jealousy and weakness that gave birth to it; the pain it had engendered for all its outward success. It talked about Richter and his death, and what would have become of him had he lived, and how it fell to me to make what reparation I could. It asked – perhaps begged – Theresa to forgive me, or at least not to hate me. Because, if nothing else, it could be said that had I not been drawn to her from the moment I set eyes on her, nothing untoward would have happened and I would have had nothing to confess. I even talked about my childhood at some point in the letter, my misadventures among the ruins, my great-uncle's death, my years of searching with nothing but bitterness to show for it, although it is beyond me now to explain the relevance of those particular digressions. Finally it set out my hopes for the future, for a fresh start, for a new life of clarity and openness, for a life without secrets.

It was a letter that could never be sent, at least not by conventional means. It gave voice to thoughts and feelings that demanded expression, that I could no longer stand to keep inside. I did not even read it through. As soon as it was done, I tore it up and burned it in the ashtray. As I watched my words blister and blacken in the flames, I knew I still had to write *something*. I had to write enough that by the time I arrived in the West, Theresa would know I was a changed man, a better man.

So I began a new draft. I knew by now how it would be delivered: the same way Theresa had sometimes communicated with me, via Anton. This draft I remember more clearly. It was shorter and less explicit, and in its own way equally unwise.

*Dearest Theresa,*
*I am hoping this letter reaches you before you return to East*
*Berlin – because that's something you must not do. I know*

*that it must sound crazy, but a lot has changed since your
last visit. You see, I am likely to forgo the favour of the
authorities here very soon, having at last decided to leave.
Those authorities may assume you are the cause of my
treachery and the nature of their retribution could take
almost any form. That is why you must stay away. I am very
sorry for ruining your studies – studies which you undertook,
in part, I know, to be near me and to carry on your role as
my literary champion in the West. But there is nothing that
can be done. I will find a way to make it up to you.*

*During your time away things have come to a head. I
have learned that your suspicions regarding a certain young
writer (of whom we spoke last time) were well founded. I
should have listened to you. His is a story that must be told
and only I can tell it, from the safety of another country.
This is the reason for my coming – or, at least, my reason for
my coming now. To keep silent would be to join in a lie and
I have put too many of those into the world already, as I
will make plain to you very soon.*

*I have asked a lot of you this past year: not only to
change your plans and your career, but to play-act and to
lie, not once but a hundred times. This cannot have been as
easy for you, or as amusing as you said. Now that the whole
world is watching, I can only imagine what a burden it has
become. It is my failing that I did not foresee any of this, but
whatever the future holds, you will not have to carry that
burden much longer. This I can promise. Though there will
be a price to pay, my leaving here means nothing if I do not
speak out.*

*My feelings for you are the same as ever. My love is as
strong. If it is the same with you, and remains the same even
after the truth is told, I will count myself far luckier than I
deserve to be.*

*I will contact you as soon as I can.*
*With love always,*
*Bruno*

\*

A few days before Theresa's scheduled departure, in the early
evening, my doorbell rang. I buzzed open the front door, but nobody
came up. After a minute or so I went out on to the landing and

looked over the banisters. Below me the lights in the hallway cut out with their habitual clunk. Everything was quiet. I went downstairs and there, in my letter box, I found a copy of *Die Union*.

I knew at once that it had come from Anton. I was not a subscriber to that newspaper (or any newspaper, for that matter, except *Neues Deutschland*, which I took for the sake of appearances) and this edition was a day old.

Near the back, a small item in the Events section had been circled in blue ink. It announced a chamber concert by a group calling itself The Florian Quintet. The event was to take place at the Lutheran church in Weisser Hirsch about two miles away. The programme comprised works by Dvořák and Shostakovich, and started that evening at eight o'clock.

I checked my watch: Anton had given me just an hour to get there.

# 51

It was drizzling as I made way across the river, following the dim lights of the Loschwitz Bridge, the letter for Theresa hidden inside my coat. The traffic was sparse and I soon found myself alone on the gangway, the Elbe moving slowly beneath me, silent and black. As I turned up my collar I was struck by an unnerving coincidence: Weisser Hirsch (the name means 'White Hart') was a part of Loschwitz, that once salubrious district that proved to be Wolfgang Richter's final destination. He had gone to a party there on the evening of his arrest, almost exactly one year earlier – had perhaps crossed on this very bridge. I pictured him now, a figure in a long coat, drifting in and out of the mist. I pictured the distinctive Richter swagger, the young artist striding out into the night, his head full of dreams about the new life to come, already looking at the valley as a place that belonged to his past – the inescapable past that forever haunts the vision of the writer-in-exile.

In my mind I travelled back a year. I was racing to catch up with him. He couldn't miss the pounding of my footsteps. Sure enough, he slowed, turned, looked back along the bridge: a handsome man, young, overconfident, vulnerable. I opened my mouth to speak, to warn him of what lay ahead. But he couldn't hear or see me. Even in my imaginings the gap between the living and the dead, the spectral and the actual, was unbridgeable. Richter frowned and continued on his way, his story already written, if as yet untold.

Theresa had thought Richter arrogant and unfeeling. He wasn't *nice*, she'd said. But she was an outsider. She didn't understand what it took for a man of his talent to survive in the Workers' and Peasants' State; to refuse, as he had done, to live in fear. Richter's arrogance masked courage. He had shown it from the beginning: courage in his attacks on me, courage in his work, courage when they dragged him away for interrogation, courage when they tortured him and broke his skull. That Anton and his network were still at liberty was the proof of that courage. Wolfgang had not betrayed them. He had died with his lips sealed – his silence more eloquent than a lifetime of literature.

Now I was following in Richter's footsteps, just as he had followed in mine. He had wanted to be my heir. Now I was his. It did occur to me, as I passed by the sooty, half-timbered houses on the far side of the bridge, that the fate awaiting me might also mirror his. I was taking the same chances on the same people. Anton hadn't completely trusted Richter, or so Theresa had told me, but perhaps it was Anton who could not be trusted. Who *was* he? Whom did he answer to? What was he part of? As I began the long climb up the hill, the dark slopes of Oberloschwitz towering above me, I was forced to admit the possibility that the network Richter had trusted with his future, and which I was now trusting with mine, was an illusion, its sole purpose to smoke out unreliable elements among the artistic elite, citizens whose unscheduled departures so embarrassed the state. But if that were the case, it meant Theresa was part of the scheme, knowingly or unknowingly. She was camouflage, or, in my case, bait. And I was not ready to believe that, even for a moment. Such elaborate schemes and deceptions might have appealed to fantasists and authors of unserious fiction (they had a certain appeal to me), but they had no place in real life.

This conviction, bolstered by hope, had just enough force to keep my feet moving along the steep cobbled streets towards the place where Anton was waiting.

I recognised the church on Luboldtstrasse from some of my longer summer walks. A Gothic fantasy in slate, lead and stone, it served as an occasional reminder of a vanished age when fantasy still had a place. A cone of light shone down from the porch. Beneath it a procession of people was making its way inside. I fell in behind them, struck by the smell of stale wax and damp. I took a seat near the back of the church. By my watch it was five minutes to eight o'clock.

In front of me, in the sepulchral gloom, sat an audience of about fifty. It was safe to assume that Anton was among them. At some point he would look over his shoulder, spot me, make eye contact. Then he would get up and exit, ostensibly for a cigarette (one between his lips, lest there should be any doubt), leaving me to follow after a suitable interval. It was sure to go something like that.

I studied the fifty candidate heads, trying to identify my deliverer. I knew nothing about Anton, but at the same time I knew what I was looking for: not the gaunt messenger who had once followed me home, but someone altogether more impressive. I pictured a solitary man in his middle years, his build athletic, his hair greying but plentiful (I could not think of Anton as bald and in that I was correct), tidy, strong-jawed, quietly formidable – an authentic champion of the people, instantly distinguishable from the counterfeit variety.

At first no one struck me as fitting the bill. Half the audience were elderly. I saw walking sticks and hearing aids. A handful of student types occupied most of the front pew. Over on one side a young couple were ostentatiously hugging each other and whispering in each other's ears. Behind them, partially obscured by a pillar, I spotted a small man roughly my age in a pale blue anorak. He sat with his hands wedged between his knees, staring ahead of him. Could this be Anton? Outwardly he lacked heroic manifestations, but he was at least alone. I watched him carefully, expecting to see him turn towards me, but his gaze, like a man in a dream, never shifted.

The lights above the nave went off. A pair of spots lit up a space in front of the altar. Greeted by a hesitant round of applause, the musicians filed out through a doorway in the side of the apse, squinting, the string players carrying their instruments. I didn't pay much attention. I was still concerned with the audience, with Anton.

The musicians tuned up. A pair of latecomers slipped through the door just before it closed: a burly man in a fawn raincoat and a younger man in denims. I knew at once that they didn't belong: their demeanours were furtive, yet stern. Taking care not to look at me, the man in denims sat down at the end of my pew, quietly clearing his throat, as if preparing like the rest of us to listen. I couldn't locate the older man. He was suddenly nowhere to be seen. I was sure no one had followed me from Blasewitz, but now I had the clear and unnerving sensation of being surrounded, hemmed in, all exits covered: me and Anton both.

The music began. A sweet, Victorian hearth-and-home melody played on the cello; a lilting piano accompaniment. It was hard sitting still, hard pretending to listen, even as the melody gave way to fortissimo chords and high drama. I wasn't sure I could stand an hour of it. But it was at that moment that I recognised the pianist.

I had never seen her look that way before. Her hair was tied in a spiral at the back of her head, her face pale and unpainted. She wore a frumpy charcoal-grey dress, with puffed sleeves, somewhere between evening wear and funeral wear: *Claudia Witt*.

I could account for the appearance, but not for her presence. I stared in confusion, a tumult of possibilities – all troubling – tumbling through my mind. I remembered a snatch of a conversation, the cellar bar near the medical school, something Claudia said about forming an ensemble in her spare time. Hadn't I said I would be in the audience at their first concert? And here I was, thanks to a newspaper left in my letter box. Was this Anton's idea of a joke? Was this Claudia's idea of an invitation (perfunctory to the point of rudeness – very much her style)? Was I about to be arrested? Or was I simply witness to a performance of chamber music? I could not answer these questions. I could do nothing but sit in the darkness – sit through four movements of Dvořák's homely raptures, sit through *five* movements of Shostakovich, alternately mournful and frenetic – and wait. It was in that condition of enforced limbo, powerless and scared, but with an excellent soundtrack to accompany my suffering, that I perceived the hand of Richter, the author not only of *The Valley of Unknowing*, but also of *Two on a Bicycle*, the young genius with a talent and a taste for mockery. I heard his laughter in that darkness, as close as if he were sitting in the pew behind me. This time, for the first time, I couldn't bring myself to resent it.

The music came to a close. The musicians were on their feet. The church rang with applause. The quintet nodded and bowed, the smiles fixed and tight, as if they had expected a bigger crowd or a warmer reception. The man in the anorak, the latecomer in denims, the lovers, the students, they were all still in their places, clapping. I clapped too. Someone shouted 'Encore!' But no encore was offered. The lights went on overhead. The musicians left their makeshift stage. People started filing out. Was I supposed to go with them or stay where I was?

One by one the pews emptied. The loving couple strolled out, holding hands. Old people shuffled past. By the door I caught sight of the other latecomer: he was smiling, shaking someone's hand, offering apologies. He left with his companions. The students came down the aisle. One of them cracked a joke, a burst of raucous laughter briefly shattering the mood of respectful reticence. The man in denims got up to a flurry of joshing and walked out with them. Soon there was nobody left, just me and the stranger with the pale blue anorak and the sad eyes.

This was Anton. It had to be.

He got to his feet, edged slowly into the aisle. I did the same. He walked towards the altar. I followed.

'Anton?'

He showed no sign of having heard me, but continued to walk away. I continued to follow. I had no idea where we were going. Three of the young musicians reappeared, wrapped up now in coats and scarves. One of them, a violinist, hurried over to the stranger and embraced him. He smiled and shook the boy's hand with both of his: the proud, supportive father. They all walked past me without even looking round. Then I was alone, free to go, relieved, puzzled, frustrated – but of these, alone most of all.

'Bruno.' I recognised Claudia's voice. 'So you actually made it.'

I didn't want to talk to her, but there was no way I could get out of it. 'A promise is a promise,' I said.

We made our way out together. Claudia had changed into jeans and a sweater. Her dress, I assumed, was in the sports bag she was carrying. Shakily, the adrenaline still fizzing in my veins, I congratulated her on the performance. She said the Shostakovich had needed more rehearsal, a remark typical of Theresa – Theresa whose perfectionism and self-deprecation, I now perceived, masked a hard kernel of ambition.

'By the way,' I said as we crossed the porch, 'it was you who put that copy of *Die Union* in my letter box?'

'Of course. Who did you think it was?'

'No one. Nobody.' I laughed, feeling more than usually stupid. Instead of enjoying a pleasant musical interlude, I'd put myself through an hour of paranoia and dread for no reason at all. 'You know, I didn't find your reminder until seven o'clock this evening. You might want to give me a little more notice next time.'

We passed beneath a large scotch pine, water dripping lazily from its branches. Claudia stopped, hoisting the sports bag on to one knee. The streets round about were dark and empty. 'I wouldn't bank on there being a next time,' she said.

She unzipped the bag and reached inside it. I had no idea what she was talking about or why we had stopped, not even when she produced an old copy of *The Orphans of Neustadt,* and handed it to me. It crossed my mind that she wanted me to sign it and that this request, like her invitation to the concert (not to mention its affectedly casual nature), was indicative of something other than disdain. In the time it took me to take the book and open the front cover I had recast the entirety of her behaviour towards me – the resentment, the sarcasm, the unflattering psychological profiling – in the light of unrequited love, jealousy, hurt.

'Not the most original hiding place,' she said, 'but it's better than nothing.'

'Not the most – ?' I flexed the pages, detected a telltale stiffness round one of the central folios, adjacent to the spine. It was then, at last, that I understood: once again my novel was moonlighting as a hiding place. On this occasion it concealed a West German passport with my photograph inside it. 'So . . . *you're* Anton?'

'Just take the book.' Claudia zipped up her bag. Either she was Anton or she was there on Anton's behalf. It didn't matter which. 'Your day visa's dated for Saturday week.'

I took the book. Suddenly everything was happening so quickly.

'Nine days from now? That isn't long. I'm not sure . . .'

'It's long enough.' Claudia hoisted the bag on to her shoulder. 'Goodbyes aren't recommended. It's best you don't say any. And you won't need to pack. You're a day visitor to East Berlin. All you should be carrying are vodka and cigarettes, and stuff from the Delikat.'

I followed her as she set off along the road, heading for the dim glow of Bautznerstrasse. The satirical edge to our previous encounters had vanished. Claudia was all business now. I liked her better the old way. I liked it better when we weren't both scared.

'Where do I go?'

'Your instructions are in the book. You cross at Friedrichstrasse Station. One stop on the S-Bahn and you're in West Berlin. Just make sure you stand in the right line at the checkpoint. West German citizens have their own.'

'West German citizens, right.'

'And wear Western clothes: coat, tie and shoes in particular. That shouldn't be a problem for you, right?'

I shook my head. 'I was thinking: don't they keep records, of who comes in and out? Isn't there some kind of list?'

'Your name will be on that list. You don't need to know how.'

We walked on a little way in silence. I was leaving the valley and never coming back. It was more than an idea, more than a plan: it was real. I didn't feel ready.

'What happens on the other side?'

'You take a plane if you've got any sense.'

'A plane where?'

'The choice is yours. Hamburg maybe, or Munich.'

Munich: home of Bernheim Media, powerhouse of the global Aden phenomenon. I could pay them a visit. No doubt they would extend me a warm welcome. But how warm would it remain, once they had learned the truth? How understanding would they be when I told them they'd spent a fortune on a book they didn't own, promoting an author who didn't exist?

'Then what?'

'That's up to you.' Claudia looked at me. 'That's the point, isn't it? To do what you want?'

I'd been doing what I wanted for years; right up to the moment Theresa came along. Under her influence it had turned into what I *didn't* want.

'She'll be at home by then,' I said. 'In Austria.'

'Who?'

'Theresa. I want to warn her. I want her to know I'm on my way out.'

Claudia shook her head. 'Tell her when you get there.'

'I don't know a soul in the West. Only her.' I reached into my coat. 'I've already written something, here. There must be a way to get it to her. Please.'

We were almost at the main road. Two hundred yards away, at the tram stop, a small line of people were waiting. Claudia sighed and took the envelope from my hand. 'All right. I'll do what I can.'

We stopped at the corner, beside an empty lot. A handful of old Trabants were parked on the uneven ground. Nothing moved on the wide, rain-washed street.

Claudia tucked the letter into her bag. 'Tell me something: why now?'

'Is this for your report?'

She laughed. 'I don't make reports.'

'For the record, then?'

'I don't keep records. I'm just curious.'

'It's complicated. It has to do with a book.'

'Theresa's book?'

'Not exactly.' I realised I was still carrying *The Orphans of Neustadt* in my hand. 'What I meant to say was two books.'

Claudia shook her head. 'Damned writers.'

A tram was coming down the hill, dull sparks flickering in its belly. Our meeting was at an end.

'So,' she said, hunching her shoulders. 'Any questions?'

'Yes. The same as yours.'

'What do you mean?'

'Why now? Why have you decided to trust me now?'

Claudia had already set off across the street. She looked back over her shoulder. 'What makes you think I trust you?' she said.

# 52

The preparation for my journey, for the final abandonment of my home, for the grave crime of *Republikflucht* (to give it its forensic name) was no preparation at all. As Claudia had reminded me, there could be no packing, no gathering of mementos, no farewells, tearful or otherwise. I was to carry on as normal until the moment I reached Berlin, whereupon I was to cease being Bruno Krug, People's Champion of Art and Culture, and become Werner Kleinschmidt, a sales executive at a medical supplies company near Frankfurt. This new persona was to endure for no more than a few hours. It represented a transitional phase, a chrysalis, masking my transformation from earthbound socialist caterpillar to airworthy Western butterfly. Once over the inner German border, I was to become Bruno Krug again, but beyond my name, the exact nature of that renewed identity – fighter for freedom, hypocrite, refugee, traitor – was very far from clear.

Contrary to expectations, maintaining the appearance of normality was not easy. The clinic in Loschwitz telephoned to enquire after my stool sample, which was by now long overdue (their pills had no noticeable effect). I could not afford to arouse suspicion, so I duly set about trying to provide and bottle the requested material, an operation greatly complicated by my permanent state of anxiety, which ensured that any food I did eat – and I ate very little – went through me at alarming speed. If anything, I overdid the charade of business-as-usual. At a meeting of the regional Writers' Union I made a long and boring speech about self-criticism in the workplace and the need for socialist writers to foster it, my first such intervention at that forum since the era of détente. I hung Christmas decorations and a string of coloured lights in my apartment. I committed to a plethora of plumbing jobs, enough to keep me occupied until well into the New Year. I even went as far as to get tickets to *Taras Bulba* for the following season, which entailed pulling strings with Barbara Jaeger ('Russian opera, Bruno? What next, Russian women?'). By my standards this level of activity was frenetic and would have suggested to any conscientious observer a transition of some kind.

I had other tasks, besides play-acting at normal life. The first was to assemble an outfit of suitable Western clothes. I owned a number of items already – most usefully the raincoat I originally gave Michael Schilling and had not yet returned – but no shoes and no tie. The latter I found at the Intershop, a gaudy floral affair in Italian silk, but the range of footwear on offer was small and almost exclusively for women. I had to settle on an ancient pair of black leather lace-ups, which I recovered from the back of the wardrobe and polished for hours on end, hoping the resultant oily shine would convey an adequate sense of prosperity and bourgeois materialism. I had also to learn my part. Anton's instructions contained a detailed biography of Werner Kleinschmidt, which I was to memorise: information about his family, friends and employment, addresses and phone numbers, and his purpose in East Berlin, which was to visit grieving relatives in Prenzlauer Berg (it seemed Kleinschmidt had missed the funeral). This was to be the basis of a more detailed persona, which my instructions said I should develop for myself, just in case I was questioned. This part of my task held none of the pleasures that normally accompany the development of a fictional character. I was aware at all times of how brittle my creation was and how easily exposed for a cipher – the price for my lack of prowess being potentially greater than any number of bad reviews. With this in mind I finally destroyed the slender file I had stolen from the clinic in Radeburg, tearing it into little pieces and dumping it into the communal skip, concealed inside an old detergent bottle. It was, I reasoned, hardly proof of anything in itself – certainly not an unlawful killing – and if it were found on me, disaster was all but certain to follow.

Theresa's silence added to the torment of those nine days. I had no idea how long my letter would take to reach her. It was unreasonable to expect a reply in so short a time. But she had promised to write to me as soon as she was safely in the West and so far I had heard nothing. It was possible the post was responsible. Correspondence did not always make it across the inner German border. It was a busy time of year. But there were other possibilities I found difficult to exclude: that my letter had silenced her, the momentous news that I would soon be in the West myself, intent on killing off Eva Aden for good. Maybe Theresa didn't like the idea of that. As Eva Aden, she had told me she felt free. Free, famous and potentially well off. It was a lot to give up.

The day before I was due to leave I went in search of Claudia Witt. My head was full of questions that only she could answer – questions about the border, questions about Theresa – and she would surely know by that time that I posed no threat. But what I really wanted was reassurance. I wanted to hear that my method of escape was tried and tested. I wanted her to tell me that nothing could go wrong, so long as I kept my head. Above all, I wanted her to tell me that Theresa would be waiting for me on the other side – because all this, everything I was doing, everything I was leaving behind, it all meant nothing if she wasn't there to witness it.

Having no home address for her, I returned to the cellar bar near the medical school in the hope she would show up there. Four hours went by without any sign of her. I was on the point of giving up when a florid young man came down the steps, polishing his spectacles with a handkerchief. I recognised him as one of Claudia's birthday companions: Johann or Johannes or Jürgen. He seemed pleased to see me and readily accepted the offer of a drink. In the ensuing conversation it emerged that Claudia had gone to Berlin for an audition six days earlier and not come back. No one had heard from her since then.

The young man made light of the news, but I could tell that behind his breezy delivery he was concerned.

'That quintet she's in, they were supposed to have a rehearsal today, but she didn't show.'

'I expect she stayed for some sightseeing. She'll be back.'

He nodded. 'I expect so. She certainly isn't the type just to take off without saying goodbye.'

# 53

smudged text at top of page, partially legible lines forming a paragraph fragment

Claudia Witt was a prisoner of the state security apparatus, undergoing interrogation at the prison in Hohenschönhausen. She was enjoying a stay with friends in East Berlin, having decided to extend her visit for a few days. She had crossed the inner German border using a forged passport, just like the one she had given me, and was now safe in the West. As I hurried home, sweat turning cold on my skin, these were the notions that jostled for traction in my sleep-deprived brain: Claudia at the Christmas market, cheeks aglow; Claudia split-lipped, eyelids purple and swollen like ripe plums; Claudia reunited with Theresa, drinking champagne and toasting freedom – which vision was the true one? Which was the most natural, the most unforced? Which one would you believe, if you read it in a book? I couldn't tell. Two possibilities gave me no reason to call off my departure; the other gave me *every* reason. But the ratio was two to one. In the absence of aesthetic or intuitive guidance, I fell back on the laws of probability. By Claudian criteria, my escape route was twice as likely to be secure as not. Were they such very bad odds? Wolfgang Richter wouldn't have thought so. He would have taken them every time.

If there had been time for second thoughts, perhaps I would have had them. But there was no time. My train for the capital left at eight the next morning. I managed at most two hours of wretched, fitful dreaming, and rose at half past five. I had been afraid of feeling drowsy, but on waking I found myself strangely alert, as one emerging from an ice-cold swim. I heard everything, saw everything with stark clarity, as if it were being carved into my memory with shards of glass. Methodically I dressed, shaved and gathered my things, knowing as I left each room in turn that I would never see it, or its contents, again. It struck me as an unnatural departure – a disrespectful one, to the past, to my life's history – to be so final and yet so casual at the same time. It was a struggle to leave the bed unmade, more than I could manage to leave dirty dishes in the sink.

At seven, I turned off the lights one by one, locked the door of the apartment and went downstairs, carrying a shopping bag, in which I had placed Schilling's English raincoat, my Italian tie, my best black velvet jacket and a bottle of expensive cologne. It was with these that

I planned to manifest my brief insertion into the ranks of Western middle management. By the front door I found one of my elderly neighbours wiping the seat of his bicycle. He must have been surprised at seeing me up so early. It took a small effort of will to say good morning, because what I wanted to say to him, he who at that moment embodied everything I was forsaking, was goodbye.

The tram came at once. I arrived at the central railway station by the first light of dawn. It was then, as I paced the empty platform, that I became aware of having neglected something. I had not been allowed to say goodbye to anyone. My departure had to appear casual, my absence temporary. But there was one goodbye I could say without risk of betrayal, one goodbye I *had* to say. I checked my watch. The train wasn't due to leave for more than half an hour. I hurried out of the station and through the streets, my pace picking up as the minutes ticked by. In the end I was running, the shopping bag clutched to my chest, my shiny shoes slipping on the cobblestones.

The heaps of masonry looked the same as always. In the grey-blue light they were stubbornly untransformed; the grass a little browner, the brambles on the southern side a little deader. But what a pull they had, those blackened stones, what *gravity*. The sight of them – I am ashamed to admit this – brought a sob to my throat and for a moment I was a boy again (Thomas in my book, Alex in Richter's), chest heaving, all at once alone in a place of strangers. There was a difference, though, and it came to me as I traced the site perimeter in my usual way: this time, for the first time, I had somewhere else to go.

I made it to the train with a minute to spare. Most of the seats were taken, and I was obliged to insert myself between an obese woman who smelled of bacon and the enormous trunk she had parked in the gangway. I wanted to take one last look at the city skyline as it slid away into the distance, but I was afraid the obese woman would think I was staring at her. So I took out a copy of *The Orphans of Neustadt* – first edition, first impression, the first copy I ever laid eyes on, now obscured behind a plain brown paper cover – and pretended to read it. The one time I did look up, I saw only derelict warehouses sliding by. '*Fine cookware*' announced an old pre-war advertisement, still faintly visible on the brickwork: '*Repairs carried out professionally*' boasted another. The one I remember most clearly read '*Coffins at all prices*'.

If anyone followed me on to the train I did not see them.

*

In Berlin, the Anti-Fascist Protection Wall ran along the banks of the River Spree not two hundred yards from the Hauptbahnhof. For this reason I did not take the shortest route to my first destination, but instead went north for a few hundred yards towards the Karl Marx Allee, before once again heading west towards the city centre. According to Anton's instructions I was to arrive outside the Friedrichstrasse checkpoint between half past four and a quarter to five. With some hours to go, I had decided to approach my point of exit by degrees, my first stop being the Pergamon Museum, home to the Pergamon Altar and a range of archaeological treasures too large for the victorious Russians to loot. It was there that Wolfgang Richter had first set eyes on Theresa, but it was not out of any desire to visualise the encounter (an encounter that led Wolfgang back to the valley and to his death) that I was going there.

I bought a guide pamphlet and wandered around the exhibits – the altar, the Ishtar Gate, the Aleppo Room, the exhibition of Old Berlin – accompanied by a steady stream of tourists, some of whom appeared to be Western, judging from their superior photographic equipment and superior teeth. I was accosted by a young Asian couple wearing jeans and ski jackets that appeared to be cut from a duvet. They asked me to take a picture of them hugging each other beside a martial Greek frieze, which I did with trepidation, being unsure whether or not photography was permitted. The sights duly seen, I then wandered into the men's lavatories, found a spare cubicle and locked myself in. From a previous visit, years earlier, I remembered that the sanitary facilities at the Pergamon were unusually private and secure. I was relieved to discover that nothing had changed.

A few minutes later I emerged in the cologne-soaked guise of Werner Kleinschmidt, my old coat, along with the shopping bag, now hidden on top of the cistern. Finding myself alone, I risked a hasty check in the mirror. The raincoat looked expensive, but needlessly dressy; the tie expensive but effeminate. It crossed my mind that I might be taken for a homosexual. I was about to remove the tie when it occurred to me that this might be a good thing. In state-sponsored critiques, the decadence of the Western lifestyle had often been illustrated with reference (oblique or otherwise) to homosexuality and the feminisation of manhood. To a well-indoctrinated border guard a Western male was quite likely to have homosexual leanings. If I appeared homosexual, therefore, I was more likely to be perceived as a Westerner.

At four o'clock, by which time it was getting dark, I left. I crossed over the canal and walked a few hundred metres along a dark, narrow road, following the brick arches of the Stadtbahn towards the west until I came out beside the mainline station on Friedrichstrasse. It was a busy thoroughfare, cars and taxis queuing as they passed beneath the railway bridge, streams of East Berliners heading for the S-Bahn, silhouetted against brightly lit shopfronts. I went into a store, paid over the odds for three bottles of Russian vodka and continued on my way, carrying the bottles in a reinforced paper bag. As I advanced towards the checkpoint I felt my confidence slowly ebbing away. Were the *Grenztruppen* supposed to be deceived by an Aquascutum raincoat and a floral tie? I tried to pick out returning Westerners in the crowd, men in particular. How did they walk? Did they look around? What did they do with their hands? I needed to observe their manner, their style. But it was hard in the deepening gloom to tell the transient Westerners from the Actually Existing Socialists.

On the north side of the railway, beside the river, stood a modern building with three glass walls and a sloping concrete roof. The authorities called it a border control pavilion; ordinary Berliners, who had always tended towards theatricality where their own city was concerned, called it the *Tränenpalast* (Palace of Tears). It was there that people heading into the West queued to have their documents checked; there that they said goodbye to friends and relatives who could not follow. According to Anton's briefing, my passport would be inspected three times, the third inspection being the most thorough. The queue outside was fat and long. It snaked for a hundred metres through the sparse landscaping of the square. Christmas was coming: the season for delivering gifts from the West, the season for picking up Cuban cigars and liquor from the East. It made sense for me to cross now. There had to be greater safety in numbers, pressure on verification procedures. In a cross-border rush hour my odds were better: but better than what? On that point Anton had offered no guidance.

After a few minutes of negligible progress I noticed that the queue was getting longer. If half past four was busy, half past five would have been busier. But my instructions had been specific as to the time of my arrival: it was to be no later than a quarter to five. What happened, I wondered, after that? Did a particular guard go off duty, a guard who had to be *on* duty? Claudia had told me: *make sure you stand in the right line.* These thoughts provoked a new anxiety: that Anton had failed to anticipate the length of the queue. Was I going to reach the third passport check too late? Was I about to present my forged documents to the wrong guard?

These conjectures, I learned later, were wide of the mark. In the queue, about forty-five minutes behind me, stood the real Werner Kleinschmidt, medical supplies executive from Frankfurt, who had just returned from one of his regular meetings at the Ministry of Health. When contacted by a conscientious Dutch reporter years after the event, Herr Kleinschmidt said he was unaware of having played any role in my flight, but that his passport had gone missing from his office a few months beforehand, obliging him to apply for a new one. He also reported that, upon reaching the Friedrichstrasse checkpoint forty-five minutes after I did, he was taken in for questioning and held for several hours, which had never happened before.

Time shuffled by, one nervous step at a time. At five o'clock I stood on the threshold of the *Tränenpalast*. At a guard post they were checking passports. Farewells were taking place outside: hugs, handshakes, audible sobbing. Many of the people in the queue had only been there to say goodbye, prolonging contact with their loved ones for as long as possible, squeezing every last second out of the precious day. Up ahead I saw grown men with tears in their eyes, though they tried their best to hide them, hastily reaching into their pockets for handkerchiefs and scraps of tissue. I envied the simplicity of their predicament, the purity and force of their feelings. It was something I wished I still knew.

I had entertained vague hopes that Theresa might come to meet me outside the *Tränenpalast*. Two Westerners crossing together, I thought, might have been less conspicuous than one Westerner crossing alone. On the other hand Herr Kleinschmidt was a married man with two children. A young female companion might have complicated the story. But that didn't mean Theresa couldn't be at the station. Several of the lines and half the platforms were for Western passengers only, being securely fenced off from the rest. At that very moment she might be waiting a few yards away on the westbound S-Bahn platform. The more I thought about it, the more likely this seemed. Why *wouldn't* Theresa come to meet me, now that I had proven my love by giving up everything to be with her? The border had divided us. The border had held us back, posing questions about the future that we weren't yet ready to answer. If there had been equivocation and concealment, this was the reason. Without a border between us, everything would be out in the open. Everything would be different.

Even as I reassured myself with these candied visions of the life to come, I was uncomfortably aware of following in the footsteps of young Thomas Schwitzer, the protagonist of *The Orphans of*

*Neustadt*. My ideological direction of travel was the reverse of his, but in other respects the parallels were striking. Thomas too gave up a comfortable, narrow, morally agnostic existence for the dream of a better world – and did it for love (or, as some feminist critics would have it, for lust). At the end of the story his happiness, like his devotion to the cause, is hanging by a heartstring. So it was with me. Over the years, many commentators have asked if Sonja, the object of Schwitzer's desire, is naive in thinking the young leopard has really changed his spots, that the black marketeer will go on loving her once the going gets tough. The question few have ever thought to ask is whether *she* will go on loving *him*.

The first inspection was cursory: no questions, no searches. The queue divided before descending a flight of steps. The interior of the building was brightly lit. Cameras looked down from fixed points on every side. A chemical taint cut through the ambient fug of sweat and damp footwear. Ahead were the customs checks, officials in short jackets lined up behind tables. I could spot the Westerners now: they had a preference for natural fibres and the men had layered haircuts that gave them an appearance of vigour. I needed to look like them, to pass unnoticed beneath the lens. A man my age in a smart green overcoat was reading a paperback book, frowning between audible yawns. I took out my book and copied him in a pantomime of distaste. What a dull and dated fiction was *The Orphans of Neustadt* (modern classic or not), how overrated was its author. Wolfgang Richter would have enjoyed the spectacle, the involuntary self-criticism. It would have appealed to his satirical sense of humour.

It took twenty minutes to reach the customs check: twenty minutes under bright lights, being watched on monitors, studied for telltale signs of fear; twenty minutes' worth of adrenaline building in my system. My memories of the customs inspection are fleeting. I recall a fat man in a wool coat counting out tins of caviar and cartons of cigarettes; a guard with a burn scar on his face in the shape of Lake Balaton; a child pulling at his mother's arm and shouting urgently 'Pee-pee! Pee-pee!'; my bottles of vodka clanking like fractured bells as I placed them on the counter. I can picture the guard examining the bag, picking it up and carefully handing it back to me. I may have wished him a happy Christmas.

'Passport!'

Another guard was sitting behind a desk between the two queues. I'd walked right past him without stopping.

'Sorry,' I said.

He looked at me, looked at my picture in the passport, looked at me again, turned to the page with the visa. He was the oldest official so far. On his uniform were several discreet emblems of rank.

He handed my passport back. I said thank you, hardly able to hear the words over the thumping of my heart.

The two queues divided again: one line each for foreigners, East German citizens, West German citizens and residents of West Berlin. I followed Herr Caviar into the West German line. A train rumbled into the station, shaking the floor.

One more inspection: the most thorough.

The queue was down to single file. It wound slowly one way, then another, no sight of the end. I heard doors open and close, the sound repeating in cavernous, invisible spaces. Minutes went by. The line shuffled forward. I took out my book again then put it away, took it out, put it away. How much longer? How much further? I was sweating inside my English raincoat and my writerly velvet jacket. Then Herr Caviar was striding away, hefting his holdall of booty. My turn now, sooner than I thought. I stepped across the white line on the floor.

Two officers occupied a booth; a young one seated, an older one standing behind him. I said good evening. I slid my passport under the glass: Werner Kleinschmidt, sales executive, forty-nine years old, residing at 25 Im Kirschenwäldchen, Kalbach, Frankfurt; married, two children: Klara fourteen, Sebastian eleven. The mantra went round and round inside my head. The seated officer stared at me, picked up the passport, turned over the pages. In all, there were eleven old visas, with their accompanying entry and exit stamps. Herr Kleinschmidt had been a regular visitor to the Workers' and Peasants' State. The officer looked at me again. I smiled wearily, feigning incipient impatience.

'Reason for visit?'

'Death,' I said.

'A funeral?'

I simultaneously nodded and shrugged, as if that was close enough. The officer looked squarely at my floral tie.

'Relation?'

'A cousin.'

'Where's your cousin buried?'

'She was cremated. At Baumschulenweg. I wasn't there, but . . .' I shrugged again. Shrugging seemed the best available camouflage. Terror and shrugging were unlikely bedfellows.

The older guard was looking at a clipboard. He leaned over the other's shoulder, closed my passport and handed it back. 'Good evening,' he said.

And that was that. The interrogation was over. Four questions. *Four*. I could hardly believe my luck. I said good evening as evenly as I could manage and walked on. All I had to do was find my way to the platform, get on the first S-Bahn train for Westkreuz and it was done.

A tunnel led below ground, cement-lined and echoing. Travellers from all the other queues were heading in the same direction, East Germans, West Germans, Berliners and foreigners, walking out of the Workers' and Peasants' State without ceremony or celebration – as if this privilege of crossing borders were no more unusual than the daily journey to work. I inserted myself into the stream, my every step marked by the vodka bottles clanking at my side.

I walked down a flight of steps, turned a corner. The air smelled of scorched soot and bubble gum. The ground was shaking. Another train was rolling in, brakes squealing, wheels clattering – an S-Bahn train, heading into West Berlin. I kept walking, barely glancing at the signs. Herr Kleinschmidt wouldn't need them. He already knew the way. Up ahead was the platform, yellow carriage windows sliding by, people waiting, silhouetted against them. There was no ticket barrier, no barrier of any sort. The train pulled up. The doors opened with a pneumatic hiss. Curious faces peered out: eager for a glimpse of the other side.

I decided to run for it.

A man stepped in front of me. He had an unlit cigarette in his mouth; quite a young man, with brown sheepskin gloves. I thought he was going to ask me for a light.

'Herr Krug?'

There was another man at my shoulder. He wore a raincoat too; a cheap one without belt or buttons. It was a little too short for him.

The first man said. 'It would be best not to make a scene.'

# PART SIX

# 54

They took me through a door at the side of the tunnel. We walked along a narrow passage and up an iron staircase. Nobody passed us on our way out of the station; nobody saw us leave. It wasn't until I was sitting in the back of a Wartburg staring at the pedestrians on Friedrichstrasse that I saw another human being besides my two companions. We drove at speed along Unter den Linden and, within a few minutes, were back on the Karl Marx Allee. I wondered, briefly, if we might be going to the Hauptbahnhof, but we passed the turning and continued east into districts I didn't know, where dim red lights marked the tops of factory chimneys and the air tasted of sulphur.

My arrival at the facility – I had no name for it then – was equally devoid of potential witnesses. We drove through iron gates into a large bare courtyard and from there into a garage where a line of identical vehicles were parked. We went on foot through more doors, along more empty passageways, sometimes halting for reasons connected with the approach of footsteps and the red lights screwed at intervals into the walls. It seemed a matter of importance that my presence, like my arrest (I assumed I had been arrested, though the word had not been used) should go unobserved. As I shuffled down those endless corridors, the phrase that I could not get out of my head was: *Fracture to the left temporal lobe.* Instinctively I touched that cranial spot, recalling in the same moment Theresa's habit of doing the same.

I was shown into a room. It was dark except for an anglepoise light on a desk. On the other side of that desk sat a man in uniform. He was my age, with tidy grey hair and glasses in heavy black frames. He was reading the contents of a file, rubbing his chin with his thumb as if perplexed. There were no blunt instruments in immediate reach, at least none that I could see.

'Sit down,' the man said without looking at me. The light from the lamp reflected off his lenses, hiding his eyes.

I sat down. The two men from the station waited for a nod from their superior and left. I never heard their names.

The uniformed man held out his hand. 'The passport.'

I handed it over. In the back of the Wartburg I had considered throwing it out of the window, but the window wouldn't open, there being no handle on the inside of the door. My interrogator opened the passport and flicked through it, returning to the photograph at the front.

'You were younger then,' he said. 'When was this, ten years ago?'

'Eight,' I said. 'I was wearing make-up.'

Michael Schilling had made the same observation. Was this what had tripped me up: that sliver of vanity? Of course it wasn't. They had called me by name, those men in the tunnel. They had been waiting. How had they known to expect me? The simplest answer was that Claudia Witt had told them to, under interrogation. Of the three possible explanations for her disappearance, I felt sure the worst one had befallen her: she had been arrested. Were they still keeping her here? Had she been questioned in this very room, sitting in this very chair? A wave of hopelessness broke over me. All the precautions Anton had employed to guard against discovery and betrayal I had considered theatrical and excessively elaborate. Now it turned out they were not elaborate enough.

My interrogator closed the passport and moved it aside. To my surprise he did not ask me how I had come by it or who had supplied it. This confirmed my fears regarding Claudia. The only possible explanation for not asking such questions was that the answers were already known.

The interrogator stared at me. 'The normal sentence for *Republikflucht* is three years' imprisonment,' he said. 'I expect you're aware of this.'

'I am now.'

'It might further be considered appropriate to make an example of a case like yours by extending that sentence, given the elaborate manner of your deception and, more importantly, the many privileges and honours bestowed upon you by the state – honours that apparently mean nothing to you.'

He was right. At that moment they did mean nothing to me, which is not the same as saying they never had.

The interrogator consulted a file that lay in front of him. It was, I noticed, a fat file. 'Only a year ago you were awarded the title of People's Hero of Art and Culture.'

'Champion,' I said. 'People's Champion. The last Hero of Art and Culture was Manfred Dressler, the sculptor.'

A small muscle flexed in the region of my interrogator's jaw. 'The

Cultural Association should bestow its favours with more care. Two artists honoured for their service to the people, both of whom turn out to be' – he hesitated before pronouncing sentence – '. . . shallow and self-serving.'

I felt a scintilla of relief. I had expected to be called a traitor. Traitors were the lowest of the low. There was no fate they did not deserve. 'Shallow and self-serving' was not so bad. It wasn't so very far from the truth.

'Why have you turned your back on your country?' My interrogator seemed genuinely perplexed. 'It makes no sense.'

'For a woman,' I answered.

As I said those words it came to me that I would never see Theresa again. She would soon learn of my arrest – Anton's network would see to that. They would tell her it wasn't safe for her in the East. Even if she ignored them and tried to return, how far would she get? No further than this place, no matter how accommodating or useful her father might be. The inner German border had finally put paid to our affair once and for all.

My interrogator was staring at me through his blank lenses. 'Is that all there is to it? You fell in love?'

'I fell in love.'

My interrogator consulted the file. 'The music student.'

'I'd hoped she would settle here. But it became clear . . . It became clear . . .'

'Yes?'

It became clear that my hopes were unrealistic; that the love I had inspired in Theresa was not the kind that overcomes all obstacles, regardless of cost. It was not, for instance, like Thomas's love for Sonja, or Sonja's love for Thomas. It was a judicious, circumspect love, the kind that authors of fiction do not traditionally concern themselves with.

'It became clear that she was not prepared to sever her ties in the West.'

The interrogator shook his head, expressed neither scepticism nor scorn, only a bottomless disappointment.

'You want me to believe that your attempted desertion wasn't motivated in any way by ideological considerations.'

'Desertion' was a more menacing description. Deserters in the Workers' and Peasants' State could, in certain circumstances, be shot.

'It's the truth.'

'Then you'll have no difficulty in cooperating on certain points of information of interest to the authorities.'

I shook my head. Whatever treatment Wolfgang Richter had stood up to before he died, I knew it would be too much for me. I would surrender everything in the end: every who, where and when. Besides, I wasn't sure if I had anything to tell the authorities that they didn't already know: because Claudia Witt knew much more than I did.

'You would be advised to answer my questions fully and honestly.'

I said I would do my best.

My interrogator picked up a pen. 'Name your contacts in Switzerland.'

'In Switzerland?' The question struck me as bizarre. 'I don't have any. None that I know of.'

'In particular Zürich. Who do you know in Zürich?'

'No one.'

'In the administrative district of' – my interrogator consulted his file again – 'Erlenbach. Was that where you were planning to go?'

Erlenbach. It took me a moment to place the name.

'I had in mind to go to Munich,' I said.

The interrogator adjusted his glasses. 'Is this your idea of co-operation? If so –'

'I don't know anyone in Switzerland,' I insisted. 'I know *of* someone. That's the best I can do.'

'Name?'

'Martin Klaus.'

'Spelled?'

'K – L – A – U – S. He's an agent.'

My interrogator looked up from his writing. 'An intelligence agent?'

'A literary agent. He's quite famous in artistic circles.'

'Western artistic circles.'

'Yes. He was in *Stern* magazine a few months ago – his house too, in Erlenbach.'

What had prompted this line of questioning? How had Klaus's home town been connected to me? Some fragment of information regarding Theresa's arrangements in the West had reached my captors, but they didn't know what to make of it. That, at least, was my impression.

I waited for the questions that would lead us to the issue of Richter's book. I had already decided to tell the whole truth, humiliating though it was: in the Workers' and Peasants' State a deception in the cause of love (in telling Theresa that the book was mine) was less reprehensible and less dangerous than a deception in the cause of freedom.

'Did this' – my interrogator read the name from his notes – 'Martin Klaus know of your plans to cross the border?'

'No.'

'Who did you tell? Specifically who in the West?'

'I told no one in the West.'

The interrogator sighed. 'I will ask you again. Who did you contact in the West concerning your defection? The truth, this time.'

I wasn't trying to be evasive. I wanted my interrogator to know that, abject as it may seem. I had decided entirely against a futile act of defiance.

'I made one attempt,' I said, remembering my letter to Theresa. 'I wrote to my . . . to the music student. About a week ago. But I'm sure the letter never arrived.'

'Because?'

'Because the person I gave it to was arrested a few days ago, this side of the border.'

'Arrested for what reason?'

'For the same reason as me.' My interrogator looked unimpressed. 'For *Republikflucht*.'

The interrogator sighed as if this were a diversionary tactic, one that, under the circumstances, was beneath us both. 'Name?'

*Fracture to the right temporal lobe.* How exactly had it happened? Had Richter seen the blow coming? Had it come as a complete shock? Had there been time to flinch? Maybe they had deliberately made him wait for it, just to prolong the terror. These questions, I realised, would never leave me. Once, when I was a boy, after a raid I saw a man's head lying in the gutter with his hat still on. For years afterwards I wondered what he had been doing when the bomb fell and where the rest of him was. I wonder still.

'*Name*?'

'Claudia Witt.'

I had the impression, even through the fog of dread, that my interrogator knew this name, but that he had not expected to hear it from me.

'Claudia Witt,' he said. 'Another musician.'

'Yes. Recently graduated from the Carl Maria von Weber College of Music. She plays the . . .'

'Who told you she'd been arrested?'

'I just assumed . . . Why else am I here? How else did you know to expect me?'

The interrogator took off his glasses and looked at me. He had pale, sad eyes. 'We have reason to believe Claudia Witt crossed the border illegally seven days ago, using forged papers. Unfortunately she was *not* apprehended.' He reached under his desk. I heard a faint buzz in the corridor. 'Perhaps that will teach you not to make assumptions.'

A guard entered the room and led me out by the arm. I preferred not to think where he was taking me. It was all I could do not to volunteer more details about my escape plans in the hope of prolonging what might turn out to be my last conversation this side of the grave.

# 55

In the prisons at Hohenschönhausen and Lichtenberg most of the cells were bare, freezing and unsanitary, with hardly enough space to lie down. I have seen them since in books and magazines. Some have been preserved in their original state and opened to the public. The flavour of dictatorship is now on the tourists' menu, along with the zoo and the pressure-sprayed glories of Hohenzollern architecture. But the cell I was taken to – I am still not clear as to its location – has not featured in any magazine or tourist guide. The colour scheme might have elicited the odd pang of nostalgia among former citizens whose memories of the Workers' and Peasants' State are still clouded with affection. But it would never have provoked the frisson of pity or horror that the tourist is looking for. It was the size of a modestly priced hotel room and furnished in much the same way: a single bed with a wooden headboard, beige carpeting, a corner sofa, an upholstered upright chair, a coffee table upon which sat a carafe of water and a glass. A large window with lace curtains looked out over the yard some thirty feet below. There was even a small television with a pot plant resting on the top of it, and a shelf of books: a smattering of the classics, texts on Marxism and revolutionary theory, several modern novels, including works by Christa Wolf and Johannes R. Becher, and finally a complete set of the *Factory Gate Fables* in paperback. Most unexpected of all, I found a small bathroom, equipped with a lavatory, sink and shower, and a single towel in chemical pink.

I did not find these luxuries reassuring. Traditionally it is a condemned man who is given a hearty meal and it seemed obvious to me that my accommodation had been arranged on a similar principle. Looking out at the empty street, at flurries of snow caught in the downcast glow of a solitary street light (the window was not barred; but neither would it open), I became convinced that this was the case. They were not keeping me in an ordinary prison because ordinary prisons were populated with prisoners and guards who might recognise me. That would never do. My disappearance was to be unexplained, my final resting place unmarked and unrecorded – exactly like my mother's.

I don't know how long I spent in that commodious condemned

cell: my watch had been taken away upon arrival, along with the vodka and my English raincoat. It was a long time before I was calm enough to make use of the bed. It was only then, as I lay staring at the white textured ceiling (reminiscent of a holiday boarding house, like the floral pattern on the lampshade) that I began at last to assemble the pieces of my exploded plan, to ask myself where I had gone wrong. The most striking scrap of information was that Claudia Witt had not been arrested, but had made good her escape to the West. This was good news not just for her, but for me: because it meant I could not betray her. I could not, in fact, betray anyone – anyone except Theresa and she was out of reach. I had never been fully trusted by Anton's network, which had irked me at the time, but a clear conscience was the result.

This, however, left a troubling question: if Claudia had not betrayed me, who had? Who had made contact with the authorities and told them of my plans? Someone else in the network, perhaps – that was possible – someone I had never met or seen or heard of. My face was recognisable. Anyone involved in the preparation or delivery of my passport could have been responsible: a back-room traitor, a mole. But then, why was I the one singled out for betrayal? Why me and not Manfred Dressler, or, for that matter Claudia Witt?

Mentally I reran my truncated interrogation. From the start the man behind the desk had focused on my supposed contacts in the West. Whom did I know in Switzerland? With whom had I shared my plans? The secret police had made a connection to Martin Klaus's home town, the location of his lakeside villa, but not to Klaus himself. How could they have known about the location, but not about the location's significance? Wasn't that the wrong way round? And what made my melancholy examiner so certain I had failed to keep my intentions a secret? How could he be sure of that?

Answers – plausible and implausible – crowded into my head. It was a question of arranging the evidence in a credible sequence, like the scattered pages of a story. This was the metaphor I clung to. If I could correctly order those pages, I might be able to discern the narrative as a whole; its shape, its direction, its message. Stories were my business, my lifelong preoccupation. I sat up. I drank some water – at least, I recall having a glass of water in my hand. (Have I given the impression that I was calm in those first hours of captivity? If so, the impression is misleading.) When I put the glass to my lips, it rattled against my teeth. It was fear, naturally, but something else too: a gradually unfolding horror. Because already a story *was* taking shape, the fragments coalescing of their own accord into a sequence. And the logic of that sequence was undeniable – irresistible, in fact, though I tried to resist it. One by one the fragments became pictures, the pictures became scenes; plot points in a dark and squalid tale, one which I, in my innocence, could never have dreamed up: a story of the modern world.

I can still see it played out, as if on the big screen. First scene, final act: Claudia slipping through the border control in a suit of Western clothes, concealed in her pocket a letter for a friend. Then the surprise arrival in Austria; embraces and celebrations. Her friend is no longer the impoverished student, living off casual work and pocket money. Her friend has her own car, her own flat. Her Western clothes look a lot more expensive than Claudia's Western clothes; and she has a wardrobe full of them. It's all the money from her book, which is enjoying its fourth month on the *Spiegel* bestseller list in Germany.

Claudia doesn't hand over the letter straight away. The letter will shift attention away from her, to the lover still waiting on the other side. She wants Theresa to herself for a little while. What about the musical career, she asks? Has Theresa anything lined up for the coming year? Any auditions? Her friend says no. Things have slipped a little on the viola front. Since the summer, the book – the signings, the interviews, the promotional tour – has taken up almost all her free time. She may be going to America soon. Besides, the money even in Western orchestras is terrible. You practise like a slave for thirteen years and you end up with the pay of a postman.

Claudia puts on a brave face, but she knows things have changed. This isn't the Theresa she knew in the East. Back in her element, Theresa is a very different creature. She detects a brittleness, a forced jollity that conceals – she sees it, finally – a sense of obligation. It comes to Claudia that their friendship is already a thing of the past. In the East they had been united by music; but here in the West such cultural adhesives cannot be counted on. In the West there are other considerations, social and material; and those considerations divide them just as The Wall divides their country.

Claudia produces the letter. 'I've news,' she says.

As she watches her friend read, she wonders if the lover will fare better with this new Theresa when the roles of native and visitor, guest and host, are reversed. Will their bonds prove more durable? For all the ensuing excitement, the breathless interrogation – When is he coming? Where will he cross? When was this all arranged? – she senses that the answer is no. In Theresa's excitement there is the same brittleness, punctuated by moments of anxious cogitation.

At one point she sits down suddenly with her fingers pressed to her mouth.

'Aren't you pleased?' Claudia asks.

'Of course I am,' Theresa says. 'I'm just worried. In case something goes wrong.'

'Nothing will go wrong,' Claudia says. 'It's all been worked out. Less than a week from now he'll be here. Or in Munich.'

'Munich?'

'I think he said something about Munich.'

Munich means Bernheim Media, means Konrad Falkner, means everything unravelling to the point of no return: no chance for Theresa to shape events, to manage this dangerous unmasking. Eva Aden's death sentence is to be a fait accompli. Her point of view, her interests are surplus to requirements. Is this the reason Bruno is coming: not for her at all, but to reassert control of the enterprise, an enterprise in which she's already invested much more than time?

She gives Claudia some notes from her purse, says goodbye quickly, sends her back to the hostel where she's got herself a bed. No sooner is the door shut than she's on the telephone to Switzerland, tearful, contrite, more than a little scared. Her name is on all these contracts. A lot of the money has been spent. How is she going to protect herself? What should she do? Klaus understands her reasons for secrecy – secrecy maintained for the author's sake above all – but with regard to her immediate predicament he is less than reassuring. The matter needs to be handled carefully, he says. In fact, it needs nothing less than complete orchestration. As things stand, Bruno Krug is no one's idea of a dissident; nor is *Survivors* an obvious example of dissident literature. The Workers' and Peasants' State hasn't been mentioned in the press releases or on the packaging; and so far the reviewers have made little of the allusion or missed it altogether. If they aren't careful, Theresa's fronting of the book could end up looking like a scam, a marketing ploy aimed at maximising exposure and international sales. If that were to happen, they could really be in trouble. Bernheim Media would seek to distance themselves from the whole affair, for fear of being seen as a co-conspirator. Other publishers would follow. Law suits and ruin lie in wait.

'I thought he'd at least consult me,' Theresa says, the tears welling. 'I thought we were partners. I suppose I should have seen this coming.'

'No,' Klaus says, manful and protective instincts getting the better of him. '*I* should have seen it coming. For what it's worth, it sounds like we've both been used.'

'Do you really think so?'

'It would be as well to assume the worst.'

Then they're on to the details: the when, where and how of the imminent migration.

Klaus has always felt the presence of a significant other in Theresa's life. He sensed it in her reticence on matters of the heart. Now he has a name and a face to go with it. 'Try not to worry,' he says, already anticipating how this crisis will bring them closer together. 'I'll make some calls. See how the land lies.'

He means Bernheim and certain trusted contacts in New York (Americans being litigious and unsentimental in matters of business), but as he thumbs through his Rolodex it comes to him that there are other parties he could contact, another call he could make – a call that would put an end to their problem once and for all; an anonymous call, one that could never be traced to him. Will he have to tell Theresa? Will he have to lie to her? Probably not. Because she will never ask him about it. It will be something they deliberately never discuss. Upon reflection, he is quite certain about this. There are some things it is better not to know and, as far as Theresa is concerned, this will be one of them. He isn't even sure, as he ponders the means of execution, if the idea wasn't really hers in the first place, if he hasn't merely reached the conclusion she wanted him to reach.

The next morning – a beautiful, clear morning, the sunshine sparkling on the frosted trees, the mountains snow-capped and magnificent on the skyline – Martin Klaus drives into the middle of Erlenbach. Within sight of the elegant baroque church he steps into a phone box and makes an international call to the Ministry of State Security on the far side of the inner German border.

He is completely unaware that the prowess of the Ministry's technicians is such that his call will subsequently be traced to the local exchange.

# 56

My interrogation turned out to be the first of several, the others being lengthier by far. This was not because my interrogators repeated many of their questions in an attempt, perhaps, to winkle out inconsistencies, but because there were no inconsistencies, or very few. I had no reason to withhold information on my attempted defection; and so, with a bitter, purgative relish, I chronicled the affair in the fullest detail, such that my interrogators (working in shifts) often struggled to keep up with me.

I told them how I had met a young music student from the West and fallen in love with her; how I had grown jealous of Wolfgang Richter, a younger and more talented artist; how, little by little, I had sacrificed everything to the Theresian cause: my honour, my loyalties, my self-respect and finally my way of life. And how, in the end, I had been betrayed, as a man without honour deserves to be betrayed – and must be, if his story is to serve any purpose or make any sense. I did occasionally edit, embellish and, where necessary, expurgate the tale, and not only for reasons of economy or style. I did not, for instance, reveal my theft of Richter's medical file, nor how Michael Schilling had helped procure my photograph. Nor did I reveal that Theresa had believed *Survivors* to be my work, rather than Richter's. From such a piece of information it might be inferred that I had been planning to go West for years. Otherwise, my aim was to concentrate blame upon myself and to avoid implicating others.

This part of my task turned out to be quite easy, if only because my interrogators were almost completely in the dark. They appeared to know nothing of my scheming, of Richter and his book, of the literary phenomenon that was Eva Aden, or of the money that had been made. So when I told them of the hard currency piling up in the West they seemed quite ready to accept that this was the driving force behind everything that had happened. Richter's book had been smuggled out of the country to make money (because a Western girl could not be kept happy without it); the alluring persona of Eva Aden had been created in order to maximise the take; I had been tempted to abandon my country on account of the resulting fortune, at least partly; I had been betrayed so that Theresa would not be obliged to give it up. Successfully shorn of all ideological and ethical dimensions, my story emerged as one of vanity, corruption and greed; merely squalid. This, I expect, was what saved me.

Self-evidently, I was not disposed of. I was not put on trial, or held on permanent remand, as so many were. I did not disappear. After less than three days in my not incommodious rooms, I was ushered into a large, airy office with a flag beside the window. My first interrogator was present, but standing. Behind a desk sat a plump, moustachioed man in a civilian suit. He did not introduce himself, which I understood to be the custom among officials in this branch of the government service, but – most unusually – addressed me by name. He told me that I had taken a very serious 'wrong turn', but that the state was capable of recognising human frailty and believed in giving valued citizens a second chance, provided they were able to demonstrate a renewed commitment to the founding principles of the Workers' and Peasants' State. Then he looked me in the eye and asked me if I would seize such a chance if it were offered me, to which I dared not answer in the negative.

There then followed quite a lengthy discourse on the progress of socialism and the difficulties necessarily encountered along the way (to wherever it was going). I do not remember the details. I was too busy at the time wondering how a renewed commitment to the founding principles of the Workers' and Peasants' State would be demonstrated in my case. A lengthy period of manual labour was sure to be involved, in a cement works or a mine or – more likely still – on a collective farm, the kind of place where, in Richter's imagination, unpretentious peasants wiped their backsides on my prose. It was often said of intellectuals that their alienation from proletarian labour led to alienation from proletarian values, and that the best way to restore the correct perspective was to hand them a spade or a pickaxe and set them to work. But I was wrong. What was demanded of me was only that I write – not a eulogy to the Party Secretary on the occasion of his sixty-fifth birthday, nor a hymn to the soldier guardians of the inner German border, but something even less appealing and even more difficult – the latest instalment of the *Factory Gate Fables*.

I should not, in the meantime, make any application for foreign travel, not even to other socialist countries, no matter who proposed it. Invitations to conferences or symposia were to be turned down. At the same time the facts of my transgression and detention were not to be disclosed to anyone. I had taken care to keep my departure a secret; I should continue indefinitely in the same vein. If it became apparent that I had not observed this condition of secrecy, if word got out that I had attempted to defect, my exceptional pardon would be revoked and the appropriate sentence imposed. I agreed to all this readily and not just out of fear. My betrayal had left me strangely numb; two competing emotions (rage at Theresa, fury at myself) enforcing a tenuous, unnatural calm that left me indifferent to the finer points of my release.

'Everything will continue as if nothing has happened,' the moustachioed man declared, looking at me over the tips of his fingers. 'You will put the whole unfortunate episode behind you. You will go home and return to work. Only work – work for the common good – can redeem you, comrade.'

From a distance I see now that my detention was not deemed to be in the interests of the state. In the dwindling artistic firmament of the Workers' and Peasants' State, mine was still a star that would be missed. In my character and my motives a chance had been seen to smooth over the whole affair without embarrassment. The authorities – at what level I do not know – had decided to take it. Yet this was not how I saw things at the time. Sitting in the middle of that stately office, I perceived my treatment as an act of indulgence, such as might be extended to a mischievous child, a confused adolescent, or a harmless clown. I felt simultaneously slighted, patronised and grateful.

'As a token of the state's faith in you, you will be allowed to retain your titles and awards,' the moustachioed man declared. 'You will remain a People's Hero of Art and Culture. But you must strive anew to deserve that honour.'

I said I would. I didn't correct him on the nomenclature.

The interview was concluded. The door opened. I got to my feet.

'Should I take a train today?' I asked, because I had momentarily lost the power of decision-making and because it was already beginning to get dark.

'Today, tomorrow, it's up to you.' The moustachioed man looked at his watch. 'You're a free man, Herr Krug,' he added, without a touch of irony.

# 57

Everything was different. Everything was the same. On what turned out to be Christmas Eve, I returned to the valley, without my vodka and my English raincoat, but in all other respects unharmed. I went back to my old apartment with its futile camouflage of tinsel and lights. I went back to my old routines and my old horizons, to a life I thought I had left behind for ever. If the events of the preceding year could have been torn up and thrown away, like an unrewarding storyline, it might have been easy to carry on. By objective standards my life was not so terrible, or so lonely. But this particular narrative had been written in stone. I could not erase or redraft it, or tack on a happy ending; and the weight of it bore down on me, sapping my strength and my will, diminishing the significance of the present. It is a dangerous thing to put your happiness at the mercy of external events, but that was what I had done – a fact I saw plainly as I stepped off the train, still wearing my Western garb, by now grimy and rank. On the platform before me I had once spent a whole day waiting for Theresa's return, clutching a wilting bunch of chrysanthemums – a wasted day, a day without value. It was days such as this that now lay ahead of me in an endless procession.

This was not quite the ending to the story that I had expected and which, I'd come to believe, justice demanded. Mine was supposed to be a story of sin and redemption in the best Western traditions. I had sinned against Wolfgang Richter, delivering him carelessly into the hands of his enemies. The path to forgiveness and inner peace was one requiring bravery and sacrifice – the redemptive arc, incarnate. The material goal was to expose the truth of Richter's death and the lies told to hide it. Object achieved, arc completed, the pot of gold awaiting me at the end of my journey should have been Theresa's love, love which I was worthy of at last. It hadn't turned out that way. Instead of love I'd been met with betrayal – and not even betrayal as retribution, as a deliberate act of revenge. My betrayal had no significance outside itself, outside Theresa's preference for her new incarnation and my inability to see it. The redemptive arc did not exist. At best, it dangled uselessly in space, like a bridge that ends midstream. The only thing left to do was get off.

For a long time I heard nothing more from my one-time lover, either through conventional means or via the covert delivery network she had used in the past. (It was possible the authorities were confiscating her letters and blocking her phone calls, but I saw no particular reason why they should go to the trouble.) She did not return to her studies in East Berlin – enquiries at her previous lodgings established that. As far as I was aware, she never attempted to cross the inner German border again. It was possible she assumed I was in prison and didn't try to contact me for that reason. More likely, I thought, she couldn't face the prospect of maintaining the lover's charade: of feigning concern and disappointment and continued devotion. That would have been too much pretence, even for her. Instead, she had left me to draw my own conclusions, knowing that for as long as the death strip remained in place I would never have the opportunity to act on them. Even the authorities in the East were in no position to point the finger. How could they support a claim that she had not written *Survivors*? They had no proof, no material evidence whatsoever. In any case, to make trouble would only draw international attention to its real author (in her eyes myself) and his motives for seeking to publish abroad.

For Theresa, the one inconvenience in our changed circumstances was that she would not now have the sequel I had promised her and which she had promised the world. But hadn't the profile in *Stern* revealed that she was backing away from that idea already? Besides, was that really a problem now that Martin Klaus was in on the game (perhaps he had been in on it from the beginning)? A sequel, after all, is a mere extrapolation; the characters, the setting, the style, all these were already in place. She and Klaus could write it together, working as a team. And if that didn't work, they could always call in a ghost, some bright young wordsmith in need of money.

Did all this lead me to hate her? Did I rage at the injustice of my betrayal? Was my head filled with thoughts of revenge? The answer to these questions is no. I did hate her periodically in the months that followed my arrest. I burned her photographs, while mentally rehearsing a variety of exotic counter-strikes, usually involving an ambush at a public event, the vanquished Krug appearing before the literary usurper like Banquo's ghost. It pleased me to imagine her tortured by conscience and the inescapable knowledge of her own selfishness, but these indignant fits soon gave way to simple regret. I still loved her, you see. To be more precise, I loved the Theresa Aden I had known in the first months of our affair, the viola player with the shy smile and the tangled hair; the diffident, clever girl who so clearly didn't know what to ask of life, or what to take; the girl who was, above all, afraid to shine. And if that particular lover had been a dream, a fantasy corresponding to my desires and my tastes, it was a fantasy I had hastened to an unnecessary end with my scheming. For who but me had given birth to Eva Aden, literary sensation? The old Theresa might have lived on if I had only let events take their natural course, instead of trying to prolong an affair whose season could not have been other than brief.

As for the cash – the Deutschmarks and dollars accumulating, I assumed, in Switzerland – I wasn't sorry to find it beyond my reach. Perhaps this is hard to believe (scrupulous honesty, I have observed, is common when it comes to small sums, but much rarer when it comes to large ones), but as far as I was concerned it was blood money. Knowing what I knew about its origins, I couldn't have spent a pfennig of it without deepening my complicity in Wolfgang Richter's fate. His mother and father were entitled to profit from the success of *Survivors*, if anyone was. In ideal circumstances the money would have gone to them. Still, my regrets over that were tempered by the undeniable fact that their son had planned to abandon them, most likely without saying goodbye. Was this proof of indifference? Certainly not. But neither did it suggest devotion.

In the interests of thoroughness I should record that I saw them once again, that sad old couple, in the grounds of the Tolkewitz Crematorium, where I occasionally strayed on my way across the river. Since the funeral a small stone plaque had been laid in the shadow of a yew tree bearing Wolfgang's name, beneath which lay his ashes. It was an awkward encounter, a dank and windy day in late March. Herr Richter, I am sure, saw me from a distance. He took his wife by the shoulders and tried to steer her away so that we should not have to talk. But then she too saw me and could not be prevented from raising a hand in greeting. A stilted conversation followed, one which I found intensely uncomfortable, though the promised *Eingabe* was never mentioned (for fear, no doubt, of embarrassing me). As I was about to take my leave, Frau Richter took me by the arm and asked if I remembered 'that girl' Wolfgang had been seeing before he died.

'Would you believe, she's famous now? In the West. For writing books.'

I expressed surprise, wondered if there could already be more than one book in the Aden canon.

'Now I know what she was up to,' Frau Richter added. 'She was picking our Wolfgang's brains.'

I agreed with her that this was very possible, at which she began quite suddenly to cry.

I didn't go back to the crematorium after that.

I got into the habit of drinking a good deal during those two years. If I avoided clinical alcoholism, it was not because alcoholism did not officially exist in the Workers' and Peasants' State; it was thanks to my weakened stomach, which had the habit of becoming irritated when pickled. All the same, I worked on the latest instalment of the *Factory Gate Fables* in a haze of misanthropic inebriation. Under this new influence the fable turned slowly and irresistibly into a farce. I broke with tradition and relocated the action to a collective farm. A bookish newcomer from the city attempts to seduce a sturdy peasant girl with another man's love poetry passed off as his own. At a certain point in the action chickens escape on to the roof. (I *wanted* people to be reminded of *Two on a Bicycle*. In a small, sly way I thought it might help to keep the memory of my protégé alive.) In the end the peasant girl makes a fool of her pseudo-poetical suitor, leaving him penniless and suicidal.

Michael Schilling, with unusual directness, told me the story lacked warmth. None of the characters was likeable: the lover arrogant and dishonest, the object of his attentions shallow and grasping. More importantly, it showed the agricultural proletariat in such a bad light that it was unlikely to secure ministerial approval. I had better redraft it, he said, introducing a little more in the way of working-class solidarity, if I didn't want 'questions asked'. I laughed when he said this. My whole life, it seemed to me, had been lived out in the shadow of questions; how could a few more make any difference? But since martyrdom was, it seemed, unavailable to me (and pointless in the circumstances), I did as he suggested to the best of my abilities, leaving him to improve on the laboured language and the tortuous tangles of grammar.

Schilling was, of course, the only person who knew of my abortive plan to go West. I had told him long since that I had simply changed my mind, partly in the light of his advice – an explanation he accepted readily and without a hint of criticism. Since then he had never raised the subject again, as if, like his failed marriage, it was something painful, best left alone for both our sakes. I was grateful for his perspicacity.

By chance, the day I finally finished the second draft of my new fable – which is to say the day I could no longer stand to have it in my apartment – turned out to be one of historical significance.

I had decided to deliver the manuscript to Schilling's office in person, not because I was terrified of losing it, but because I was out of liquor and needed to make a trip to the Intershop in any case. My priority being the alcohol, I went to the shop first and it was not until late in the afternoon that I reached Ferdinandsplatz. I hadn't gone far when I realised that the number of pedestrians passing through the square was greater than usual. Stranger still, they all seemed to be heading in the same direction: when I looked back I saw only their faces; when I looked ahead I saw only the backs of their heads.

Whatever the attraction, it wasn't located in Ferdinandsplatz. The straggling columns converged on the south-west corner of the square and disappeared down a narrow side street. Curious, infected by the novelty of the spectacle, I followed. Soon I stood at the heart of a monumental modern zone: a showcase of Corbusian tower blocks and concrete plazas. People were spilling into the area from every direction. On Prager Strasse I saw a crowd of thousands gathered outside an international restaurant (hard currency only), but they weren't after a table. They were just standing around. From further up the street came the sound of singing. I couldn't make out the tune, though it reminded me of a hymn. I continued walking, almost bumping into a young man with, of all things, an altar candle. He was struggling with a cigarette lighter. 'Here, hold this, will you?' he said.

Without thinking, I took the candle, tucking the manuscript under my left arm. The young man lit the wick, cupping his fingers round the flame. It was only then I noticed that most of the crowd were young, like him. In the fading light I searched in vain for grey hair, high foreheads, lined skin, the haggard badges of middle age – feeling suddenly out of place, as if I'd stepped uninvited into a student party. I returned the candle to its owner.

Then the crowd was moving; shuffling forward at first, then picking up the pace, buoyed along by its own momentum. A petite woman in a white ski jacket put her arm through mine, so that my shopping bag of vodka bottles clunked against my thigh as we walked. Everywhere people were linking up, making human chains, adding reinforcement to the mass of flesh and bone, as if anticipating resistance. A banner was unfurled behind me. It read:

**ALLE MACHT IN EINER HAND
GEHT BERGAB MIT UNSERM LAND**

As slogans went, this was quite poetic: the rhyming, the meter, the use of opposites. *All power in one hand, (means) going downhill with our land* would be an ungainly literal translation. Only after I had finished being impressed by the form did I ingest the content. In whose hands was power in the Workers' and Peasants' State? In the Party's, of course. The Party enjoyed the leading role, by consti-tutional right – which could only mean one thing: I was participating not in a procession but in a protest. I had never seen a protest before, let alone taken part in one. Under Actually Existing Socialism the right to peaceful protest did not exist. The thrill of sheer novelty and the female arm clamped round mine were all that kept me from taking to my heels right away.

'Where are we going?' I had to shout. Around us people were chanting.

'To the Hauptbahnhof,' the woman said. I remember clearly her avian delicacy – the pale skin and dark eyes, the slight build. One good blow with a nightstick would have been enough to break her in two.

'Why the Hauptbahnhof?'

'The freedom trains,' she said. 'From Prague. Didn't you hear?'

What I hadn't heard was that thousands of my fellow citizens had crossed the border into the socialist republic of Czechoslovakia, a journey for which no visa was required, and there set up camp in the grounds of the West German embassy. After negotiations between the three relevant governments, they were now being rail-roaded to the West so as not to spoil the upcoming season of revolutionary anniversaries. The trains, it had been agreed, would pass through the territory of the Workers' and Peasants' State on their way, not out of geographical necessity, but so that their passen-gers could be officially expelled, rather than simply being allowed to escape. A high price had been paid for this political fig leaf: protests and violence had erupted at stations all along the way, where hundreds more of my fellow citizens had tried to break into the carriages.

This I learned later. That evening I was clear about only one thing: that we were collectively asking for trouble. In the early history of the Workers' and Peasants' State there had been instances of unrest, or so I had heard. They had always ended in bloodshed.

'What about the police?' I asked.

'They can't arrest us all.'

I wondered if that was true. How many people *could* they arrest? A hundred? A thousand? Where would they put us all?

'What about the Russians?'

'Just let them try!' the bird woman said, throwing back her head.

I hoped they didn't try. The Russians, I was fairly certain, could roll over anyone or anything if they put their minds to it. Numbers were no impediment. But it wasn't a vision of tanks or machine guns or tear gas that was responsible for my slipping away. Nor was it my burden of vodka and double-spaced fiction, though my arms were beginning to ache from carrying them. It was not an emotion or a feeling of any kind, but rather the *absence* of a feeling: an absence of belonging. I admired this youthful, defiant crowd. I was astonished by their bravery. I hoped the bird woman was right, that she and the other marchers would get everything they wanted without getting their skulls crushed. But as we walked on together, away from the Altstadt, away from the ruins and the part-ruins and the reconstructed grandeur of a fallen kingdom, towards the central railway station – now a metaphorical gateway to a freshly minted future – I found it impossible to share in that dream. You see, I had already been to that station, to the metaphorical reality as well as the physical one, and it had not delivered on its promises. It had not gifted me a new life. It had only made a wreck of the old one. I found, even on that extraordinary night, that I had no stomach for another disappointment.

A couple of blocks from the station I broke away from the crowd. It rolled on without me, brave and hopeful, buoyed along by candlelight and song. From the shadows I watched it go by, still full of wonder and not a little envy; and that was when I knew what it was that divided us more than anything. For the people on that march the war – the firestorms, the rapes, the endless, numbing vistas of ruin – was just a story. It had no hold over them. They could leave it and forget it, just as easily as they could forget the fallen masonry of the Frauenkirche. Their appetite was for experience, their *own* experience: raw, direct and unpredictable. Stories, for this new generation, were for bedtime; things to be bought and sold and tossed away once they had been consumed.

And this was unfortunate, because stories, which had been my refuge and my anchor for so long, were all I could ever hope to offer them.

A few weeks later Herr Andrich and Herr Zoch failed to turn up for our regular meeting. This had never happened before in all the years of our acquaintance. I sat waiting in my apartment for most of the afternoon, periodically checking and rechecking the date and time (it was possible I had lost track, one day being much like another). Finally, at around six o'clock, by which time it was dark, the telephone rang. It was Herr Andrich.

'Are you coming over?' I asked innocently.

'No.'

'Herr Zoch, then?'

'No. We can't. We're needed here. We're all needed here.'

He sounded grim and slightly out of breath. He didn't explain what he meant by 'here', or, for that matter, 'we all' and I preferred not to ask.

'I just wanted to tell you, comrade, that whatever happens we'll do whatever we can to protect you.'

Herr Andrich did not normally call me comrade and I was suspicious of this sudden familiarity. In any case why should I need protecting and from whom?

In the background I heard voices, the pounding of footsteps. 'What are you talking about?' I asked. 'What's happening?'

'We may not speak again. For your sake we must never speak again until . . . until this is all over.'

'Until what's all over?'

There was a heavy clunk on the line, but we were still connected. I became aware of a new sound: like a badly tuned radio, like interference. It took me a moment to realise that the source was organic, human.

'They're here.' It was Herr Andrich again. 'They're at the gates. There's no one to . . . I don't know how long it'll hold them.'

I understood now where he was: at the regional headquarters of the state security apparatus on Bautznerstrasse. I could picture the scene outside, the crowds, the banners, the multitude of faces – perhaps the very same young faces I had seen on Prager Strasse: the boy with the candle, the bird woman in the white ski jacket.

'Herr Andrich,' I said, in spite of myself. 'Whatever happens, don't let anyone shoot.'

I don't know if he heard me. There was a lot of shouting going on.

'I must get back to the files. Goodbye, comrade,' he said and hung up.

That was the last I ever heard from him.

As history relates, the bird woman's optimism turned out to be well founded. There were beatings and arrests during that first night's demonstration and others that followed, but the Russians stayed in their barracks. Without the guarantee of fraternal heavy armour the governing apparatus of the Workers' and Peasants' State found itself unable to govern. In a matter of weeks it vanished into memory, just as surely as if sixteen million people had simultaneously woken from a dream. For many employees of the state security apparatus their final act was to burn and shred as many records as possible before their premises were stormed (an epic task, given that the totality of the files, laid side by side, would have stretched for seventy miles). It was this that must have occupied Herr Andrich and Herr Zoch in their final operational hours.

According to press reports there was some method in this hasty bonfire of hearsay and history. The priority was to protect the identities of foreign agents and, on the domestic front, of *Inoffizielle Mitarbeiter* – that is, citizens who provided confidential information to the authorities on a regular basis – citizens like me.

# 58

In December, following a visit to the site by the West German Chancellor, an appeal went out from the parish of Weisser Hirsch for the rebuilding of the Frauenkirche. Money poured in from all over Germany and from all over the world, but I was long gone before the first new stone was laid. The great baroque dome, images of which sprouted up everywhere on hoardings, in magazines and in tourist brochures, was alien to me, part of a reassembled past that pre-dated my arrival and my adult life. Perhaps, as many said, it was part of our heritage and therefore part of mine; but heritage, like beauty, is in the eye of the beholder. I was a child of those ruins. They spoke to me. In their eloquent desolation they consoled me. Now they were being swept away with unashamed haste, making me an orphan all over again.

I had other reasons for leaving. The new government of all Germany had decided that the personal files of the state security apparatus would be made available to the public. Anyone who turned out to have a file could apply to view it and to learn what investigations had been conducted into their lives. Such information would include the identities of all relevant informers. It was also decreed, with some hesitation, that the files shredded in the final days of the *ancien régime* should be unshredded. The task of sticking them back together was given to forty-five civil servants, stationed in the Bavarian town of Zirndorf. Even at a rate of one hundred thousand pages a year, it was calculated that their work would take ten times longer to complete than the entire forty-year lifespan of the Workers' and Peasants' State. Still, the fact remained that with every passing year, with every new application, the chances of my being revealed as an *Inoffizieller Mitarbeiter* grew. Such unmaskings happened every day, in a more or less public way, the revelations creating a feeding frenzy in the press. There were dismissals, divorces and suicides. Explanations were demanded, but rarely if ever listened to. The authors of the system got off lightly. The lower ranks were left to fend for themselves. This, at least, was my impression in those early months, when hope and fear went hand in hand.

I migrated across Europe in stages, my freshly converted Ostmarks being supplemented by a healthy trickle coming in from *The Orphans of Neustadt.* This proved more valuable than I had supposed, thanks to the incompetence of the old Ministry of Culture. An agency I turned to in London discovered unclaimed and unpaid royalties in a dozen territories, some going back more than a decade. These eased my passage westwards. I stayed a while in Amsterdam, until I was tracked down by an aggressive young reporter. In France, which was my home for two and a half years, I was treated successfully for a peptic ulcer, my stomach problems turning out to be neither metaphorical nor psychosomatic in origin. England was too hectic for my taste and there seemed to be journalists everywhere. I was in London when the newspapers learned that Christa Wolf, our most famous female novelist, had been an informer for the state security apparatus. In the space of a week four different reporters approached me, asking for my opinion on the matter. I declined to give it and was forever afterwards described as 'elusive'.

So I went west again, to Ireland, a place of bad weather and good books; and, having got there, maintained my intermittent line of march until I had reached the Atlantic Ocean. There, in west Cork, before the great grey horizon, among the low, sturdy houses and the drystone walls, I stopped. Except for one return trip to the valley, which honour demanded, I have yet to retrace my steps. In Ireland I have been left to live privately and in peace; and no has ever found me here, until now.

One place I did not visit on my long migration was Munich. I stayed away from Bernheim Media. I made no attempt to establish Wolfgang Richter as the true author of *Survivors*. For one thing, I had no way of proving such a claim. My only supporting witness would have been Michael Schilling and he had expressed no great interest in setting the record straight. He was struggling to find work by then and had no time for the finer points of cultural record. Perhaps his attitude would have been different had *Survivors* become recognised as a permanent addition to the German literary canon. But it hadn't. The book chalked up excellent sales for a couple of years, but with no sign of a sequel, or a successor novel of any kind, it was slowly superseded by works of a less pessimistic hue. Thereafter it was generally referred to as a popular hit; rarely, if ever, as a classic. This rendered any intervention on my part academic. Even if Bernheim had believed me, what commercial incentive would there have been to produce a new edition?

As for Theresa Aden, I made no attempt to seek her out. Nor, when messages from her reached me via Michael Schilling, did I respond. This is not to say I didn't think of her. I thought of her every day and dreamed of her every night (in my dreams my desire for her was always unqualified and unambiguous). But I couldn't picture a real-life encounter with her that wouldn't be either squalid or sad. I couldn't stand to hear more lies, to be pacified or bought off. Nor was I in any hurry to draw a line under our affair, to shake hands and part – nominally but not actually – as friends. I was sure that somewhere in her soul Theresa must have craved absolution, an acknowledgement at least that there had been fault on all sides, but I saw no reason to oblige on either count. It seemed fair to me that she should live in suspense, not knowing how or in what way the fraud of Eva Aden would be revealed, because I was living the same way, courtesy of the puzzlers of Zirndorf and the open archives of the state security apparatus. In this way Richter's book would do a little of what I had intended it to do: namely bind together Theresa's fate and mine in a way that could not be easily undone. Was this selfish of me? Was it unforgiving? To both questions the answer is yes. But among the great panoply of sins being uncovered at that time, these seemed inconsequential and easily borne.

I made myself invisible to Theresa Aden, but she was not invisible to me. Newspapers and magazines continued to mention her name in various cultural contexts. A motion picture based on *Survivors* won several awards for production design and music, but disappointed at the box office. Critics complained that by adding a happy ending (a change made in haste after ominous test screenings) the producers had confused the central message of the film. Theresa attended the premiere at the Venice Film Festival and was quoted as saying she was 'impressed'. I searched for photographs of the occasion, but the ones I found were all of the director and the cast. Eighteen months after that Theresa was living in Berlin. By that time the absence of a new book had become a talking point. In a feature entitled 'New voices for a new world' Theresa conceded that *Survivors* had been a difficult act to follow.

I laughed when I read this (partly out of amusement, partly out of relief), but my laughter was cut short by the revelation that Theresa was cohabiting with an unnamed boyfriend. This turned out not to be the agent, Martin Klaus, but a jazz pianist named Rolf. Rolf was succeeded by a property developer called Oscar Schmidt, then by no one. A year later the concluding paragraph of a brief colour supplement profile described Eva Aden as living alone. In the photograph she was depicted sitting on a park bench staring straight at the camera, as if posing for a passport. Over the years she had lost weight. Her face had a hard, sculpted look, the youthful roundness of her features having all but disappeared. The girl, I supposed, had become a woman and, as such, more of a stranger than ever. The year she had spent with me was now just one year among many; our mutual involvement an interval, an episode that could be recounted without emotion, as if it had happened to someone else.

Slowly the press mentions dried up. The occasional passing references added nothing to the sum of my knowledge. In Germany the Zirndorf effort began to wind down. Departing staff were not replaced and soon the number remaining had dwindled to less than twenty. The unmaskings and retributions gradually ceased. Meanwhile in west Cork, at the suggestion of some local residents (admiring ladies of a certain age, for the most part), I took up teaching at an adult education establishment, my subject being 'creative writing'. A good portion of my students had never heard of me before. I preferred it that way. *The Orphans of Neustadt* remained firmly off the syllabus.

It was in Ireland, after seven years' residence, that I finally began work on this account of my last years in the East. I set out to write it not to justify myself, or to reanimate a vanished career, but in part-fulfilment of a debt. This is the story Wolfgang Richter wanted me to write (in a dream, but also in life), or as close as I can make it. I began, I persevered through the yawning middle, but the problem was always in finishing it. The difficulty lay not in my choice of language (I chose English, partly for the challenge; mostly for the sense it gave me of a fresh start); it lay in the fact that until you came along, Miss Connolly, hot from Zirndorf and the Berlin archives, I could identify no clear or satisfying ending. My story was like a country whose borders are invisible beneath an impenetrable fog. This failure, this narrative irresolution, has tormented me more than I can say.

I had been gone more than ten years from the valley when I found a letter waiting for me at the adult education college. The stamp was German and the post mark said DRESDEN. I knew at once that it was from Theresa. I stood in the corridor, staring at the unopened envelope, trying to pretend that everything was normal as my students filed past on their way into the classroom, bestowing their usual cheery greetings. It took a feat of willpower just to smile back at them, a still greater one to leave the envelope unopened until the end of the class. Still, I doubt if anything I said that day made sense.

The letter had been written in Berlin, months before it was actually posted. It seemed Theresa had been carrying it around for some time, searching perhaps for a reliable address. The tone was strangely formal to begin with, but beneath that stiffness I detected bewilderment and anguish – and felt it too, just as if it were my own. Most of the money arising from our venture was still intact, Theresa said, and awaiting my instructions. She needed to know where to send it. Then came the questions: why had I never come forward to reclaim my book? Why had I remained silent? Why had I avoided her for so long? If she had angered me, she had a right to know how and why. She had respected my decision to disappear, she said, and to put the past behind me, but now circumstances had changed. She was sick and needed to put her affairs in order 'just in case'. If she had ever meant anything to me, she asked that I reply.

This mention of sickness had all the hallmarks of a ploy. Perhaps the undertones of indignation were a pretence, a carapace of bluster. But such reservations hardly registered. I was overwhelmed by this simple appeal for clarity. I ran out of the college and into the street, needing to be alone and unobserved. I ended up in a churchyard. Was it possible I could still hurt Theresa after so long and from so far away? Was her eagerness to clear things up prompted by a bad conscience? Or was it possible that her feelings for me – never unmistakable, never couched in grand declarations – had outlived the satisfaction of her new-found freedom? Had our love, by some miracle, survived?

And so, in spite of all I had learned, in spite of the wounds I had determined never to reopen, in spite of the years invested in forgetting, I crumbled. The next day I sat down within sight of the sea (it was a clear, cool day in September, gulls looking over my shoulder as they drifted by on the wind) and wrote back. I told Theresa I would meet her, in Berlin if that suited her. It would be good to see her again. I was eager to know her plans for the future, I said, and if she had found happiness in our time apart. In that regard I couldn't help adding one sentimental observation: that many of the hours I had spent with her were, with the benefit of hindsight, the happiest of my life.

I sent the letter by airmail. Weeks went by and I received no response. I wondered if Theresa might be on her way – the troublesome journey, perhaps, a small act of contrition on her part. I pictured her arriving on my doorstep, freshly soaked from an untimely downpour. I didn't go out for days at a time, in case she should arrive while I was away. When the telephone rang (which was not often in the normal course of events) I found myself disappointed when the voice at the other end wasn't hers. Such occasions betrayed a disturbing reality: that, like many a battered wife or bullied husband, my irrational feelings of love were stronger than any rational assessment of the facts. In such cases the imbalance lies in a general expectation of abuse or betrayal, a deep-seated conviction that the treatment is merited. But not in my case. My opinion of myself had always been higher than that. Besides, in this world what we deserve and what we get have no more relation to each other than one roll of the dice with the next – except, of course, in fiction.

Eventually my letter came back to me unopened. Accompanying it was a note from a Frau Hanssen, who turned out to be Theresa's aunt. She told me that Theresa had succumbed to ovarian cancer some months previously. At her request the funeral had taken place at the Johannis Cemetery in Tolkewitz, close to where she had spent the last months of her life. It seemed, in the months prior to her illness, that she had just taken up a teaching position at the Carl Maria von Weber College of Music.

It was two days after I received this news that you first contacted me, Miss Connolly, with your request for an interview. You wondered if I could shed any light on some bizarre discoveries among the scrambled files of Zirndorf; in particular about a book smuggled out of the Workers' and Peasants' State and published under a false name, of a planned defection by myself, of a hitherto unknown informer at the heart of the literary scene, living and working in my city. My regular dealings with the state security apparatus were, I assumed, about to be made public. You were fortunate. At any other time I would have refused your request. But at that moment I could not summon the will for evasion. My mind was elsewhere – on the past, to be precise, on what could have been and never was. The future was no longer of any great concern.

You arrived the next day. You were afraid, I suppose, that a rival would get to me first. As a journalist, as a dealer in discovery, it must be hard, when you have a secret, to know how long it will remain one; when to keep it as a means to uncover still more secrets and when to cash in. Still, you surprised me with your courtesy and your eagerness to listen. Maybe you were wearing a disguise, but I didn't sense that you had plans to judge me. Even when you talked about *The Orphans of Neustadt*, it was with nostalgia and regret at time gone by, which is much how I think of it myself. Perhaps, in different circumstances, we could have become friends.

Eventually, sitting at the kitchen table, you shared with me what your sources at Zirndorf had shared with you. Among the scraps of intelligence, of briefings and action plans, there was, after all, no reference to Herr Anders or Herr Zoch, or any of my conversations with them. Your interest was in an informer whose name was 'Nachtigall'.

It was his or her file that had been partially reassembled, not mine. It was reports made by 'Nachtigall' that told the authorities about the smuggled book, and of my plans to cross the inner German border.

Could I shed any light on the identity of 'Nachtigall', you asked me? His or her cooperation had been secured following the arrest of a son on narcotics charges. I was not sure if I fully believed you until you showed me that sheaf of photocopies, the fuzzy, reassembled type, enlarged beyond its original size. The son, it seemed, had been a heroin addict. He had stolen a gun and attempted to rob a pharmacy. The authorities had promised 'Nachtigall' a reduced sentence for his son, and treatment with methadone, in return for regular intelligence on the cultural community. Then, on one of the copied pages I saw the report of a conversation between the informer and me. It concerned a forged passport, my need for a photograph and the authorship of a book published in the Federal Republic under the title *Survivors*.

At the end of this report was a note from the handler, one Lieutenant Ulrich. In it Ulrich wrote that he had rebuked 'Nachtigall' for not coming forward with his information right away, given the imminent possibility of *Republikflucht*, instead of waiting for the scheduled monthly meeting. 'Nachtigall' had expressed regret and requested permission to visit his son in prison at Christmas. In the light of his recent lapse, permission was refused.

I am sorry, Miss Connolly, if the rest of our interview did not go as well as you'd hoped. I didn't mean to be uncooperative, but forty years of circumspection has lasting effects. The consequences must always be considered, even if they cannot be foreseen. The habit is hard to break. Besides, I was in a state of shock. I know you went back to Dublin disappointed that so many questions remained unanswered. A more ruthless soul might have pressed me harder on the meaning of 'Nachtigall's' reports, with all their details so tantalising to the investigative mind. I wonder, in fact, if your sensitivity makes you ill-suited to your trade – if you had not better been a doctor, a teacher or, better yet, a musician. But these professional shortcomings do not discourage me from sending you this manuscript, which I have finally finished. Far from it. There is no one better to receive it, no one better to decide its fate – if only because in some small way you remind me of her, of my Theresa, and because in visiting me, Miss Connolly, here in my valley of unknowing, you have brought structure and form to my story, and made clear to me at last how it should end.

# Afterword

*Liebermann & Klaus AG*
*Heliostrasse 32*
*8032 Zürich*
*Switzerland*

*6 July*

*Dear Miss Connolly,*

   *Thank you for the proofs which you were kind enough to send me, and for this opportunity to comment on their contents. While the speculations regarding myself contained in the work may not be technically libellous, there is a danger that some readers will be left with a wholly inaccurate impression of my conduct and that of my firm. As you will understand, this could prove very damaging.*
   *I should like to state at the outset that at no point did I knowingly make any communication with the East German security services regarding a possible escape attempt by the late Bruno Krug, or any other matter. Until now, I was only dimly aware that Herr Krug had ever planned to defect from the then German Democratic Republic (even assuming the claim is credible). I would suggest, since Herr Krug failed to suggest it himself, that the idea of my involvement, and of Theresa Aden's complicity, was deliberately planted in his mind by the security services themselves. Their intention, I feel sure, was to undermine his reasons for leaving the country and thereby retain his loyalty. It seems to me that Krug's description of his interrogation in Berlin reveals, perhaps unintentionally, how this manipulation took place – manipulation which the information from 'Nachtigall' made possible. I can see no other rational explanation.*
   *I was also completely unaware, until many years after publication, that the novel Überlebende ('Survivors') had not in fact been written by my client, Theresa Aden. It was more than ten years later, by which time Theresa was gravely ill,*

*that she confided in me that the real author was, as she
thought, Bruno Krug. This she did in the strictest confidence
– confidence I breach now only with great reluctance.*

*By this time Theresa had ceased to be an active client,
having turned back to music. I had given up hope of seeing
another novel, but we had remained friends. In our final
encounters she described to me her time in the GDR and
her affair with Herr Krug. She told me that she had seriously contemplated moving to the East permanently so as to
be with him (a move to the West, she was convinced, would
snuff out Krug's resurgent creativity, of which he openly and
repeatedly boasted). She also told me that she had become
pregnant with Krug's child, but miscarried while in the West.
I believe she must have kept this from Krug himself, since he
makes no mention of it, but she told me the incident trig-
gered a period of depression and doubt, which she found
difficult to hide – and which I myself recall. From what she
told me, I estimate that Theresa's miscarriage took place a
few weeks before her final visit to Krug in Dresden.*

*I would like to add that in my opinion Theresa Aden kept
the secret surrounding the authorship of* Überlebende *not
out of greed or fear of censure, but out of loyalty. I believe
her love for Bruno Krug was genuine, and that his resolute
and inexplicable absence following the collapse of the GDR
may have contributed to the illness that eventually killed
her. Though medical opinion might dismiss such an idea, I
believe it is an idea Bruno Krug came to share and that his
death can best be understood in that light. The coroner may
have recorded an open verdict, but I firmly believe Krug
took out his dinghy that day with the firm intention of never
returning to land. The fact that you were sent his last work
immediately beforehand provides further supporting
evidence.*

*There remains one awkward matter, to which I plan to
attend. If the claims in this book are true, the estate (if such
exists) of Wolfgang Richter are due, morally if not legally,
whatever royalties can be recovered from the past and
present sales of his novel. I have already begun preliminary
enquiries in Dresden and while I have not yet identified the
next of kin – Richter is not an uncommon name – I have
made one surprising discovery: that of a public swimming
pool in the district of Blasewitz that was reportedly*

reopened a matter of weeks before German reunification. It is known officially as 'The Wolfgang Richter Hallenbad'. Whether or not the late Herr Krug was responsible for this unusual name is not something I have been able to establish. Either way, only time will tell if the facility will prove a more lasting memorial to the young writer than any work of fiction he may or may not have written.

    Yours very sincerely,
    Martin Klaus

# Acknowledgments

My wife Uta grew up in the former German Democratic Republic, and without her recollections, inspiration and support, this book would not have been possible. I would also like to thank other members of the Bergner family for sharing with me their memories of life in the GDR, most especially my father-in-law, Jürgen Bergner, whose extensive Stasi file provided an indispensable insight into the workings of the Stasi informer network.

I should also like to acknowledge the generous assistance of Christopher Zach, whose constructive and imaginative critique of the first draft was absolutely invaluable; and of Claudia Geithner, another former East German citizen, who not only lent me her excellent PhD thesis on East German novelists, but who carefully checked the manuscript for cultural and historical accuracy. Finally, I should like to mention Liz Foley at Harvill Secker and Alison Hennessey at Vintage for their astute and sensitive input into the final draft.

# Note on the Type

This book has been typeset in Drescher Grotesk and Excelsior. These were commonly used typefaces in the German Democratic Republic, featuring in publications ranging from children's books and high-profile Communist publications to the humble Trabant car repair manual.

Life was frugal for designers (and everyone else) in the GDR. Typeface licences were very expensive and with little money available to pay for them, type designers were instead ordered to design their own version by state publication authorities. Drescher Grotesk, originally designed by Arno Drescher around 1932 and redrawn by Karl-Heinz Lange as Super Grotesk at VEB Typoart (the state-owned type foundry), was the East German response to Futura. Excelsior, designed for optimal readability, was most likely a very close copy of the original 1930's version by Chauncey H. Griffith.